the Dream Merchant Saga

BOOK FIVE
World's End

Written by
L.T. Suzuki
in collaboration with
Nia Suzuki-White

Book Cover, graphic design and layout:
Scott White
Shinobi Creative Productions
www.shinobicreativeproductions.com

Note for Librarians:
A cataloguing record for this book is available from the Library and Archives Canada at: www.collectionscanada.ca/amicus/index-e.html

ISBN 978-0-9921265-2-0

Dedication

To Scott,

for all he does and all he's done.
With love,

Lorna and Nia

Contents

Contents

1

An Inconvenient Hour

"I hate this!" groaned Rose.

In the most undignified manner, she staggered about in the middle of the royal courtyard, only to collapse onto her hands and knees. The dizzying influences of the Dream Merchant's power to transport her and her comrades back to this country taxed her delicate constitution to the limits of what she deemed humanly bearable. And now, all hopes of impressing the heir apparent to the throne of Axalon by appearing as a regal princess should, only served to undermine her pride and self-confidence.

"We're not accustomed to this mode of transportation, that's all," reminded Tag. Drawing a deep breath to clear his rattled mind, he tried valiantly to sound unaffected by the assault his body had been subjected to.

With a grunt, Tag shoved Harold's tree-trunk legs off his chest as the large man struggled to gain his bearings. Harold's eyes were bulging like a freshly landed codfish. The colour drained from his face as he fought the urge to vomit.

In contrast, Rainus Silverthorn managed to arrive looking his dashing self. The moonlight illuminated him in all his Elven glory and more importantly, highlighted the fact he was still standing, unassisted. He glanced down to see his mortal comrades sprawled upon the ground before him. Myron, Harold, Tag and Rose appeared as though they had been unceremoniously dumped here from the back of a turnip wagon drawn by a team of deranged horses that had stampeded about in tight circles before coming to an abrupt halt to dispense their load.

"It is sad to note that even our animals fared better than you four," commented Rainus. He glanced over to observe their horses and Harold's donkey. These creatures were unfazed, peacefully nibbling on the neatly manicured lawn.

Extending his hands, Rainus hoisted Rose and Tag onto their feet as Myron and Harold leaned against each other for support. All four wavered about like drunken sailors forced on to dry land after battling the high seas during gale force winds while thoroughly inebriated on spirits concocted from questionable ingredients. They struggled to regain their composure and balance, steadying their legs before venturing into the castle.

"Had I been permitted to use my final wish of the day to deliver us here rather than allow that sorry excuse for a Wizard to transport us, we would have all arrived looking as dignified as you do now," responded Rose. She eyed the Elf with a degree of envy.

"We all agreed that you were not to use the Dreamstone unless it was an emergency," reminded Myron. "If it is of any consolation, I am confident Captain Ironwood and his warriors endured the same when Silas Agincor *wished* them back to the Enchanted Forest to ready for our return."

"I think not," said Rainus.

"They are Elves! Of course they fared better than us," grumbled Rose, brushing the dust from her apparel. "Look at me! *This*, I would have considered an emergency."

"Are you fit to walk?" asked Rainus, steadying her as she squeezed her eyes shut.

Drawing a deep, calming breath, she gathered her shattered nerves and prayed the spinning sensation in her head to stop.

"I believe so," she sighed. "But first, how do I look?"

Rainus scrutinized her, attempting to select only the adjectives that would least offend her, but will still ring true.

"Well?" she asked expectantly.

"You look like *you*," interjected Tag, before Rainus could say a word.

"I was not asking you. I was asking for the opinion of one with refined taste and a genuine sense of style."

With one hand, Rainus gently lifted her chin. With the other, he licked the pad of his thumb, using it to wipe away the most noticeable smudge of dirt from her dusty forehead.

"As our young friend said, you look like *you*," assured Rainus. "Other than the redness and slight bruising around your neck from when that crazy Witch tried to throttle you, you look none the worse for wear, my lady. You look fine."

"That was not the answer I was hoping for." Rose huffed as she tamed the stray wisps of hair blowing across her face. "I must look better than *fine*, especially if Prince Percy is waiting to see me."

"We are in the middle of a quest. So what if every strand is not in its proper place or you got a bit grubby?" grumbled Tag. "If Prince Prissy cannot understand this, then you're too good for that fool."

"What do you know? I must look perfect for him," insisted Rose. She corrected her posture, standing straight and tall in an effort to appear regal and dignified. This illusion was effectively shattered as she tried to walk. She staggered, wobbling about with the grace of a drunken bar wench as she tottered toward the fountain in the centre of the courtyard.

"All things considered, I think you're lookin' rather beautiful, Princess," called Harold. He suddenly turned away to retch, clutching his queasy stomach as he dropped to his knees.

"Perfect answer, wrong response, Harold," sighed Rose.

Hurrying off to the fountain, she hovered over the water to scrutinize her reflection. Rose's face scrunched up into an expression of utter condemnation. Her normally perfect features wrinkled in distaste to see a less-than-pristine image blinking back at her. Unkempt and covered in dirt and grime except for the one spot Rainus had wiped clean from her forehead, Rose's likeness grimaced back at her. She shuddered to see this reflection. It was greatly distorted by the splashing of the water erupting from the top of the fountain and this irregular surface only served to exaggerate her true condition under the celestial light provided by the night sky.

Focusing upon the dried twigs and grasses protruding every which way from her dishevelled hair, Rose plucked them out before hastily braiding her tresses neatly into place.

Returning her attention to her face and neck, Rose was disgusted to see the grime smudged across her face and the dark trail of dried blood from the small laceration on her neck. This thin, crimson crust served to draw attention to the bruising created by the Witch's hands when the demented hag attempted to strangle her.

Rose dipped her hands into the chilly water. Cleansing her face and neck, she was careful not to splash her raiment as she freshened up. The dirt and blood quickly washed away, leaving her dewy-faced once more.

Staring at her reflection, Rose smiled in approval. She now saw the flawless face of a princess, rather than that of a dirty commoner, even if she was dressed like one. Her smile dissolved into a frown as her eyes scrutinized the still-prominent bruising. Tugging at her collar, Rose tried her best to conceal the contusions on her slender neck.

"Be quick about it, Princess!" hollered Tag. He took a moment to adjust the scabbard of his sword to make sure he looked presentable and that his weapon was at the ready, should he be forced to use it. "Stop fussing. You look fine."

"I do now," responded Rose. She gave her trousers and cloak the once over, inspecting for them for unsightly dirt or noticeable tears.

"Do hurry, Princess," urged Myron. "Let us be away from this courtyard before Maxmillian's soldiers descend, marching us into the throne room again like we are nothing more than common criminals to be charged for tax evasion."

"Too late," groaned Rainus. He raised his hands in surrender as a dozen soldiers armed with pikes charged toward them, the tip of each weapon pointing dangerously as they surrounded the group.

"What sorcery is this?" shouted an angry voice. "The gate is closed; the portcullis, secured. How did you come to be here?"

Glancing over to the castle keep, they watched as the captain, sword in hand, stormed down the stairs. This knight was without his suit of armour, but his vest of mail worn beneath his surcoat rattled and clinked just as loudly as if he had.

"No sorcery involved, my good man," promised Rainus, motioning the soldiers to lower their weapons. "It was merely a bit of magic employed by a powerful Wizard to deliver us here for an audience with your king."

"A brilliant flash like lightning and a din as resounding as the roll of thunder, but nary a cloud in the sky? Man and horse abruptly appearing in this courtyard?" snapped the captain. His eyes narrowed in suspicion as he hoisted his sword. "It looks like dark magic to me."

"I assure you, sir," said Myron, raising his hands higher to show he meant them no harm and had no intention of reaching for his weapon, "we were sent forth by the Wizard, Silas Agincor to meet with King Maxmillian."

"You don't say!" snorted the captain. "At this ungodly hour? I think not!"

"Why not?" asked Harold. He used his forearm to wipe away the thread of saliva that stretched down his chin. "It's not like we haven't been here before and he doesn't know who we are."

The captain frowned. He scrutinized the large man reeking of fresh vomit and those in his company.

"My friend speaks the truth," stated Myron.

"Well, what do you know, men? If it isn't Fleetwood's knight of renown, Sir Myron Kendall and his merry band of rabbles!"

A murmur of surprise rippled through the knot of soldiers tightening their circle around the intruders.

"Due to unforeseen circumstances, we were made to return.

We mean to have an audience with King Maxmillian," said Tag.

"It is nigh on to the midnight hour, young man." The captain glanced up at the moon glowing brightly against the cobalt sky. "And I, being of sound mind, will not be the one to disturb my liege from his slumber."

"You must! We demand a word with King Maxmillian, immediately," insisted Myron.

"Demand all you want, Sir Kendall. I'm thinking a meeting tomorrow, when he is good and ready, is more likely."

"We cannot wait," responded Rainus. He jumped with a start as a soldier impeded his advance, thrusting the tip of his pike in the most threatening manner toward the Elf's chest.

"Yes, you must wait," countered the captain. "Now go find some rest. Return when the hour is more reasonable."

"You mean to say *go away*, so you and your men will be left undisturbed to steal away with some sleep rather than tend to your knightly duties!" snapped Tag.

"Watch your mouth, boy!" growled the captain. "Your insolence shall see you and your cohorts spending the night as King Maxmillian's *guests*, perhaps in one of his gloomy dungeons, if you persist."

"You'd jail us?" gasped Harold. His eyes grew wide with horror at the prospects of spending the night in the bowels of the castle keep. "For doin' nothin' but inconveniencin' you?"

"Demanding an audience with King Maxmillian, especially when you request that I disturb His Royal Highness from his bed, to meet with you vagabonds is far from *nothing*. It shall only see me hanged by my neck in the public gallows, if I were to appease you by displeasing my liege."

"And when the safety of the entire realm is in jeopardy, I should care about one man?" questioned Rainus, thoroughly irked by this mortal's attitude.

"Obviously, you don't," snorted the captain. Tightening his grip on the hilt of his sword, he glared in contempt. "So, I shall make this easy for you and your comrades, Elf!

With a snap of his fingers, the soldiers rushed in to seize them.

"I have the perfect dungeon waiting for you unfortunate blokes!" declared the captain. "Each prison comes with its own filthy straw for bedding, rats to keep you company throughout your stay and a stinking trough you can use as your privy! If you're lucky, you may even have a cellmate waiting to make a new *friend* of you!"

"Unhand us!" shouted Tag. He struggled against a soldier's grip on the scruff of his neck. "You will not be locking us up like criminals!"

"I can and I will!" growled the captain.

"No, you will not," demanded Rose, as she marched over from the fountain.

"Who are you to say?" grunted the captain, spinning on his heels to confront her.

"I am Princess Rose-alyn of Fleetwood. We are here on a matter of great urgency. We *must* see King Maxmillian."

The captain laughed at her proclamation as one of his soldier's mocked her, "Well, my lady, we won't be taking orders from you, as you are no princess of ours. Is that not so, Captain Loftus?"

"My friend is right," responded the captain, as he nodded in approval to his soldier. "Your title has no bearing on us."

"You impudent fool! I am betrothed to Prince Percival. I will indeed be *your* princess sooner than you think! And consider this: When you treat my friends with such disrespect, it is no different than treating me, King Maxmillian's future daughter-in-law, with the same disregard. I will not stand for it, and neither will my prince!"

The captain blinked hard. It was as though her words alone verbally accosted him, cutting him to the bone and parcelling up his pride for good measure.

"What is your name, sir?" Rose demanded to know.

"Loftus, my lady, Captain Gilbert Loftus." His words were now thoroughly contrite as he considered the young woman before him.

"So, what will it be, Captain Loftus?" Rose's arms crossed her chest as she demanded his answer. "And just keep in mind, I hardly think your liege will be pleased to find out you had us locked away for *your* convenience because you felt we arrived at an inconvenient hour."

Captain Loftus raised his hands in surrender, ordering his men to lower their arms and to release these late night visitors.

"It was a simple misunderstanding, my lady." The captain bowed low, almost seeming to grovel before her. "Allow me to appeal to your good senses and understanding. King Maxmillian has a fine selection of bedchambers ready to play host to such esteemed guests during occasions such as this!"

"That sounds like a fair compromise." Rose gave him a judicious nod. "Suitable accommodations in exchange for my silence and an audience with King Maxmillian in the morning sounds reasonable to me."

"Reasonable, indeed! A very wise decision, my lady!" With a wave of the captain's hand, two soldiers gathered the animals to house in the stable for the night while the rest of the soldiers dispersed to resume their watch. "Follow me, my friends."

"Tell me, Captain Loftus, is Prince Percival about?" queried Rose. She discreetly pinched her cheeks, giving them a blush in case she chanced upon her love.

"Yes, my lady. However, I dare not disturb him, lest I desire an early death. Where King Maxmillian can be quite the bear when disturbed needlessly, Prince Percival is more like the angry, wounded bear prodded by a sharp stick to drive him from his den. He is *very* insistent that he not be disturbed from his *beauty* sleep."

"Oh…" Rose's heart sank.

"Come now, Princess! You know how important that beauty sleep is," teased Tag. "Just be glad your prospective husband appreciates the importance of sleep, allowing you to rest all you want, just to retain your youthful appearance to keep up with his."

"I suppose you have a point," sighed Rose.

"Of course I do." Tag gave her a knowing smile.

"If you wish to wake him, who am I to stop you, my lady?" Loftus shrugged his shoulders as he removed a torch from its wall sconce. "Just know that if you raise his ire, princess or not, his betrothed or not, *you* will be the one to deal with the consequences when Prince Percival lashes out as only he can."

"Oh, my!" groaned Harold. "Sounds like the good prince has a bad temper, my lady."

"Nonsense, Harold," assured Rose, as she dismissed his concerns. "I know exactly how Prince Percy feels to be disturbed from a good night's sleep. Even I admit I am not in the best of moods when I have been cheated out of much needed rest, however, being a little cranky does not mean I have a bad temper."

"A bad temper does not even begin to describe your mood when you've been forced from your bed before you're ready!" exclaimed Tag.

"And on this note, we should all find a restful night of sleep while it is afforded to us," suggested Myron, ushering the others on to follow the captain as he directed them through the main hall and up the grand staircase to the guest rooms.

"I have no qualms about taking some rest," confided Rose. "It will feel so civilized to sleep in a comfortable bed with a sound roof over our heads than to sleep out in the wilds."

"It's just for this one night," reminded Tag. "Tomorrow, you can explain your need to cancel –"

"*Postpone,*" corrected Rose, as she shot a mincing stare at him.

"Yes… to postpone formalizing your planned nuptials, for we must resume with our quest right away."

Rose unleashed a dreary sigh upon hearing Tag's words, but she understood the sooner the quest was done, the sooner she'd be able to return and begin planning for her life of wedded bliss.

"Here you go," said Loftus, as he reached the top of the staircase. Pushing open the door to a small, modestly furnished room there was a narrow bed pushed against the far wall and a small table against the other. He ushered Harold in. Using the torch, the captain lit the tinder and dry pieces of wood already in the fireplace to provide this humble bedchamber with generous light and heat.

"We can take the floor and you can have the bed, Princess," offered Harold, placing his pack next to the small table.

"This room is for you, sir," explained the captain.

"For me?" Harold frowned in bewilderment.

"You each get your own room. And should you be in need of anything, just pull on this to ring for service," instructed Captain Loftus, pointing to a length of silken rope. It disappeared through a small hole in the floor to terminate with a brass bell that hung with all the other room service bells in the kitchen area that was open night and day, should King Maxmillian or one of his guests desire a late night snack. "A servant is always on call. Ring, should there be anything you require."

"*Anything?*" gasped Harold, astounded by this offer.

"Within reason, sir. If you require more firewood, additional bedding, food and beverage, or whatnot, it is but a *ring* away."

"That's good to know. I've got no money to pay for any of this, but it's good to know, indeed," said Harold. "Mind you, I do have a fine selection of headpieces I can barter with."

"There is no need for that. You are King Maxmillian's guest on this night. As a testament to my liege's generous hospitality, you are welcome to all the fine amenities afforded in his castle."

"*Wheeee!*" squealed Harold. Like an exuberant child destined to be locked in a toyshop after hours, he spun about in the centre of this room.

"We should leave him be," whispered Rose, motioning for the others to come away. She was equally embarrassed and mortified by this large man's enthusiastic display.

"Good night, Harold," called Myron, as he closed the door behind him. "Sleep well, if you find sleep at all."

From the corridor, they heard Harold's bed frame squeak in protest. He bounced onto the thick, down counterpane covering the feather-filled mattress as he tested the softness of his bed. Turning down the soft quilt, he giggled in delight to find clean linens of the finest quality waiting to envelop his large frame.

One by one, Captain Loftus delivered each guest to their room, appointing them to quarters he felt was in line with their social status. Tag was the next to be housed, his room slightly larger and better furnished than Harold's. Myron was delivered to a finely appointed room of grander scale than the last, as was Rainus.

"Sleep well," Rose called to her friends, as they each closed the door to their bedchamber.

"This way, my lady." Loftus escorted her to the largest of the guest chambers at the far end of a long corridor.

He pushed the door open, entering to ignite the wood in the fireplace and to light the candles for her. "I hope this room meets with your approval."

Rose stepped in as the warm glow of the fireplace and the many candles filled the room. Rich tapestries, a fine wool rug and sumptuous velvet drapery, along with the ornately carved, gilded furniture made this room stand out from the others.

"I have stayed in finer accommodations, but this shall suffice as it is only for one night."

"Lovely," muttered Loftus. "If you had demanded a more opulent room, it would mean I'd be forced to remove Prince Percival from his royal bedchamber just to appeal to your exquisite tastes."

"Oh, we would not want to disturb the Prince, would we now?" said Rose, as she stifled a great yawn.

"Under the threat of death, no, you would not." Loftus gave her a judicious nod. "I shall leave you to your rest now. A servant will come to wake you in the morning so you can break your fast with your comrades before meeting with King Maxmillian."

"Please have the servant wake me at sunrise."

"But that is well before the breakfast hour."

"I know," said Rose, freeing her tresses from the ribbon that held it in a simple braid. "It will take me at least that long to make myself look presentable to Prince Percival, for I do not want to disappoint him."

"Very well. I shall alert the chamber maid of your request." Captain Loftus bowed politely as he backed out of the room, closing the door behind him.

In her solitude, Rose breathed a sigh of relief, grateful that she'd not be made to sleep under the stars on this night. And, as exhausted as she was, her heart fluttered with excitement. Knowing how close she was at this very moment to her future husband was almost unbearable.

Rose dashed across the room. Peering out the tall window, the moon was almost at its height. She estimated that in about ten minutes the final wish allotted to her in this current 24-hour cycle threatened to vanish, unused and wasted. She would be granted another three wishes at the stroke of midnight, but she had also promised her friends that she would not use any more of these wishes without their collective approval or in the case of a dire emergency, to be used at her discretion.

With time ticking away and with the prospect of this last wish of the day going to waste needlessly, Rose decided this was indeed an extreme emergency that needed to be dealt with before the coming of morning. Drawing the drapes across the window to obliterate the light of the moon that flooded into this bedchamber, she pulled out the Dreamstone that was tucked away beneath the simple, linen blouse she wore. Clasping the magic crystal against her chest, Rose set to work.

"I am surprised King Maxmillian, or at the very least his son, did not grace us with his presence to break fast together on this morn," commented Rainus. He glanced over to the large, gilded chair sitting vacant at the head of the table.

Rainus set aside his empty bowl that had been filled with hot porridge studded by a selection of dried fruits, drizzled in amber honey and bathed in warmed cream. It made for a filling meal, but there was room still for a cup of tea and a piping hot biscuit served with freshly churned butter and sweet strawberry preserves.

"I know neither of them well, but I'm not surprised," said Tag, his words smug. "The need for excessive sleep seems to be a common malady amongst those of royal blood."

"What is more surprising is that Harold is not here," noted Myron, helping himself to another rasher of smoked bacon that was fried to crispy perfection. He dipped it into the warm, creamy golden yolk, using this instead of a spoon to finish off his soft-boiled egg. "He is usually an early riser."

"Perhaps the excitement of spending the night in a castle was too much for him," said Tag, passing the basket of freshly baked biscuits to Rainus, along with the dish of creamy butter. "Most likely, he fell asleep late in the night, surrendering to exhaustion in the wee hours of the morning."

"Truth be told, I am more surprised Princess Rose has not graced us with her company," stated Rainus, staring across the table to the vacant chair meant for her. "I would have thought she'd be the first one at this table, especially as the prospect of dining with her fair prince was so high on the list of her priorities."

"Hey... You're right, Lord Silverthorn," said Tag. He glanced up from his plate as he nodded to the Elf. "Maybe she is skulking through the castle as we speak, hunting about for her Prince Charming."

"A princess does not skulk, you dolt!"

All eyes turned to the entrance of the grand dining hall.

There stood Rose; resplendent in a frothy, pale pink gown encrusted with diamonds embellishing the full skirt and form-fitting bodice that was a deeper pink tone around the middle to give the illusion of a wasp-like waistline. A dazzling diamond choker-style necklace adorned her slender neck. Its sheer size and glittering spectacle made the Dreamstone non-existent to the eyes of all and served to conceal the lingering contusions and healing laceration on her throat.

A matching pair of diamond earrings and a regal tiara crowned her golden head of hair that was now twisted, twirled and teased into an elegant up-do complete with delicate ringlets to frame her face.

Her skin glowed, her eyes sparkled and a demure smile creased her dewy lips as she searched the room for Percy.

"He is not here," stated Tag. His words were blunt as he stood up, pulling out from the table a chair for her to sit upon.

Rose stared innocently at her friend as she responded, "I know not whom you speak of."

"Prince Percival, he is not here," he said again.

As Rose sat down, Tag pushed her chair closer to the table.

"Oh! Was there any talk he will be joining us for a morning meal?" queried Rose, trying her best to sound only mildly interested.

"No. But I know you and that's certainly what you were hoping for."

"I cannot deny it would have been lovely to engage in sparkling conversation with him first thing in the morning, but Prince Percival is a very busy man."

"Yes," said Myron, with a nod and a chuckle. "He and King Maxmillian are so diligent in their royal duties, they are busy being served breakfast in their beds, rather than to join us at this table."

"It is the prerogative of the rich and famous," Rose said, shrugging her shoulders in empathy as she motioned for Tag to serve her a cup of tea.

"More like the powerful and shameless," muttered Tag, obliging Rose by pouring from the silver teapot a steaming-hot, fragrant blend into her porcelain cup that she already half-filled with honey and cream.

"Jealous, that is what your are!" rebuked Rose. She shot a baleful glance at Tag as she filled her breakfast plate with biscuits, spooning practically the entire bowl of strawberry preserves atop.

"How about a serving of eggs and bacon to start your morning?" suggested Myron, pushing the platters toward her.

"Or a healthy serving of porridge?" suggested Rainus.

"Lest it is to ply onto my skin for a facial, I avoid porridge whenever possible," explained Rose. "And, as there are no desserts at this moment, this will have to do. The eggs and bacon can wait, if there is room."

Rose used her knife and fork to devour these sweet biscuits than to get her fingers sticky.

"I suppose that is a good thing," said Rainus. "We should save some food for our large friend."

So intent on seeing Percy this morning, Rose did not even notice that Harold was absent.

"Where is that big bugbear of a man?" she asked, glancing over to the empty chair next to Myron.

"He failed to answer the servant's call to break his fast with us," answered Rainus. "We believe he chose to steal away with extra sleep than to indulge in a hearty meal in our company."

"I mean no disrespect, but both the breakfast and the company are somewhat wanting at this moment, but each to his own, I suppose," said Rose. She eyed the basket of remaining biscuits she may not have to share with Harold, if he did not come down in time to join them. "There is nothing wrong with getting more rest."

"Yes, and yet surprise, surprise! Here you are," said Tag. "I'm amazed you found time to get all fancied up and still make it down in time to eat with us."

"I *do* look fancy, do I not?" Rose beamed like the first light of the morning sun as she revelled in her formal attire.

"I'm more surprised Prince Percival found the time to get his royal seamstress to fashion this extravagant gown for you, not to mention cracking open the royal vault to gift you with these fineries," noted Rainus. He admired these exquisite pieces of jewellery as Princess Rose was quite literally dripping in diamonds.

Rose's eyes suddenly stared down at her plate. There was a trace of guilt shadowing her face as she used the fork to poke at her food.

"I know that look," grumbled Tag, as he shook his head in disappointment. "For shame, Princess! For shame!"

"What are you speaking of?" asked Myron, as he glanced at Tag, and then over to Rose. "What does she have to be ashamed of?"

"I do believe the young sir means to say these jewels and that fancy gown were *not* gifted by Prince Percival," surmised Rainus. He could not help but notice how perfectly everything fit her, like they were custom-made specifically for the Princess.

"You used a wish?" asked Myron, sitting tall in his chair as he stared across the table at Rose.

"Before you get angry, yes, I did use a wish, but it was not squandered! Just know I did *not* break our agreement. This was an emergency, if ever there was one. After Prince Percy took issue with my apparel when we first met, I thought it was important for him to see me, his prospective bride, in all my glory, dressed as a princess should dress."

While Tag's eyes rolled in frustration, the palm of Myron's hand soundly slapped his forehead as he groaned.

"Men!" grunted Rose, her tone indignant as she shook her head. "None of you will ever understand, except perhaps Lord Silverthorn, but in my world, this was indeed an emergency, a dire one to be circumvented and easily rectified, thanks to my quick thinking. Plus, if it is of any consolation to you, I thought it made good sense not to allow the final wish of the day to go to waste needlessly."

"Oh! So don't tell me, you squandered another wish to ready yourself to look like this for Prince Prissy?" snorted Tag.

"I am proud to say I did all this on my own," insisted Rose. "Waking early allowed me to create these lovely results."

"So, there are still three wishes for this day?" asked Myron.

"Yes."

"Hmph!" grunted Rainus, as he peered over the rim of his teacup at her. Surprised by her words, he nodded in approval. "That is good news for a change."

"I suppose you are mad at me nonetheless for using that final wish," decided Rose, as she glanced over at Tag.

The young man unleashed a sigh of resignation. "Truth be told, I really have nothing to be mad about. There was nothing pressing, so that wish would have gone to waste, had you not used it. There are far worse things you could have used it for, so no harm done, I suppose."

"This time," chimed in Rainus.

"Speaking of time, when will we have our audience with King Maxmillian?" queried Rose.

"His personal servant stated that His Highness will do so when he is good and ready," answered Myron. "That means after he has had his morning ablutions, breakfast in bed, been briefed of today's events and is dressed to receive us."

"And the same goes for Prince Percival," added Tag. "And we were told by his manservant that this royal requires even more time than *you* to get ready to meet the day."

"So… it will be some time before I, I mean *we*, meet with King Maxmillian and his son," determined Rose.

"We have time to kill, Princess," assured Rainus.

"Yes, and before more of this day is wasted waiting about for our royal hosts, perhaps we should check on Harold," recommended Myron. "Make sure he wakes with enough time to dine before we have our audience with King Maxmillian."

"Well, while you see to Harold, Tag and I will go to the stable; tend to our horses," offered Rainus. "We shall make sure the animals are ready to go when we are."

"Good plan." Myron nodded in approval.

"What about me?" asked Rose. She daintily sipped her tea to chase down the sweet biscuit.

"Did you want to help us with the horses?" questioned Tag. "They need their hooves cleaned before we take to the roads."

She stared with raised eyebrows at Tag as he pretended to use his knife like it was a pick to remove dirt and pebbles packed against the frog of the hoof.

"I think I should accompany Myron," answered Rose. "Make sure Harold is up and about, instead of wasting away the morning luxuriating in his bedchamber."

Rainus excused himself from the table, bowing his head in polite parting salutations as he left the dining room with Tag following close behind.

"You know where we'll be when we are finally granted an audience with King Maxmillian," called Tag, as he disappeared with Rainus.

Myron nodded, and then glanced across the table to Rose as she swallowed another mouthful of biscuit. "Are you done?"

"Almost," she mumbled.

"Why do you not just stay here?" asked Myron, as he stood up from his chair. "No need to rush your meal on my account."

"I think not! It will not reflect well on me."

"How so?"

"How do you think it will look if Prince Percival should wander into this room to find me alone, stuffing my face? Even though I arrived later than the rest of you, he has no way of knowing that. He will likely assume we were all seated at the same time and, while the rest of you finished, it will look like I've been abandoned because I am still eating like a hungry, little pig."

"If you must worry about what that young man will think of you just because you are having breakfast, then perhaps he is not the right suitor for you."

"Bite your tongue!" snapped Rose. She crammed half a biscuit into her mouth, mumbling once more as she spoke, "I am done now. We shall leave together."

Chewing as she gathered up the hem of her gown, she followed Myron up the grand staircase. They came to a stop at the first bedchamber situated at the top of the stairs.

"Do you hear that?" asked Myron, cupping a hand to his ear as he listened intently.

Rose pressed an ear to the door.

"It sounds like moans... moans of pain!" she gasped. "Something is wrong with Harold!"

Not waiting for an invitation to enter, with the hilt of his sword in one hand Myron used the other to work the door latch. The crunch and clatter of scattered objects being shoved aside as he forced the door wide open was followed by an obnoxious stench, like the curdling, stale reek of a public drinking house on the morning after hosting a bevy of late-night revellers bent on drinking the establishment dry.

The overwhelming pong billowed forth, rolling out like an invisible fog to accost their olfactory senses. They recoiled, assaulted by the foul odours reminiscent of fusty ale, acrid smoke and sweaty, unwashed bodies crowded into a small, sweltering room heated by stale pipe smoke and firewood. Stepping inside, Myron and Rose gasped as a strange and disturbing scene unfolded before their eyes.

Amidst the carnage, sprawled out in the middle of the floor was Harold. With nothing more than a black and white pelt of a striped skunk on his head and the counterpane from his bed draped loosely around the lower half of his doughy, naked body, he lay lifeless. His half-closed eyes stared vacantly at the ceiling. Crusty trails of saliva that radiated from the corners of his mouth, like the telltale dried slime left by slugs, were made all the more apparent against his skin that had taken on a sickly pallor in the harsh light of the morning sun streaming in through the window. This great beam shone down on Harold as motes of dust floated like Fairy's dust in this radiant light.

"Good gracious! He was robbed! Beaten and robbed!" gasped Rose. The sight of this ransacked room strewn with debris shocked her. "Is he even alive?"

In a daze, Harold lifted his head upon hearing the dull drone of voices. Seeing it was only his two friends standing at the doorway, he moaned in a failed bid to greet them. His eyes rolled to the back of his head as it flopped, striking the floor with a hollow 'thud'.

"Clearly, he is alive, but Harold shall only wish for death once he comes to his senses," muttered Myron, shaking his head in disgust.

"And I hardly think the man was robbed, perhaps of his dignity, but not of his personal belongings."

Glancing about, Myron spied upon a small, empty keg of ale on the dishevelled bed, its mattress hanging half off the frame. Dirty dishes and empty tankards that could find no space on the table had spilled over onto the floor. Stale crusts of bread, hardened crumbs of cheese, and great bones of ham hocks gnawed bare lay scattered around Harold. It was as though he had been trampled in a stampede to a banquet, and then fell victim to a feeding and drinking orgy.

Myron stepped over the clutter. Using the edge of his boot to sweep aside the dishes and scraps of food, he cleared a path to his friend. Prodding Harold's rib with the toe of his boot, the only response Myron could solicit from the man was a cough and a snort, followed by a long, loud snore as he drifted off to sleep once more.

Nudging him again, Myron called, "Wake up, Harold. It is time to make ready for the day."

The knight's demand was met with the smacking of thick lips, followed by another low, droning snore.

"Well, this is truly disgusting, and I am not just speaking about the condition of this bedchamber," grumbled Rose. She refused to take another step into the carnage to follow Myron.

"Once Harold wakes, not only will he get cleaned up before he leaves this room, I will make sure he straightens up the worst of this mess."

"Good luck just trying to wake him." She shook her head in disapproval. "The man is dead to the world."

"Worry not, Princess. I will rouse him from this alcohol-tainted slumber."

Picking his way across the room, Myron lifted the pitcher of water. It sat in the matching porcelain washbasin, waiting to be used for morning ablutions. Both were pushed to one side of the table that was now burgeoning with dirty dishes.

"What are you doing?" queried Rose, watching as the knight hovered over his inebriated friend. "Judging by that empty keg and all these dirty mugs, I hardly think he is thirsty. I would not be surprised if he even sopped up the dregs at the bottom of the barrel."

To her astonishment Myron deliberately and purposefully poured the entire contents of the pitcher onto Harold's sleeping face.

The chilling brace of this cold water caused the prostrate man to bolt upright, sending his now wet skunk headpiece flying toward Rose. The counterpane fell away from Harold as he coughed and sputtered, wiping the water from his startled face.

"Look away!" Rose squealed in disgust, averting her eyes and turning her head, but too late.

Myron flung the soggy skunk pelt back over to the naked man as Rose fled from the room, crying: "Woe is me, my poor eyes! This cannot be unseen!"

Suddenly sober, Harold was overcome by a sense of modesty. He snatched up his headpiece, holding it before his shrivelled manhood like he was wearing a boldly striped merkin. He shuddered as the water trickled down his goosy, pale flesh.

"That was Princess Rose, wasn't it?"

"It most certainly was," confirmed Myron.

"You saw nothin', my lady!" Harold shouted behind her, stumbling toward the door with nothing more than the skunk pelt to cover his nether regions.

"For pity's sake, get back in here!" ordered Myron. Grabbing the pair of trousers his friend had abandoned at the foot of the bed, he tossed it to Harold. "Put some clothes on before Princess Rose demands I gouge out her eyes so she will not be subjected to more of you in this sorry state."

"Sorry state, indeed," moaned Harold. A resounding belch rumbled forth, escaping him to pollute the air they breathed. "You don't suppose she saw anythin' in the way of twig and berries, do you?"

"Twig and *what*?"

Harold glanced down to his manhood.

"For your sake and hers, I hope not." Myron shook his head. "Mind you, she did complain about her eyes."

"She's like a delicate flower. I'm thinkin' her eyes were stingin' as the air isn't exactly fresh in here." Harold's nose wrinkled as he sniffed the stink hanging heavy in the chamber. This odour continued to linger long after his solitary party of binging was done.

"What happened in here?" Myron glanced about, inspecting the aftermath of Harold's nocturnal activities. "Did you host a party in your room after we retired for the night?"

"A party?" repeated Harold. He shook the fog from his throbbing head. Dropping the skunk pelt, he used the trousers Myron tossed to him to blot his face dry.

The sight of this large man standing with his feet splayed wide apart as he teetered to and fro, struggling to find his balance; the wet hairs now dark and matted against his pasty-white body that stood out against his tanned arms and face, this was a vision Myron preferred to forget. He shook his head in a failed bid to dispel the sight of Harold that was now indelibly etched in his mind.

"Yes, did you make merry?"

"No," admitted Harold. "But by the way things look, someone got a bit carried away."

"You mean to say that *you* got carried away."

"It was quite by accident, my friend," insisted Harold. "It started out all quite innocently with me pullin' that service bell. The captain wasn't foolin' when he said a servant was always on call. In fact, he showed up right away, askin' me what he could get for me. I felt silly sayin' I just wanted to see if someone would come."

"So you felt compelled to order a keg of ale and a whole roasted pig?"

"Oh no! All I asked for was a cup of warm milk to help me sleep."

"Then how do you explain this big mess?" Myron used the toe of his boot to nudge a well-gnawed bone off the floor onto the plate it fell from.

"Well, when the servant delivered the milk and asked me what else could he get for me, I told him I was feelin' a wee bit peckish," confided Harold.

"And that's when the keg of ale was delivered."

"Well, no… the servant delivered a nice, big tankard of ale, plus, a plate full of bread, cheeses and a ham hock. It was delicious!"

"And so you felt compelled to request another serving?" determined Myron.

"Truth be told, I was hungrier than I thought. After the poor fellow delivered food and drink for the fourth time –"

"The *fourth* time?" Myron's eyes bulged in surprise.

"Oh, yes! All this questin' business gave me a huge appetite, but with the last order, it was the servant who delivered that keg and a platter of food to keep me tied over 'til mornin'."

"Goodness," sighed Myron, with a dismal shake of his head.

"When I thought about it, it made perfect sense. Spared him more trips up and down that big staircase and he seemed so keen on pleasin' me, how could I say no? And who was I to stop him from feelin' like he was doin' a good job?" responded Harold, glancing about to see where he had shed the rest of his apparel during his night of monumental gluttony.

"I'd say the man performed his job too well."

A balled fist thumped Harold's chest as he belched in agreement. Glancing around, he heaved a disheartened sigh. Taking in the condition of this bedchamber, as the alcohol induced haze lifted from his throbbing brain, it was evident just how much he had indulged.

"Methinks I ate too much."

"Methinks you drank more than you ate." Myron removed the small keg from the bed, shaking it to hear only the splash of dregs that couldn't be poured from the spigot. Other than that, there was nothing left inside.

"Not so!" protested Harold, as he fumbled about to pull on his trousers. "I swear that keg was not full to begin with. By its heft, I'd say at least four tankards of ale were already drained from it."

"Yes, undoubtedly those four tankards were delivered to you before the servant decided to spare himself further trips up the staircase by delivering the entire keg, so you could help yourself."

Harold heaved a troubled sigh. "You think so?"

Myron cast a condemning stare at his large, naked friend sitting in a dejected heap with trousers tangled around his ankles.

"I know so," he answered. "Now, get dressed and before you decide to join us, you will clean up this mess."

"Absolutely! This was my doin' after all," said Harold, struggling to sound enthusiastic even in his less than lucid condition. "I have no intention of leavin' this for that kindly servant to deal with."

"Good on you, my sorry friend." Myron stepped over the scattered plates and drinking vessels. "Breakfast will be waiting for you in the dining room."

"I do believe I've eaten more than I should these last few hours."

"Well, if you're still hungry, there's still plenty of eggs and bacon, albeit cold now."

In response, the thought of dining on cold, congealed eggs and greasy bacon made Harold lunge for the water pitcher Myron had emptied on him.

Myron grimaced in disgust as Harold heaved, vomiting into the container. Closing the door behind him, he left his friend to wallow in his self-induced misery.

"When you're up to it, you will find me in the stable with Lord Silverthorn and Tag, as we ready the horses," said Myron.

Harold responded with an explosive, *"Blaaaah!"*

It was a retched sound that echoed from the depths of the water pitcher and was undoubtedly heard around the world.

2

A Tangled Mess!

"It is time," announced Captain Loftus. He rounded up the late-night visitors as they made final adjustments to their horses' saddles. "King Maxmillian is ready to receive you."

"Huzzah!" cheered Rose. She eagerly thrust her mare's reins into Tag's hand as she addressed the captain. "And Prince Percival? Will he be receiving us, too?"

"Prince Percival stated that he will be there only if his father deems it necessary, otherwise, he asked that he not be disturbed."

Rose frowned in confusion. "He does know that I am here, does he not?"

"He does, my lady."

"And?" Rose probed for details.

"And what, my lady?" responded Loftus.

"What reason did he give you for not gracing us with his presence?"

"None."

"*None?*" she gasped. "He must have a very good reason not to see me. Perhaps he intends to have a private audience with me?"

"It is not my place to speak for Prince Percival. Just know that he said nothing about a private meeting and he is a very busy, young man. I suspect he is preoccupied with other matters more dire at this moment."

"What can preoccupy his time this early in the morning? I demand to see him!"

"Rest assured, Princess Rose, if Prince Percival has the time to devote to you, or should his father demand his presence, then he will be in attendance. Otherwise, the young sir is *not* at your beck and call. He is not a well-trained dog that will heel by your side because you insist on his obedience."

"Help me understand, sir. You informed him that I, Princess Rose-alyn of Fleetwood, his intended bride, is here in this very castle?"

"I did."

"Was he pleased or surprised to find this out?"

"Most definitely, by the expression on his face, he was very surprised to hear this news, my lady."

"In a good way, yes?"

"I hesitate to speculate, but I would assume so."

"Well, I will take it as a good thing!" declared Rose, nodding in approval. "I am confident he is as eager to see me as I am to see him. Perhaps, as he is so busy, I should go and surprise him? I can have a private meeting in his bedchamber, with a chaperone, of course."

"Prince Percival does not take well to surprises. Never has. Never will. Unless he is forewarned, he will not take kindly to it," insisted Captain Loftus.

"Yes, but I am speaking of *me*, not some tawdry harlot or cheap plaything here for his amusement. I really must see him."

Loftus moved quickly before Rose, blocking her way. "That would be unwise, my lady."

"But you said he knows I am here."

"Yes, but he is adamant when it comes to his private space and the violation of unsolicited intrusions of any kind," stated the captain.

"I am confident he will make an exception for me. He will understand that I am eager to see him, as we are here for only a brief time," reasoned Rose. She tried to skirt around the man, only to have him block her path once more.

"Be warned, my lady, none, not even his father dare intrude on the Prince's inner sanctum without his prior permission. It is not the done thing."

Rose's shoulders drooped, her lower lip protruding in a pout of disappointment.

"I'm confident he is just as eager to see you, but if protocol demands that you wait, then so be it," said Tag. He offered Rose a consoling smile to cheer her up. "Perhaps that fancy lad requires more time to make himself presentable to you."

"Say... I do believe you are correct, Tag," said Rose, smiling once more. "He just wants to look his very best before I see him."

"He did come across as one to engage in excessive preening," added Myron, recalling Prince Percival's grand entrance the first time they were introduced.

"I have no doubt this young man will want to impress his ladylove," said Rainus.

"Believe me, Lord Silverthorn, Prince Percy's regal bearing is enough to impress any lady," assured Rose, as she and her comrades followed the captain to the throne room.

❀ ❀ ❀

Harold drew in a deep breath. He exhaled slowly in a bid to cleanse away the fog still swirling through his aching head. Rarely was there a time when he regretted his actions, but now, leaning heavily against the door to his bedchamber as he prepared to meet the new day, his body and conscience lamented over his poor decisions of last night.

He could not remember the last time he drank to this excess, enough to make him feel this poorly the following morning. His tongue felt fuzzy, like dry wool and swollen at least three times its usual size. It stuck to the roof of his parched mouth. And the throbbing in his head went unabated even now, standing in an upright position.

When he had forced himself to crawl about the room on all fours, piling up the dirty plates and empty tankards onto the serving platter, he was sure his brain was going to explode from his skull. Now, standing before his relatively tidy room, Harold squinted as the morning light flooded into the corridor. He had drawn the heavy drapes in his bedchamber to lessen his misery as he cleaned up, but the tall bank of windows had no curtains to shield his eyes and lessen the pounding in his head against the sun's brilliant assault.

Hearing a loud giggle, he struggled to stand upright to adopt a more dignified stance even though he did not feel it. This tinkling laughter sounded from the opposite end of the corridor where the royal bedchambers were situated, secluded from the rooms intended for guests. This lilting giggle was followed by the sound of a heavy door being shut and the metallic *clank* of a latch locking behind it.

Harold sucked in another deep breath, doing his best to stand upright and appear halfway human again. He shielded his eyes from the glare of sunlight as he squinted, staring down this long hallway. Blinking hard, he could make out the silhouette of a young woman coming his way.

Prying his pasty tongue from the roof of his mouth, Harold called out, "My lady, apologies are in order."

His greeting went unanswered, but the footfalls grew louder. These deliberate steps marched in his direction. By this chilly reception he had no doubt his slovenly and uncouth appearance of this morning had put her off. He was confident he had lost what little respect he had garnered during their quest in that instant she saw him not only stripped of his dignity, but of his clothes, too.

Harold used the sweaty palms of his broad hands, pressing the wrinkles out of his trousers in a desperate bid to look more respectable before he apologized to her.

"Beggin' your pardon, my lady," said Harold. He felt his face burn a feverish shade of red as his personal shame gnawed at his conscience while he forced his eyes to meet hers.

Instead of a forgiving smile, this comely young maiden stared, branding him with unfriendly, scrutinizing eyes that burned with utter disgust. She hastily knotted the strings of her apron before primping and tucking the loose curls of hair behind her ears.

"You fool! How dare you intrude?" she scolded him as she swept by this behemoth of a man. "The horses are in the stable, not in the castle! Get back to work."

Harold bowed in apology. "Forgive me! I thought you were my friend."

The young lady flashed him a frown and a sideway glance that spoke of her apparent disdain for him. This cursory inspection of his tatty apparel and the stale reek of ale that wafted around him only served to reinforce her belief he was as oafish and stupid as he was large.

"I hardly think you're the type to have friends in such high places, if any friends at all. You best get back to the stable; start mucking out those stalls before Prince Percival catches you trespassing in here."

"But I'm his guest," insisted Harold. His feet shuffled about nervously as she approached to scold him. He was now painfully aware he did not belong in the opulent surroundings of this castle, invited or not.

"So you say! Now, shoo! Get to your station before I report you for neglecting your duties!" ordered the maid.

"Well… I suppose I'll head to the stable, get my donkey ready for another *quest*." He was sure to emphasize this word in the hopes it would lend credibility to his character that was somewhat tarnished after his late night, solitary carousing. To Harold's disappointment, his words fell on deaf ears.

The young lady picked up her tray of cleaning utensils she had abandoned on a narrow table situated against the wall at the top of the stairs. "We all have our duties. Now get to work before we both get into trouble."

"And the stable?" Harold called to her as she hastened down the staircase to put as much distance between them as she could. "Where is it?"

"Are you an imbecile?" she snapped with mounting impatience. "It is where it's always been; around to the back of the castle!"

"Thanks," said Harold. He lumbered down the stairs as she rushed off. "And I'll have you know I'm not a stable boy, even though I'm headin' that way."

His words were ignored as the young lady hurried across the main hall to disappear into one of the many rooms.

Shouldering his pack with one hand, the other pressed against his belly in hopes it would help to stop the incessant churning of his queasy stomach. With slow, steady steps meant as much to ease his aching head, as it was to prevent attracting unwanted attention from others doubting his invited presence in this castle, he crossed the main hall of the keep. He crept by the double doors of the dining hall where the young lady that had verbally accosted him was now at work.

She scowled in disapproval at the sight of him once more, but Harold noticed how quickly her disposition shifted. She was now smiling, as though thoroughly pleased with herself, as she worked. Orders being barked at her by another maid, an older, stern looking taskmaster, seemed to go ignored as the young lady helped with clearing the table. They were loading dirty dishes onto a trolley and dumping food scraps into the slop bucket to be fed to the pigs.

The sight and sound of the cold eggs splatting into the wooden pail caused Harold to hasten his pace. Exiting the keep, he gingerly made his way down the steps into the courtyard. Shielding his eyes from the glare of the sun, he spied upon Captain Loftus heading his way; his comrades following close behind this knight.

Harold winced in pain; his head throbbing as Rose wagged an admonishing finger at him as she snapped, "For shame, Harold Murkins, for shame!"

His ears burned, turning as red as his cheeks. Too embarrassed to look her in the eyes, Harold stared wistfully at the ground as Rose marched by him. Glaring in disapproval, she stomped up the steps into the castle.

"Why the foul mood?" asked Tag to anyone with a possible answer, as he observed this one-sided exchange.

"I believe it is a story best left untold," sighed Myron. Glancing over, he noticed Harold's pleading, bloodshot eyes. No words were needed to see this large man did not want the others to know about his shameful, nocturnal exploits fuelled by ale. "We have more pressing matters to contend with at the moment."

Peering up at the fuming Princess, Tag then glanced back to see the look of exasperation clearly etched on Myron's face and the unadulterated shame radiating like a warning beacon from Harold's reddened visage. Knowing there would be no further explanation for now, Tag decided it was best to let the matter rest and allow his imagination to speculate what had come to pass.

"This way," said Myron, waving Tag onward. "We have an audience with King Maxmillian. It is wise not to keep him waiting lest he changes his mind."

Tag nodded. He jogged up the stairs two steps at a time only to stop midway. Turning about, Tag asked, "Harold, are you not joining us?"

"I should really check on Sassy," declined Harold. Sheepishly he added, "Besides, the skunk headpiece I like to wear for formal occasions is in no condition to be worn right now."

He lowered the pack from his shoulder. The matted plume of black and white fur, still damp with water, dangled pathetically for all to see.

"There's no need to worry about appearances," reasoned Tag. "None of us, with the exception of Princess Rose, are properly dressed for an audience with royalty, but we don't care."

"It's fine," said Harold, unleashing a dismissal sigh. "I should finish readyin' the horses while you have your meetin'."

"The horses are prepared, but you are right. It will serve you well to check on your donkey," recommended Myron, as he directed his friend toward the stable. "She was raising quite the fuss when Tag was loading her up. Just make sure you're satisfied with how Sassy was packed, and then just wait for us. We shouldn't be long."

With Myron's voice echoing in his ears to make his head ache all the more, Harold merely nodded in response. He shuffled off to find solitude in the stable.

As Captain Loftus escorted the party by the dining hall on their way to the throne room, Rose felt the chill of an icy stare fixed upon her. Peering into the room, her eyes locked with those of a pretty maid. The young lady greeted the Princess with a forced smile and a curtsy, as protocol would demand it of her.

Sensing there was nothing sincere in this greeting; that this maid was required to treat all guests with a level of respect and civility, Rose glanced away. She felt no need to treat her any differently than had this maid been in her service at Pepperton Palace. Ignoring the young woman, Rose marched along, close on the heels of the captain leading the way.

As they approached the grand throne room, the two guards in attendance threw the double doors wide open. Captain Loftus made the formal introductions as he ushered the guests forward to meet with his liege.

"I am delighted to see you again, Princess Rose!" King Maxmillian waved them forward to approach his throne. "I see you have improved slightly on the company you keep, exchanging that large buffoon of a man for Lord Silverthorn."

"That *large buffoon* is tending to our mounts," explained Rose. "Lord Silverthorn is here now because we have pressing business to attend to."

"Greetings, Elf Lord, it has been a long while since you had last graced this castle with your presence," said Maxmillian, as he struggled to sit upright on his throne. "I see you have remained unchanged; none the worse for wear despite the ailment to plague your people."

"Of course, I am unchanged. I am an Elf after all." Rainus nodded politely as he spoke. "You on the other hand – "

Myron placed a firm hand on Rainus' shoulder; an unspoken demand that he resist from insulting the corpulent king by speaking his mind.

Maxmillian stared suspiciously at the Elf. "Business, you say? Do you mean to impose a tax on the Troll-made cheese being transported through your forest?"

"That is a fine idea, but our presence has nothing to do with that damned cheese you so covet," answered Rainus.

"So you are here because your quest is done!" determined Maxmillian, sighing in relief as he glanced over to Rose. "Very good! I have a formal announcement regarding your engagement to my son already prepared, the one you had demanded to approve of before it is delivered by my royal messenger to your parents."

"There is no need for that," responded Rose.

"If you *do not* wish to read it, then I will take this as a sign of trust between our royal houses." Perplexed, but inwardly pleased, Maxmillian smiled upon hearing this news.

Tag seized Rose by the wrist, squeezing it as he spoke, "She means to say, there is no need for your royal messenger to deliver it on her behalf."

"I mean to say what?" She glared at Tag, taken back by his words.

Myron raised his hand, motioning for her to be silent. "Due diligence, Your Highness. Princess Rose believes this announcement to her parents was drafted by you with good intentions, but it is her duty and responsibility to review it before it is delivered, just in case there was an oversight of sorts."

Myron then turned to Rose, discreetly whispering to her, "You were tricked once by this man, for your sake and our sanity, take measures to ensure it does not happen again, my lady. I urge you."

Rose looked sheepish as she addressed the King. "Come to think of it, Your Highness, it would be prudent to peruse this message. If anything, my parents will not accuse me of shirking my responsibilities in doing so."

"Plus, it will be in bad form for such an important message to be delivered by an absolute stranger," added Tag. "The wax seal bearing your heraldic symbol to be used on the message is very official looking, but a stamp can easily be forged."

"And why would anybody do that?" grumbled Maxmillian.

"Usurpers and malcontents," replied the Elf, his words matter-of-fact. "Every kingdom ruled by man seems to have those lurking in the shadows; those wishing to undermine the monarchy."

"I am adored by my subjects! My people are loyal to me!"

"Are you positive?" said Rainus. His piercing sapphire eyes stared through this mortal, as though searching his soul for the truth. "It is my understanding there are rumours of discontent, that your people are being taxed beyond reason. Rulers have been overthrown for less, Your Highness."

"Rumours, indeed!" Maxmillian snapped, dismissing Rainus' warning with a wave of his soft, plump hand.

"If your royal messenger is intercepted, the message replaced with one to undermine your intentions, precautions must be taken to prevent this," advised Tag. "Plus, if you are sincere in your motives to see this marriage come to fruition, you must make all efforts not to offend the King and Queen of Fleetwood."

"And how can a message sent forth by me cause offence to King William and Queen Beatrice?" Maxmillian rubbed his beard as he pondered the young man's warning.

"Any message, especially a proposal of this significance, must be delivered by a person *they* hold in trust, one that has a sworn oath of allegiance to them," explained Myron. "In this case, an individual they know will consider their daughter's well-being of highest priority is the one person they will entrust to deliver news of such importance."

"I hardly think her parents would take issue with forming a strong and lasting alliance, one that will benefit both our countries. And how can they say no to such a fine specimen of a prince that is my son?"

"That may be so," responded Myron. "But they are sticklers for adhering to protocol. If you wish to appeal to their senses, it is best to consider our recommendation of sending word via a person they trust unreservedly."

"Then Princess Rose will be the one to present them with the news," said Maxmillian. "Coming straight from her, they will know the proposal is sincere; my intentions honest."

"Sincere?" scoffed Tag, rolling his eyes in cynicism. "Princess Rose's relationship with her parents is such that they will likely believe her wish to marry Prince Percival is rooted in spite, that she made this decision on a whim to stymie their efforts to arrange a marriage for her of their choosing."

"They will not believe in their daughter's sincerity?" questioned Maxmillian. "How is this even possible?"

Rose's eyes were like daggers as she glared at Tag, angered that he revealed too much.

"Does this young man speak the truth, Princess? You have fallen from favour in their eyes? You are no longer in good standing with your parents?"

"It is better to say that my relationship with them has been strained of late," admitted Rose, blushing with embarrassment. "It is nothing to be concerned about and, if I get my way, I intend to rectify this matter once and for all."

"Oh, my!" chuckled Maxmillian, surprised by the conviction in her words. "What are you up to, young lady? I hope you are not planning something as sinister as murdering your mother and father to get your way!"

Upon hearing these chilling words spoken in jest, Rose's comrades exchanged uneasy glances.

"I assure you, it is nothing as drastic as that, Your Highness!" said Rose. "But it does bring us back to the matter of the quest we had embarked on when we were last here."

"Ah, yes! You and your cohorts returned late last eve, hale and hearty, none the worse for wear. So what is there to discuss, other than formalizing plans for the nuptials?"

"These plans must wait for now," answered Rose.

"For what good reason? There is no harm in getting things underway in preparation for the celebration of the century."

"Your Highness, her parents must approve of this proposal first," reminded Myron. "I guarantee you, King William will be most displeased if you proceed to arrange marriage plans for his daughter without his consent."

"And her mother promises to be offended beyond words, if you started making plans for this gala without Queen Beatrice's input," added Tag.

Maxmillian sat back, contemplating the ramifications should he proceed.

"Trust me, Your Highness, there is nothing worse than in-laws feeling like they are being treated like outlaws," said Rainus.

"I suppose you have a valid point, Lord Silverthorn." He gave the Elf a judicious nod.

"Fear not, Your Highness," said Rose, "we can begin planning for the grand nuptials soon enough."

"How soon?" queried Maxmillian.

"When the quest is done," she answered.

Maxmillian raised his hands, motioning her for silence as he spoke, "Are you saying that you returned, even though you claimed you'd not be back until your mission was done?"

"That was the original plan, but circumstances changed things," said Tag, his shoulders rolling in a shrug.

"We were able to deliver aid to Lord Silverthorn and his people as we had intended, however, the fiend behind the deadly malady that befell the Elves, not to mention the tragic deaths of the Trolls, is still at large," explained Myron.

"You are speaking of other Trolls, correct?" Maxmillian's well-padded heart skipped a beat. "You are not referring to Tiny and his cheese-making brethren?"

"Sadly, a necromancer murdered them," explained Tag. "All indications speak of poison."

"Woe is me!" wailed Maxmillian. He struggled to mentally take stock of his supply hoarded away in the castle pantry. "Say it isn't so! What will I do now? My cheese stores will dwindle in no time!"

"You will be relieved to know Tiny managed to evade death," said Rose.

"He did?"

"Yes, Your Highness. Tiny now resides with the Dwarves, taking refuge in the Mines of Euphoria for his safety," informed Rainus.

"And his special goats?" asked Maxmillian, leaning forward to learn more. "Were they harmed?"

"My men helped to corral those little beasts," replied Rainus. "You will be pleased to know Tiny has found companionship with Giblet Barscowl and his kin. They will take care of each other in these difficult times."

"So all is not lost." Maxmillian sighed with relief. In his mind, he rationed out his stock to make it last for the time being.

"I take it, you were referring to access to your special cheese supply?" said Tag.

"Of course not! I was speaking out of compassion. But now that I think about it, with at least one surviving Troll and the herd he continues to maintain, I suppose my cheese supply will flow once more in due time."

"You do understand Tiny lost all his kinfolk, right?" questioned Rose. She stared at the corpulent man as he salivated at the mere thought of this special delicacy.

"A tragedy, indeed, Princess! But life goes on. It would serve Tiny well to pick up the pieces and strive to resume a normal life, and that would include partaking in activities that were common place for him before his tragic loss."

"I believe some time to grieve is in order," said Myron, inwardly appalled by Maxmillian's insensitivity.

"I suppose Tiny needs a day or two to mourn, but nothing is better for the soul than keeping one's mind and hands busy. In that Troll's case, it will be to his benefit to resume crafting that delectable cheese."

"I am sure Tiny will do so when he is good and ready, but just know that when he does, this cheese you prize so much will be in short supply," cautioned Rainus.

Maxmillian glared at the Elf. "Are you saying you intend to impose an embargo on this cheese when it is transported through your domain once more, Lord Silverthorn?"

"Not at all, Your Highness. I am just saying that Tiny must work alone now."

"Trolls, in general, are slow of wit and action," said Maxmillian. "However, I am certain Tiny can be encouraged to work harder, with the proper motivation."

"Just to meet your quotas?" asked Tag. He was appalled, but not surprised by this royal's greed.

"You make me sound so very insensitive," grunted Maxmillian.

"You did state the importance of 'supply and demand' when we were here last," reminded Rose.

"What of it?"

"You said that you were the lone distributor of this product beyond your realm," answered Rose.

"Yes, a deal I struck up with that Troll earlier this year. As far as I am concerned, this deal still holds true, tragedy or not."

"Then all is not lost," said Rose. "Just do what you do best; increase the taxes on your existing stock of cheese, but only after you raise the prices to reflect just how *rare* this product has become. Those with deep pockets and discriminating taste, as well as a reputation to uphold, will spare nothing to buy it."

Maxmillian slapped his meaty thighs that jiggled from the impact as he praised her. "Brilliant, my dear! You are going to fit right in with that head on your shoulders! I swear, when it comes to generating revenue, you have more business sense than my son!"

"Are you bragging about me again, Father?"

All eyes turned to the doorway upon hearing Prince Percival. Like a vainglorious rooster, he strutted into the throne room.

Rose flushed, her knees weakened upon setting eyes on him for the first time since returning to this castle. Her heart raced; the sensation of a thousand butterflies taking flight in her stomach made her feel giddy with excitement. Her adoring eyes admired the young man decked out in the finest of silk brocades embellished with gold and silver threads and a rich, deep purple velvet cape draped majestically over his shoulders.

Abiding by protocol, all in attendance bowed in respect. Rose curtsied as Percy paraded by her, not even acknowledging those in his father's company.

"My son!" greeted Maxmillian, motioning Percy on to the dais so he, too, may stare down at those before him. "Step forward, join me by my side."

Percy did not hesitate. Like a proud cockerel perched above the lowly hens, he stood on this platform; hands on his hips, chest puffed out as he flicked his golden locks off his shoulders like he was posing for an official portrait to be painted.

"Did you hear the news?" asked Maxmillian. His beady little eyes almost disappeared in his plump, round face as he beamed at his son.

"I heard rumours about late night visitors arriving in our courtyard at an ungodly hour," answered Percy. "It is my understanding that my dear Princess Rose-alyn was amongst them."

"Indeed!" said Maxmillian. Nodding vigorously, he sent his generous jowls a-wobbling.

"Where is she then? Where is my fair princess?" With those steely blue-grey eyes Rose found so mesmerizing, Percy scanned the room, pretending to search for her. "For all I see is this lovely blossom amidst a miserable tangle of thorns."

Rose took a dainty step forward. She curtsied once more as she spoke, "I am here, Prince Percival."

Pretending he did not recognize the young lady in the feminine pink gown and sparkling tiara, Percy stared through narrowed eyes as he scrutinized her. "Rose-alyn? Is that really you?"

She bowed her head in respectful greeting.

"I did not recognize you in this fine gown and those beautiful jewels! You are truly stunning… a vision of beauty to match mine own! In every sense of the word, you look as a princess should; perfectly attired and suitable to be seen in public by my side."

"Thank you, Prince Percy." She blushed, trembling as he took up her right hand into his to plant a gentle kiss upon it.

"In our circles, appearance is everything. I am pleased you have done away with that appalling raiment you were wearing when we were first introduced!"

"Though it was less than eye-pleasing, those trousers did do the job for the mission."

"Well, I am glad the quest is done and you are safe, my dear," said Percival.

"She is safe, but the quest is *not* done," interjected Tag. His skin crawled as he was made witness to this public display of affection.

"Say again!" demanded Percy. He scowled as he stared down his perfect nose to glare at Tag.

"The quest is not yet done."

Percy glanced over to Rose. Perplexed by Tag's statement, a look of doubt was clearly etched across his handsome face as he confronted her. "Is this true, my dear? This is a mere stop, a momentary respite, before you go gallivanting off once more on another one of your rollicking adventures?"

Myron's hand rested on Tag's shoulder; a silent order not to provoke the Prince with words spoken out of anger as he responded, "I hardly call a mission to capture a deranged murderer a rollicking adventure, my lord."

"A murderer, you say? My father informed me that you were on a mercy mission to aid the Elves."

Rainus stepped forward to address Percival. "They did, delivering much needed medicine."

Percy scrutinized the Elf. In his opinion, this was a being that appeared to match him in perfection, but not quite. "And I am to believe the words of Silverthorn's lackey?"

With one raised eyebrow, Rainus stared at the impudent royal.

"I *am* Lord Silverthorn of the Woodland Glade, the very forest that provides safe passage for the cheese your father so covets."

Maxmillian reached over, pulling his son close as he whispered, "Do not raise the ire of this Elf. Relations are tenuous enough as it is. Do not give him reason to slap an embargo on my precious cheese shipments. I beg of you."

Percy nodded in understanding, turning his attention back to Rainus. He sounded contrite as he spoke. "I beg your pardon, Lord Silverthorn, please forgive my ignorance. We have never been formally introduced, nor am I well acquainted with your kind, apart from what I have read and had been taught by my scholarly tutors. For some reason I thought the Elf Lord would be more youthful and ethereal in appearance. I was not expecting someone quite so *ordinary*; an above average looking mortal with pointed ears."

"And this is the reason why I do not like most mortals," Rainus muttered to Myron.

Myron spoke up before this exchange became more heated. "Lord Silverthorn's people did receive the medicine before more lives were lost, but now, we are on the hunt for the instigator of this treachery."

"This demented soul also kidnapped our friend, Loken of the Fairy's Vale," added Tag.

"Really?"

"The perpetrator of these crimes, including the poisoning deaths of the Trolls, must answer for these acts of murder," continued Myron.

"Oh, my!" gasped Percy, as he turned to his father. "I do hope your cheese is still in good supply!"

"I shall ration out what is in stock until the surviving Troll can replenish it," answered Maxmillian.

"What is wrong with you people?" snapped Tag. "Forget about that stinking cheese! We have a deranged killer on the loose, one that must be stopped before more innocent lives are lost."

As Percy and Maxmillian gasped, appalled by Tag's antagonistic demeanour, Rose motioned for calm.

"Be reasonable, my friends. Prince Percy is just concerned about the economic ramifications to his realm should his father's business be affected," said Rose, wishing to pacify her comrades while boosting Percy's flagging image that was compounded by his poor choice of words.

"Ah! My dear Rose-alyn understands what you commoners cannot," sniffed Percy, his tone condescending. "But if the original quest was to deliver medicine to Lord Silverthorn's people, and this was accomplished, why should Princess Rose-alyn be forced to continue on with another quest to capture this villain?"

"This is not a new quest," replied Myron. "The original one just took another unexpected twist, one that must be resolved, once and for all, before others die."

"So, because the mission did not meet with a successful end, you are forcing her to go with you, as a form of punishment for whatever reason."

"I am not being forced," explained Rose. "I suppose you can say I am obligated to aid in this mission."

"Ob- obligated?" sputtered Percy. He frowned at her as he digested this news. "You are a princess! How can you be obligated to any one of these ne'er-do-wells you pass off as your friends?"

"It's complicated," answered Rose, as she fought to maintain her composure under Percy's biting tone.

"Were you the one to set this deranged soul on a killing spree?" queried Percy.

"Pretty much!" Tag piped up, only to be punched in the arm by Rose.

"If you speak ill of my bride-to-be, I shall use a dull knife to carve out that tongue from your smug face," warned Percy, casting a baleful stare in Tag's direction.

In a meek voice, Rose admitted, "In a round-about way, it was slightly my fault. But rest assured, Prince Percy, with the help of Silas Agincor, we shall bring this murderer to justice."

Percy frowned as he turned this name over in his mind. "Are you speaking of *the* Silas Agincor, the wily Wizard that also goes by the title of Dream Merchant?"

"Yes, the one and the same," confided Rose. "He has come to our aid, and even now, Master Agincor works to help us bring the murdering miscreant to justice."

"This is truly bizarre, my dear Rose-alyn." Percy's index finger tapped his perfectly cleft chin as he pondered this mystery. "How did this Wizard become embroiled in this misadventure you call a quest?"

"I summoned him." Rose placed her hand over the Dreamstone hidden beneath the bodice of her gown.

Percy shook his head. "That is impossible! It is my understanding the Dream Merchant can only be summoned by either one in dire need, or when this purveyor of dreams is being summoned to have one of his magic crystals returned to him."

"You would know, wouldn't you, my lord?" snipped Tag. His tone was icy as he cast an accusing stare at the Prince.

"I already have power, wealth, an abundance of charm and good looks, more than you can shake a stick at! And let us not forget, I now have a lovely, prospective bride." Percy's tone was matter-of-fact as he winked at Rose. "Why would I need the magic from a Wizard whose power is to grant wishes when I have all I will ever want or need in my lifetime?"

"You tell us!" snapped Tag. Percy's coyness only served to agitate him all the more.

"What are you speaking of?" asked Rose, bewildered by Tag's accusing words and cynical tone.

"This fool of a knave speaks of nothing because he knows nothing," dismissed Percy. "If anything, he delves into dangerous rumours. But I say again, it is not any person who can summon the Dream Merchant. It is my understanding he only appears if one wishes to bargain with him or to return a Dreamstone."

"Very true," admitted Rose.

"Are you saying you possessed one of these magic crystals?" Percy gasped with surprise.

"That was part of the reason this quest was first initiated," disclosed Myron. "Due to a cavalcade of misfortune brought about by the Dreamstone, part of our mission was to help Princess Rose reclaim it from an evil Sorcerer, Parru St. Mime Dragonite, so she can return that cursed thing back to its rightful owner."

"Tut, tut! You speak ill of something you obviously do not understand, Sir Kendall," chided Percy. "The Dreamstone is not an accursed object. It is a powerful and awesome tool that can be used to affect great change. However, when its powers are abused in the hands of a witless fool, that is when bad things can happen."

"I mean no disrespect to you, Prince Percy, but I am not a witless fool," said Rose. "The powers of a Dreamstone can cause those of the strongest will and the most honest of intentions to be reduced to making foolish wishes."

"Hush, my dear Rose-alyn, say no more! A delicate creature like you is not meant to wield a powerful crystal. Only a man with the moral scruples and know-how to best utilize such a weapon, I mean *gift*, can take proper advantage of a Dreamstone. It is a pity you had forfeited such a wondrous prize."

"I have plenty of scruples! It was always with the best intentions that I had used the Dreamstone, and yet, practically every wish came with dire consequences," lamented Rose.

"So you say!" Percy shrugged. "However, I sense your wishes were not practical to begin with. Most likely, they were based on emotional needs, and we all know emotions can be a very messy thing."

"Here! Here!" Maxmillian agreed with a nod as his fist pounded the armrest of his throne. "If it is to wish for something practical, like more cheese, a Dreamstone would be a stupendous thing to possess. However, it is obvious to all that in the wrong hands, this crystal can be a dangerous thing."

Rose was stunned. Her mouth drooped open upon hearing Percy's damning comments that were reinforced by his father's. They were meant to put her in her place and keep her there.

"That is an unbecoming sight, my dear," groaned Percy, motioning for Rose to close her gaping mouth. "Just know that decisions based purely on emotion or avarice often have terrible consequences."

"Princess Rose can be accused of making some poor decisions in the past, but she was not behaving like some hysterical girl acting on a whim. Overall, she meant only to do good," countered Tag, coming to her defence. "But that is neither here nor there at this point. What is for certain is we must capture a demented murderer before it is too late!"

"Good gracious!" exclaimed Maxmillian. "If Dragonite still roams free, armed with the Dreamstone no less, what are you still doing here?"

"Yes! Why are any of you here, loafing about, if the peril is so dire?" questioned Percy, staring down his nose at Rose and her comrades. "Capture that deranged Sorcerer, reclaim the Dreamstone, *and then* return to us when your task is done."

"It is not Dragonite we are after," disclosed Myron. "The Sorcerer is dead."

"Are you sure?" asked Maxmillian, as he mulled over these foreboding words.

"Yes, Dragonite is quite dead, but we are now challenged by another taking up his mantle," answered Rainus.

"And this foe has proven to be as dangerous as the Sorcerer," stated Tag.

"Say no more!" urged Maxmillian. "Spare your comments. Use this time and your energy to bring that murderous fiend to justice before this evil spreads to my realm."

"That is our plan," said Rose, "but I felt it would be a show of courtesy and respect to come by this way first; to update you on our progress before we head off, rather than have you think I had abandoned my promise."

"It was considerate of you, my dear. Now, be on your way. Do what must be done to end this madness," urged Percy, waving Rose and her comrades off. "Reclaim the Dreamstone, and only then we will meet again."

"We shall not be long," promised Rose.

"If you and your comrades have yet to capture this killer and take back the Dreamstone, even with the help of the Wizard, I highly doubt you will be back any time soon," determined Percy. "Just consider yourself lucky that I am such a patient man. I shall dutifully await your return."

"But half the quest is already accomplished," said Rose, even as Tag and Myron rushed her away, attempting to steer her toward the doorway and beyond.

"We really must be leaving now," said Rainus, quickly bowing to Maxmillian and Percy as he backed away. "There is still so much to do."

"Halt!" demanded Percy. He stormed down the dais to yank Rose free of her friends' grip. "What do you mean the quest is half done?"

"I already reclaimed the Dreamstone," explained Rose.

Before Tag could stop her, she fished out the magic crystal from her bodice, letting it dangle on its chain before Percy's astonished face. His eyes bulged in amazement. Even against the glitter of her dazzling, diamond-studded necklace, this simple bead of crystal had its own special allure.

3

A Clash of Swords

"Why… *(Thump!)* did… *(Thump!)* you… *(Thump!)* do that?" groaned Tag. He banged his forehead one more time for good measure against the stable door. *(Thump!)*

"Do what?" With a coy smile Rose blinked innocently at her friend.

"Tell Prince Percival that you have the bloody Dreamstone, that's what!"

"So what if I did?" snapped Rose.

"You must admit, my lady," said Rainus, "it was not the wisest thing to do."

"And just what was I supposed to do?" asked Rose. "I was not about to begin lying to the man destined to be my husband! If I start deceiving him now, it will be a relationship built on lies. I will not have that."

"I'm not saying you had to out-and-out *lie* to him," grumbled Tag, his face flushed with annoyance. "I was just saying you didn't have to tell him you already possess the magic crystal. There are some things he just does not need to know."

"Why?" she asked.

"Because the Dreamstone can be a great and dangerous temptation to someone like him," answered Tag.

"I think not! I am the only real temptation Prince Percy is faced with. Thankfully, he is a true gentleman with moral scruples of unquestionable integrity. And as he said before, he has no need for the Dreamstone; he already has everything he desires."

"If he's not interested in that crystal, then why, out of the blue, is your prince tagging along on this quest?" argued Tag.

"He means to keep me safe."

"That's what we're for!" Tag's angry eyes flashed over to Myron and Rainus before defiantly jabbing a thumb to his chest.

"Well, I have no doubt he would like to experience a life of adventure firsthand," added Rose.

"You bloody well know he'd rather be left in that castle with his big nose buried in his books; living a vicarious life of adventure than being subjected to the hardships of a real quest," fumed Tag.

"What do you know?" snapped Rose, snatching her mare's reins from Harold's hand.

"There is nothing we can do about it now," said Myron, passing the gelding's reins to Tag. "We must make the best of a bad situation."

"Did I hear correctly? Prince Percival's joinin' us on this quest?" asked Harold.

"Sad, but true," muttered Tag, as he led his horse toward the courtyard. "He insists on coming with us."

"The more the merrier! That's what I always say," chirped Harold. He was only too glad that the attention no longer focused on him and his sorry state of earlier in the morn. He tugged on Sassy's reins as the little donkey snorted in protest for being made to leave her cosy stall.

"Not in this case," stated Rainus, speaking with all certainty. "I have a bad feeling we shall only be burdened by the demands made by this young royal."

"Don't you go worryin' about that, Lord Silverthorn," urged Harold. "You just worry about the business of savin' Loken and capturin' that crazy Witch. I'll see to Prince Percival's needs along the way, if he be needin' anything at all."

"See! Problem solved!" declared Rose, nodding in approval to the large man. "Harold has kindly offered to act as Prince Percy's personal manservant; we shall have an extra sword should there be danger; plus, it will give me an opportunity to become better acquainted with the man who will one day, as my consort, rule this realm *and* Fleetwood. The time we spend together will give him a chance to reveal his true and noble qualities that I know are there, but you all seem to feel he is lacking in."

Tag heaved a disheartened sigh as he grumbled, "True qualities, indeed! In time, I'm confident Prince *Prissy* will reveal all this, and more."

This would be the only consolation for Tag and his comrades; the cad of a prince would show his true character, revealing his real motive for coming along.

Rose nodded in gratitude to Tag. "I am grateful you are willing to give him a chance, but please, at least in his presence, do address him as Prince Percival."

"Prince Percy," bargained Tag.

"He allows *me* alone to address him as Prince Percy, a term of endearment really. You shall not address him so informally. Instead, you will address him as either *my lord* or Prince *Percival*, or do not even bother speaking to him."

"I prefer not to talk to him at all," sniggered Tag.

Myron and Rainus smiled at him in agreement while Harold frowned in confusion at this veiled hostility directed at their new travel companion.

"You are all acting like insolent, childish brats," admonished Rose. "Prince Percy only means to aid us on this quest, to help me, if nothing else, being his betrothed. I demand you pay him the level of respect he is deserving of."

"I'll be happy to give him exactly what he is deserving of," offered Tag. He waved a clenched fist into the air before following Rainus to the courtyard.

"You better be nice to my prince, or so help me, Tagius Yairet!" demanded Rose. She shook an angry fist right back at him.

"As long as *your prince* does not provoke me, we're good," Tag said with a shrug of indifference.

Rounding the castle, Tag's troubled heart plummeted into his stomach. The sight of Prince Percival's smug grin as he waited in the courtyard served to rankle his nerves.

There he was. The hubris, young man looked as pretentious and pompous as did his mount. Percy was perched upon a magnificent, snow-white specimen of a warhorse with an elaborately braided mane and tail adorned with royal purple ribbons to match his cloak that was lined with luxurious sable and trimmed with the white fur of the ermine. An intricately embossed bridle, reins and matching saddle made this horse look like it was prepared for the pageantry of a fancy parade rather than a long and gruelling trek into the wild.

As Rose strolled forward with her mare to greet him, Percy stared at her. His steely eyes inspected her from head to toe.

"What happened to your lovely gown, my dear Rose-alyn? Where are your fine jewels and your sense of good taste and fashion? Have they been abandoned for this atrocity you wear now?"

She glanced down at her riding attire, brushing the dust from the leather trousers that paired perfectly with her riding boots and the simple linen blouse she wore. "I am dressed appropriately for the quest, my lord. That pink gown was not designed for riding on horses."

"It is, if you ride sidesaddle, as a proper, young lady should," countered Percy.

"Surely you do not expect me to ride sidesaddle in a formal gown for league upon league?" Rose was stunned by his suggestion.

"Surely you do not expect *me* to be seen in public with *you*, my prospective bride, dressed as a man and riding like one, to boot?" responded Percy, staring down his nose in the most condescending manner.

"Hey!" snarled Tag. "Princess Rose is suitably dressed for this mission. Leave her alone."

Percy's eyes narrowed as he glared in contempt at Tag. "You will not address me with a *'hey'*. I am Prince Percival to you, and you shall address me with the respect I am deserving of!"

Tag swallowed his pride as he made another appeal. "Prince Percival, I apologize for my abruptness. I insist you leave Princess Rose alone on the matter of her dress for, in all likelihood, we will be venturing into rough terrain and inclement weather as autumn settles quickly on the lands and winter comes early to the regions far to the north."

Percy's tone was uncompromising and authoritarian as he responded to Tag's words. "*I* am the one in the position of power here; the one to insist, request, order and demand, not *you*. I will be taking command of this mission, so you and your cohorts best learn to be mindful of me. In short order, you will learn to follow my directions and do so with utmost obedience."

"Brilliant! I'm sure, under your command, this quest will meet a triumphant end with little or no casualties." Tag's words were tainted with cynicism and spite.

"Absolutely!" declared Percy. He gave Rose a confident wink upon his sudden, self-appointed promotion. "I promise to make for a worthy commander to lead this mission."

"I'm just glad you have ample experience leading a dangerous quest to capture a demented murderer armed with dark magic," said Tag, as he grinned at Percy. "Skills on the battlefield and an excellent strategy can mean the difference between life or death, especially if this trek takes us deep into dragon country. You do have experience leading such an expedition, right?"

"Perhaps not firsthand experience, but I have read plenty of books of adventure; tales filled with acts of derring-do," confided Percy. "Besides, how hard can it be to order people about?"

"Oh, I'm confident you're very good at that, if nothing else," muttered Tag.

Myron threw himself onto his stallion, steering his mount before Percy's to confront the young man, eye-to-eye. "I mean no disrespect, Prince Percival, but when was the last time you brandished your sword or fought in a battle? For I have no recollection of you in attendance by your father's side during the last skirmish against Dragonite that united us with Axalon's army, Lord Silverthorn's warriors and Tiny's brethren early in the spring."

"I used my sword just the other week, I will have you know!" With great pride, Percy puffed out his chest.

"In a terrific fight?" questioned Myron, genuinely surprised by this news. "A brawl in the local public house, perhaps?"

"How very uncivilized!" Percy grimaced in disgust at the mere thought of engaging in a scuffle against a ruffian of questionable pedigree in the lowly arena of a neighbourhood tavern. Given the choice, he'd select a formal duel against a fellow royal, or at the very least, a worthy knight. "It was during a respected tournament, of course! It was the final and largest competition of the season to be hosted in Axalon."

"You competed in a contest of swords?" queried Myron, hoping to be pleasantly surprised.

"I used my sword to appoint a new champion to the knighthood. The young sir did an outstanding job doing battle on my behalf," explained Percy, his hand proudly patting the hilt of his weapon.

"So, you *did not* actually compete?" asked Myron.

"That is so, but having witnessed many contests of skill with lance and sword, you can rest assured, Sir Kendall, I have become an expert when it comes to these deadly weapons and their proper implementation."

Rainus steered his mount next to Myron's as he spoke with concern. "What Sir Kendall means to ask, my lord, is when did you last ride into a *real* battle? Used your weapon to take the life of another in an actual fight to the death?"

Sensing doubt in the Elf's line of questioning, Percy responded with a question of his own. "Why do you ask, Lord Silverthorn?"

"I ask because a contest of skills is not the same as a genuine battle to preserve one's life. We fear you will not be prepared for a clash of swords, should we be faced with even a small skirmish."

Percy grimaced in distaste as he pondered this possibility. "I do not partake in such menial and brutish acts of violence. Such demonstrations of savagery are reserved for those already predisposed to pugilistic tendencies."

"Are you saying that if Princess Rose's life is in danger, you'd stand aside, allowing her to come to harm just to spare you from engaging in a *menial, brutish* act?" questioned Myron.

"Even though I am fully capable of fending off an attack, even by many at once, I am merely saying that this is when a knight or soldier intervenes on my behalf. Being the sole heir to the throne of Axalon, I cannot deliberately place my life in jeopardy, even for her," reasoned Percy, as he glanced over at Rose to make sure she understood royal protocol. "Some lucky soul will step forth to champion my cause."

"He speaks the truth," wheezed King Maxmillian, motioning for an aide to deliver a chair so he may sit while seeing his son off. "The heir apparent, my only son at that, cannot and will not be placed in harm's way. As capable as we all know he is, he is not even permitted to enter jousting tournaments for this very reason."

"Interesting," commented Rainus.

"It does make sense, when you think about it," said Harold. He nodded in understanding to Maxmillian, as the mortally obese king plopped down gracelessly onto a chair; his heavy legs seemingly to give out from supporting his immense weight after the short stroll from the throne room.

"If that is the case, why do you even carry that fancy sword?" asked Tag. He stared at the golden hilt of Percy's armament that hung at his left side from a fancy, embroidered baldric. This hilt was encrusted with rubies and the pommel of this magnificent sword was adorned with the largest scarlet gem he had ever seen.

Percy patted this ornate scabbard decorated with gold filigree scrollwork. "This beauty is a gift from my father; purely for ceremonial purposes, of course. Consider it an unspoken testament of my true power and wealth wherever I go."

Tag unleashed a disgruntled sigh as he grumbled to Rose, "So, are you still feeling safe with *him* by your side?"

"I heard that, you insolent knave!" snapped Percy. "And did you not already claim that King William personally appointed you and Sir Kendall to keep Princess Rose-alyn safe during her travels?

"Yes, he did," answered Tag. "That's exactly what we plan to do."

"Well then," sniffed Percy. "If harm should come to her, then you two will be the ones to blame for failing in your duties, not me!"

"Well said, my son, well said!" praised Maxmillian. With a wave of his hand he ordered a servant to deliver him a goblet of wine to toast their departure.

"Thank you, Father." Percy nodded his head in respect to him before turning his attention back to Rose. "As for you, my dear, we have had this discussion before. A change in apparel is in order."

"Can you not make an exception this one time?" she pleaded.

"To make an exception is to make a compromise. Do I look like the compromising sort?" Percy snorted with indignation as he adjusted the golden crown perched on his head. "If you are to be seen in public with me, you will dress as a princess should."

"But –"

"But nothing, Rose-alyn! Return to the castle, don an appropriate gown, and then we shall be ready to leave," demanded Percy.

"That first impression is ever so important, my dear child," averred Maxmillian. "To avoid embarrassing my son before his adoring public, it is best to look the part of a princess if you wish to be seen by his side outside the walls of my great castle."

"I understand the importance of appearances, Your Highness," said Rainus, "but you do understand Prince Percival has volunteered to join us on an important mission, one that can possibly take us into dangerous territories during the height of winter?"

"Of course, my son is aware of that," responded Maxmillian. With a clap of his pudgy hands a royal entourage paraded into the courtyard. "That is why he is going on this quest well prepared."

Rose and her comrades watched in amazement as a team of a dozen servants, each leading a packhorse, trotted into the courtyard. The animals were loaded down with Percy's personal grooming supplies, an extensive wardrobe suitable for every possible occasion he may be called upon to attend along the way, two crates containing bottles of wine representing their best vintage, as well as numerous tents to comfortably house Percy and his staff at the end of each day.

This procession was followed by a large wagon bearing the royal cook, his assistant and an assortment of cooking utensils and food supplies taken from the castle pantry and root cellar.

Behind the cook and his supply wagon appeared Captain Gilbert Loftus, leading a contingent of Maxmillian's army. Riding in on a great ebony stallion, he held high for all to see the standard bearing the heraldic symbol of Axalon. This knight and captain who had reluctantly welcomed their arrival late last night was now appointed to escort Prince Percival and those in his company.

Marching in behind Loftus was a small army of three-dozen knights, hand-picked for this very quest. Each man was decked out in full battle regalia and each led a black mount that was identically saddled and bridled so horse and rider would appear as one powerful, cohesive unit. Man and beast fell into an orderly formation. Snapping to attention and saluting their liege, in one crisp, synchronized movement, all thirty-six knights mounted their steeds. They awaited Maxmillian's inspection and approval before striking out on this adventure.

"What is the meaning of this?" gasped Myron. He stared at the assortment of men and horses now assembled in three perfect rows in the middle of the courtyard.

"It is called leaving nothing to chance," explained Percy, gazing proudly at his followers that will cater to his every whim and fight his every battle. He was confident this show of power would impress Rose as greatly as it would humble her comrades and their motley crew that consisted of nothing more than Harold Murkins and his lowly donkey.

"Are you serious?" asked Tag.

"Unlike you, you useless rapscallion, I am always serious," sniffed Percy. "And while you are woefully unprepared for this quest, whatever the weather, whatever the danger, I will be prepared for every and any situation to arise along the way."

Myron's only response was to drag his hand down his fretful face.

"You must really want us to die on this quest," grumbled Tag, with a shake of his head.

"And you are an idiot!" snapped Percy. "My knights will not only keep me safe, but all of you will be kept alive should danger strike. And there is nothing wrong with having creature comforts while away from the security of this mighty castle, especially for a member of a royal house."

Tag turned to his comrades to pose a question to them. "Tell me, my friends, in all our travels was it ever necessary for us to be accompanied by so many and to be loaded down with so much?"

"We have always travelled with only the necessities and we always moved in secret," replied Myron. "Discretion is a necessity best undertaken with as few as possible."

"Yes, a difficult feat to accomplish with such a large contingent of knights and servants dogging our heels," added Rainus.

"We should light a huge beacon as we travel," scoffed Tag. "Along with the great standard carried by your captain, we can announce to our enemy exactly whom we travel with, where we are and that we are closing in!"

"Brilliant!" exclaimed Percy. "A beacon to announce our coming is just the thing to keep that murderous villain on the run!"

Tag's palm slapped his forehead as he groaned in frustration. "You don't get it, do you?"

"Get what?" snapped Percy, as he sneered at Tag.

"The purpose of this mission is to *capture* this fiend, an impossible feat if evil is always one step ahead and we are unable to catch up because we forewarn of our coming."

"Oh," said Percy. "So, you mean to use the element of surprise to sneak up on this culprit?"

"That was the plan," stated Myron.

"And it promises to be a hard feat, if not totally impossible, to accomplish when trying to conceal the many servants, knights and horses in your service," said Rainus.

"Mind you, if we keep our distance from the Prince and his company, their bold and obvious presence can be used to draw the attention of our enemy," suggested Tag, his index finger tapping the side of his nose as his eyebrows bobbed up and down in mischief. "They can be used to lure that maniac out of hiding, and if we time it just right, we can attack before it's too late."

Rose gasped, appalled that Tag would even dream up such a scheme that would endanger her prospective husband. She smacked his arm. "How dare you?"

"Well, you must admit, Princess, we've survived the quest so far with minimal manpower and resources, moving about in secret," responded Tag. "This certainly cannot be achieved with so many in our company, especially if we're forced to venture to the Fire Rim Mountains far to the north."

"A journey to faraway lands; a likely chance of dreadful weather; the growing potential for danger," announced Percy. "All the more reason to advance with a full complement of knights and servants to make the trek a little more bearable."

"This is not about travelling in comfort," stated Myron. "This is about undertaking a mission and doing whatever it takes to capture this demented soul and to save our friend."

"So you say, but who said one cannot marry comfort *and* adventure to accomplish this deed, and do so in style?"

"I agree," said Rose, as she nodded to Percy. "Why can we not have both?"

"Yes, why not?" Tag smiled, nodding eagerly.

Rose's eyes narrowed in suspicion as she glared at Tag. "You never agree with me unless you are up to something. You are trying to trick me!"

"I would never dream of doing that," said Tag, suppressing his mischievous grin.

"If you mean to trick or manipulate my dear Rose-alyn, then I shall consider this an act of treason!" snapped Percy. "An offence punishable by death, need I remind you?"

"How is agreeing with you two considered treason?" questioned Tag, his tone matter-of-fact.

Myron raised his hands, gesturing for calm. "Let us not speak of treason. Instead, let us use reason."

"Hey! That rhymes!" exclaimed Harold. "I like that."

Percy glared at Harold. This look of utter contempt caused the large man to shrink under the Prince's withering gaze.

"As I was saying," said Myron. "Do we all agree it is paramount to bring this evil to a stop and to rescue Loken?"

"Absolutely!" answered Rainus.

"Of course!" said Rose.

"Without a doubt!" chimed in Tag.

The general consensus was positive, but amongst all these words of agreement, Percy raised his hands for silence.

"I can understand the need to stop this maniac, to end the killings before this lunatic chooses to run amok in Axalon. This, I have no issue with," confided Percy. "However, I feel no responsibility in helping you to rescue that pesky Pooka."

"Fine," snapped Tag. "We'll be the ones to rescue Loken. Just promise to stay out of our way."

"Gladly!"

"The point being," said Myron. "We are not pitted against a typical killer. We are up against one using the powers of the forbidden arts to wreak havoc on the innocent."

"Yes, a cunning necromancer with a penchant for pure evil," stated Rainus. "This deranged killer must be approached with utmost stealth. An army, even a small one, will warn of our approach, tipping this fiend off to take the appropriate actions to repel our efforts."

Percy glanced over to the captain and this conservative show of military might. "Too much?"

"Far too much, by thirty-seven to be exact," averred the Elf.

"Then who will keep me safe?"

"Princess Rose is scary accurate with her sling," stated Tag. "She will keep you safe, if we neglect to do so."

"No offence to her, but she is just a girl!" protested Percy, as Rose frowned to hear these condescending words.

"Yes, a *girl* with an aim that can knock that ruby from your sword's pommel at fifty paces," assured Myron. "I am getting the sense she is better equipped to fight than you are."

"You are that good?" He stared doubtfully at Rose.

"Better," she answered, her hand patting the sling and pouch containing her endless supply of ammunition. "I have had years to perfect my aim."

"Where this necromancer is concerned, there is no such thing as safety in numbers, if that's what you were hoping for," stated Tag. "We found, in dealing with those wishing to conjure dark magic, our best defence has been to move in secret, striking quickly when they are caught unawares."

"So, no show of military might?" asked Percy.

"To be accompanied by so many is an invitation to be attacked," said Myron.

"Mind you," added Tag, "if we are forced to journey to the lands in the north, deep into dragon country, with so many to choose from, all these knights and servants can serve as a distraction."

"Distraction? What kind of distraction?" asked Percy.

"We call it dragon fodder," answered Tag. "If we're caught out in the open with your large company, the dragons will be so distracted with the selection, we can make good our escape while those monstrous reptiles dine."

"Suppose I take half the men?"

"Suppose you take none of them?" countered Myron.

"How about if Prince Percy brings his captain, as his personal bodyguard," negotiated Rose.

"You do not speak for me!" scolded Percy. He glared at her, motioning for silence before turning to Myron. "So, Sir Kendall, one is better than none. Suppose I bring my captain? He will be my champion, if need be."

Myron glanced over to Tag and Rainus for their approval. Both nodded.

"Your captain is permitted to accompany you," answered Myron.

"Very good! He can oversee my servants along the way!"

"I hardly think your servants are capable of handling a sword, should danger come in the way of dark magic or attacking dragons," said Myron.

"It is best to leave them behind," said Rainus. "We travel light and quick. They will only slow us down."

"This is barbaric!" protested Percy, his fair complexion reddening with anger. "Who will manage the supply wagon? Cook my food? Set up my tent?"

"We hunt for our food, cook what we catch and we sleep under the stars," answered Tag. "Surely, if Princess Rose can endure such a rough and tumble existence on the road, you can do the same?"

"Obviously the Princess is far more hardy than most and far less discriminating that she is willing to put up with such a meagre existence," argued Percy.

"She does what she must in order to see this fiend brought to justice and to help secure Loken's freedom," stated Tag.

"It is really not that bad," insisted Rose. "We always manage."

"We are royalty, my dear! We should never be made to just *manage*."

"Just know that I have ways of coping," said Rose. Her hand discreetly rested over the Dreamstone hidden beneath her blouse as she smiled sweetly at him.

Percy nodded in understanding.

"It is obvious to all that you are not cut out for the hardships of a quest," assessed Rainus. "If you feel such a great need for so many just to travel outside of your castle, perhaps it is better for you to remain here."

"Yes," agreed Myron. "It is not like we were unable to cope without you before."

"And nobody is forcing you to come with us in the first place," reminded Tag.

"Perhaps Princess Rose's comrades are right, my son," said Maxmillian, his hand rubbing his generous chin in pensive thought. "I do not fancy the idea of you traipsing about to who-knows-where for who-knows-how-long without a full contingent of men to keep you safe."

"But I have a genuine interest in this quest, Father. I mean to keep our investment safe from harm; impressing the King and Queen of Fleetwood in the process of doing so. If there is no princess, there will be no marriage. Without this marriage, there will be no lifelong alliance between our countries."

"Is that the only reason?" questioned Tag.

"It is the only reason that truly matters," replied Percy. "I mean to stay close to my future bride; keep her safe should you and your friends fail to do so."

"Ahhh! True love!" exclaimed Maxmillian, nodding in approval to his son. "A noble cause and a wise decision when it comes to securing a powerful alliance."

Rose smiled with delight. She elected to ignore Percy's words of protecting his 'investment', choosing instead to dwell on Maxmillian's declaration of his son's love for her, as indicated by his great sacrifice in coming on this quest with so little in the way of protection and creature comforts.

"True love can be a fine motivator, but it can also be the death of you," warned Rainus. "If you are not prepared to join us on this quest, then so be it. Do not subject yourself to the misery of a long and dangerous expedition for altruistic reasons."

"I beg to differ," countered Percy. "In my way of thinking, such a noble act will only prove to the Princess, and more importantly her parents, that my words and deeds speak of my love and devotion for their daughter. Surely, this will win their approval and secure my good standing in their eyes."

"What would win their approval more, and impress the heck out of all of us, is if you were able to prove you can survive such a quest without such a huge party to coddle and cater to your every whim," stated Tag.

"I am a prince, therefore, I am pampered, never coddled! Coddling is for babies."

"The point being, a resourceful, able-bodied prince would have far greater esteem in her parents' eyes, than one that proves to be whining, whinging and full of demands, especially if both suitors are of equal status and wealth," responded Tag.

"So they will require proof of what I am willing to endure to win their daughter's hand in marriage, as well as earn their approval that I am indeed a fitting suitor for her?"

"Any decent parent would only want what is best for their child," said Myron. "Even your father would agree!"

"Sir Kendall does have a valid point, my son," said Maxmillian. "Perhaps a quest is exactly what you will need to bolster your standing amongst those who vie for the Princess' hand in marriage. It will certainly speak of your willingness to prove your worth as a husband to King William's only daughter."

Percy drew a deep breath, exhaling as he considered his father's advice. He weighed and balanced the reward and hardship he'd be forced to endure in the company of Rose's friends against the difficulties of having just one manservant, his captain, in this case, to tend to his needs.

"It is not looking very tempting, is it?" asked Tag. "Not everyone is cut out for a life of danger and adventure."

"Well, if Princess Rose-alyn can do it, then so can I!" declared Percy, as he glared at Tag.

"Are you sure?" asked Maxmillian, pleased, but apprehensive of his son's bold declaration. "I know it will elevate your standing in winning King William's approval, but is the reward worth endangering your life?"

"The reward is much greater than you will ever know, Father." Percy smiled at Rose to send her heart skipping in delight.

"Then it is settled," announced Myron. "If you dare come along, you will be following *our* lead. You are permitted to bring your captain, but you will rest only when we rest; eat when we eat; sleep when we sleep; and stand watch when it is your turn for sentry duty."

"Oh, yes!" added Tag. "One of the rules of the road is our standing in life or title have no bearing. On this quest, we are all equal and share in the responsibilities of caring for the horses, cooking, gathering firewood, and so on."

"I can handle that," insisted Percy. He smiled while his captain's face was suddenly shadowed with woe.

It was apparent to Captain Loftus he'd be made to carry the brunt of Percy's weight, as well as his own, for the duration of the trek.

"And I can help you," offered Harold, with a congenial smile.

"Problem solved, then!" chirped Rose, pleased to see her prince measured up to her expectations when the others hoped he would decline. She mounted her mare with a leg up from Harold. Steering her horse next to Percy's, she said, "This is your chance to show my friends exactly what you are made of! You can prove to them your resilience; that you are perfectly capable of enduring a rugged lifestyle just as well as any of them."

"I am royalty," Percy growled beneath his breath at her. "I need not prove a thing to them."

"Let us waste no more time," called out Myron, as he reined in his horse. "We ride for the north."

Myron and Rainus guided their horses out of the courtyard at a canter. Urging the gelding to follow, Tag's horse trotted close behind the duo. Prodding the flanks of her mare with her heels, Rose followed behind Tag. This abrupt departure from his side prompted Percy to dig his heels into his stallion's flanks to keep up with the Princess. Joining her once more at a quick trot, Percy reined in his mount to keep in step with the Princess. Behind the royal couple, Harold trailed along with Sassy, clucking his tongue against the roof of his mouth to motivate the donkey to keep up with the others as Captain Loftus rode his great, ebony warhorse next to this man and his little donkey.

As they rode, Percy's eyes narrowed. Scrutinizing the party at the front where Rainus and Myron led, followed by Tag, to the back where Harold took up the rear with his captain, Percy decided the order of this procession was a reflection of status within this motley crew.

The cogs in Percy's mind turned as he ruminated on this perceived pecking order, seeing that to boldly take the lead promised to establish him as the boss, the cock of the flock so to speak. However, to do so will be to put him first in line for danger. As he thought on this conundrum, his eyes landed upon Tag. Glaring at the back of this pest's head, Percy made his decision.

He dug his heels into his stallion's flanks, urging this steed to pick up its pace. Abandoning Rose, he quickly gained ground, guiding his mount up next to Tag's.

Seeing Percy from the corner of his eye, Tag urged his horse on.

Soon enough, Tag and Percy were engaged in a race of dominance, neither letting the other pass in front. The horses continued to pick up speed, a continuous ebb and flow of each until their horses' snouts were nearly up the rumps of Myron and Rainus' steeds.

As the iron-shod hoof of Percy's snowy mount clipped the heels of Myron's stallion, the incensed knight reined in his steed.

"Enough with this childish behaviour!" snapped Myron, wheeling his horse about to confront them both.

"You heard the good knight," said Percy, sneering in contempt at Tag. "Grow up, will you?"

"I was speaking to the both of you!"

Percy frowned. He was appalled upon receiving this scolding while Tag merely smiled a smug grin, accepting Myron's words for exactly what they were.

"This rapscallion, I can understand, for he knows nothing about social status nor the true meaning of fealty!" Percy snorted with indignation as he glared at Tag. "But you, Sir Kendall, will not use that tone on me, for you know better!"

Rainus unleashed a disheartened sigh as he muttered beneath his breath, "We have barely even left the castle grounds and already there is dissension amongst the ranks."

Myron steered his stallion up to Percy's mount to address the young man. "I owe my fealty to King William, not to you. And you, my lord, had been forewarned that on a quest such as this, we are all equal. Titles mean nothing to a rampaging dragon or a necromancer bent on revenge. You are welcome to return to your father's side and remain safely behind the walls of your castle."

The knight turned his steed about, resuming the trek but hoping in his heart to be relieved of this royal burden that was sure to slow their progress.

"It's better to turn back now while you have a chance," chided Tag. "Just know that only those with true resilience are cut out for the gruelling and perilous demands of a quest. You're better to live your life of adventure vicariously through the pages of your books."

Tag's damning tone set Percy's nerves on edge. With a disgruntled huff he was determined to prove he was as capable, if not more so, than this commoner or a mere princess for the rigours of a deadly mission.

"What now? Are you going have your captain slap us with his glove for insubordination?" Tag taunted Percy a little more.

"You insolent whelp, Yairet," muttered Percy. "I am a bigger man than that."

"Prince Percy will be more mindful of his words," promised Rose, not wishing for him to be banished so early in the quest.

Percy raised his hand to Rose, motioning her for silence. "You may indeed be a princess, Rose-alyn, but make no mistake, you *do not* speak for me."

"I am sorry," whimpered Rose. These three words were contrite indeed, as she had no intention of offending the man of her dreams.

"As I was going to say," said Percy, as he addressed his reluctant travel companions, "I will be more mindful of my words in the future. I will not allow such pettiness and these verbal fisticuffs to tear asunder this fine fellowship. If I mean to remain by Princess Rose-alyn's side to keep her safe along the way, I must learn to cooperate with all of you."

"Brilliant!" exclaimed Rainus. "That was the smartest thing to come out of your mouth thus far, Prince Percival."

The Elf urged his mount on to keep in time with Myron's steed as Tag followed close behind to put some distance between him and the pretentious royal.

"It was big of you to speak up as you did, Prince Percy," praised Rose. "My friends mean no harm. They are just easy to ruffle and are a little rough around the edges when it comes to dealing with those of higher social status."

"Do you really allow your *friends* to treat you as an equal?" His tone was sour as he questioned her.

"Yes, but only because they *are* my friends and because it has served us well in the past, especially when we first embarked on this quest," explained Rose. "I suppose, on an equal footing, it made all of this not so unbearable."

"Speaking of unbearable, is it true what my father said, that Dragonite surrounded himself with useless mimes?" asked Percy.

"I take it, you did not ride by his side when he first came to our aid along with Lord Silverthorn and the Trolls when the Sorcerer first attacked us earlier in the year?"

"Though my father did offer me the courtesy of riding with him in his fine carriage when he mustered his forces to come to your aid, I had to decline that opportunity."

"You were already engaged in other diplomatic duties?" queried Rose.

"No. Truth be told, that little skirmish held little interest for me, as it had nothing to do with furthering my interests nor was it benefitting my people. In fact, I even took issue with my father for becoming embroiled in that farcical show of force, all for the sake of ensuring his silly supply of cheese would not be affected, if he did not come to the aid of the Elves in a show of good faith."

"But I was there. I was in grave danger!" exclaimed Rose, stunned to hear of Percy's lack of interest.

"Yes, well… had I known you were there, and more importantly, had I known we were destined to be together, I would have had no qualms about overseeing the military manoeuvring required to rescue you."

"I suppose that is comforting to know," said Rose.

"Comforting, indeed! How many damsels-in-distress have the auspicious honour of having a genuine prince, never mind a lowly knight in shining armour, come to her rescue."

"True, but you were not actually there to rescue me."

"It is the *thought* that counts, my dear Rose-alyn. That is what truly matters. Always keep in mind, the intentions of a prince have far more bearing than the acts of a common man." These words were followed by a contemptible scowl directed at Tag.

For a fleeting moment, Percy's cavalier attitude and his haughty tone stabbed at her heart and conscience. Rose was silent as she pondered his comment.

"I am your prince, am I not, my dear Rose-alyn?" He cast a charming smile at her, one intended to melt her heart should she have doubts about his meaning.

"Of course!"

"In hindsight, I do regret having not been there," admitted Percy, heaving a sigh for her benefit.

"You do?"

"Yes! My father told me that through some strange magic, you had transformed into a magnificent, but pink, dragon. You were doing battle with the very Pooka you seek to rescue now. Is it true? If so, it would have been a spectacle worthy of my time to have witnessed with mine own eyes!"

"You would have wanted to see me as a hideous dragon?" gasped Rose.

"If I can handle being seen with you while you are dressed in this atrocious riding garb, then believe me, seeing you as a dragon, albeit a pink one, would have been spectacular! Can you imagine if I had you on a leash, leading you about like a gargantuan pet? If that did not garner respect from the people, then what would?"

"You would have put me on a leash?" Rose was appalled at the thought he'd take pleasure in leading her about like she was an oversized dog. "Parade me about before your subjects for their amusement?"

"For their amusement? I think not! Had you been this horrific dragon, having you on a leash would have struck fear in the hearts of my subjects. Now that would have been for my amusement!"

"I was hardly a great and dangerous beast." Rose's face reddened, prickling with embarrassment.

"Come now! My father said you put on quite the show, especially when that demented Pooka gave chase as an even larger dragon! I would have paid good money to have been a spectator."

"It was not as though we were engaged in a sport," said Rose.

"Well, had it have been, the most important thing is that you won! You defeated that worthless, shape-shifting miscreant!"

"In Loken's defence, he was forced to do the Sorcerer's bidding to keep his love safe," explained Rose.

"Are you justifying his action in attacking *my* ladylove?"

"You did not even know me then," argued Rose. "But yes, I would have done the same, if it meant to keep a loved one safe."

"So tell me," asked Percy, "exactly how did you transform into a dragon?"

Rose was reluctant to answer. She stared at the back of Tag's head as he rode just before them.

"Come now, my dear! You can trust me. It was with that marvellous Dreamstone, was it not?"

"Perhaps."

"Do not be coy with me, my dear! So, how does that clever little trinket work?" probed Percy. He stared intently at the magical bead, although it was hidden from his eyes.

Hearing this exchange, Tag twisted about in his saddle. He cast a threatening gaze at Rose. The expression on his face said all that he did not, and there was no mistaking what was on Tag's mind.

Having already endured a scolding from her comrades for simply showing the Dreamstone to Percy, Rose felt it unwise to reveal how this magic crystal was used.

"Come now, be a lamb," whispered Percy, giving her a charming smile. "You can tell me how it works."

"I know what you're up to!" Tag snapped upon hearing his muted words.

"You know nothing," argued Percy.

"Even if she wanted to Princess Rose is not permitted to reveal to anyone how the Dreamstone works," said Tag.

"I am not *anyone*. I am the Prince of Axalon."

"Big, hairy deal!" grunted Tag, reining in his mount to bring his gelding to a halt. "Even if you were the king of the whole, damned world, she would not be able to tell you. Call it a vow, a promise she made to the Dream Merchant, so the Dreamstone is not abused by some unscrupulous soul with nefarious plans to manipulate its powers."

"Do I look like the type?" sniffed Percy, his back straightening with indignation at the sting of Tag's words.

Simultaneously, as the Princess said *"no"*, Tag gave a resounding *"yes"!*

Rose raised a hand to Tag, motioning for silence as she explained to Percy, "What Tag means to say is that *yes*, I cannot share with others this secret about how to use the Dreamstone. A promise to Silas Agincor upon being the recipient of the crystal, prevents me from doing so."

"So you cannot deliberately break this vow made to the Dream Merchant?" questioned Percy.

"Yes, that is so."

"But should you reveal it, say by accident, you would not be deliberately breaking your promise to that Wizard," pointed out Percy, his words discreet.

"By accident?" repeated Rose, as she pondered his words. "I suppose if I revealed anything and it was by accident, it is not really like deliberately breaking this vow."

"I heard that, Princess!" Tag called over his shoulder. "That's what we're here for, to make sure that does not happen, not even accidentally, until you can return that cursed thing back to Master Agincor."

"Fetch off! Turn about and keep moving, you nosy git," demanded Percy, waving Tag and his horse to continue on. "I never invited you to speak. This conversation is between Princess Rose-alyn and me, so shut your gob and mind your own business!"

"My business is to keep her safe, that includes from unsavoury characters of all ilk, royal or not," snapped Tag.

"Oh, shut it!" grumbled Percy. "What do you know?"

"I know *unsavoury* when I see it." Tag was smug as he prodded his gelding on.

Rose gasped, frowning in exasperation at her friend's candid comment. "Just ignore, Tag. He takes his post as my personal bodyguard too seriously at times."

"To ignore that incorrigible lout is the perfect advice, my dear Rose-alyn." Percy shook his head in disapproval at the knight-in-training. "But as I was saying, it is a shame, an absolute shame. The Dreamstone is a kingly gift! As far as I am concerned, it would be terribly rude to return such a wondrous thing that is capable of providing the beholder with so much."

"I hate to admit it, but Tag is quite correct where the Dreamstone is concerned," confided Rose. "I thought it would be a wonderful gift, being able to wish for whatever I want, but often, the reward was not worth the calamity that often ensued. In the end, it was not worth the cost that cunning Wizard demanded to make the deal binding."

"So you say, but some things are worth the sacrifice," stated Percy, watching as Tag urged his mount on, riding up to Myron's side as the knight led the way. "It is a matter of balance; understanding and believing with utmost conviction what truly matters and what is considered trivial in the big scheme of things."

"I thought, even believed with all my heart at that moment, I was making the right decision and the sacrifice was minimal, but I was so wrong," lamented Rose. "It has become such a burden."

"My dear, such negativity shall only artificially compound the situation. In the hands of the wise, this burden can be a boon!"

Rose smiled at Percy, giggling as she spoke, "You silly goose! I learned firsthand that simply wishing for what you want is a poor substitute for earning what you desire."

"That sounds like something Yairet would say," muttered Percy.

"True enough, but I cannot say he is entirely wrong on this matter." Rose sighed as she glanced up to see Tag conversing with Myron, no doubt sharing his concerns that she was about to either hand the crystal over to Percy as proof of her love or that she was going to reveal to him how to use the Dreamstone. "It has been far more trouble than it has been worth."

"So you say, my dear girl, so you say," muttered Percy. With a disheartened sigh, he pressed his steed on as a jumble of thoughts churned through his troubled mind. "I am sure you'd think differently if I were ever able to show you exactly how best to utilize that magnificent gift."

Taken by his charismatic smile, Rose giggled at his suggestion. She was just delighted to know her prince was by her side for this next adventure.

4

Trouble and Strife

'There must be an easier way,' thought Loken, as he drew a weary breath.

He blinked away the rivulets of sweat that beaded on his forehead, trickling down to sting his eyes. With wrists bound behind his back to pin his wings down, the Sprite's hands grew numb as he frantically scraped the twine against the rough, iron bars holding him prisoner. The thin twine, a hefty rope to a being of his size, rubbed and chafed his wrists after countless hours of this futile struggle. All efforts to break this restraint only served to polish these iron bars smooth than to fray and snap the twine.

Earlier efforts to use the soles of his boots to rub out the runes drawn with charcoal onto the wooden floor of this cage led to his captor taking appropriate countermeasures.

The tip of a knife was used to permanently carve the empowered runes into the wood to ensure he did not regain his ability to shape-shift. And Loken's attempts to hurriedly shovel out with the edge of his boots the grains of pink salt used to reinforce this spell only forced much of the crystals to become permanently lodged. The granules were now jammed in the seams between the steel bars and the cage floor, forming a crusty ring of salt that was nearly impossible to remove now without the use of his hands.

In another frantic effort that caused this cage to rattle and vibrate on this uneven shelf, Loken leaned back against the roughest bar. With grim resolve, he resumed sawing the wrist-binding twine against this barrier.

"It is useless."

Loken froze. He listened intently to these solemn words reverberating through the chamber. They faded away, drowned out by the splashing of waves breaking against rocks before surging forth to spill into a tidal pool.

"There is no escape."

Fearing the Witch had returned to vent her wrath, Loken threw himself against the far side of his prison. He raised his left shoulder, wiping off the last of the thick, sticky pitch that was smeared over his mouth to keep him silent.

"We are doomed..."

The tips of Loken's pointed ears pricked up as he listened. There was a foreboding melancholy to these words as they echoed only to evaporate into the rocky walls. It was not that dry, rasping tone issued by the Witch when Sin would curse at him or muttered to herself now that she no longer had her sock puppet to speak to.

"Doomed to die in misery and despair..."

Though this lament was truly sad, there was a pure, lyrical quality to this voice, and by these sentences, Loken knew it could not be the Witch. Sin would have said that *he alone*, not *we*, would be doomed to die.

"Where are you?" asked the Sprite. "I hear, but I cannot see you."

His question was answered by a dismal sigh followed by gentle sobs. Loken straightened up upon hearing the metallic clank and rattle of chains sounding through the chamber as the flames of the wall-mounted torches spiralled in an erratic dance as a salty draft rushed in. This damp air, riding on the crest of a foaming wave, swirled about as the water heaved itself upon a boulder, breaking apart before tumbling into a great tidal pool.

Straining to hear more, Loken crept up to the edge of his prison. Pressing his face between the bars, he glanced about. From this rocky shelf he could make out details of this sea cave wherever torchlight pushed against the shadows. At one end, he detected a narrow tunnel connecting to this chamber. By the sunlight that flooded into that passage, Loken could tell this cave was not deep underground.

Freedom was possible, if only he could escape.

This light glowed like a beacon at the end of the tunnel, but it did not extend into the chamber. The natural light of day was exiled to this passageway, unable to bend around the corner to light up this space. At the opposite end, the belly of this cave narrowed, opening to the sea, but with the high tide moving in quickly, whatever sunlight coming through was now underwater, blocked by the encroaching cold, murky sea that surged to and fro.

As though this chamber was a living, breathing thing, the flickering flames guttered, twisting about at the mercy of the damp, salt air each time the tide receded, sucked out in a swirling whirlpool through the opening to the sea. Each time a wave rushed in, breaking against the rocks, the flames swelled, feeding on the fresh air. The expanding glow of the torchlights helped to push against the gloom, allowing Loken fleeting glimpses of the darkest recesses of this chamber as he searched for this mysterious voice.

"I am not ready to die just yet," declared Loken.

"I thought that too, but I now invite death."

Loken stood on his toes, craning his neck to see where his fellow prisoner was being held as he called, "Where are you?"

"Down here... in the water."

The Sprite followed the sounds of this defeated voice. He gasped in horror to see slender arms shackled behind a narrow, rocky pillar, the hands bound at the wrists by salt-rusted iron chains. Where this jagged rock, encrusted by sharp barnacles, scraped against these arms and hands, fresh blood mingled with trails of darker, dried blood now rehydrated by the surf splashing up against her.

He now knew where the clatter of chains came from and where he stood caged, this prisoner was in a far worse predicament. If she did not drown first, then the icy grip of the sea was sure to take its toll, as the tide crept in ever higher.

Loken watched in dread as a wave larger than the last crashed against the rocks forming the rim of the tidal pool, but as this catchment filled, the water rolled forward, breaking against the pillar and the poor girl shackled to it.

"You're going to drown!" cried Loken.

"I can only wish for death," she sobbed.

Partially immersed in this tidal pool, Loken determined she was sitting waist deep in the chilling embrace of the sea. He shivered involuntarily as the breaking surf, now splashing up against her torso, slapped at her neck and face, thoroughly drenching her.

"Sit taller!" shouted Loken. "Try to get out of the water as much as possible."

His words went ignored. Instead, she slumped down, sinking deeper into the pool of frigid water. He cringed in sympathy to see the barnacles cutting deeper into her arms as she struggled against these iron bonds.

"Don't give up! Perhaps the tide is already at its height and will now recede."

Loken's heart jumped to the back as his throat as he struggled to see. Though the pillar of stone she was chained to obscured his view for the most part, by her great gasp as a wave broke over her, she seemed intent on drowning herself.

"Stop!" cried Loken, alarmed by this desperate act. "Stop it!"

Rocking the cage to and fro, the Sprite backed up as far as he could.

Charging forward, he leapt up high, ramming his shoulder against the bars. For a moment, the prison teetered on the uneven shelf. Loken's wings, though still firmly bound, vibrated with excitement. Backing up again, he charged once more, leaping high and timing his movement to the rocking of this cage. He was confident if he timed it just so, this prison would fall over, smashing open on the rocky floor of this cave.

Loken whooped in victory as the cage tipped over. Just as suddenly, he groaned in pain as his prison crashed to the ground. To his dismay, the steel bars smashed against the rocks, but would not yield to the impact. Instead, the cage tumbled, rolling toward the tidal pool.

"No!" cried Loken. Banging against the bars, he scrambled to stop the cage as it careered on a deadly path toward the icy water.

With a loud clatter, the cage crashed against the pillar, bouncing off the tangle of chains. Loken caught a fleeting glimpse of bloodied hands reaching out, struggling to snag his cage as it rolled by.

It was too late.

A wave crashed over the prison, swallowing it up and dragging it into the tidal pool as the sea retreated. Loken instinctively inhaled, but the freezing water snatched his breath away. He and the cage plunged to the rocky bottom as sand, silt and seawater swirled all around him.

"I will tell you now, that dandy of a fop is more trouble than he is worth," whispered Rainus. "The strife he is sure to stir up can break our fellowship, if we are not careful."

"There is no denying he will bring trouble and strife," admitted Myron, his words were hushed. "All that is left to do now is to pray the Prince grows weary of this quest before too long. Let's hope he chooses to abandon this mission, leaving us to resume without him."

Tag steered his horse between the two, as he whispered, "Why do we not tell Princess Rose the truth? If she knew, she'd be the one to drive him off, if she doesn't outright strangle him with her bare hands first."

"We discussed this before," reminded Myron. "The girl is smitten, absolutely besotted by love. This infatuation she mistakes for love is rendering her blind, deaf *and* dumb, where we are concerned."

"You feel she is that far gone?" questioned Tag.

"Rest assured, the more charm Prince Percival exudes, the more charismatic he becomes, the greater his hold over her," averred Myron.

"She'd rather abandon us than believe her prince is a conniving, murderous villain with his sights on the Dreamstone," stated Rainus.

"You truly feel she'd rather believe in him than us?" Tag's troubled heart sank to hear his friends' concerns.

"What do you think?" asked Rainus. His tone was dismally smug as he glanced over his shoulder to where Rose and Percy rode side by side, engaged in private conversation.

"I must say, Prince Percy, that is a magnificent cloak you wear so regally," praised Rose. She smiled demurely, hoping to gain his favour through flattery.

"Thank you, my dear. I had it specially tailored for adventures such as this." Percy sat tall in his saddle so Rose could better admire him in all his glory.

"It is quite becoming on you," commented Rose. "Nothing speaks of royalty more than that fine ermine trim."

"Well, if I had my way, the entire lining would be ermine rather than sable," huffed Percy. "Apparently, the royal seamstress claimed she lacked the time to make this adaptation before we departed from the castle."

"That would not give her much time indeed!"

"Time?" snorted Percy. "I would say it had more to do with her lack of competence and skill. If she had both, time would not have been an issue."

A forced smile curled her lips. Inwardly, she felt regret for asking a question that would cause him such irritation. "I suppose -"

"Ineptitude of the highest order, I'd say!" grunted Percy. "It would seem that half the domestic staff are cursed with cloth ears, a penchant for idle chatter and equally idle hands. Lest one holds a brand to their backside to keep them motivated, they are a lost cause."

"They can pose a challenge at times," said Rose.

"I am surprised my father has not already fired everyone in the palace, twice over. But I suppose in a world mired in incompetence suitable help is hard to find even on a good day," sighed Percy. His comment was followed by his braying laughter as he thought on the domestic staff being marched out of his home, if they could not defend their purpose or define their skills.

Myron and Tag glanced behind to witness this exchange between the two royals as Percy chortled loudly.

Tag heaved a disheartened sigh as he spoke, "I suppose you're right, Lord Silverthorn. They are like two peas in a pod."

"Rest assured, my young friend, she will only hate you, if you were to disclose the real reason that scheming cad is by her side now," cautioned Rainus. "You must take comfort in knowing that even a pea pod will ripen over time, bursting open to send its seeds scattering when the conditions are just right."

"At this point, it is best not to make comments that will give Princess Rose reason to hate us where Prince Percival is concerned," suggested Myron.

"So you say, but as best as I can tell, she already hates me," stated Tag, speaking with utmost certainty. "So what if she hates me all the more? If anything, I'd get certain pleasure in revealing to her what a weasel her charming prince really is."

"To what end?" questioned Rainus. "True, she will hate you more, but ultimately, it will not change the fact she would rather believe in a lie from him, especially if he says all the things she wants to hear, than the truth from any one of us."

"Suppose we allow the Wizard to reveal the truth to the Princess about his dealings with that fool?" asked Tag. "Surely, if the news comes straight from the source, she will believe it to be true."

"This is Princess Rose you speak of," reminded Rainus. "There is no love lost between her and Silas Agincor. She will brand him a liar, accusing him of wanting nothing more than to ruin her chances of happiness as a form of punishment for one reason or another."

"You're probably right," conceded Tag, heaving a troubled sigh.

"Besides, this quest will prove to be daunting enough," warned Myron. "If the Wizard is waylaid somehow, we may be forced to rely on the Princess and her Dreamstone to wish us out of trouble along the way. Impossible to do, if she turns against us in favour of her prince."

"But suppose Prince Prissy somehow finagles the magic crystal away from her?" questioned Tag.

"That is why one of us shall remain close to her at all times, to be mindful of the Prince and the words he will weave to beguile her into foolishly handing over the Dreamstone to him," said Rainus.

"And how do we plan to do that without raising her ire or suspicions?" asked Tag.

"Ire, or not, we were appointed as her personal bodyguards," responded Myron.

"True enough." Tag answered with a nod.

"Then, as her personal bodyguards, it is our duty to act as her chaperone. Her parents would expect at least one of us to be in their presence at all times, just to keep unsavoury rumours soundly squelched when it comes to their daughter and keeping her good virtue intact."

Tag nodded once more. "That would work."

"It *must* work," said Myron. "It will be the only way to keep an eye on that royal interloper."

"It will have to do for now," said Rainus. "At this point it is becoming painfully obvious Princess Rose will only believe such wicked news if the Prince were to admit, without coercion, that he covets that crystal. He must reveal to her that he even went as far as having his mother murdered to prove to the Wizard he was worthy of a Dreamstone."

"I suppose such news from us will only sound too far-fetched for her liking," conceded Tag. "She will most likely view it as us merely undermining his character; besmirching his good name just to spite him."

"I'm afraid so," said Myron. "For now, we must be patient. Keep a close eye on Prince Percival, even more so than the Princess, in case his motives are as devious as we fear them to be."

"What I truly fear is explaining to Silas Agincor the presence of Prince Percival on this quest," muttered Rainus. The Elf shot a baleful glance at Percy as this mortal unleashed a loud guffaw. Not only did it rake at his nerves, his boisterous voice sent ravens perched in the overhead trees to take flight, alarmed by Percy's braying laughter.

"Ooh..." said Tag, with a nod of agreement. "The Wizard will not be pleased."

"We shall have to be careful how we break this news to him when we meet again," decided Myron.

"I say we be honest with the old chap," suggested Rainus. "He may take pity upon us and take appropriate action."

"What kind of action?" asked Tag.

"I am hoping the Wizard will see fit to cast an enchantment on the Prince, turning him into a lowly frog or another benign creature that will not get in the way of this quest."

Tag snickered as he imagined Percy as an amphibian the Princess was sure to find detestable. "I can see it now! Maybe if the Wizard can include a way to remedy his condition, like a kiss for example, Prince Percy will be doomed to be a frog forever!"

"Are you sure about that?" asked Myron.

"She will rather roast up his little frog legs and eat them with a side of garlic butter, than to kiss him as a frog," chortled Tag.

"Your friends appear to be in fine humour," noted Percy. He shifted uncomfortably in his saddle as he caught snippets of their muted exchange and the sudden bursts of laughter the trio was quick to stifle. "It is a pity we are not privy to the camaraderie they share."

"It is more idle chatter than camaraderie. It helps to pass the long hours," responded Rose, ignoring their seemingly infantile shenanigans and the furtive glances directed at them as they rode. "But do you really want to be a part of *that*?"

"I would much rather be a part of their conversation than to engage those two," said Percy. His eyes narrowed in contempt as they sized up Harold. The large man trundled along at a steady pace as he chatted of mundane things with Captain Loftus as the pair took up the rear. "Perhaps we should ride ahead, join in on the conversation. I am positive Lord Silverthorn, at the very least, can impart some wisdom on us. In fact, this is our chance to rescue the Elf Lord from having his ears mauled off by that knight and his lowly cohort."

They glanced up the road where the Elf shared in a chuckle with his comrades as their horses plodded on.

"Believe me, you do not want to be a part of their conversation or you may well end up being the subject of their mindless prattling," warned Rose.

"So, they speak of matters irrelevant to those of royalty?"

"That is a polite way to say their inane topics of conversation would mean nothing to us," answered Rose. "I swear there were times I practically fell asleep on my mare, listening to them discuss strategy, where to camp for the night, what to eat for dinner, and so on and so forth. The topic of conversation can be trite at times."

"There is nothing worse than being bored than to be subjected to boring company," stated Percy, with a prudent nod. "Thank goodness I have you by my side to share in sparkling conversation."

Rose blushed upon hearing his flattering words.

"Their topic of conversation can feel taxing on one's ears at times, but my friends do have some fine qualities in spite of their pedigree, or lack thereof."

"You are such a generous soul, much too kind for your own good, my dear Rose-alyn," sighed Percy. "It is with a humane heart you endure their company to boldly undertake this quest."

Though said as a compliment, his words prickled at Rose's conscience.

"I fail to understand, Prince Percy. What do you mean by that?"

"This quest I have embarked on with you and your comrades of questionable repute, it was based on humanitarian grounds, was it not?"

"Yes, to spare those being tormented by the evil necromancer we seek now, and to make sure no more harm is inflicted on the innocent," explained Rose.

"I understand this criminal must be brought to justice, more importantly, to prevent this evil from spreading to my father's realm," said Percy. He spoke loudly enough so the others would be privy to his opinion. "But care to remind me why this quest is so urgent, as you claim it was initiated on *humanitarian* principles?"

"The fiend we pursue must be made to answer for many atrocious crimes against humanity," answered Rose. "Lord Silverthorn's people have suffered enough and the Trolls have suffered a terrible loss there is no recovering from."

"But you said these were crimes against *humanity*," said Percy.

"I speak the truth," insisted Rose.

Overhearing this exchange, Tag addressed the Prince's concern. "Cold-blooded, premeditated murder against the Elves and the Trolls and now, our friend Loken is in danger for coming to our aid. Are these not reasons enough to act?"

"I suppose, but how can these acts be considered crimes against humanity?"

Rose brought her mare to a standstill, staring in confusion at Percy.

"Murder! Cold, calculated murder!" repeated Tag. He swung his mount about to face him. "You do know what these words mean, right?"

"Of course, you dolt! I am saying, why are we embroiled on a quest to capture a deranged killer to make this villain answer for crimes against *humanity* when technically, that is not so?"

Tag reined in his gelding as Rainus and Myron came to an abrupt halt. They were just as perplexed as Rose, struggling to make sense of Percy's words.

"Humanity, my good people!" exclaimed Percy, grunting in utter frustration. "There was no crime against *humanity* because *humanity* implies the crimes were committed against those of the human race."

"So?" responded Tag. "What are you getting at?"

"*So?* I will have you know the Elves, Trolls and Sprites, especially shape-shifting Pookas, are technically *not* human in the truest sense of the word, as we are," explained the hubris, young man.

"The point is, innocent lives were being endangered because of this crazed necromancer," stated Tag.

"No offence, especially to Lord Silverthorn, as he and his kin possess some fine qualities that extol the very best of my race, but it does not change a very important fact."

"What fact is this, dare I ask?" queried Rainus.

"Even though the Elves are almost perfect, it does not change the fact you are *not* members of the human race," reasoned Percy. "It is like comparing an apple to, say a... pear! Both crisp and sweet, very similar and yet, quite different."

"I have been compared to many things before, but never a fruit," muttered Rainus.

"It was a great comparison, was it not?" asked Percy, quite proud of his choice of words.

"Yes, it is like me comparing you to an ape in fancy dress," answered Rainus.

Percy frowned as he silently mulled over the Elf's words.

"The point being, all those opposed to dark magic and the genocide of innocent people deserve to be treated with compassion and humanity," argued Tag.

"What's happenin'?" asked Harold, as he and Captain Loftus caught up to them.

"I am sharing in an important observation related to the significance of this quest," revealed Rainus, his tone raked by frustration.

"Care to share?" queried Harold.

Percy stared with raised eyebrows at the big man. "I can, Humongoid, but I hardly think one of your intellectual capacity will have the ability to understand what I speak of. I mean, look at the vacant expression on Yairet's face. If he can barely comprehend the meaning and relevance of my statement, I hardly think you will."

"I understood exactly what you said," snapped Tag, before turning to address his friend. "And Harold, what Prince Percival said had little relevance to begin with. If anything, it spoke of the true level of his ignorance and *lack* of humanity."

Rose gasped, appalled by Tag's candour in blatantly insulting her man.

"I beg to differ," grunted Percy. "Your inability to see the obvious speaks soundly of *your* ignorance!"

"So these folks differ in appearance," said Harold, his broad shoulders rolling in a shrug. "Thing is, whether Elf, Sprite or Troll, they all have the capacity to feel loss and love, to share in common beliefs when it comes to doin' what's right. Isn't that the most important thing?"

"You gullible fool! You are too trusting and open-minded to truly understand the relevance of what I say." Percy's tone was dismissive as he waved off Harold. "And beware, for when you have an open mind, you never know what refuse will fall into it."

"Begging your pardon, my lord," said Loftus, raising his hand to speak, "but when you think about it, Harold does have a valid point."

"You will not be pardoned, for it is obvious you lean to the absurd!" snapped Percy, waving an admonishing finger at the captain. "And you are supposed to be on my side. This is a poor demonstration of your loyalty, Loftus!"

"I am sorry," apologized the captain.

"As you should be! I swear, Loftus, I should send you back to the castle just to teach you a lesson!"

"If that is your desire, my lord, I will be happy to return."

Percy's eyes narrowed in contempt, as he considered weathering this mission without a manservant and personal bodyguard by his side. "No, that will make you *too* happy. As your punishment, you shall accompany us. Continue on with this wretched quest and serve me as you should."

"As you wish, my lord." With a curt bow, Loftus issued a muted sigh of disappointment.

He fell back in line with Harold to take up the rear.

"Yes, take your rightful place. I will call on you when you are needed." Percy dismissed Loftus with a wave of his hand like he was shooing away a dog before turning his attention back to Tag and his cohorts. "As for you three, like that big lout of a man, you are much too open-minded for your own good."

"Being open-minded allows for us to act out of compassion," said Myron.

"As I said before, being open-minded, especially when one is weak-willed and easily influenced by others, can also mean absolute rubbish can be dumped into that mind to cloud your judgement!"

"Compassion is what makes us all, the Elves, Sprites and Trolls included, *humane*," stated Rainus. "In fact, it is when mankind is lacking in this compassion that it makes them less human, even more so than the other races you had maligned."

"High words spoken by a high Elf," snorted Percy. "You speak with such wisdom, yet I see straight through you, Lord Silverthorn."

"And what do you see?" questioned Rainus.

"My intuition warns me that you venture forth on this mission for personal gains. In fact, I am confident you are all motivated to embark on this miserable expedition for your own personal reasons."

"They are here to help me," stated Rose, baffled by Percy's accusing tone.

"So they'd like you to believe, my dear Rose-alyn!"

Myron turned his steed about, refusing to hear anymore from this royal blowhard.

"I am not done speaking!" snapped Percy. His face reddened, incensed by the knight's cavalier attitude.

"Well, I am done listening," muttered Myron, his heels prodding the stallion's flanks to move on.

"You shall hear me out," demanded Percy.

In response, Tag and Rainus wheeled their horses about, trotting away to catch up to Myron.

"You are welcome to keep talking," invited Rainus. "You cannot be swayed by reason, but you are entitled to your opinions, as wrong as they are."

"Yes, keep talking, but nobody is listening," mocked Tag.

Percy exhaled a disgruntled huff as he grumbled to Rose, "You are quite right."

"I am?"

"Yes, my dear. I am quite above their level of thinking and I shall rue the day I ingratiate myself to be party to their lowly, inner sanctum."

In the swirling confusion of bubbles and churning sediment, the icy seawater rushed in, engulfing Loken and his prison. These iron bars far outweighed the wooden floor. In a heartbeat, it caused the cage to sink to the bottom of the pool. As the ebbing tide rushed out through the now submerged entrance of this sea cave, his prison bounced and banged at the mercy of the retreating waters. The hollow echo of the iron bars striking the barnacle-encrusted rocks resonated through the water as the cage tumbled along to send saltwater sculpins trapped within this tidal pool scattering in fear. The school of spiny-finned fish darted away, seeking refuge between the dark rocks and boulders forming this pool.

Unable to morph into a sea creature to save his life, Loken's chest ached. His lungs felt like they were ready burst as he held his breath. His mind raced, fighting to come up with an escape plan. Though he had no doubt the ring of salt used to reinforce the spell conjured by the carved runes was washed away with the pummelling waves, this freezing water and his depleting air supply made it impossible to concentrate on harnessing his powers of shape-shifting.

Either he was going to drown at the bottom of this pool or this retreating tide was going to sweep him and this prison out to sea. He'll be lost forever in the briny deep where no doubt crabs and fishes were going to dine on his corpse in the end.

Tumbling helplessly in this cage, the spent air slowly streamed from Loken's lungs as the icy embrace of the sea seeped through his flesh, chilling him to the bones. Bubbles escaped from his mouth and nose, his senses growing dull while his mind began to swim in growing darkness as fond memories of Celia Feldspar filled his heart with both love and sorrow.

As though these dying thoughts imbued him with newfound powers, with a final, valiant struggle against these wet bonds, Loken thrashed about. He could feel this twine beginning to stretch from being soaked in water, but the effort required to work the knot loose would be his final act. Even if he were able to be free of this rope, it would be these iron bars to seal his doom.

He resigned to his fate, closing his eyes as he waited for death to make its claim.

Loken's eyes suddenly flew open. A moment of lucidity fuelled by desperation forced him to fight again, his wrists wrenching and twisting against the twine to be free as he tried to morph into a fish.

As the last of the air floated free in a shining bubble from his parted mouth, Loken's eyes closed as he surrendered his life.

With the surge of an incoming wave, this small cage rolled, its prisoner tumbling along at its mercy. Suddenly, this iron enclosure was airborne, bursting through the surface of the tidal pool. A great force propelled it from the depths of this watery grave. With a loud clatter, the cage landed upright on the edge of the tidal pool.

"Breathe, little Sprite! Breathe!"

These pleading words droned in Loken's ears as the chilling brace of the sea released its hold on him. He coughed and sputtered, a flood of salty water gushing from his nose and mouth as the dreadful sensation of drowning continued to squeeze his heart and lungs.

"Breathe!"

This order caused Loken to cough once more, and then he gasped, sucking in a great breath of air. For the longest moment, the Sprite lay at the bottom of his prison. He was cold and shivering, but very much alive. With his wrists still tied behind his back, the twine had stretched. Before it could shrink and tighten as it dried, Loken sat upright. Wriggling about, he slipped his legs out so his bound hands were now before him.

Grabbing a hold of one of the iron bars, he slowly pulled himself onto his feet.

"You're safe now. Thank goodness for that!"

Panic filled Loken's heart as another great wave broke over the rocks. The foaming water filled the tidal pool before rushing toward his fellow prisoner and this cage that now perched dangerously close to the water's edge. Instead of surging forward to sweep this prison back into the water, the wave splashed up against the girl, washing away the trails of blood along her arms and the barnacle-covered rock she was chained to. To his relief, the water merely lapped at the bottom of his cage, splashing over his feet before receding with the tide, but he could only imagine how this saltwater stung at this girl's fresh wounds and how its frigid touch stole her breath away each time it washed over her.

"It was you!" said Loken. He pressed his face against the bars, straining for a better look at her. "You saved me."

"I did."

"But how? Your hands are chained behind you," said Loken. He held his breath in empathy as the sea rushed in, splashing over her once more.

The girl shook her head, flicking the water from her face as she answered, "With this."

The fan-like tail flukes broke the surface of the water.

"I was saved by a fish?" gulped Loken, momentarily baffled as the tailfin disappeared into the cloudy water filling the tidal pool.

"No, not quite." Her words were indignant. "I am a Mermaid."

"Forgive me! Of course you are. What a fool I am for not knowing that from the start," sputtered Loken. He was genuinely stunned by this revelation.

Staring at what should have been legs, these limbs were fused together as one, terminating with a powerful, translucent tailfin. There was no mistaking she was a creature of the sea. The scales, dulled by prolonged exposure to air, regained their beautiful, iridescent sheen thanks to the rejuvenating seawater replenishing the tidal pool she was chained to. Wallowing waist-deep in this water, it swirled and foamed as though the sea itself was a living organism. The level of water at low tide was just enough to keep her alive, but he knew prolonged exposure to the air would take its toll, if the waters should recede to the lowest tide, taking half the day to come back in again.

"What is your name?" asked Loken.

"My name?"

"Surely you have a name."

"Elee."

"I wished we had met under better circumstances, Elee. My name is Loken."

The Mermaid uttered a sad sigh in response.

"How did you come to be here?" asked Loken.

"I was tricked, but there is no time for questions. Quickly! Free yourself before the Witch returns!"

"Sin did this to you?"

"Yes, but there is a chance for you to escape, Loken. Do so before she returns."

"Once I free myself, I can help you," said Loken. Raising his bound wrists to his mouth, he set his teeth on to the knot to loosen it. "I can set you free."

"How can *you* help *me*?" These sad words tinkled like silver bells as she spoke. "I mean no offence, but you are just a tiny Sprite."

"I am no ordinary Sprite." He grunted as he tugged at the twine. "I am a Pooka."

"A genuine Pooka?" She glanced over her shoulder, straining to peer at the diminutive being. Elee was just as surprised to discover this about her fellow prisoner, as he was to learn she was a Mermaid. "I thought your kind was no more."

"I am only one of a few left in this realm."

"I suppose that is why my people believed the Pooka were no more."

"Just as I believed it was only a rumour that Mermaids still swam the seas," said Loken, struggling to push the end of the twine through the loosened knot. "It is hard to believe unsubstantiated tales from unreliable sources, especially when they are usually from drunken sailors, but I cannot dispute what I see with mine own eyes."

"My people now shun the warmer seas plied by mankind and their intrusive ships. We found safety and solitude here."

Loken stopped his work for a moment as he mulled over her words. "So, we are far to the north."

"As far north as you can travel. Some say this is the world's end, if your world is that of dry land."

"Oh, my!" said Loken, heaving a disheartened sigh. "Even if my friends knew where I am now, I doubt they'd get here in time before that crazy Witch does away with me."

"You have friends searching for you?"

"Yes! Wizard, man and Elf, some are more friends than others, but yes! I'm sure they are looking for me as we speak."

"I shall pray for your rescue, Loken, just as I shall pray for my demise before that Witch returns to inflict me with more torment."

"But my friends can help you, too, if you just hold on," said Loken. "If I cannot free you, then my friends surely well."

"The Wizard and Elf, perhaps, but I have heard terrible tales about the treachery of the human race," she said with a shudder. "They will be no better than this Witch in their treatment of me."

"My human friends are not monsters, I promise you. Once I free myself, I can prove my words to be true."

"No need for that. Just free yourself; fly away from this place, if you can."

"I am indebted to you, Elee. I owe you my life," said Loken. "Once I can get out of this cursed cage, I'll be able to break the bonds that bind you to that rock."

"You can change into a key to open this lock?" she asked, as she glanced down into the water at the heavy, rust-pitted padlock that sagged from the chain about her slender waist.

"No, I cannot change into an inanimate object, but I can certainly morph into a creature that will be strong enough to break those chains that bind you," answered Loken. "Once I do, you'll be able to swim away from this cave; be free once more."

"I can only hope," she prayed wistfully.

"This hoping will not be in vain, if I can help it. This knot is getting loose now." Loken bit at the twine, tugging hard with his teeth.

Loken suddenly fell to his knees, groaning in pain as his head slammed against one of the bars as the cage was lifted off the ground. With a sinister cackle, the Witch hurled this prison across the cave. The cage smashed against the rock wall, crashing to the ground with a loud clatter as Loken's limp body tumbled about helplessly. The Sprite landed hard, slumping over, he fell unconscious.

The Mermaid cringed, recoiling with fear as the hag abruptly pranced about in a frenetic victory dance that was devoid of all sense of rhythm. Using her obsidian-topped staff as a dance partner, she frolicked and chanted in a nerve-raking, singsong voice, "Just in time! Just in time! I came back just in time!"

Elee shrank down, squirming to sink deeper into the tidal pool that was both her prison and her salvation. The ends of her long, dark hair floated on the surface, swaying like seaweed drifting with the current. Bending forward as far as she could, no matter how hard she tried, she was unable to dip her face into the cold water; unable to cry out so the sea could carry her pleas for help to her sisters.

She shrieked in pain as Sin's boot pushed hard against her shoulder. Thrusting her back against the razor-sharp barnacles that grew from the rock she was chained to, Elee bit her lower lip, refusing to shed tears in spite of the pain.

Sin snorted in bitter disappointment as she glared at Elee's face. It was beautiful, but it also spoke of her stubborn refusal. The Mermaid now gritted her teeth as she scowled in resentment.

"Not going to cry, eh? Getting too used to this pain, dearie? Well then, you force me to be inventive. I shall find other ways to make you shed those precious tears."

"Please, no..." whimpered Elee.

"For now, it can wait. In the meantime, make yourself useful; sing for me," demanded Sin. "Sing me a song while I tend to some chores."

Knowing a blatant refusal would only incite vengeful punishment, Elee reluctantly obeyed. Like a musical instrument, a beautiful, but haunting lament flowed from her mouth as she began to sing. It was a sad ballad telling of how the first Naiad, the most beautiful of the

Water Nymphs, became cursed as a Mermaid, forced to forever live her life in the briny sea.

Though this lament spoke of love, betrayal, murder and the Naiad's attempt to drown herself in despair, all Sin could hear was the mesmerizing tone that echoed through this chamber. It was a pitch that was so perfect, clear and sweet, it was easy to understand how sailors, so beguiled by the Mermaid's legendary song, had, over the ages, dashed their ships upon jagged reefs, drowning in the sea while embraced in a stupor that lulled their minds than to make them panic at the thought of a watery death.

Sin drew a cleansing breath, shaking off this sensation that could only be described as a form of intoxication. Each concise note was enchanting, vibrating to her very soul, if this Witch had one.

While Elee continued with her sad song, Sin went about her business. Using the staff as a walking stick, she limped over to where the cage had landed after her spiteful act to end Loken's attempt to escape. Just as she bent down to pick up this small prison, she moaned in pain. Cursing beneath her breath, she lurched to a stop. Using her staff, she leaned heavily against it, preventing her lanky body from keeling over from the sharp pain. Pushing against the staff, Sin gingerly stood upright once more.

Her one good eye stared with contempt at her unconscious prisoner, while her blind, clouded one seemed to come alive. As though a mist swirled over the surface of this milky white orb, the more she thought on the large mortal who accosted her when she was so close to throttling the life from Princess Rose, the shadowy form of Harold Murkins took shape over this murky iris. Her most recent aches and pains were all because of this interloper; a hulk of a man that easily picked her off of the Princess to toss her aside like a ragdoll. This ghostly form of her assailant dissipated as her thoughts turned back to this cage and how to retrieve it from the cave floor without enduring more pain than necessary.

Utilizing what was at hand, Sin used her staff. Reaching down, the obsidian crystal tipping this staff hooked the handle of the cage. Lifting it off the ground, she took this prison in her hand. Holding it up to the light of the torch, her good eye narrowed as it scrutinized this prisoner. In her angry outburst, there was a very real chance she had killed the tiny being this time.

Rattling the cage, Loken, having flopped against the bars, landed in a silent heap on the floor of the cage.

"You better not be dead just yet," growled Sin.

Upon closer inspection, she watched as the Sprite's chest rose and fell with each slow, steady breath.

She snorted in glee and astonishment! Loken was indeed alive and would live for at least another day. For Sin, it also meant another day to torment the powerless Sprite while retaining this valuable hostage, a bait to lure her foes into a deadly trap.

A cursory inspection of this prison revealed that in spite of her rash and violent actions, the iron bars held true after being battered against the cave wall. Some of these bars were now dented and marred by the abuse, but overall, they were still holding strong.

Staring at the ancient runes she carved into the floor, she was pleased to see the Sprite's bid to scrape them away had proven futile. These symbols remained, but all traces of the pink salt she had painstakingly harvested, dried, and then poured in a perfect circle around these runes to reinforce the spell had been washed away, leaving only traces of the pink-hued salt grains.

"Oh, my! This will not do!" Sin muttered as though she was speaking to an invisible friend. "We shall have to make sure this little vermin does not escape when he comes to."

Absentmindedly, the old Witch's gnarled hand pressed against her bony chest. She had forgotten the Dreamstone was stolen during her bid to escape capture. A hiss of disdain seethed forth between her rotting teeth as words curdling with malice growled, "I no longer have the Dreamstone, but I still have this."

Pointing the jagged, black crystal topping her staff at a pile of driftwood she had collected and tossed carelessly into a jumbled heap in the centre of the cave, Sin worked her magic. A blue flash of light, like a bolt of lightning erupted from the obsidian; the intense heat it exuded caused the meagre kindling to ignite instantly. Within seconds, the pile of wood was set ablaze, expelling warmth and light to fill the chamber with a modicum of cheer.

Forced to find comfort in the fact that she had managed to escape with this tiny hostage and her brother's staff of power, Sin's thin, cracked lips pressed against the obsidian in a grateful kiss. She carefully rested this weapon against the cave wall before turning her back to warm away the ache with the heat of this fire.

"Better! Isn't that much better, my dear pet?" asked Sin, as she peered out of habit at her left hand.

A shadow of hatred darkened her face as she scowled, abruptly gnashing her teeth in bitterness. She forgot that her beloved sock puppet and only *friend* had fallen victim to Princess Rose, the only other person aside from Silas Agincor to become the bane of her existence.

"Curse that miserable girl and her cohorts! They have been nothing but trouble, trouble and strife, from the start of my mission."

With a resentful sigh, she took a moment to contemplate her next course of action. Sin's good eye rolled about as she glanced at her surroundings. The flames of the campfire added to the torchlight, banishing the deepest shadows of this chamber serving as her secret lair.

While Elee lost herself in the sad lament, Sin resumed talking aloud, even though she was not muttering to anyone in particular.

"First, we shall make sure that damned Pooka does not regain his powers. Once that is done, then we shall teach him and his friends a lesson they will never forget, especially as it'll be the last lesson of their sorry lives."

She limped over to a crooked row of rickety shelves constructed from salvaged planks of wood and broken pieces of timber. Much of it was riddled with tunnels bored by marine worms, and most were almost completely waterlogged before being washed ashore from an old shipwreck.

Sin fumbled about. She searched through a collection of containers for a specific ceramic jar that was sealed with a beeswax plug to keep the moist air out of this container. Finding what she sought, she held it to her right ear. Giving it a vigorous shake, the Witch listened to the loose granules rattling within to determine how much she had left.

"Should be just enough to do the trick," mumbled Sin, "but I'll definitely be needing more."

Placing the cage upon the shelf, she sank her teeth into the wax plug, yanking it free. She carefully tipped out the contents of the jar. Sprinkling the pink-hued salt crystals to encircle the runes once more, the spell to prevent Loken from using his powers was reinforced. Using the tip of her index finger, Sin pressed this circle of salt into the narrow crevice where the ring of iron bars was embedded into the wet wooden floor of this cage.

"There! That should do nicely," said the Witch, slapping the salty residue from her hands before picking up the cage for final inspection.

Holding it before her haggard face, Sin's good eye narrowed as she scrutinized the thin twine securing the Sprite's wrists together. If she were going to attempt retying this, she'd be forced to work quickly, while Loken was still rendered unconscious, otherwise the chance of him escaping should she attempt it once he was awake was just too great. Inserting an index finger between the bars of the cage, her long, claw-like nail snagged Loken by his bound wrists.

With no concern for his comfort or condition, she dragged his limp body closer to the edge of the cage to examine the twine. Sure enough, even though the Sprite had initially worked it loose enough to slip his legs out so his hands were no longer bound behind his back she knew the twine was shrinking as the saltwater dried from the fibres. By the time Loken woke, she was confident the knots securing the twine would shrink and tighten accordingly.

With a grunt of approval Sin was satisfied that between these iron bars and the circle of salt crystals, her prisoner would be securely confined. She was confident it was more than enough to keep him imprisoned until it was time to put her next plan of action into play.

Assured Loken was in no need of further attention, Sin glanced about, searching for a safe place to leave this cage. Whether it was by accident or the Sprite had somehow managed to knock this cage from the shelf, Sin decided to find a more secure location to leave this prison than to chance it rolling away on her again.

With the cage in her hand she limped over to the wall where she had rested her staff next to a torch. Examining the crude, hook-shaped sconce supporting this torch, Sin decided this was the perfect place to hang this little prison. Under the glow of the flame, she can keep her one good eye on her prisoner while the angle of the hook should make it impossible for the Sprite to work the cage free. Also, the warmth exuded by the flames of this torch would not only hasten to dry this fresh circle of salt into a hard crust onto the still-wet wooden floor, it would help to shrink and tighten the knots securing her prisoner's wrists together.

The rusted handle of the cage creaked as Sin hung it from the sconce. The noise caused Loken to stir, but he did not wake. This unnatural sleep maintained its grip on him. Confident he would not be going anywhere once he woke, Sin ambled over to her narrow worktable that was just as rickety as the shelves above it.

Pushing aside the stone mortar and pestle, the dirty dishes and pots, Sin found what she was looking for. Taking up a small knife with a rust-pitted blade into one hand, in the other, she picked up a small vial.

"Here it is," she muttered to an invisible friend. "Now we can get to work."

With silent, loping steps, Sin pounced. She landed at the edge of the tidal pool, next to the Mermaid. Her abrupt appearance took Elee by surprise. Her beautiful song was replaced by a shrill scream of fright as the Witch thrust her ugly visage into Elee's startled face to shout, *"Boo!"*

In a panic, the Mermaid thrashed about. The chains shackling her to the rock bit into her flesh as she struggled.

"Freedom is but a dream." Sin mocked her by adopting a sympathetic tone that rang hollow.

"I would rather die trying than to give up; surrendering to your abuse."

"The abuse you speak of is self-imposed," growled Sin, shaking the blade of her knife before Elee's face. "If you had only learned to cooperate, there would be no need for me to be forceful to get what I want from you."

"I know what you do with my tears. I know what vile magic you conjure with it! I will give you no more. Burn me again, if you wish, but I will give you no more."

Sin issued an angry snort. She stared dejectedly at the charred remains of wood she had tossed into the tidal pool after she was done with the last torture session. The blackened sticks bobbed about, floating on the surface. These once red-hot pieces of wood initially solicited plenty of tears when pressed against the Mermaid's flesh, but the severity of this repeated punishment was now losing its impact. Sin hoped this form of torture would be compounded, the pain intensifying when Elee's burned flesh was immersed in the briny seawater. Instead of stinging these fresh wounds, the seawater served to soothe the burns, rapidly speeding the healing process.

With stubborn determination, Elee forced herself to tolerate this abuse. She refused to shed the copious quantities of tears the Witch so desired.

Unleashing a dismal sigh, Sin glanced over at the pile of burning driftwood, watching as glowing embers caught up in a draft swirled, chasing each other until their amber light burned out. She realized using a larger piece of wood to inflict more grievous wounds would cause greater pain, but it was undoubtedly the kind of pain that would render the Mermaid unconscious rather than generating a flood of tears.

The Witch snarled at Elee.

In a blatant act of defiance, the Mermaid raised her fanned tail. With wild abandon, she deliberately slapped the surface of the tidal pool to splash her captor with the icy seawater.

"Stop it!" growled Sin. She used her forearm to wipe away the water dripping down her face. "Stop it, you wretched creature!"

"I am a Mermaid! You are the creature!"

"I am a powerful Sorceress!"

"According to whom?" Elee's tail slapped the water again to douse the old woman.

"Once I am done, the whole world will know me for the powerful Sorceress I truly am!"

"So you say, but I refuse to provide you with the means to be imbued with greater powers."

"You *will* give me those tears!" demanded Sin, pressing the edge of her knife to Elee's neck. "You will give me as much as I desire! You will give those tears now! Or so help me, I will not hesitate to kill you this time."

"Then kill me!"

Sin's bony shoulders slumped in defeat as she hissed at her prisoner. "No, that is exactly what you want. If I kill you, you will only get your wish and I will be without your tears."

"So you will set me free?" Elee dared to hope.

"You will give me what I want!" demanded Sin.

"Never!" declared Elee.

"You are too stubborn for your own good!"

"Too bad for you!" snapped the Mermaid.

"No, it is too bad for *you*. I am forced to be more *creative* in my efforts."

"What?" gulped Elee, watching as a cruel glint gleamed in the Witch's good eye.

"It is obvious you have grown somewhat immune to the pain I inflict, or perhaps it is your sheer stubbornness that prevents you from complying," grunted Sin. She picked up a broken oar that had washed in with the tide, "You force me to find new ways to make you cry, and trust me; I am very good at making others cry."

"Do your worst," snapped Elee, drawing a deep breath to steel her nerves. "I will not submit!"

"Oh, I will do my utmost! And you *will* submit!"

Just as Sin hoisted the oar, bringing it down with a vengeance, Elee closed her eyes. She gritted her teeth, bracing for that first bone-shattering blow.

5
Totally Plucked

The oar's blade sliced through the air. A yelp of pain followed by a visceral wail echoed through the chamber as the crude weapon struck with no mercy.

Elee opened her eyes to see the Witch swing the oar down again as she laughed at the defenceless animal.

"Stop!" pleaded Elee. She struggled against her restraints, watching in horror as Sin struck her little seal once more.

The animal lay helpless, tangled in netting that had been dragged just beyond the edge of the tidal pool. The seal yowled in pain as the broad edge of the oar's blade slapped down, bouncing off its protective layer of blubber that had grown thin after weeks of captivity trapped in this cave along with her mistress.

"I'm betting if this pet of yours dies, you'll be shredding tears a-plenty!" snarled Sin. She raised the oar over the frightened seal as the animal cowered, issuing another pathetic cry.

"Stop!" begged Elee. "Stop it!"

Unable to endure the cruelty inflicted on her helpless companion, Elee broke down. Great, salty tears welled in her eyes as she watched her dear, little Flotsam endure another painful strike.

Upon hearing her prisoner unleash a great sob, Sin squealed with delight. The hag tossed aside the oar, scurrying to take up the small vial once more. Holding it to Elee's face, Sin followed the trails of tears, catching them as they came together to form large drops on her drooping chin.

Seizing the Mermaid by a fistful of hair, she yanked back on Elee's head to gain better access to this precious supply. "Keep it up, my dear! Now that I know what your weakness is, harvesting these tears promises to be so much easier."

Elee sobbed all the more to see Flotsam lift her small, round head.

The light of the nearby torch reflected off the seal's dark, liquid eyes that seemed to weep as much for her mistress' shared misery as it was for this fresh pain.

"This is torture! Absolute torture!"

"Forgive me, Prince Percy, but whatever do you speak of?" queried Rose. Glancing over to her riding partner, there was a look of genuine concern on her face.

"How do you manage?" He glared up ahead at Tag and her friends riding before them.

"Tag and I have been friends since we were small children, so I have gotten rather used to him. We practically grew up together, so he is like a pesky, older brother to me, really."

"I was not referring to *him*, but to be subjected to the company of that insolent dolt for any duration of time would certainly qualify as torture."

"Forgive me," apologized Rose. She was now thoroughly baffled by his complaint. "What were you speaking of, if not Tag?"

"I was commenting on how you subject yourself to these many, gruelling hours seated on that hard, uncomfortable saddle." Percy shifted about restlessly, and then in his stirrups to ease the pressure on his aching back as his warhorse plodded on. This temporary relief ended when the pain migrated to his knees and thighs as these muscles grew weary adjusting to his steed's great girth.

"Are you uncomfortable?"

"No more so than you, my delicate flower, but I must admit, I am greatly concerned for *your* comfort, being subjected to ride like this for as long as we have. It is cruel to treat those of royal blood so callously."

"I was under the impression you were a seasoned rider; accustomed to life on horseback," said Rose.

"Seasoned, as in, I *know* my horses, but riding on one is not the same as riding in a comfortable carriage pulled by these stupid beasts."

"True enough," agreed Rose. "I prefer the comfort of a carriage too, but one does get used to this after a while."

"Perhaps after an intolerably long period, but this is just so uncivilized," whined Percy. "Riding *on* a horse is for the common man who cannot afford a decent carriage and a fleet of horses to pull it. A member of a royal house, with any scruples at all, would see fit to be *in* a carriage, transported in comfort. Time may force me to grow used to riding on horseback, but it does not mean I will grow used to the stigma attached to this practice."

"But even the most noble of knights gallantly ride their horses into battle," reminded Rose, glancing up to Myron Kendall as he travelled by Rainus Silverthorn's side.

"You silly girl! We are not riding into battle. And do I look like a lowly *knight* to you?" chided Percy. "I am a royal! Nobility is an inherent quality, one I was born with!"

"Take no offence," apologized Rose. Her cheeks burned with embarrassment upon being the recipient of his admonishing words. "I am only saying that true horsemanship is a respected skill, one that is mastered by all great men."

"I possess skills a-plenty, more than you can imagine, my dear Rose-alyn. I am just saying that those of royal blood should not be expected to endure such barbaric conditions. It is not because we are weak. It is because ordinary folks lacking in pedigree have no qualms about enduring such insufferable conditions. They are predisposed to enduring such hardships. It is their pre-ordained lot in life, to suffer so we do not have to."

"I think I see your point," said Rose, mulling over Percy's words. To hear him echo her former sentiments, she was inwardly troubled to hear these very words spoken by another. There was a level of callousness to Percy's claim.

"If you hope to be my bride, it is expected that you come to see, as well as support, my views on such worldly things that you have little knowledge of."

"Even if it is wrong?" she asked innocently.

"I am Prince Percival, heir apparent to the throne of Axalon. I am *never* wrong."

"You sound so very confident."

"I am the very embodiment of confidence, my dear girl! It is a quality that comes with being *me*." With a forced smile, he sat perfectly straight on his uncomfortable saddle in hopes this posture would ease his aching back and weary thigh muscles, but more importantly, make him look more dashing in her eyes.

Rose smiled sweetly, hearing her man speak with such poise. It filled her with a sense of security knowing her brave prince exuded such self-confidence and undoubtedly, the gallantry she always associated with those held in such noble esteem. These qualities would surely come in handy during times of danger.

"And I am confident my royal bones can handle little more of the drudgery that comes with sitting on this beast of a horse," groaned

Percy. He spoke loud enough for Rose's comrades to hear him issue this complaint.

Myron reined in his mount, turning his stallion about to face the Prince. "Are you saying that you're getting tired?"

"I am *not* tired," insisted Percy, annoyed this knight would reduce his suffering to a minor irritation that sounded so very petty. "I am merely saying that we have *all* endured too many hours confined to the backs of these horses. Look around us! We have journeyed almost the entire span of Axalon and soon, night will be upon us."

Tag merely shook his head as he corrected Percy. "Your father's castle is almost smack dab in the centre of Axalon."

"So it is," sniffed Percy.

"Then how is it even possible *you* had travelled across the *entire* country?" questioned Tag. "Most certainly *we* have, but you just joined us this morning."

"As you are such a simpleton, let me explain it to you, Yairet." Percy sneered at Tag as he spoke. "I meant to say, we have travelled non-stop from the castle and now, we near my country's border as night approaches."

"I'm no simpleton, and believe me, I understand that what you say and what you mean are two different things," responded Tag.

"How dare you speak to me with such impudence! Are you so stupid you keep forgetting that I am a prince and you are an absolute nobody? I should have Captain Loftus punish you for your blatant show of insolence!"

Percy twisted about in his saddle, waving for the captain to approach.

"You are the stupid one to mistake my honesty for impudence," countered Tag. "And besides, what kind of man asks another to fight his battles?"

"A man who is a *prince* does, that's whom!" snapped Percy. Thoroughly agitated by Tag's tone of indifference, the Prince glowered at his foe all the more when it became apparent this knight in-training was unmoved by his threat.

"Oh no, my friend!" scolded Tag, waving an admonishing finger at Percy. "In joining us on this quest, you were forewarned titles mean nothing; that we are all equals in undertaking this mission. Your princely title, and all it entails, was left behind the portcullis of your father's courtyard. You, me, Harold… all of us, in fact, are now on equal terms and an equal footing as far as status is concerned."

Percy scowled in resentment at Tag.

"I do recall these words being spoken, my lord," said Loftus.

"Tag is quite correct," agreed Rainus, as he nodded to the captain. "We made this clear from the onset, and yet, you still chose to accompany us. Therefore, you must abide by *our* rules, if you wish to continue on."

"In fact, Captain Loftus does not even have to punish Tag on your behalf, if he wishes not to," explained Myron, his words matter-of-fact.

"Say again!" gasped Percy. His already fair complexion took on a sickly pallor now knowing they had not spoken in jest when it came to this matter of equality.

"Fear not, my dear prince," Rose cooed in a sickly sweet voice in a bid to pacify him. "It is simply a way of showing mutual respect for all in our company."

"Thank goodness for that! For a moment, I thought you were putting me on the same footing as your manservant," Percy sighed in relief as he glanced back with a look of repulsion at Harold as he trundled up to them with his little donkey.

"In terms of seniority and experience within our group, technically, Princess Rose, and even Harold Murkins is a step above you," noted Myron, "but as we said, overall, we are equal."

"I shall treat you like a brother!" said Tag. In feigned glee, he threw his arms wide open to offer Percy a welcoming hug.

"And I shall treat you like the insolent fool that you are!" snapped Percy, motioning Loftus to approach him for instructions.

The captain steered his mount next to Percy's horse as he queried, "You beckoned, my lord?"

"Teach this ne'er-do-well a lesson!"

Loftus glanced over at Tag as he asked Percy, "What lesson do you deem appropriate, my lord? A brief lesson on Axalon's colourful history? Perhaps some basic arithmetic? What is your wish?"

"*ARGH!* If I were not so gentlemanly, you would be met with blows for your incompetence, Loftus! I meant for you to be *my* champion. You are to give this insolent whelp a thorough bruising to remind him of his place."

"What say you, Captain Loftus?" queried Tag, his lips twisting into a smirk of a grin as he continued tormenting Percy. "How do you feel about punishing me for sharing in honest words with Prince Percival?"

The pauldrons, those pieces of articulated steel and leather protecting his shoulders and upper arms, creaked as Loftus shrugged. He asked, "How am I, a respected knight, expected to punish you for your honesty? That would be absurd and far from gallant."

Percy snorted, "*You* are being absurd, Loftus! Though you agree to being treated as one of *their* equals in partaking in this quest, we are still in Axalon! You are still under my command. I demand that you put this arrogant sod of a ruffian in his rightful place on my behalf."

The group watched with interest as Captain Loftus responded by coaxing his mount, and the packhorse following behind him, on just beyond Rainus' mount that was now in the lead. To Percy's surprise, the knight wheeled his horse about as he announced, "I am now officially outside the borders of Axalon, my lord. Being as such, I will continue to do all that I must to keep you safe, but more so than ever, I am forced to comply with the wishes of those party to this quest so we can remain as a unified front against evil. I refuse to jeopardize the lives and well-being of all, just for the sake of one man."

"I am not *one man,* you dolt! I am a *prince,*" snarled Percy, his face burning red with embarrassment as his captain abandoned him.

"Now, now!" said Rose. "You are making something out of nothing."

"I am?" Percy scowled in resentment now that his princess sided with the others. "How can you say that?"

"I say this because I care for you. We, this little fellowship of ours, have endured much and survived thus far because we care equally for each other," explained Rose. "What my friends are trying to say, in their rather unorthodox way, is that by putting your wants and needs before everyone else, it can potentially cause undue stress to the entire group, thereby putting all in danger."

"Plus, by putting you on a pedestal, as you seem intent on doing, it can single you out. It will make you more vulnerable and the likely target for an attack," added Myron.

"I never thought of it that way," said Percy.

"Of course you didn't," muttered Tag.

"Because you never had to before," reminded Rose. She flashed an angry glance at Tag. It was a non-verbal cue for him to stop antagonizing her man.

"I suppose it makes sense," conceded Percy. "If marauding brigands should attack, they will try to abscond with the most valuable person to hold as hostage or to rob. If I appear to be just one of the gang, blending in with all of you, if that is even possible, it will be most difficult to make the distinction."

"Precisely," said Rainus.

Percy reached up, removing the golden crown from his head. He flung it to Loftus, instructing him, "Be a good man, keep this safe for me."

"Yes, my lord," said Loftus, nodding in approval as he tucked the crown into his saddlebag. "A very good plan."

"Now I truly understand why you are dressed so slovenly, my dear

Rose-alyn," said Percy, his index finger tapping the side of his nose. "You mean to become one of *them*, so your title and manner of dress does not scream out to the world that you are a worthy victim for thievery!"

"Well, yes," said Rose. "That, and the inclement weather we are sure to encounter."

Percy's eyes scanned the twilight sky. "The weather should hold through the night, but darkness will soon be upon us."

"True enough," said Myron. "If you can endure just a little longer, we shall set up camp just beyond this border."

"In truth, I would feel safer spending the night in my own country," admitted Percy, glancing over his shoulder. "Perhaps in closer proximity to the official visitor's centre, where two soldiers are on guard at all times, will be a better place to spend the night."

"To turn back would be counter-productive." Rainus shook his head in disapproval.

"I agree, and there is no place to set up camp in this immediate area," added Tag, as he glanced at the trees crowding the roadside they travelled. "If we go just a little further, there is a clearing that's suitable for our needs. We can picket the horses for the night, too, as there's plenty of grass for them to graze on."

"I believe I see this clearing you speak of, just up yonder," said Loftus, nodding to Tag as he urged his mount and the packhorse on, not even waiting for Percy's approval or instructions.

"You better be speaking the truth, Loftus!" Percy hollered behind the man. "If Princess Rose-alyn is made to endure longer in her saddle than you claim, there will be hell to pay."

"I am fine," insisted Rose, prodding her mare on. "And Captain Loftus is quite correct. It is just up ahead to the left."

"If you say so," said Percy, the heels of his boots rapping against his horse's flanks.

They caught up to Loftus in this clearing just as the captain dismounted from his steed. Removing two thin metal stakes strung together by a length of rope from a pack carried by the horse burdened with the Prince's many belongings, he proceeded to use a large rock to pound them into the ground. Satisfied, he tethered his mount to this picket before taking the reins of Percy and Rose's mounts. Securing these horses, he worked with the others to ready the horses for the night.

For the longest time Percy stretched, twisting about to ease the stiffness in his back and legs. With a dreary sigh, he plopped down onto a log. Just as he was about to give Rose permission to massage his aching shoulders, he spied upon her, busy with the others.

Inwardly, he was disturbed watching Rose toil amongst the commoners. There she was, on her hands and knees, repositioning the rocks around an old fire pit while Harold scooped out the cold ashes and set aside unburned pieces of wood to add to the tinder when he was ready to start a fire.

"What are you doing, my dear?" questioned Percy. He motioned for her to come sit next to him than to toil with the fool.

"I am helping Harold."

"You are getting dirty," countered Percy, his perfect nose wrinkling in disgust.

With a disgruntled shake of his head he sat there, watching Rose as she continued to help the large man. Glancing about, Tag and Myron were busy stripping the saddles from the horses while Lord Silverthorn and Captain Loftus worked together to set up his tent.

Percy sidled over on the log, making room as Tag used the natural curve of the trunk to keep the saddle's form. The Prince promptly stood up, claiming this seat. He perched himself upon the saddle as though he was riding sidesaddle on a wooden horse.

"Not exactly a throne, but still, it is better than sitting on that dirty old log or upon the filthy ground," said Percy.

"There are other horses to strip down, if you want to make yourself useful," said Tag, as he brushed the dirt and dust from his hands.

"You and the others appear to have things under control," responded Percy, waving Tag along. "I believe I will only get in your way, so carry on."

Tag shook his head in disgust. His concerns about Percy's laziness and unwillingness to contribute were now evident, and this was only the first night in his company.

"You can help me," offered Rose, rising up from the fire pit.

"With what?"

"We need wood for the fire," said Rose, following Harold as he headed off to begin collecting fuel, "plenty of wood, for the nights are getting longer now."

"I believe you are quite capable, my dear. I am hardly needed to supervise you two for this task."

"I need no supervising. Instead, you can help us *collect* the wood," corrected Rose, as she motioned for Harold to stop and wait for them.

"I do not partake in such menial tasks," stated Percy, "and neither should you."

Overhearing this conversation, Myron felt compelled to speak his mind. "Do you wish to stay warm tonight? Share in a hot meal with the rest of us?"

"Of course," answered Percy.

"Then you will do your share of work," stated Myron.

"Well I – ah! Owww!" yelped Percy. Grasping his right calf, he rocked back and forth on the log. "My leg! My leg is cramping up!"

"Oh, dear!" gasped Rose. She rushed over, dropping to her knees by his side.

Percy continued to nurse his feigned injury, rocking to and fro to elicit sympathy. He peered up to gauge the reaction of the others.

"Please!" scoffed Tag. He shook his head in disgust at the lengths Percy was willing to go just to avoid work. Removing his sword from its scabbard as he spoke: "This will fix what ails you."

Rose jumped to feet to defend her prince's honour, "Tag! I hardly think this is necessary!"

"My leg is feeling much better now," insisted Percy, scrambling to stand before Tag could take another step closer with his weapon. "There is no need to amputate my limb."

"I am pleased to see you've made a full and sudden recovery," said Tag. "And as much as I'd like to take my sword to you, I was merely going to suggest resting the cold metal of this blade against your cramping muscle to ease the pain."

"Oh," squeaked Percy. Inwardly, he was appalled he had been foiled in his bid to avoid being assigned a menial task.

"And now that you are able-bodied once more, go make yourself useful," suggested Tag, as he sheathed his weapon. "Gather some firewood, if you think your feeble body can handle it."

Percy's face reddened as he fumed. "I am not feeble! I can undertake this task *and* endure the rigours of a quest better than you, you impudent whelp!"

"If you say so." Tag dismissed these words with a wave of his hand. "It's not as if you'll be able to prove it."

"I have nothing to prove, especially to you!" growled Percy. Grabbing Rose by her wrist, he pulled her along. "Come, Rose-alyn. We must fetch firewood so this knave may keep warm through the night. It would be a shame if he were to catch the chills. Bear-man, accompany us on our search."

Harold glanced about in confusion, searching for this supposed Bear-man when Percy aggressively pointed at finger at him, gesturing for the large man to follow.

"Well, I suppose that's that," sighed Myron, shaking his head in exasperation as he watched Percy sulk, stomping away with Rose and Harold in tow.

"And about time," sighed Tag, as he turned back to the fire pit, "or I'd be compelled by the tip of my sword to persuade him to work."

As Loftus went off to hunt for dinner with bow in hand and Rainus directing him to where his keen ears detected the sounds of grouse roosting in a nearby tree, the others continued to pull their weight.

Myron wiped down the horses while Tag fished out his flint. He prepared the tinder of dried moss and wood shavings within the circle of stones Rose had carefully repositioned.

Tag glanced up to see Rose return with Harold and Percy after their wood-gathering foray. Harold placed his great armload down next to Tag. Rose dumped her armload of wood onto Harold's pile, as Percy strategically placed his contribution on the very top for all to see. It consisted of a single, spindly stick atop of the firewood.

"That's it? That's all you collected?" asked Tag. "One measly toothpick?"

"I did more than my fair share," declared Percy.

"I think not!"

"No worries, young sir. Prince Percival did help us," said Harold, plopping down on the ground to assist Tag. "When our arms were gettin' full, too full to pick up any more wood without droppin' everythin', he kindly loaded more into our arms, pickin' up anythin' that we did drop along the way. That's how we managed to get so much firewood at one go."

"Yes, and it is not my fault that by the time their arms were full there was no more wood left to be collected," grumbled Percy, reclaiming his seat on the most comfortable saddle to straddle the log before the fire pit.

"We are surrounded by forest! How can there be no more wood?" questioned Tag, frowning in agitation.

"You are getting yourself worked up over nothing, Tag," insisted Rose. She motioned for calm as she sat on the saddle next to Percy's. "There will be other opportunities for my wonderful prince to show his finer qualities and his great work ethics."

"Not that I even need to prove anything to this ruffian," grumbled Percy. With obvious contempt, he stared down his nose at Tag as the young man knelt, using the back of his dagger's blade to strike against the piece of flint.

"So you say, but just know that what you do, or fail to do, will be more telling than mere words," responded Tag. He gently blew on the smouldering tinder to ignite the sparks into flames.

Harold helped Tag to place more kindling, and then larger pieces of wood, onto the growing fire. As fate would have it, the single stick

Percy had contributed was damp and rotten. Added to the pile, the amber flames lapped at this piece of wood and as it reluctantly burned, a thin trail of acrid black smoke drifted from this stick.

The evening breeze sent this smoke wafting toward the hapless prince. It caused his eyes to water, instigating a fit of dry, raspy coughing as Percy tried, for as long as he could, to endure the exposure to this foul air.

Cursing beneath his choking breath, Percy finally jumped to his feet. He marched across to where Captain Loftus had settled down on a log next to Rainus, engaged in a pleasant conversation with the Elf. To the surprise of all, Percy deliberately shoved the man aside when the captain was too slow to acknowledge him by relinquishing his smoke-free spot by the campfire.

Loftus fell backwards off the log as Rainus' eyes darkened, ablaze with anger as he snapped at Percy, "That was uncalled for! I do believe an apology is in order."

"You are absolutely correct, Lord Silverthorn," agreed Percy. He watched as Rainus offered his hand to Loftus, pulling the humiliated man onto his feet. "This fool should apologize immediately for failing to relinquish his seat to me when he first heard me cough."

"All you need do was to ask, my lord," said Loftus, brushing off his embarrassment and the dirt from his raiment.

"Had you been paying attention, there would be no need for that. You would have been ready to relinquish this seat to me."

"No worries," said Harold. He dragged over a third log around the fire as he extended an invitation, "Gilbert can sit here with me."

"Gilbert? Who is Gilbert?" questioned Percy, staring in confusion at Harold.

"Captain Loftus, of course! We're on a first-name basis now, havin' spent time chattin' up a storm durin' our trek to here."

"What is the meaning of this?" asked Myron, casting an incredulous stare at Percy. "You do not even know your captain's full name?"

"Why would I? He's always been just *Loftus* to me. Captain Loftus, if the occasion calls for it, so his men maintain a level of respect for him, should he be made to lead my father's army into battle."

Tag rolled his eyes in frustration as he glanced over at Rose, knowing how she was just as guilty as Percy for this demeaning habit.

Percy suddenly burst out laughing as he stared in disbelief at his captain, snorting as he guffawed. "So, that is your given name? Gilbert? Who in their right mind names their son *Gilbert*?"

"Apparently, my parents did, as did my great grandfather's parents, for I was named after my grandfather, Sir Gilbert Tomalie Loftus."

"It's a very respectable name," said Harold, speaking with utmost esteem as he swept away the dried moss to make room for the knight.

"Yes, like *Hairy Merkins*," snickered Percy. Slapping his thigh in delight, he mocked both the captain and his new, simpleton friend.

"You are such a jokester," giggled Rose, attempting to downplay Percy's condescending words directed at these two men.

"He was not joking," grunted Tag, shaking his head in disapproval, as much at Rose as her prince.

"Of course he was!" insisted Rose, refusing to believe her intended betrothed was anything but charming and only wanted to bring a bit of levity to an otherwise awkward situation.

"I do not need you to come to my defence," snapped Percy, pointing a damning finger across the fire at Rose. "I stand by my words."

"You keep standing by those words and soon, you will find no one willing to stand by *you*," cautioned Myron, as he tossed a log onto the fire to send orange embers swirling into the velvety night sky.

"Are you threatening me, Sir Kendall?" Percy stared with resentful eyes narrowed at the knight.

"I am merely sharing in some words of wisdom you are in sorry need of. If you wish to survive this trek with us, it would be prudent for you to learn some manners," responded Myron. His tone was the kind concerned parents used to scold their unruly children to bring them back in line. "If you feel this is a threat, then I hardly believe you will be in a position to deal with *real* danger during this quest."

Appalled by this rebuke, Percy's mouth drooped open.

"It is one thing to look the fool, but if you act like one, you shall surely die the fool," added Rainus.

Percy raised his hands in surrender. "Look here! All I am saying is that I have never had a need to know Loftus' full name. Why should I, when the most important thing is that *he* remembers my name and my title?"

"Because this is the man you rely on to champion you, preserve your life and honour, if need be," reminded Myron. "It would serve you well to treat Captain Loftus with the level of respect he is deserving of."

"Thank you, Sir Kendall." Loftus bowed his head in reverence to his new friend.

"Please, call me Myron." He tipped his head in acknowledgement to Percy's long-suffering captain.

"I am bold enough to speak my mind, but wise enough to know when to hold my tongue when words are wasted on deaf ears," muttered Percy. "I am merely saying that as a prince, my duties and responsibilities are many. I am surrounded by a large staff, so large in fact, it is nigh on impossible to remember each and every one of them by name."

"Oh, I know exactly what you speak of!" declared Rose. "I've had the same problem, but with some effort, I've been able to recall the names of those I am made to interact with on a regular basis."

Percy nodded in approval. "At least you understand, my dear Rose-alyn. Though it is obvious my requirements are greater than yours, accordingly, my staffing needs are much larger. Being the case, it makes it very difficult to become acquainted with any of them on a first-name basis, even if I wanted to."

"That is understandable," said Rose. She edged away from Harold's side as he began to pluck the feathers from the five grouse Rainus and Loftus returned with earlier after a brief, but successful hunting expedition.

"Toss me one of those birds," said Tag, raising his hands for Harold to throw a grouse in his direction. "I'll help you ready them for dinner."

Percy grimaced in repulsion, watching as a lifeless bird flew from Harold, over the campfire, to land in Tag's outstretched hands. Loftus took up one of the grouse, joining them in preparing dinner for roasting over the open fire.

"There appears to be an abundance of down and feathers," noted Percy, as he watched Harold, Tag and Loftus pluck the grouse clean. "If you collect them into a bag, I can use it as a pillow tonight."

In response, as though he did not hear this request, Tag suddenly gathered up the feathers he plucked. The campfire blazed, erupting with heat and light as he tossed the feathers into the flames.

Percy looked aghast when Tag gave him a smug grin as he said, "Did you say something?"

"Never mind," muttered Percy.

"If you be wantin' feathers, my lord, I've got a grouse or two that still needs pluckin'. I'll toss them to you, if you like. You can do whatever you want with them feathers," offered Harold, holding up the largest of the game birds for Percy's consideration.

"That is quite fine. I am in no mood to pluck." Percy's nose wrinkled in disgust at this offering. Never in his entire, privileged life had he ever been asked to pluck, let alone cook, his own meal.

"Perhaps you'd rather gut and clean them instead, once they're totally plucked?" asked Harold, holding forth a grouse that was now denuded of feathers except for the little tufts still on its head.

Percy looked queasy. He paled as his eyes bulged at the prospects of undertaking this gruesome task.

"Never mind, Harold," said Myron, as he drew his hunting knife from its leather sheath. "Better to give them to me. I'll get them ready for the spit."

"How dare you?" gasped Percy. "I refuse to eat food that has been spat upon!"

"You must be used to it by now," teased Tag. "I'm sure it's a regular occurrence amongst your kitchen staff vested with the onerous task of cooking your meals."

"Myron was speaking about the simple utensil used to roast the grouse over the fire," explained Rose. She managed to contain her laughter as she shot a mincing stare in Tag's direction.

"Oh, of course he was," said Percy, hoping the flames of the shared campfire would help to hide his embarrassment as his cheeks burned red.

"In fact, I packed some metal spits just for this purpose," said Loftus.

"Just you relax, my lord," said Harold. He motioned to Percy with one hand as the other rummaged through one of his many bags to dig up a selection of spices and herbs perfect for flavouring these birds. "We'll be eatin' succulent, flame-roasted grouse in no time."

"Excellent! I have the perfect vintage of wine for the occasion," said Percy, hoping to win over Rose's comrades with quality libation. "I will be happy to share this fine nectar with new friends."

"That would be lovely," said Rose, smiling with delight at her man for his generous hospitality.

"Loftus," called Percy, "go fetch us a bottle of wine. Serve up the good stuff."

"Of course, my lord." The captain handed over the freshly plucked grouse to Myron for cleaning. Wiping the downy feathers from his hands, Loftus searched through the supplies.

He returned with the roasting spit and the wine.

"The goblets, you fool!" snapped Percy. "Where are they?"

"Back at your father's castle. There was no room for goblets," explained the captain, as he passed the spit to Myron.

"Blood hell!" cursed Percy. "How are we expected to partake in wine, if there are no goblets to drink from?"

Loftus issued a disheartened sigh. Then, to Percy's surprise, the captain clenched the cork between his teeth, wrenching the stopper free. Holding the bottle to his mouth, he took a deep draught.

"That's how you do it!" praised Myron, as he and Tag applauded Loftus' act of rebellion.

"How uncivilized!" declared Percy.

"It is called making-do," grunted Loftus. He wiped away the dribble of wine from his bearded chin before passing the bottle to Rose. "Here you go, my lady."

Having been reduced to drinking water out of streams as they roamed through the wilderness, at this point, Princess Rose was hardly fazed by the idea of drinking wine directly from the bottle.

In a bid to demonstrate to Percy it was acceptable behaviour to share in drink, whether it was from a water flask or wine bottle, when forced to endure life on the road, Rose accepted the bottle from Loftus. She held it to her lips, taking a dainty sip without spilling a drop.

She passed the bottle on to Percy, encouraging him to share in a friendly, bonding drink with Captain Loftus and her friends.

Percy was reluctant, but with all eyes on him, seemingly to gauge his worth by his actions, he felt pressured into partaking in the wine in this most uncivilized manner.

Using the sleeve of his shirt, Percy first wiped the mouth of the bottle clean of any potential, unwanted residue left by Rose and the captain. Planting his lips over the opening to create an airtight seal and using the tip of his tongue as a stopper to prevent a torrent of wine from spilling forth to permanently stain his apparel, he carefully tipped the bottle. When only a meagre taste of wine seeped through into his mouth, he began to suck on it like a starving calf nursing at the teat of a dried up cow. Instantly, the vacuum he created pulled the tip of his tongue into the opening of the bottle.

"H-elp me!" he cried, with words stifled by his immobilized tongue. "Elp!"

Percy frantically tugged, trying to remove the wine bottle that refused to relinquish its grip. A mysterious force continued to suck his tongue in deeper, as the chill of this night air served to cool the wine inside.

Tag keeled over, howling with laughter, while Rose grabbed the end of the glass container. She began pulling in a bid to free her prince from the offending bottle's tenacious hold. To her horror, as he worked his lips over the mouth of the bottle, hoping to use them to help pry his tongue free, the vacuum created by that first attempt to drink caused his lips to be sucked into the opening of the bottle once his tongue was freed.

"Don't just sit there gawking at Prince Percival! Help him!" demanded Rose. She twisted this glass *leech* that only inflicted more pain as its victim shrieked for her to be gentle on him.

"Remain calm, the both of you," ordered Rainus, as he marched over to offer his assistance.

Selecting a slender twig, he stripped it clean of its bark. Taking the bottle from Rose's hand, he gently wedged the smooth twig into the mouth of the bottle. Working it in between the smooth glass and Percy's compressed lips, with a gentle pry, Rainus broke the seal. The

Prince yanked his lips free of this glass prison, waving it off when the Elf offered it back to him.

"I think not!" muttered Percy, thoroughly rattled and embarrassed by this unfortunate mishap. "This bottle has been hexed. It wanted to devour my face!"

"If you had only tipped the bottle to your lips and *sipped*, than to *suckle* at it like a voracious piglet, this would not have happened," explained Rainus, demonstrating how to properly drink from the wine bottle.

"So you tell me now," muttered the red-faced Percy.

As Harold helped prop Tag back onto the log as his fit of laughter subsided, the young man burst out laughing once more upon seeing Percy's face. A perfect circle of mauve created by the vicious vacuum action left Percy with a deepening bruise around lips so swollen, they protruded like a duck's bill.

"What?" grumbled Percy.

He glared in absolute contempt at Tag, and then he noticed the pursed lips of all those sitting before him as they struggled to stifle their laughter.

"It is nothing," assured Rose. "The red wine merely stains your lips."

Using her silk handkerchief, she gently dabbed away the carmine liquid. To her surprise, the traces of wine lifted immediately however, that perfect circle of mauve Tag was so quick to point out that extended just beyond his upper and lower lips remained, only growing darker with her gentle ministration.

"Oh, my…" she gulped.

"What? What is it?" asked Percy, his eyes growing wide in horror. Pushing away her handkerchief, he pressed his fingertips to his mouth that still tingled with a numbing sensation.

"I… Well… Ah…" stammered Rose.

She flashed an angry glance at Tag. He collapsed from his perch once more, laughing unmercifully upon seeing the evidence left on Percy's perfect visage of this brutal, but hilarious assault inflicted by the wine bottle that was now in Rainus' hand.

"Speak up!" demanded Percy. "What is so funny?"

"Nothing is funny, Prince Percy, nothing at all!" assured Rose. She desperately struggled with her own battle to contain her laughter at the expense of offending him.

"It's just that you got some serious bruisin' action happenin' on your mug," chirped up Harold. "Nothin' to fret about, at least it's not a misshapen blob of a bruise."

"As for those swollen lips, I'm sure it'll be fine by tomorrow," added Tag. "If not, it's not as though it's so bad that you'll be mistaken for a duck."

"Bruising? On my face? The horrors!" gasped Percy, slapping a hand over his mouth to conceal the contusion. It was only at this very moment when the palm of his hand pressed against his engorged lips did he realize how truly swollen they were.

"Trust me, my lord, it's nothing that will kill you," said Loftus. A great smile creased his face as he waved off Percy's concern. "It is just a little discolouration and swelling that should disappear in a day or two."

"Or three or four!" Tag chortled, gulping down a deep breath as he pressed a hand to his aching side.

"Is it that bad? Loftus, fetch my hand mirror!"

"Sorry, my lord, but there was no room for such trivial items on this quest," said Loftus.

"My dear Rose-alyn, do be a lamb. Lend me your looking glass, so I may gaze upon the atrocity that is my face!"

"I did not bring one."

"Nonsense! You are a girl, and a princess at that! Of course you have one."

"Yes, she has several of them back at her palace," snorted Tag. Wiping away a tear that rolled down his cheek, he gawked at Percy's face that reddened with anger. It was a hue that served to temporarily diminish the true level of bruising around his lips.

"Woe is me!" wailed Percy. In melodramatic fashion, he cupped his hand over his wretched mouth so none would see to further mock him.

"Woe-ho-ho, indeed!" chuckled Tag.

"How dare you make a mockery of my misfortune?" snarled Percy, these stifled words seeping through his fingers. "I shall teach you a lesson!"

"Like that *bottle* taught you a lesson?" snickered Tag, extending his hand to Rainus to receive the wine from him.

"You impudent sod!" declared Percy. He jumped to his feet, almost bowling Rose over in his anger.

"Steady on," ordered Myron. "It is not as though you are permanently disfigured, Prince Percival."

"So you say, but I have had enough! To be asked to prepare dinner, and then drink in this uncouth manner after being ordered to collect firewood, it is more than a prince can or should be expected to bear in a single night!"

Percy glowered in anger at the dangerous bottle of wine that made its way into Tag's hand, and then he stared in repulsion at the pile of grouse now denuded of feathers that Myron was preparing to skewer onto the spit as Harold proceeded to grease them with bacon lard for added flavour and for the perfect coating that the spices and herbs can cling to.

Rising to his feet, Percy announced, "I shall retire to my tent until dinner is ready."

"Shall I accompany you?" asked Rose. Though her tone was meek, her hopes were high that her efforts to comfort Percy would help to further endear her to him.

"You shall remain here. Summon me when dinner is ready."

"As you wish," said Rose, in a timid voice that squeaked of disappointment.

"It is not a wish. I demand it!" snapped Percy, as he stormed off to find refuge in the solitude of his private tent. "Call me when dinner is done. If you are fortunate, I shall grace you with my company then."

With a disheartened sigh, Rose sat down next to Tag to scold him. "You were so rude, laughing as you had."

"Sorry, but I just couldn't help myself."

"Where is your sense of deportment? Where is your self-control?" admonished Rose.

"They are both at the same place yours are," answered Tag. With a wicked grin, he glanced at her face. His eyes bugged out as he puckered his lips as though they were stuck in a bottle.

"You are terrible!" snapped Rose. In retribution, she smacked Tag on his arm.

He leaned into her disgruntled face to see a small smile curl her lips as she resisted the urge to giggle aloud.

"Ha!" snickered Tag. "You must admit, it was rather amusing, especially that perfectly round bruise encircling his lips."

"It was *not* funny, not at all!" sulked Rose. Her words were sincere, and yet, her body deceived her. Her lips quivered as she fought a losing battle to not smile.

"Ah… Yes! There it is! You do want to laugh!" Tag pointed at her face.

Rose slapped her hands over her mouth so Percy would not hear this eruption of giggles spouting forth.

"Stop it!" These muffled words squeaked between the seams of her fingers.

"Come now, Princess," said Tag, "it is only human to want to laugh at him."

"I was *not* laughing at Prince Percy, nor his misfortune, I was laughing at that ridiculous face you made." She smacked his arm again.

"No harm done," insisted Loftus. "Prince Percival claims to be a grown man. If he cannot handle a little laughter at his expense, I hardly think he will survive life in the big, wide world outside his castle, and especially during a quest such as this."

"If anything, it will help to harden him for life on the road," said Myron, watching as Harold carefully turned the spit, roasting their meal over the flames.

"I do not need Prince Percy *hardened* by any of you or your foolish shenanigans," insisted Rose, removing her hands from her mouth after that urge to giggle subsided sufficiently. "And if anything, prolonged exposure to all of you shall only harden him to *everything,* including me! He is sure to find me guilty by association, if you keep up with this dreadful behaviour."

"You worry all for naught, my lady," said Loftus, accepting the bottle of wine from Myron. "Trust me when I say it will be a positive experience for Prince Percival to endure some good-humoured ribbing. It will help build his character."

"So the young man's ego is slightly bruised," said Rainus, his shoulders rolling in a shrug of indifference.

"But not more than his lips," quipped Tag.

"The point is," continued Rainus, with a knowing smile, "consider it an initiation into our fellowship. It is the very nature of this camaraderie that allows us to endure together the rigours of a quest."

"I suppose," said Rose.

She glanced over to see Percy's silhouette backlit by the candles burning in his tent. His shadow, cast against the wall of the tent, paced to and fro, mimicking his every move. Undoubtedly, he was still angst-ridden by the incident involving the wine bottle.

"It's nothin' that can't be cured by a hot, delicious meal shared in good company," promised Harold, his mouth watering involuntarily as the aroma of roasting grouse permeated the night air.

"Is it ready?" asked Rose. The seasoned skin sizzled as the flames gently lapped at the skewered game.

"In a bit," answered Harold.

In time, once thoroughly golden brown, with his knife Harold pricked the largest of the birds in the thigh, inserting the tip of the blade to the bone. The juices ran clear, causing the fire to flare as it dripped onto the burning pieces of wood.

"Cooked to perfection," announced Harold.

He carefully lifted the hot spit off the pronged sticks that supported their meal over the campfire. Tipping one end of the spit into a shallow pan Tag held steady for him, Harold used his knife to loosen, and then slide each roasted fowl from this cooking utensil.

"Excellent!" said Tag. Placing the pan before his friends to share, he tore off a chunk of bread to complete this meal before passing the loaf on to Myron. "Tuck in! Eat while it's hot."

"I shall let Prince Percy know," said Rose, excusing herself from the campfire to extend a personal invitation.

As Rose approached the opening of the tent, she called to Percy as he continued to brood in silence. Pushing against the tent flap, she discovered he had secured it from the inside.

"Dinner is ready, Prince Percy! Please, come join us."

"No!" An insolent voice thundered from within.

"No? Are you not hungry?"

"Of course! I am famished after this long and trying day!"

"Then come! Join us! Eat while dinner is fresh and hot," invited Rose.

"No," pouted Percy, sounding like a spoiled child on the verge of a tantrum. "You shall go; fetch my dinner. Bring it to me."

"Pardon me?" gasped Rose.

"You heard me. Bring me my dinner. I wish to dine alone on this night."

"Do not be silly," said Rose.

"*What did you say?*" roared Percy. He was infuriated by her words.

"I said – "

"I know what you said! I am never *silly*! I am always serious!"

Rose jumped with a start, hearing a loud clatter from inside as though an object was thrown in the heat of anger.

"If you mean to be my bride, then you will learn to serve me well! Go fetch my dinner! Now!"

Rose blanched, for she knew all had heard his ranting. Swallowing her pride, she slunk away. Pursing her lips, she held back her tears. Struggling to retain her dignity, she was sure Tag was only going to make fun of Percy's rude conduct toward her with little regard that the whole world, her prince included, would hear him.

"Princess, there's no reason to put up with such rudeness, especially from that guy," said Tag, appalled by Percy's callous treatment.

"That *guy* you speak of shall one day be my husband," whispered Rose. She motioned for Tag to lower his voice, and the others not to say another word, in case it further raised Percy's ire.

"Still, there is no reason for him to treat you worse than he would a maid," whispered Tag.

"I beg to differ, my friend," chirped up Harold. "From what I've seen, he treats his maids well."

"What do you mean by that?" questioned Rose, frowning in

bewilderment on hearing Harold.

"This mornin' when I was leavin' my bedchamber to join you all, I met up with one of the maids leavin' Prince Percival's bedchamber. She was all smiles and giggles, but wasn't too friendly to me though. She basically chased me out, thinkin' I worked in the stable and had trespassed into the castle."

All seated around the campfire fell silent. They, with the exception of Harold, stopped eating while Rose's mouth fell open in stunned surprise upon hearing this news.

"What was that girl doing there?" asked Rose.

A fleeting recollection of the comely, young maid tidying up the dining room flashed through her mind. Their eyes locked for only a brief instance as Rose followed Captain Loftus to the throne room for their audience with Percy's father.

"I can't rightly say," answered Harold, stuffing a small drumstick into his mouth as he spoke. "I imagine she was probably deliverin' breakfast to him, being that time of the day. She just grabbed up her cleaning utensils and headed off toward the dinin' room, when I last saw her."

Rose's heart sank to the pit of her stomach as she mulled over this information.

"That cad of a dolt!" denounced Tag, rising to his feet before Rose. "Clearly, Prince Percival was being unfaithful to you, his intended bride."

Rose drew a deep breath, pushing any dark thoughts to the farthest reaches of her mind as she selected a more fitting possibility.

"I believe you are jumping to the wrong conclusion, Tag. You just want to believe in the worst when it comes to Prince Percy," insisted Rose. "He would never do that to me."

Tag turned to Loftus, "Captain, speak true to Princess Rose. Tell her the Prince was engaged in an illicit affair with this maid."

"I am not aware of any affairs, if Prince Percy does indeed dabble in such things," answered Loftus. "Mind you, he is a young buck. What red-blooded royal doesn't indulge in a harmless dalliance or two?"

"But there is nothing to say that maid was not merely delivering breakfast to him, as it was pointed out that both he and his father prefer to dine in the privacy of their royal quarters, is that not so?"

"Very true, Princess Rose," replied Loftus. "That girl may well have been doing just that."

"See, Tag!" said Rose. "I refuse to think the worst of Prince Percy, and so should you. That maid was probably smiling and giggling because he shared in a joke with her."

"Hopefully, the joke won't be on you," sighed Tag. With a dismal shake of his head, he sat back down. He now knew just how futile any attempt to make her see the truth would be.

"I would be gullible to believe a prince, as dashing and charming as mine, has never been in the company of a woman, but now that he has plighted his troth to me, Prince Percy is above such low-brow affairs. He would never jeopardize our relationship, nor would he discredit his standing in my parents' eyes, all for a tawdry affair with a commoner!"

"Then I pray you are right, Princess," said Tag. "I hope that maid was delivering breakfast to him, and nothing more."

Rose's back straightened, holding her head high as she adopted a regal stance. "A lowly scullery maid over a genuine princess? I know what my Prince Percy would choose. The answer is obvious!"

"You are obviously in denial," countered Tag.

"Do you not think that if Prince Percy was carrying on with his maid, that he would have confessed this to me?" asked Rose, her eyes narrowing with resentment as she glared at Tag.

"Not if he had no intention of telling you in the first place. Besides, why would he confess to such a thing when he is attempting to woo your hand in marriage? I believe he is a fool, but I don't believe he is that stupid."

Rose stomped her feet as she snapped at Tag, "You are being unreasonable *and* impossible!"

"I am trying to open your eyes to what *he* is capable of," argued Tag, as he shot a baleful glance at Percy's shadowy form.

"I say we give him the benefit of the doubt," suggested Rainus. "Give the young man time and he shall reveal his true character."

Myron and Tag nodded, but in their minds, Rainus' words really translated into: *Give the young man enough rope and he shall hang himself.*

"No harm in easing off on the Prince, for all will be revealed in good time," agreed Myron, as he motioned for Tag to end this verbal jousting. "Being his first real quest, he needs time to adjust to the rigours of life in the wilds. It was something even Princess Rose had to grow accustomed to."

"Thank you all for your understanding. I only ask that you be patient with him," urged Rose. As the others, with the exception of Rainus Silverthorn, tore into the roasted grouse to resume their dining, she searched about for something to serve Percy's dinner on.

"A plate?" asked Rose, looking to Harold as he licked his greasy fingers.

"For what?" asked Tag, twisting off a wing at its joint to chew on its crispy tip.

"For shame!" admonished Rose. "You are all behaving like a pack of wild dogs tearing into a fresh kill!"

Tag and Harold stopped eating just long enough to howl like they were wolves baying at the moon.

"Carry on like the animals you are," dismissed Rose. "Just remember, there is nothing wrong with being civilized, even if we are forced to endure uncivilized conditions."

Harold dug about in one of his packs, pulling out a dented tin plate. "Nothin' fancy, but it'll do."

"Thank you," said Rose, as she selected the largest thigh and drumstick to serve to Percy.

"Breasts," said Loftus, as he pointed toward her.

"Pardon me!" gasped Rose, staring down at her chest in case a button had come loose.

"Prince Percival does not eat dark meat. He is partial to the tender, white meat, hence the breasts I had suggested," responded Loftus, his words matter-of-fact as he used a drumstick to point at the roasted grouse.

"Oh, I see." Rose nodded in understanding.

She dumped the pieces she had selected back into the pan. Borrowing Harold's knife, she sliced off the largest breast portion she could find that wasn't already mutilated by the others diving in to devour this shared meal.

Satisfied with her selection, she took what was left of the round loaf of bread, placing it on the plate strategically so it made the helping of food look more generous than it really was. Pinching off the tip of a small, weedy plant sprouting beside one of the logs, she hoped it was not poisonous. She arranged it on the plate as a garnish to make the meal look more palatable before delivering it to Percy.

The tent flap wavered soundlessly under Rose's attempt to knock. "Prince Percy, I have your dinner ready."

She listened, hearing footsteps approaching the entrance. Rose quickly smoothed out her tresses, attempting to look presentable. Instead of inviting her in, Percy made his order: "Slide my meal under the flap."

"Pardon me?"

"Do you have cloth ears?" snapped Percy. "I said, slide my dinner under the tent flap! I wish to dine in the pleasure of mine own company on this eve."

Rose unleashed a sigh of resignation as she knelt down. Lifting the bottom of the flap with one hand, the other slid the plate into the tent.

"What is this?"

"Your dinner," answered Rose.

"This is it? On a sorry tin plate to boot? What about a helping of roasted vegetables? Where is dessert?"

"On this night, we are dining on roasted grouse and bread," said Rose. "There is no dessert, unless you desire some dried fruit."

"Damn it!" cursed Percy. "I should have insisted on my personal cook to come with his supply wagon. How are we to exist on this?"

"The poor exist on less," said Rose.

"And deservedly so!"

"That is an unkind thing to say," admonished Rose.

"Good gracious, now you are sounding like one of them!"

"Them?" repeated the Princess, as she frowned in confusion.

"Yes, *them*! Like you are degenerating into a lowly commoner!" complained Percy, using the chunk of bread to push the meat about his plate as though he was expecting to find a serving of rich gravy or perhaps a dessert hidden underneath it. "And where is the cutlery? Surely you don't expect me to eat like an animal?"

In a disgruntled huff, Rose reached under the tent flap. With no regard to where he was standing, Percy jumped with a start as she rammed the knife she had borrowed from Harold, stabbing the ground at his feet.

"Here's a knife! Stop complaining; eat your dinner!" snapped Rose.

Vexed by Harold's seemingly harmless revelation, Tag's obvious contempt for her Prince, and now Percy's pathetic whining, she had about enough for one night. Rose promptly stood upright. Mustering her dignity, she marched back to the campfire to enjoy the scraps left by her comrades.

6
Into the Night

As the night wore on the chorus of yawns around the campfire grew longer and louder as the waning full moon climbed into the deep cobalt sky.

"I shall take the first watch," offered Rainus. Standing up from the campfire, he gathered his bow and quiver of arrows. "The rest of you should find some sleep while you can. Dawn will be here soon enough."

"We should keep watch in pairs," suggested Loftus, securing the scabbard of his sword to his baldric. "I shall join you on this watch, if you will allow it, Lord Silverthorn."

"The nights grow long." Rainus nodded in approval. "Your company is most welcome."

"Excellent," said Loftus, bowing his head in gratitude to those sharing the campfire, meal and friendly conversation with him. "Allow me to check on Prince Percival first, make sure he is in want of nothing before I assume this post with you."

"Of course," said Rainus, he pointed with the tip of his bow to the edge of the clearing facing north. "I will be over there when you are ready to join me."

The captain nodded to the Elf, as he turned away to check on his royal charge.

While Myron and Tag inspected the horses and the donkey to make sure they were securely picketed for the night, Rose neatly stacked the pile of firewood so it could dry out while Harold carefully arranged more pieces in the fire pit for a larger flame to provide warmth and light, instead of the lower, steady heat that was perfect for cooking.

Loftus quickly returned to the campfire. He discreetly whispered to Rose that Prince Percival had extended an invitation for her to share his tent than to leave her in the cold, sleeping under the stars on this chilling autumn night.

Rose's face glowed upon receiving this news. She leapt to her feet, almost knocking over the neatly stacked woodpile. All thoughts of Percy's harsh words and transgressions were overshadowed by his willingness to open his heart and arms to her, protecting her within the walls of his tent on this brisk night.

Snatching up her bedroll she tucked it beneath her arm.

"And where are you off to in such a rush?" queried Tag. His eyebrows furrowed in suspicion.

"Prince Percy has kindly invited me to join him in his temporary domicile," informed Rose. Before Tag could voice his concerns, she waved him off. "And worry not, it shall all be very innocent. The only thing we shall be engaged in is delightful conversation before drifting off to a night of sound sleep."

Dumbfounded, before Tag could stop her, she was gone, slipping into Prince Percy's tent without so much as a 'goodnight' to them.

"Oh my…" murmured Rose. "It is quite dark in here, is it not?"

Her eyes adjusted to the gloom. The only light to seep through the canvas walls to illuminate her surroundings came from the communal campfire and the cold light of a clear, bright moon.

"Worry not, my dear. This lighting is rather romantic and more appropriate for the occasion," reasoned Percy, when in reality the lack of candlelight was to prevent her from gawking at his bruised and swollen lips.

"So true!" Rose smiled demurely. She unfurled her bedroll opposite to Percy's. Removing her cloak and riding boots, she climbed in. She lay on her side to face him.

"I must say, Prince Percy, I was honoured to receive this invitation to join you. Perhaps we should take advantage of this time to become better acquainted."

"Yes, yes. That sounds all well and good," agreed Percy rather brusquely. "I feel we would be more comfortable talking if we were more cosy, perhaps lounging on down-stuffed mattresses set upon cots elevated off this cold, hard ground."

"I agree, but these are luxuries your staff dispensed with when they repacked for this quest," reminded Rose.

"I know, but these are meagre necessities that Dreamstone of yours is capable of conjuring, is that not so?" whispered Percy.

"Of course."

"Well then, have a go," urged Percy.

"But I made a promise to only use the powers of the Dreamstone in an emergency. My friends would hardly deem our comfort, or lack thereof, an emergency."

"I beg to differ," countered Percy. He scowled as he considered changing his approach, and then he smiled as he continued with his coercion. "Come now, my dear Rose-alyn, all I ask is for the comfort of my future bride. If you truly love me, the man destined to be your husband, you will have no qualms about using the Dreamstone in my presence, especially if it is to better our circumstances."

Rose's heart and resolve began to melt under Percy's persuasive words. She fingered the fine chain the Dreamstone dangled from. "Well... I suppose -"

"Make room!" demanded Tag. "I'm coming in!"

Unwanted and never invited to begin with, this young man barged straight into Percy's dark, private domain. Armed with his sword in one hand and his bedroll in the other, with a grand flourish, Tag unfurled it. Laying this bedding down in the very centre of the tent, he boldly claimed his space.

"Get out!" shouted Percy. Appalled by Tag's intrusion, he pointed toward the tent flap for this interloper to leave.

"No," grunted Tag. He stashed his sword beneath the bedroll.

"Just what do you think you are doing?" snapped Percy.

"Yes, Tag! What are you doing here?" Rose tucked the Dreamstone back under her blouse, sitting upright on her bedroll to confront her friend.

"I am doing exactly what your parents had appointed me to do from the very start, when this whole nonsense of matchmaking and the supervision of appropriate suitors was first broached by them," explained Tag. Snorting with indignation, he crawled into his bedroll, getting cosy between the two royals. For his part, Tag did his best to sound thoroughly agitated that this onerous task was hoisted upon him and now, he was made to fulfil this portion of his duties.

"You were appointed to keep me safe during this quest," insisted Rose, as she shooed the young man away. "Intruding on me, when I am in private conversation, is hardly keeping me safe from harm."

"If a madman should skulk by, undetected by those on night watch, to attack this tent," said Tag, patting the weapon he hid under the bedroll, "my sword will be at the ready. I am prepared to keep you both safe from danger."

"I hardly think that will happen," countered Rose. "You are not here to keep me safe. You are here to intrude on a matter that is of no concern to you."

"To the contrary! Not only am I present to save you from physical harm, I am here to safeguard your good name and to preserve your reputation, all to keep the salacious tongues of others from wagging to tarnish your good character."

"But nothing has happened and nothing is going to happen!" protested Rose, growing more agitated by her friend's unwanted presence.

"And I am here to make sure of it!" Tag rolled his cloak up, tucking it under his head to use as a pillow. "You, Prince Percival, will remain on that side of the tent, while you, Princess, shall stay right where you are. None shall cross this border that is me."

"How dare you order me about?" growled Percy, jumping to his feet to confront Tag.

"Oh, I dare." Tag's words were indifferent. He remained unmoved, ignoring the fast-building undercurrent of animosity thundering his way. "I will be the third wheel on this love wagon, all to make sure it does not go astray, landing in the proverbial gutter."

"You are a blithering idiot! A wagon has four wheels," snorted Percy.

"Yes," agreed Tag. "That *fourth wheel* goes by the name of Sir Myron Kendall. He will also be keeping a watchful eye on *you*."

"On me?" gasped Percy. "But I am beyond reproach!"

"So you say, but how do we know for sure? I have reason to trust in her. However, it is *you* that Sir Kendall and I have no reason to trust, especially where Princess Rose is concerned. Even if she disapproves of my presence, or Sir Kendall's, we intend to keep her safe in more ways than one during this quest, for it is our sworn duty to do so."

"You are being impossible!" declared Rose.

"Your parents are the ones who will be *impossible* to deal with, if I am made to explain your presence in *his* tent, without a chaperone at that! Come to think of it, it shall prove to be more impossible for you, in explaining *this* to your mother and father, should they catch wind of this little tryst."

"This is no tawdry tryst! It is all very innocent. We were merely sharing in some delightful conversation when you came barging in," explained Rose.

"That may well be true, but consider this, Princess," cautioned Tag, "perception is everything where you royals are concerned. Need I remind you of how this *innocent* moment can be easily misconstrued for something that will not be perceived as being so innocent by those more anal than this prince of yours?"

In the darkness of the tent Tag could still make out Percy's angry form. The Prince stood there, his silhouette backlit by the moonlight seeping through the canvas. His shadowy form trembled with barely contained rage as these accusing words soundly accosted him.

"I will have you know I am an absolute gentleman! I would never take advantage of her!"

"Excellent! Then that will be in your favour, when I report back to the King and Queen of Fleetwood," responded Tag. "However, keep in mind they will not take *your* word for this. They will take *mine*."

"They will believe in a lowly knight-in-training over the words of a genuine prince? I think not!" scoffed Percy. His shadow stood in defiance, hands now resting on his hips as he puffed out his chest in inflated pride.

"Trust is earned. It is never given freely, except by a fool. King William and Queen Beatrice are not foolish. They had placed their trust in *me*, not *you*. You are a prince they know by title only, not by reputation or personal interaction. They trust me to hold at bay those of unsavoury character, title or not; reporting to them of their conduct before their daughter."

"You exaggerate your role," grunted Percy, dismissing Tag's warning with a wave of his hand.

"If you wish to challenge me on this matter, then indirectly, you are challenging my liege. Is that what you want? Is this how you intend to ingratiate yourself to her parents in a bid to woo their only child?"

Rose unleashed a sigh as she spoke, attempting to quell Percy's mounting anger. "Tag is quite right. At this time, my parents will be more inclined to believe in his words than mine, until I can return this Dreamstone to the Wizard."

"We do not want that," said Percy, giving a thoughtful nod to Rose.

"Want what?" probed Tag. "That she returns the crystal to the Dream Merchant or that her parents trust in her words and judgement more than mine?"

"Of course I was not speaking about that supposedly magical bauble!" blustered Percy. "I meant I do not want her parents, possibly my future in-laws, to discount her words or judgement; trusting less in her, than in a ne'er-do-well like you!"

"No need for harsh words between friends," urged Rose, motioning for Percy to remain calm.

"That knave of a fool is no friend of mine," grunted Percy, his once perfect face twisting into a sneer of contempt made more ugly by the gloom of the tent and the fresh bruising.

"Friend, or not, Tag is quite correct on this matter. My parents are sticklers for protocol, appointing my *dear* friend to this very task to ensure societal correctness, especially where I am concerned, is not breached."

"Then it is settled," announced Tag, tossing the covers over his body as he hunkered down for the night. "I will remain here, as a physical barrier, to remind you both of this protocol, and especially to keep you, Prince Percival, on your best behaviour. If you plan on violating this, going against the very proprieties as sanctioned by her father, then by all means, go head. Test my patience."

"Is that a dare?" snorted Percy, his tone mocking as he stared down at this intruder infesting his private sanctuary. "Are you threatening me with physical harm?"

Tag sat up, addressing the royal in a calm, steady voice that spoke of his conviction to this cause, "Make no mistake, Prince Percival, if you hurt the Princess in any way, then I will not simply *harm* you, I shall out-and-out *kill* you."

"Another one of your damned threats!" snorted Percy.

"It is not a threat. It is a promise of things to come, should you tempt fate."

"Your insolence will be the death of you," snapped Percy, pointing an accusing finger at his nemesis.

"My sword will be the death of you, if you intend to break with protocol," vowed Tag. The calmness with which he delivered these words was more than a little unsettling to the Prince.

Watching Percy's dark form trembling as he fought to contain his rage brought a smug grin of satisfaction to Tag's face. He just regretted that the darkness in this tent would not allow Percy to see this smile that would have surely rattled him to his very core.

"Damn you!" snapped Percy. "I shall put you in your place, you insolent whelp!"

"If you mean to call on Captain Loftus, he is busy, keeping watch with Captain Ironwood, so I hardly think he'll come rushing to your aid."

Percy stammered, stomped and fumed in response to Tag's terse words.

"Prince Percy, just ignore Tag," urged Rose, as she motioned for calm.

Just as she was about to step over Tag's body to cross the tent in a bid to comfort her man, Tag's arms and legs popped up. Like a dog sleeping on its back, now engaged in a wild chase, his limbs waved to and fro to create a physical barrier as he warned her, "Stay on your side of the tent, Princess!"

Rose stepped back as she continued to pacify Percy with her words. "In Tag's unorthodox way, he only wants to ensure he has nothing but good things to report back to my parents. And as much as my parents are sticklers for protocol, Tag is just as persistent when it comes to obeying orders, especially when they are issued by my father."

"Is King William a wrathful man?" questioned Percy, drawing in a deep breath to calm his nerves.

"My liege is only wrathful if your intentions for his daughter are called into question. *Do not* make him question your integrity!"

Rose downplayed Tag's pointed remark, "My father is not a wrathful man, but there is no doubt he expects me to conduct myself in a fitting manner, just as he will expect the same from you. He also anticipates Tag and Myron will fulfil their promise to make sure this protocol is maintained."

"Very well, then," grunted Percy. In reluctant surrender, he flopped down onto his bedroll, his mood as black as the night as he sulked in this dark tent. His arms folded across his chest in brooding defiance, even as he yielded to Tag's annoying presence. "I will be the bigger man; ignore your silly ranting, for you have no substance. You are all sound and thunder."

"I am, especially when I break wind in the dead of night while I sleep," chuckled Tag, his hand waving before him as though he was fanning away a noxious odour.

"You are so disgusting!" scolded Rose. Her nose wrinkled in repulsion even as she giggled at Tag's self-deprecating comment that was meant to lighten the mood at his own expense.

"Indeed!" declared Percy. Rolling over so his back was to Tag, he wished this ruffian would just vanish. "Disgusting *and* deplorable."

"And disgusting, deplorable me is here to stay," announced Tag. "As of now, there is an invisible line running through the centre of this tent. You two will remain on your appointed side, not to pass through this neutral ground I am guarding. Failure to comply will be considered a declaration of war."

Tag glared in Percy's direction, watching as the Prince's form shrank as he unleashed an exasperated sigh upon being the recipient of this verbal lashing.

"Yes, yes!" grumbled Percy. "At this point, I would rather escape in my dreams than to endure more of your hollow threats and mindless ranting."

"There will be no escape, not even in your dreams," hissed the Witch. Glancing over her shoulder, she spied upon Elee as her tail flapped about sluggishly in this prison tidal pool.

With great effort the Mermaid splashed some of the refreshing seawater onto her pet seal. The icy water helped to soothe Flotsam as she whimpered in pain and misery, hopelessly tangled in the net Sin used to capture her.

"I am no fool. I know I cannot break these bonds that shackle me," snapped Elee. "I am only trying to keep Flotsam alive. She needs to be in the water or she'll die."

The Mermaid stopped to catch her breath. With the receding tide, the incoming waves were no longer large enough or strong enough to break over the stones and rocks to replenish this tidal pool that kept her alive, but had become her prison nonetheless.

"For pity's sake!" exclaimed Sin. She abandoned her work by the fire to limp over to the edge of the pool where the seal lay. "We can't have this critter die on us just yet."

Flotsam cowered, shrinking away from this threatening form hastening her way. Issuing a yelp of fear, the little seal anticipated another beating. Instead, Sin snatched up the tail end of the netting to avoid the seal's sharp teeth. She dragged the animal closer to the edge of the tidal pool. With a hard shove the Witch kicked the seal in.

Flotsam landed in the water with a great splash that splattered both the Mermaid and the Witch.

Where Elee revelled in the refreshing brace of this salty water, Sin snarled in annoyance. Using the back of her hand, she wiped away the water streaming down her haggard face. She took up the oar once more to punish the seal, this time, pushing the animal down to the bottom of the pool and holding her there.

The frigid seawater was invigorating to Flotsam, instantly cooling down her blubber-insulated body and flippers that were becoming uncomfortably warm in this cave due to the torches and bonfire the Witch used to heat and illuminate her lair.

Rather than panicking on being completely immersed in her watery surroundings, the seal's large, ebony eyes watched as sculpins, shore crabs and sand flounders scattered along the bottom of this tidal pool. The pangs of hunger forced Flotsam to forget her pain and fear. Feeling little crabs scuttling about, brushing by her whiskers, the seal worked her snout between the mesh of the net.

Snapping up the crabs scrambling to find refuge in her shadow, Flotsam munched on these crustaceans, crushing their carapace with her teeth to devour them whole. As a small flounder settled in the sand nearby, the vacuum created by the seal as she snapped her mouth wide open drew the fish inside. Flotsam quickly slammed her jaws down on the flounder, swallowing this fish.

"Show some mercy," pleaded Elee, watching as Sin used the end of the oar to hold Flotsam beneath the surface of the water. Though she knew this seal could hold her breath far longer than any human or Elf could stay alive underwater, eventually Flotsam would need to come up for a breath of air. "If you hold her down, she will die."

Sin complied. Reluctantly, she removed the oar, leaning it against the cave wall. Flotsam splashed about in this net, feebly chasing down a sculpin to devour.

"Thank you," said Elee, breathing a sigh of relief to see Flotsam still possessed the will and energy to feed.

"Do not be so quick to thank me. If this seal dies, it might inspire a final bout of tears from you, but I'll be needing more, much more, now that I no longer possess the Dreamstone."

Elee's heart dropped into the pit of her stomach. Her emotions were torn. She understood Sin's actions were motivated by her need to keep her pet alive for the sole purpose of torturing Flotsam, just to drive her to tears.

Was it better to let her dear seal die a cruel death now, or was it better to fight to keep Flotsam alive only to endure more punishment, while she clung to hope? Was it foolish for her to hope salvation would come in one form or another, sooner than later? So far, her prayers had gone unanswered.

Elee knew this refreshing dip and quick feed would revitalize Flotsam, sustaining her for a while longer. However, this knowledge was tempered by another concern. No longer numbed by her miserable existence, Flotsam would now be keenly aware of the punishment this Witch was sure to inflict.

The tip of Flotsam's nose broke through the surface, sending a geyser of spent air gushing forth in a fine mist. With a deep breath she filled her lungs and resumed her work, desperately foraging along the bottom of the tidal pool for more tasty morsels. She struggled about in the net, still managing to catch another flounder camouflaged against the sand. Breaking through the surface, fish in mouth, the seal swallowed down her squirming meal.

It broke Elee's heart to see Flotsam's sad eyes peering at her through the mesh of this net as she wallowed about, struggling to swim.

Before the seal could snatch up more food, the Witch snagged the end of the net, dragging Flotsam back over the rocks onto dry land.

"No! Please, just a little longer," begged Elee, "at least until the tide comes in."

"Why?" snapped Sin, securing the end of the net to a wooden stake to make sure the seal did not roll back in. "So your pet can wait for a great wave to wash her out to sea, perhaps to escape only to return with help to free you? I think not!"

"That was not what I meant," said Elee, her aquamarine eyes darkened with fear for her pet. "I was hoping for her to linger in the water for a little longer, to recuperate her strength, that is all."

"That animal is fine, so shut it!" snapped Sin, brushing by Elee as she returned to her work by the fire. "Not another grovelling word from you, or I will kill that wretched beast!"

Elee held her tongue as the Witch limped over to an old, scorched cast iron pan. It did not sit directly over the flames; instead, resting on heated stones Sin had dragged from the heart of the fire. At first glance, and to untrained eyes, this pan appeared to be empty except for a thin film that shimmered in the light of the flames.

Sin crouched down. Leaning over, she sniffed at the barely discernible scent, like drying seaweed, wafting from the pan. Touching the surface with the tip of a claw-like nail of her index finger, the smooth, glass-like substance she had been painstakingly drying over this indirect heat suddenly crackled, shattering like a broken looking glass.

A cruel smile curled her thin, chapped lips as she cackled with delight, "It is done! Dried to perfection."

Wrapping the edge of her cloak around the pan's handle, she lifted it from the heated rocks. With care, she delivered it to her worktable.

Using a wooden spoon, the Witch crumbled the substance into small fragments, scraping them into the granite mortar. Setting this pan aside, Sin picked up the stone pestle. Pulverizing this substance, she smashed it into small granules rather than reducing it to a fine powder. Satisfied, she emptied the mortar onto a small sheet of parchment, using the pestle to remove any traces clinging to the worn sides of this stone bowl.

Holding up this parchment to the light of the overhead torch, Sin used the tip of her index finger. She sifted through her handiwork; inspecting the pink grains of salt she had meticulously cured to retain its potency.

"Perfect," she muttered beneath her breath as she carefully sprinkled the pink-tinted granules into a ceramic jar, sealing it with the wax plug to keep moisture from seeping in to contaminate this batch.

Taking this container of precious salt, Sin hid it behind the other bottles and jars lining her shelf. Satisfied with her work, it was time to move on to the next task. Glancing toward the entrance of this cave that faced the usually tumultuous Sea of Shadows, the tide had receded just enough to allow the moonlight reflecting off the water to shine into her lair. She knew, even though the full moon was waning, it still cast enough of its silvery light across the sea. The conditions on this fall evening would be perfect for some late night fishing.

Taking up her staff in one hand, she used the other to pick up a wooden pail. Inside this pail was a fine-meshed net.

"Be a dear, will you? Keep watch on our home while I am out." Sin's tone was mocking.

Anticipating a productive night, she scurried out of the cave, through the connecting tunnel. Her dark, ragged form melted against the deepening night sky.

When the Witch's shuffling steps and the rhythmic thud of her staff striking the cave floor as she walked faded away, Elee drew a deep breath. Sighing in relief, she knew they would be left alone for now while the demented hag followed the tide, casting her net into the sea to harvest its rich bounty.

"Psst! Elee?" This soft whisper reached her ears.

"Loken! Thank goodness you're alive!" She struggled to peer over her shoulder to where his cage now hung, secure on the wall sconce of a torch. "How do you fare?"

"My head hurts." Loken's bound hands reached up, gingerly rubbing his bruised forehead.

"I am not surprised. That was quite the blow you endured. I thought the impact had killed you, for you were still for so long."

"It may be surprising, but I am incredibly resilient for my size," assured Loken. Grabbing hold of the prison bar, he slowly dragged himself onto his feet. Pressing his face between the bars, he strained to see her. "I take it, the Witch crept up on me, catching me unawares."

"Indeed! She caught you trying to free yourself."

Loken stared at Sin's handiwork; the fresh sprinkling of salt encircling the runes had dried. Many of the crystals, partially melted by the residual moisture trapped in the wooden floor, formed a crusty ring of salt. It solidified once more, this time, cementing itself to the base of this prison.

"This is not good, not good at all," said Loken. He kicked at the salt that was now as hard as a rock to one of his diminutive size.

"What is not good?" asked Elee.

"The Witch has once more fortified the spell that binds me to this cage, rendering me impotent to use my shape-shifting powers," explained Loken.

"So, there will be no escape now."

"That is what Sin wants to believe."

"Still, you sound intent on escaping," noted Elee. She sensed the determination rising in Loken's voice.

"As long as I live and breathe, I will use this time to make good my escape. It may take a long while, but if I can deface this rune and scrape away this hardened salt, just enough to break this ring, I will be free to morph at will."

"Is it possible?"

"I am about to find out," said Loken. He tugged at the twine binding his wrists together. The knots he had worked so hard to loosen were now biting into his flesh, shrinking as the seawater dried from them.

Under the cold light of the diminishing full moon Sin used her staff for balance as she clambered over the uneven terrain. The light emitted by the ebony crystal crowning the staff helped to illuminate her immediate surroundings as she carefully picked her way over the stone-strewn shore. Making her way onto the outcrop of large, flat boulders that stretched into the mouth of this protected shoal, she squinted, straining to see into this dark seascape.

Gentle waves heaved and swelled, surging forward to wash over the sandy shore exposed only during low tides. Sin watched as the moonlight danced and shimmered. This celestial light stippling the surface served to illuminate the coastal landscape under its silvery glow. Beyond this shoal fed by the Sea of Shadows, she spied upon the ghostly, pale bluish shapes of several icebergs adrift on the dark waters. With only the tip of these icy formations protruding above the waterline, the bulk of these massive chunks of ice lurked beneath the surface of the water, creating strange shadows that changed with the angle of the moonlight and shifted with the restless tides.

Using a hand to shield her eye from the cold glare of the moon, she squinted, staring at the incoming waves gently rolling to shore.

"There they are!" announced Sin.

As a wave washed upon the beach, the water came alive; squirming and thrashing as a school of long, thin, silvery candlefish rode in on the tide.

As the females, heavy with roe, worked their tails into the soft sand, the smaller male fish followed. They simultaneously released milt to fertilize these eggs before the next wave surged in to bury the spawn, allowing for safe incubation hidden away from predators. This annual, mass mating ritual had reached its zenith during the full moon of the autumn equinox, but with the waning full moon shining bright and a significant low tide working in their favour, these slender sea-going fish, late-comers to this spawning ground after a long migration from warmer, southern waters, worked quickly.

With the next receding wave, the spent fishes allowed the current, now a cloudy white from the spontaneous release of milt, to wash them back to the sea, as the next school waited for their turn to repeat this cycle of life.

Sin eagerly clambered down from the rocky outcrop onto the exposed sandbar. She inched her way to the edge of the water, watching as the next school of candlefish tumbled toward the beach, their tiny scales shining like liquid silver in the moonlight.

Setting down her pail and staff where the waves would not race in, stealing away with them on the retreating tide, Sin carried her net to the water's edge. With the waves lapping at her feet, she held onto each end of the long rope that was threaded through the opening of this net. Casting it out as far as her lanky arms could throw, it opened wide, landing with a splash to break the surface of the water. As the net sank from her view with the receding current, she released the knotted end of the rope. Pulling hand-over-fist on this line, as the rope was gathered and pulled to shore, it tightened over the mouth of the net, like the cord of a purse being drawn to prevent coins from spilling out.

Sin squealed with delight. The weight of the net was indicative of the quantity of this catch. Dragging it on to the beach, she loosened the rope, dumping into the pail her bounty that included a sea perch and several sculpin. These two species were hoping to feed on the rich roe that escaped burial in the sand, following the school of candlefish close to shore to take advantage of this easy and plentiful, but short-lived food source.

The Witch retained the perch, but tossed the sculpins back into the water. Picking these fish up by their tails, she was careful not to be pricked by the sharp spines arming the dorsal and pectoral fins. Before tossing them away, she stared in disgust at the sculpin's little body that seemed dwarfed and burdened by an overly large, bony head.

Even with the spawning season coming to an end, this night of fishing proved even more successful than the previous evening when the full moon was at its height and the tide was at the lowest it had been in six months.

She was pleased to see the majority of this catch consisted of female fish that had not yet spawned. Though the white flesh was sweet and tender, the bones so small and delicate there was no need to remove them to eat, her favourite part that provided added nutrition was the tightly packed roe. Sin enjoyed these fish, pan-frying them whole and devouring them, discarding only the heads when she was done feasting on them.

What she did not eat right away would be salted and smoked, cured to last through the winter, and in a pinch, should her torches burn out or her supply of beeswax candles were to be depleted before spring, these fish were called candlefish for good reason. So rich in fat, the fish oil was easily rendered and stored in barrels. It was used to fuel lanterns or a single fish was simply mounted onto a candleholder. Once lit, it burned, providing more light than the wick of any ordinary wax candle. Although not as sweetly scented as beeswax, the candlefish provided light that burned just as efficiently, serving its purpose, if one can overlook the smell of burning, oily fish becoming thoroughly entrenched in one's clothing and hair.

Satisfied with this catch, just as she picked up the pail a jet of salty water sprayed up into the air, splashing her frock.

Sensing the pressure of her feet on the sand, a clam responded to this potential predator. It withdrew its siphon, forcefully expelling the water inside as its powerful foot proceeded to dig deeper into the sand to escape possible capture.

Sin dropped her pail of still writhing candlefish that now buried the sea perch. Using the end of her staff, she dug into the sand. Working quickly, she laboured until the tip of the staff struck against a hard, calcareous shell. Dropping onto her knees, she dug furiously with her hands. There it was! A clam as large as a horse's hoof with a siphon that was so disproportionately large that unlike other bivalves, it was unable to draw this siphon completely into its protective, oblong-shaped shell.

Seizing it by this siphon, Sin pulled the clam free from its sandy burrow. Its foot retreated inside as the two halves of the shell clamped shut. More seawater gushed out from the siphon as this mollusc tried desperately to retract the breathing/feeding appendage into its shell, but it was in vain. Even if the Witch was not holding tightly to the clam's oversized siphon, there was no room within this closed shell to protect this one vulnerable part of its body.

"Dinner," Sin muttered beneath her breath. Hefting the weighty shellfish in one hand, she released her hold on the clam's siphon. No longer supported upright by sand, this large appendage became flaccid, flopping to one side as the remaining seawater trickled out.

As Sin retreated from the encroaching tide, she continued scavenging, digging with her staff each time a jet of water betrayed where one of these large clams lay hidden in the sand. She continued on until she reached the rocks brimming this sandy beach that would soon be submerged by the sea.

This was the only time she was afforded the opportunity to harvest clams, big and small. When the tide had receded enough to expose the sandy beaches and sandbars dotting the shores of this northerly sea, she took advantage of this bounty.

Tossing three more large clams into the net to carry home, Sin thought on how she would shuck, and then clean the muscular, meaty foot of each clam, cooking them in a chowder to be thickened by the starch of potatoes and other root vegetables she found or stole on her travels. As for the siphons, she would clean, and then thinly slice them. Tender and sweet when eaten fresh and raw, what she could not devour in the first feeding, the remainder would be preserved. She planned to cure the thin, salty slices on a wooden rack over the heat of a slow burning fire. Processed this way, once adequately dried and already naturally salty, the clam meat would last through the winter, even into the spring, if she ate sparingly.

Unlike the meat that was tender when eaten fresh from the sea, the dried clam promised to be tougher than old boot leather. It would still be full of flavour, but it promised to wear on her old teeth and tire out her jaw just trying to chew the desiccated clam meat. Still, it was better than the prospects of starving to death, should food supplies grow lean as it often did in the unforgiving north.

With the rising tide, the sea chased her back to higher grounds. Clambering over the rocks leading to the trail that would deliver her back to her lair, under the glow of her obsidian crystal, Sin spied upon a large oyster securely anchored to the side of a barnacle-encrusted rock. This sedentary mollusc was wholly dependent on the sea to deliver life-giving moisture and food. It waited to be submerged once more by the rising tide.

A quick poke with the end of her staff caused the oyster to draw the two halves of its shell tightly together as displaced seawater gushed forth.

This was all she needed to know that the oyster was fresh, alive and safe to consume.

Pulling a small knife from the pocket of her tattered frock, she pried the bivalve free from the rock that had been its home since the oyster was a tiny, free-floating organism. Using the tip of the blade, pressing it between where the two halves of the oyster's shell were held securely together, she pried until this *hinge* snapped. Inserting the knife inside, she slid it against the flatter of the two halves, cutting through the powerful abductor muscle that controlled the opening and closing of the shells. Tossing this top half aside, she then loosened the oyster's soft flesh from the deeper shell.

Sin held it to her lips. Tipping it back, she slurped it into her mouth. It was not often she could enjoy food that did not require her decaying teeth to chew. The cold oyster slipped and rolled over her tongue, filling her mouth with the briny taste of the sea as it slithered down her throat.

Her effort to search for more oysters was effectively quashed by the unrelenting tide chasing her back to dry land. In resignation, Sin snatched up a handful of damp seaweed, placed it over the candlefish that no longer thrashed or gasped. Gathering her pail, she picked up its handle by the end of her staff. Hoisting her catch over one bony shoulder, she tossed over the other one the net holding the clams she had collected.

As she reached the narrow, pebbled trail, Sin took a moment to rest and reflect on her day.

Under this starry canvas with the moon hovering at its height, shining like a luminous pearl, Sin stared out to the north where the deep indigo sky and the inky black sea melded together as one. Here, the waters glowed. Great clouds of tiny, luminous plankton and jellyfish, drawn by the moonlight, drifted at the mercy of the currents. These aquatic life forms massed together, floating like ghostly, pale green spectres trapped just beneath the surface of the sea.

Glancing to the sky, the twinkling beads of starlight were diminished as a great show of yellow-green lights, outlined by an aura of pink and lavender, stretched and danced, arcing across the northern sky. Surging like an undulating wave of rainbow colours, and then waning against this darkness, a mysterious force was at work here.

Sin shook a defiant fist at the night sky as she snarled, "You don't scare me! You cannot touch me! You are nothing more than ghosts, spirits bound forever to this realm."

These phantom lights abruptly swelled, rippling through the dark sky as though in response to her bold words.

Sin squealed in surprise, recoiling in momentary fear of retribution. She breathed a sigh of relief as these spectral lights just as suddenly waned. She sneered at the colourful display that became more conspicuous in the northern skies as summer surrendered to autumn.

"See! No harm done! And when I finally get my way, I'll be more powerful than all of you combined when you were alive."

The shimmering waves dancing through the sky cast delicate fingers of pale purple light stretching up to the heavens. They suddenly turned an eerie green before shrinking away, almost disappearing from view. Just as abruptly, these northern lights expanded once more, glowing brightly against the darkness, but never touching down upon the earth.

"I have no pity for any of you fools," declared Sin.

The play of these ghostly lights veiling the ebony sky reflected off the surface of her good eye as she stared at this spectacle. It was a sight that would have invoked awe had it been anyone else observing this phenomenon. This rainbow flame arcing across the sky was only witnessed by the rare few who dared venture and ultimately survived trekking this far north beyond the dragon infested lands of the Fire Rim Mountain Range.

Her brooding gaze dropped from the sky to stare across the Sea of Shadows that continued to reflect the ever-changing show of light. She cocked her head, listening above the soothing, rhythmic sounds of the waves rushing to shore. The churning sounds of water mingled with those of driftwood being dragged over sand and pebbles as the currents carried them on the tide.

There it was again, that unmistakable, haunting cry.

Somewhere on the dark horizon, pods of north whales, or nor'whales as they were often called, the most northerly known species of small whales, gathered to frolic in the waves, swimming through an obstacle course studded by icebergs. These sea creatures were often referred to as the unicorn of the sea because of the long, single, spiralling tusk, some longer than the length of a grown man, which protruded from the snout of the male nor'whales.

As Sin listened, she recalled an old tale. Legend had it that one of the last great unicorn herds had been hunted and pursued, becoming trapped on the edge of a sea cliff. As the hunters closed in, rather than being killed by man, the stallion deliberately dove off the high cliff. Without hesitation, the herd followed. Mares and foals plunged into the sea.

The unicorns that did not die immediately, their bodies dashed upon the boulders below, were destined to drown in the brooding sea. With the fast-flowing currents and steep cliff wall that provided no place to return to dry land, the animals floundered on the great waves. The herd was forced to swim, following the stallion farther out to sea to avoid being bashed against the rocks.

Weakened by the chilling brace of the frigid waters and pummelled by the constant, rolling waves that now dragged them out to the open sea, death was imminent. As the herd struggled to remain afloat, when the stallion knew there was no hope, the old stallion gradually slipping beneath the surface of the water.

Surrendering to a watery death, as the entire herd sunk into the sea, fate intervened. As the disappointed hunters lined the clifftop, seeing their prize sink into the briny deep, they watched in amazement. Spiral horns burst through the surface of the water.

Now, seen by mankind as rarely as the unicorn, these nor'whales sought refuge in the northern reaches of the Sea of Shadows.

Far off in the distance, Sin heard the high-pitched, undulating whistles and squeals of these creatures. These cries were carried far and wide. Their haunting song was interspersed with the loud clatter of horns as the males jousted, vying for the attention of the females in competing pods.

The Witch cupped a hand to one ear, turning it to the sea. Mingling with the cries of these whales, Sin listened to the sad lament shared by the Mermaids. It would be a song that grew louder with the coming of dawn as they grieved for their lost sister.

7
Woe is Me!

"It's another beautiful morning!" Tag announced in the most irritating singsong voice he could muster. He threw off his blanket with great exuberance before gleefully leaping to his feet. "Time to wake up and meet the world head-on!"

Though he was still groggy, the sheer joy he derived from harassing Prince Percival so early, starting this royal's day off with an annoyingly cheerful morning call, made it all the more worthwhile.

Glancing over to Percy's sleeping form, he looked like a dead body. His back was still turned coldly to Tag, as a juvenile show of contempt. By the loud snort that was followed by the slow, steady rise and fall of his chest as he breathed, it was obvious the first effort to wake him went completely ignored. Percy lay there, like the useless lump of a man Tag always assumed him to be, totally oblivious to the world and those around him.

"It is time to wake up, I say!" declared Tag. This time, he spoke a little louder as he snapped out his rumpled bedroll, laying it flat once more before rolling up it for another day of travel.

Rose yawned, stirring upon hearing Tag's demand and his less-than-subtle movements. Prying open her tired eyes, she squinted upon being greeted by the pale morning sun glowing against the tent wall, filtering in through the heavy fabric to accost her drowsy senses.

"Come on, sleepyheads! Get up," chirped Tag. His joy only served to rake at Rose's nerves and he knew it. "Rise and shine! There is much to be done before we take to the road."

She muttered, "It is much too early to be this cheerful. Hush up, will you?"

"It is never too early to start the morning on a positive note!" exclaimed Tag.

Rather than rising and getting ready to greet the new day, Rose chose to retaliate. In a sleepy daze, she fumbled about, reaching for one of her boots she had abandoned by her bedroll. Tag laughed as he easily deflected the boot she carelessly launched in his direction. This errant footwear landed with a hollow '*thud*', striking Percy on the back of his sleeping head.

Rose cringed in horror as Tag merely laughed at her failed bid to quiet him.

Percy yelped in surprise, bolting upright from his bedroll. Even though he did not witness who the perpetrator of this physical assault was, he was ready to blame Tag.

"How dare you accost me?" shouted Percy. He glared with unadulterated hate at Tag, but his angry tone was muted by his less-than-threatening appearance: dishevelled and as rumpled as his bedding and the clothes he slept in.

"It wasn't me," answered Tag. He suddenly fell to his knees in a fit of laughter upon his first glimpse of Percy's face, illuminated by the pale morning light.

"What are you laughing about now, you knave of a dolt?" Throwing off his covers, Percy jumped to his feet, ready for a brawl.

With Tag sprawled out on the ground, overcome by laughter, Percy was now in full view for Rose to behold. Her eyes flew wide open, staring at his angry face that scowled in bitter resentment.

As a small smile unintentionally curled her lips, she was forced to act to preserve her good standing in Percy's eyes, as well as spare his ego from further humiliation. Slapping a hand over her mouth, Rose abruptly turned away. She averted her eyes, desperately attempting to stifle her laughter upon seeing Percy's face.

"What is the meaning of this? I demand to know!" ordered Percy. Stamping his feet, he was like a spoiled child on the verge of a major tantrum. "What is so bloody funny?"

"I am sorry, Prince Percy," apologized Rose, biting her lower lip to control this urge to break down in a fit of giggles. "Normally, my aim is spot on."

"Yes! So '*spot on*' in fact, you hit the Prince smack dab on the back of his head," snorted Tag. He gasped, inhaling a deep breath before another great explosion of laughter burst forth.

Percy's eyes narrowed as he glared at Tag, and then at Rose.

Raising her hands, she motioned for calm as she explained, "It was an accident! I was aiming at Tag. He moved away just as I threw my boot at him, deflecting it. That is the only reason it touched your head."

"It did not *touch* my head!" growled Percy. His hand gingerly rubbed where the heel of her boot collided soundly with the back of his skull. "It clearly struck me with force!"

"No need to get angry at her," scolded Tag. "It was an accident."

"Yes, an accident that will undoubtedly leave me with a nasty bruise as a reminder of her reckless action!"

"At least this one will be hidden by your head of hair," teased Tag, pointing at Percy's face before doubling over in another fit of glee.

"What are you talking about?" asked Percy.

This question was met with another howl of laughter as Tag struggled to answer with a straight face.

"You have a… a little *mark* on your face," said Rose. Mustering all she can of her composure, she pointed to the discolouration around his lips.

"Say it isn't so!" wailed Percy. His fingertips traced the redefined lines of his lips. He had hoped a night of restful sleep would be enough to remedy the assault by wine bottle.

"It *is* so!" mocked Tag, wiping away the tears of mirth rolling down his cheeks. "It looks like you had been kissing a suction cup on the tentacle of a giant octopus!"

"Woe is me!" cried Percy. His hand slapped over his mouth so none would see.

Though the pronounced swelling to his accosted lips had somewhat subsided, it gave rise to a perfect circle of mottled, purple bruising that had only deepened in colour with the passing of the hours.

"Tag is exaggerating," insisted Rose, smacking her friend on the back of his head as he continued to snicker over this unsightly blemish. "It is not as bad as that."

"Be honest with me, Rose-alyn, just how bad is it?" Percy reluctantly removed his hands from his mouth for her inspection.

Rose tried desperately to look more concerned than surprised or appalled as she examined his face.

"Well?" Percy asked. "How bad is it?"

"In truth, it is not like Tag said about the suction cup of a giant octopus," answered Rose, as she drew a deep breath to maintain her composure. "In my humble opinion, it is more like a *medium-sized* octopus had its way with your face."

"What?" exclaimed Percy.

"At least on a happier note, your lips are no longer protruding like a duck's bill. The swelling is nowhere near as obvious."

Her comment drew a sharp gasp of horror from Percy while Tag folded over once more, surrendering to his laughter.

"As I am now so abhorrent, I shall remain here until this atrocious disfigurement disappears." The discolouration became more evident as Percy pouted. "I do not wish to subject others to seeing what has become of my handsome face."

"What you really mean is that you do not want to subject your delicate ego to what the others will have to say about this new *look* of yours," countered Tag.

"Believe what you want!" snapped Percy. He stubbornly plopped down onto his bedroll. "I refuse to leave my tent looking the way I do."

"But we have a quest to tend to," reminded Rose.

"This quest must wait until I am ready to venture forth from here!"

"It is no big deal," muttered Tag. "It's just a bruise."

"Do not diminish the level of this disfigurement that sullies my otherwise perfect face!" snapped Percy. He gasped, appalled by the sight to greet his eyes as he stared at his reflection on the glass-like surface of water in the washbasin.

To his horror, the perfect circle of bruising was almost as dark as the wine he had tried to suckle from the offending bottle. Against his fair complexion, it was darker and the circumference was as such now that the bruising extended well beyond his natural lip line. He looked like he had the lips of a painted harlot whose exaggerated, coquettish bow-shaped splash of trolloppy red had instead, taken on a purple shade and a clownish circle that gave his mouth the appearance of permanent surprise.

"I look like a monster!"

"You look as you always did, other than that bruise. And you need not look like a monster to be one," chided Tag. "In my opinion, you look more like a pathetic clown than a terrifying monster."

"Take that back!" Percy shook his fist at Tag's smirking face.

"It is not as bad as you believe," insisted Rose, but even as she spoke, she was unable to gaze upon her prince's face without breaking down into a fit of giggles. As angry as Percy was, the colour, shape and position of the unmistakable bruise gave him a comical air, and the angrier he became, the funnier he appeared.

"How can this monstrosity of a bruise not be a bad thing?" grunted Percy. He was thoroughly annoyed she would downplay the level of damage to his once exquisite visage.

"Scars and bruises are viewed as badges of honour and courage, for those surviving great battles," answered Rose.

"And against wine bottles that attack!" snickered Tag, slapping his thigh at the hilarity of his comment.

"Har, har!" Percy scoffed in mock laughter as his purple lips served to exaggerate his sneer of contempt.

"Just be glad it is a bruise on your face and not an ugly scar," said

Tag. "Scars are permanent while that contusion on your mug will fade away over time."

"So you say, but *'over time'* will not be soon enough for me," grumbled Percy. "I have an image to uphold, and this disfigurement serves to ravage what should be exquisitely perfect!"

"Well, while you sulk over your *disfigurement*, Princess Rose and I have much to do that cannot wait," said Tag, tossing the errant boot back to her to don. "If you wish to continue on with us, then feel free to join us for breakfast."

"Are you two not going to tend to me? Ready me for the day, should I decide to venture forth from here?" questioned Percy. He frowned, perplexed by their sudden need to depart before seeing to his needs.

"I am not your manservant and neither is Princess Rose your maid. We have more important things to do this morning than to help you don fresh apparel," muttered Tag. He rolled up Rose's bedroll as she finger-combed her hair.

Tossing to Rose her riding jacket, he said, "Let us leave the good prince to contemplate his next course of action without interruption from us."

"Yes! Do leave!" urged Percy, angrily waving them toward the entrance of the tent. "And while you are at it, send for Loftus. Tell him I demand to see him immediately."

"I will let Captain Loftus know that you had requested his presence," responded Tag.

"It is an *order*, not a petty request," snapped Percy.

"Fret not," said Rose. "I will fetch Captain Loftus."

"And if he is tardy in responding to my order, there will be hell to pay!"

"What? Are you going to give the captain a *bruising* by wine bottle, too?" teased Tag.

Rose grabbed her friend by the arm, steering Tag out of the tent before he aggravated Percy even more.

"Captain Loftus," Rose called as she neared her friends gathering for breakfast. "Prince Percy requires your presence immediately."

"Very well, my lady," nodded Loftus, brushing his hands off on his trousers as he rose to his feet. "I shall see to the young man."

"Thank you." Rose smiled in appreciation as she sat down to join the others.

Loftus trotted over to Percy's tent, pausing at the entrance he called, "My lord, you beckoned?"

"Enter, and be quick about it!" snapped Percy. The irritation in his voice signalled to Loftus his young charge was already in a foul mood.

Loftus steeled himself for a verbal assault as he entered the tent, but nothing could have prepared him for what came next. The captain's eyes bulged as they gazed upon Prince Percival. Loftus was forced to bite his tongue to stifle the laughter waiting to erupt from him.

"I see you can appreciate my sorry state," growled Percy, his hand moving to cover his mouth so Loftus would not gawk at the deep purple encircling his lips.

"Sorry state, indeed!"

"Seeing how this is your fault, you shall find a way to postpone this quest until I am presentable to the world once more. You shall break this news to those idiots, and fetch my breakfast while you are at it. I wish to dine in the comfort of my lone company."

"No."

"N- no?" sputtered Percy. Shocked by Loftus' insolence, his voice increased in pitch and volume. "What do you mean, no?"

"I meant exactly what I said. The answer is no." Loftus shrugged, growing weary of Percy's whining. "This quest we embark on is bigger than any of us, with dire consequences should we fail. To delay this quest for the sake of this... unfortunate accident, particularly when it does not impair your ability to move is pure folly. As for breakfast, if you wish to be a part of this group, then you will eat with us."

Percy floundered, at a loss for words. His mouth opened and closed like a gasping fish as Loftus administered this harsh dose of reality. He frowned at the realization the captain's new friends would only side with Loftus. To save face, he grunted, "Well, the very least you can do is help me conceal this unsightly horror now marring my face."

"Perhaps you should tie this around your mug," suggested Loftus, pulling a swathe of fabric from Percy's saddlebag. Undoubtedly, it was a memento discreetly stashed into this bag by the Prince's favourite maid.

Percy scowled in disgust, swatting away the flowered, perfumed scarf Loftus waved before his face. "Absolutely not! I was thinking of something more becoming of a manly man such as myself."

"Very well. How about this?" Loftus held up a cloth used to wipe clean Percy's boots.

"That is a filthy rag!"

"A fitting symbol of a man unafraid of a little hard work," reasoned Loftus.

"I am not afraid of hard work! I meant a *noble* man exuding masculine qualities women so admire," Percy huffed, crossing his arms in defiance. Scanning the room, his eyes fell upon Loftus' stand of armour propped up in the corner of the tent. Marching over, he hefted the steel helmet.

"I shall wear this!" declared Percy. "I will look far more intimidating and battle-ready wearing this rather than wrapping my face in flouncy fabric."

"My lord, with respect, I suggest you buck up; take your lumps than to subject yourself to the capricious hold of vanity. To wear my helmet just to conceal that bruise will only draw more unwanted attention than the bruise itself."

"What do you know?" snapped Percy. He placed the helmet over his head, dropping the visor to hide his discoloured mouth. "Follow me! After last night's meagre dinner, I am famished!"

Harold, Rainus and Myron peered up from the campfire to see Percy exiting his tent. With the aroma of breakfast wafting through the air, the nagging pangs of hunger prevailed, winning over his wounded pride.

"Not a word," whispered Rose. She shot an admonishing glance at her comrades.

With a confident swagger, Percy's haughty gait was quickly reduced to a stiff, bow-legged limp. His body chose now to rebel against the long hours he spent mounted on his warhorse, compounded by the misery of sleeping on the hard ground instead of the soft mattress he was used to. Wincing in pain, he was grateful none could see his grimacing face as he abandoned his manly strut. He dragged his body, with as much dignity as he could muster, over to the campfire as though nothing had happened while Loftus, pursing his lips together in a bid to maintain his composure, followed several steps behind his royal charge.

When Loftus gazed upon the muted expressions of surprise on his companions' faces, he felt his lips stretch into a great smile. He clamped a hand over his mouth, all the while fighting the urge to break out in laughter at Percy's ridiculous and futile efforts to mask his facial contusion.

"Good morning, Prince Percival," greeted Harold, scooting over to make room on the log for this royal. "It is you, right?"

"Of course it is me, you fool!"

Percy stared through the eye slit to glare menacingly at the large man. It then donned on Percy that if he sat next to this big buffoon wearing the pelt of a dead, snarling badger on his balding head, surely Harold's odd headpiece would become the centre of attention, not this formidable steel helm commonly worn by knights.

"It is a fine thing that you decided to join us for breakfast," said Myron, as he scrutinized this odd choice of headgear, "but why the helmet? And where is the rest of your armour?"

Percy adjusted the helmet engulfing his head as he addressed

Myron. "I felt it was necessary to be prepared; properly attired as we engage in this perilous quest."

"Interesting," said Myron.

"How so?" Percy detected the knight's cynical tone.

"It is wise to be prepared, for there is no telling what dangers await us, but I take it, you either feel your body is invincible to weapons, hence the missing body armour, or you feel the only part of your anatomy worth protecting is your head."

"You do realize without the neck-guard your precious head can still be lopped from your shoulders with a well-placed blade?" queried Rainus, his words matter-of-fact.

"Are you threatening me with physical harm, Lord Silverthorn?" gasped Percy, as he glared at the Elf.

"I am merely stating the obvious that you are obviously oblivious to," answered Rainus, as he glanced over to the captain standing behind Percy. "Is this your idea of a joke, Captain Loftus? I believe Prince Percival has been poorly advised in donning merely a helmet, if he means to face danger head-on, no pun intended."

"Oh, I made it perfectly clear that a head without a body, and vice-versa, is rather pointless and of little use, but Prince Percival was the one to *insist* on abandoning a whole stand of armour to wear nothing more than a steel helm on this morning. Mind you, my suit of armour was designed specifically for a man of my proportions. Prince Percival would be floundering in my armour – "

"Being that Loftus is so *fat*, and I am perfectly lean in comparison," interjected Percy. "This is rather cumbersome, but at least my valuable head, vital for thinking up strategy and controlling my body to act on the said strategy, will be safe from a deadly blow."

"Oh, come now!" said Tag. "Even if you don't wish to tell these good people the truth about why you're really wearing Captain Loftus' helmet, how do you intend to eat with it on your head? Are you going to sieve crumbs of food through the grate?"

Percy glared at Tag, realizing this helmet encased his head in steel so thoroughly, only the narrow eye slits and the ventilation grate for his nose and mouth provided openings via this moveable visor. These provided little in the way of a portal for food to pass to his mouth.

"I never thought of that," said Percy. He scowled at the captain as he admonished him, "Why did you not say anything, Loftus, you idiot?"

"I tried, my lord, but you would hear none of it."

"Do not argue with me! It is your job to speak up and be heard when my good name and reputation are at stake!"

"That would be tantamount to ordering a deaf man to suddenly hear," retorted Tag, speaking up in defence of the captain Percy attempted to publicly shame.

"Had Loftus been more vocal and insistent, I would have been prepared to listen, rather than being subjected to further ridicule by the likes of you!"

"Well, what is done is done, Prince Percival," stated Rainus. "As it is highly unlikely we will be drawn into battle so close to your father's domain, I believe you to be safe for the time being. Remove that damned helmet; join us for a morning meal before we strike out."

Percy stared at the plump, sizzling sausages in the cast-iron pan Harold used. His mouth watered involuntarily as the spicy aroma invaded his steel helm.

"I hardly think you'll be able to slice these sausages thin enough to push through the slots of that visor," said Tag. He chomped down, enjoying the thick slab of bread he had wrapped around the piping-hot, savoury sausage to eat both at the same time.

"Come now, Prince Percy, remove that helmet and join us for breakfast," urged Rose. She motioned Harold to slide down the log so the Prince could sit between them. "It is not as though these men are so childish they are going to make fun of you."

With a disgruntled sigh, Percy plotted down onto the log; sitting closer to Rose than the strange man he detested the very sight of.

Inwardly, he was annoyed that his saddle was already on his horse than on this log for him to use as a seat as he did last night, but at the same time, it meant he would not be tasked with the menial job of saddling his own mount.

"Now, do be a dear, remove that silly helmet so you can eat," insisted Rose.

Before she could reach over to remove it for him, Percy snatched the helmet from his head. Efforts to turn away or lower his face before anyone could spy upon the nasty-looking contusion marring his puffy lips failed as all, with the exception of Rose, burst out in a fit of laughter.

"You said they would not make fun of me," pouted Percy. His face and ears burned red, muting the darkness of the circular bruise.

"You are mistaken," assured Rainus, motioning for this mortal to calm down. "We are not making fun of you at all."

"I fail to understand," grumbled Percy. He wanted nothing more than to grab a plate, fill it, and then retreat with his breakfast to eat in the privacy of his tent. "You are all laughing at me."

"If we meant to make fun of you, words of ridicule would be flying with gay abandon around this campfire," explained the Elf. "Instead, we laugh, but it is nothing more than a gut response."

"Yes," agreed Myron, as he stifled his laughter. "It is much like laughing when one is tickled or coughing when one has an itch in the throat; a physical response really, nothing more."

"Believe me, if I wanted to make fun of you, Prince Percival, I'd come up with some choice words," admitted Tag. In reality, he already said all he wanted to when he first saw Percy's face upon waking in their shared accommodation.

"What's there to make fun of anyway?" questioned Harold, his broad shoulders rolling in a shrug as he spoke with genuine empathy. "It's not like we never had a bruise or two to contend with. At least yours is perfectly round and concentrated in one spot, instead of bein' a huge, ragged, ugly blob of purple discolourin' half your face."

"See!" exclaimed Rose, her hand gently patting Percy's arm to console him. "There is no fun being made, not at all."

"I suppose," muttered Percy. He resigned to the fact his perfect face would be temporarily marred for however long it would take for this bruise to fade away.

"Had you a looking glass to peer into, I'm confident you would have been laughing just as hard as the rest of us," said Myron. He speared a sausage with the tip of his knife, resting it on a slice of bread before passing it on to the irate prince to dine on.

Percy accepted the food, handling it daintily between his fingers and thumb. He then glared angrily at Loftus, shaking a fist at him as the captain attempted to smother a broad grin that was sure to unleash another explosion of laughter from all, if he did not contain himself.

"You shake your fist now, Prince Percival, but it is a sad state of affairs when one cannot step back and laugh at one's self," said Rainus. "When you are able to do just that, you will find the world laughs with you, not at you, when you can find humour in your own foibles."

"I am a prince! I have no foibles! I am quite foible-less and more fabulous, when the need calls for it."

"Incredible!" announced Myron, giving Percy a shrewd nod. "That must mean you are not like us."

"I am of royal blood, of course I am not like you or any one of these miscreants sitting before this fire," explained Percy. "Even Princess Rose-alyn, being a girl, albeit one with a title, is lower than me in the grand scheme of things."

"Say again!" gasped Rose. Her face frowned upon hearing his pointed words.

"Worry not, my dear, take no offence! You are still above these lowly commoners, so that counts for something."

"I meant to say, my lord, that you must not even be of this world, our earthly realm, if you are so perfect, as *fabulous* as you claim to be," corrected the knight.

"Yes, it makes you totally alien and definitely not of this world," teased Tag.

"I have been mistaken for a divine being more than once," boasted Percy, puffing out his chest in pride.

"For pity's sake," groaned Rainus.

"Indeed, I do pity all of you," said Percy, proud that he came from a prominent family and endowed with a lofty title to accompany his inherited wealth.

The boisterous laughter shared earlier by all was now replaced by murmurs of discontent upon being the recipient of Percy's latest insult.

"Lord Silverthorn is quite correct," said Rose. She nodded to the Elf, but it was as much to stop Percy from saying anything else that was sure to further alienate him from the group. "You can let your guard down. There is no need for pretentious airs when you are amongst friends."

Percy's eyes narrowed as he glared at her, sensing she was siding with them, instead of him.

"Please, my lord, do listen to the wise, young lady," urged Loftus. "We have far to go and the days on the road are unknown. There is much to be gained in embracing this camaraderie that only serves to strengthen this fellowship."

"So you say," grumbled Percy.

"It's always better than bein' on the outside lookin' in," added Harold, as he glanced over to his little donkey picketed with the much larger horses. "Take my Sassy for example. She's nothin' grand like your warhorse, but once she stopped nippin' at the horses she's travellin' with, they all get along, even treatin' her as part of the herd."

Percy scrutinized the faces of those sitting around the campfire. To be compared to a donkey, a lowly ass of all things, did not sit well with him. Yet, this odd man donning the badger headpiece did have a valid point about the need to cooperate and get along with others. The idea of being part of a fellowship certainly held a level of appeal to him, but considering the present company he was forced to keep, just to stay close to Rose, it left much to be desired.

To be accepted into a brotherhood that included a big buffoon like Harold Murkins as a *brother* held no appeal. However, to be regarded with the same level of respect afforded to Myron Kendall, Rainus Silverthorn, Captain Loftus and even the lowly ne'er-do-well Tagius

Yairet, did have its charm.

"What say you, Prince Percival? It's good to put up with some good natured ribbing," insisted Tag. "It makes a long trek much more bearable for all. Mind you, not everyone is blessed with a sense of humour."

Percy scowled with disdain at Tag. "I have a delightful sense of humour! You just do not know it, for it is obviously much more refined than yours!"

"If you can laugh along with the rest of us, there's a bloody good chance you will fit right in," said Myron, raising a flask of water in good cheer to Percy before taking a sip.

"And you do want to fit in, is that not so, Prince Percy?" said Rose, staring hopefully at her man.

"Oh, come now, my dear Rose-alyn! I can never 'fit in' with these people. It goes against everything I was raised to believe that defined the very character of one with a royal pedigree."

Loftus ran a hand down his woeful face as he grumbled at his royal charge, "It is obvious you wish to make this quest as difficult as possible for yourself, my lord."

"I beg to differ, Loftus. It would be ludicrous for me to pretend I can be like any one of you. However, there is nothing that says I cannot learn to get along with you fun-loving louts."

"I will gladly accept a genuine attempt to get along," said Myron, nodding in approval.

"I agree," said Rainus. "This quest promises to be difficult enough without unnecessary distractions. At this moment, getting along is a satisfactory compromise."

"Excellent! I know how trying all of you can be at the best of times," teased Rose. "This is a wonderful compromise on Prince Percy's part and it proves the true quality of his character."

"Huzzah!" cheered Harold.

His affable grin, accompanied by a hearty slap on Percy's shoulder was met with a scowl of disapproval that this behemoth would even dream of touching him, especially in such a rough and casual manner. Leaning away from him, Percy inched closer to Rose's side.

"Huzzah, indeed," responded Tag, as he used his knife on the hard cheese to cut it into bite-size cubes to share with all. "Let us eat, and then we can strike down this camp."

"Sounds like an adequate plan," agreed Percy, taking a large bite of his bread and sausage. In his bid to *fit in* with this uncouth assortment of friends, he set aside all sense of decorum. With his mouth still full of masticated food, he addressed Tag. "Be a good chap and share in that cheese."

"Absolutely! Catch," said Tag. With a mischievous grin, he tossed a square of cheese right at Percy's mouth. To the astonishment of all, the yellow cube bounced off his face to land on the ground at his feet.

"What was the meaning of that?" snapped Percy, his cheeks reddened with embarrassment by this cheesy assault.

"Forgive me," said Tag, smiling unrepentantly. "I thought your mouth was already opened. I forgot it was actually that dark bruise making it look that way."

All chortled in amusement as Rose glared menacingly at Tag, like he was a bratty child in need of a scolding.

"No harm done, I suppose," sighed Percy. With forced affability, he laughed, taking the Elf's advice to learn to laugh with the others.

Rose beamed at her man, delighted that he was making a genuine effort to be accepted into their fellowship.

"Each day grows shorter," said Rainus, casting his eyes to the pale blue sky. "Let us make haste. We eat, then we ride."

Like feeding crumbs to a caged bird, Sin tossed a scrap of pan-fried candlefish onto the bottom of Loken's prison.

The Sprite stared at this meagre offering that had landed unceremoniously at his feet.

"Eat," she hissed. "It could well be your last meal."

"Of the day?" asked Loken.

"Of your life," answered Sin. She licked the residue of fish oil from her fingertips. "If you become more trouble than you are worth, I have no qualms about killing you."

He glared at her ugly face that peered through the bars of his prison. It was an image he had yet to become used to in spite of his long days of captivity.

"You are such a wretched hag," muttered Loken.

"Thank you! I'd like to believe I am the very embodiment of true power and all it entails."

"I said no such thing!" snapped Loken. With a shake of his head, he plopped down onto the floor of his prison. "You are as delusional as you are wretched."

"And you will be dead, if you choose not to eat."

"I will eat." Loken picked up the piece of fish. "I must keep my strength up."

"Your strength?" snorted Sin, the wrinkles on her forehead furrowed even deeper as she scowled. "For what purpose?"

"So I can kill you."

"Kill me!" chortled Sin, slapping her bony thigh as she laughed. "Oh, woe is me! I am so scared!"

"I am serious. I have every intention of killing you for what you did to the Trolls and to Lord Silverthorn's people. And now, you keep me apart from my one true love."

"This threat that rings hollow will be what kills me. It is hilarious! I might choke on my own tongue laughing at your idle threats."

"Then choke!" growled Loken. He took an angry bite from the handful of food.

Sin used the back of her hand to wipe away the single tear that trickled from her one good eye as she mocked him. "Such bold words from one so small. You are powerless; powerless to act against me."

"Believe what you want. Give me time. I will escape this prison and when I do, I will free the Mermaid and her seal. Once done, I will take great pleasure in doing away with you, in the most excruciating manner conceivable."

"You are pathetic, but bully for you, believing in the impossible," said the Witch.

"I am a shape-shifting Sprite, nothing is impossible for me."

"Then shape-shift your way from this sturdy prison that holds you now." She dismissed Loken with a wave of her hand. Picking up the pail and the tin plate of cooked fish, she turned away, limping off toward the sad lump of a seal.

Flotsam cowered.

Sin chuckled. She was pleased this animal was quick to show its fear. Reaching into the pail, she tossed a handful of raw candlefish before the seal's snout.

"Eat!" she demanded, as she tossed another handful of silvery fish before the animal.

Flotsam uttered a sad moan, but the scent of food wafting up to her nostrils pushed aside her fears. Her snout poked out from between the mesh to devour the offering.

Satisfied the seal had the will to feed on its own, Sin turned her attention to Elee.

"Your turn," growled the Witch, holding a fresh, limp fish before the Mermaid's face.

Smelling the briny scent of the dead candlefish, Elee shrugged off from this offering.

Annoyed by her reaction to this fine offering, Sin snarled at her, "Eat, damn it!"

The slender fish jiggled about, as though it had come back to life in her quivering fist she thrust into Elee's face.

Instead, the Mermaid turned her face away, her tail splashing on the surface of the tidal pool in protest.

"You nasty little creature! Eat, I say!"

"No!" shouted Elee.

Sin threw the dead fish back into the pail. Snatching up the plate of partially eaten, fried fish she grabbed a handful, mashing it into a mouth-sized ball. Thrusting it into Elee's face, the Witch repeated her demand, "Eat!"

"I told you before, I do *not* eat fish."

"You are being fussy! I know a sure cure for fussy. It is called starvation. When you are hungry enough, you will eat anything I offer!"

"I do not care what you think. I will refuse all offerings of fish, large or small, fresh or cooked. I would rather starve. If I did, my suffering would end. You will no longer have access to my tears."

Sin growled as she threw the ball of fish against the far wall.

"I have seen your kind eating fish, fish much bigger than these!" snapped the Witch. She threw down the plate of food. "Do not tell me Mermaids do not eat fish!"

"Most will eat fish, but some do not eat meat of any kind, not even shellfish."

"What else is there for Mermaids to eat in the sea, if not fish?"

"I prefer kelp, seaweed, eel grass and other aquatic plants," explained Elee.

"Well, dearie, today's your lucky day!" Sin grabbed the seaweed she had gathered last night to place atop her catch to keep the candlefish from drying out before she had a chance to eat or cure the remainder. Tearing off a manageable piece of the dark, damp seaweed, she thrust it into Elee's face.

The Mermaid turned away. Pursing her lips together, she still refused to eat.

"You miserable wench!" growled Sin. The seaweed shook in her trembling hand as she shoved it at Elee's face. "You *will* eat!"

Elee kept her mouth clamped shut. She gasped in surprise when the Witch seized her by the chin, forcefully wrenching her mouth open. Cramming the handful of seaweed into the Mermaid's mouth, Sin slapped her bony hand over Elee's mouth and nose. "I'm not letting go until you swallow! Now eat!"

Smothered, Elee quickly chewed, swallowing down the briny offering.

"So, what will it be?" asked Sin. "Will you eat like a good little Mermaid, or will you make me ram this seaweed down your throat with my fist?"

Elee's eyes were glazed with tears, but she held back, refusing to cry before the old hag. She nodded her response.

"I knew it!" declared Sin. She gleefully tore off another handful of seaweed. Balling it into a wad, she shoved it into Elee's mouth that she did not have to force open this time. "See? It is so much better when you cooperate!"

Elee said nothing. She chewed, allowing the taste and smell of the sea to fill her mouth and buoy her troubled soul as her mind dreamed of swimming in the vast, open waters.

With all three of her prisoners adequately fed, Sin was satisfied, taking a moment to wash her hands in the pool of water as she contemplated on tasks yet to be completed.

As the waves rushed in, breaking over the rocks forming the tidal pool before spilling over to fill it with fresh seawater, Sin knew they were well into the morning and the light of this new day would not hold out for long in these lands far to the north.

She picked up the plate of scraps and the pail of fresh fish she still needed to deal with. If the weather still held, it was a chance to cure the candlefish, smoking them over a slow-burning fire just outside her lair.

After setting the drying rack with this latest catch to cure in the sun and the drying heat of a fire, then it would be time for her to get to the real work awaiting her attention. There was a new kind of trap she had in mind, one to capture a very special animal.

8

An Exception to the Rule

"Over there," announced Harold. For Captain Loftus' benefit, he pointed to the west. "That's where I caught up to the gang at the ravine."

"That was during the unicorn stampede you spoke of," assumed Loftus, nodding in acknowledgment. "The herd charged after your comrades, is that not correct?"

"I can't rightly say my friends were deliberately chased down, but they were definitely in the front of the stampedin' herd. When I came upon Princess Rose, she was danglin' into the ravine, hangin' over the boulders and river coursin' down below."

"Thank goodness you were there to rescue her!" praised Loftus, nodding in approval to the large man.

Percy twisted about in his saddle, glancing behind to address Harold as he and his donkey trotted alongside the captain. "Did you say unicorn?"

"Oh, yes!" Harold nodded. "Had to be well over a hundred I'm sure, if I were able to count that high. They came thunderin' by. I followed, happenin' on my friends along the way."

"*Happened* upon us? Do not be so modest!" exclaimed Rose. "You, Harold Murkins, saved my life that day!"

"That is all well and good," said Percy, motioning for silence so he may continue his inquisition, "but this unicorn herd you spoke of, in which direction did they flee?"

"They cleared the ravine, headin' that way," answered Harold, pointing westward once more. "That's the last I saw of them."

"Perhaps we shall be lucky enough to see a unicorn or two, as we venture deeper into the Enchanted Forest," Percy hoped aloud.

"Accordin' to Lord Silverthorn, these creatures are bashful to begin with, not wantin' to be seen by most people, other than the Elves, that is," informed Harold.

"We were told these creatures are so shy they would run at the very sight of a human being," added Rose. "However, on that fateful day, those beasts had no qualms about charging straight for us, no doubt in hopes of trampling us to death."

"Sir Kendall had alluded to something evil lurking in this forest, some strange force that spooked the unicorns, causing them to stampede," said Loftus.

"Apparently so," responded Rose, "but you would think those creatures would have had the good sense to recognize a genuine princess, giving me proper leeway to escape or to go around me!"

"So, it is unlikely we shall see one of these elusive creatures?" asked Percy.

"Highly unlikely," answered Rose.

"That is a pity." Percy shook his head in disappointment.

"If we happen to spot a unicorn on our travels, we shall be sure to point it out to you," offered Harold. "They're truly magnificent!"

"Excellent! I have never had the good fortune of seeing a unicorn with mine own eyes. I can only imagine how proud my father would be if I were to kill one of those creatures of legend, gifting this prize to him, being the wonderful son that I am!"

"Say again!" gasped Harold, appalled by what he was hearing.

"It has been many generations since one on the throne of Axalon had the privilege of hunting one of these rare creatures," explained Percy, grinning as he thought about the bragging rights that would be his, should he be successful on a hunt. "If I killed one of those beasts, it'd make for a kingly trophy to display in the royal library! Or perhaps I would take its horn; have it crafted into a magnificent, one of a kind sword hilt and there'd still be enough to carve out a matching dagger handle!"

With his mouth agape, Harold stared in stunned disbelief, sickened by Percy's need to kill such a rare and exquisite animal.

"But that is tantamount to killing a horse," said Rose. Bewildered by Percy's brazen words, she attempted to reason with him. "I am not particularly fond of horses, as they are not small, fuzzy creatures that one can easily cuddle on the lap, but it would still be like killing one's pet."

"Balderdash!" Percy dismissed Rose's comment with a casual wave of his hand. "A unicorn, in my honest and correct opinion, is a very different creature. How many horses do you know have that elegant horn spiralling from its forehead? None! Besides, a horse, even that pathetic nag of a donkey, can be tamed. Throughout history not one human being had been able to tame a unicorn, never enough to ride on one."

"I've ridden a unicorn before," said Harold.

Percy glanced over his shoulder to frown at the behemoth of a man. He was perplexed that Harold would make such a bold claim before all. "How is it that *you*, of all people, were able to ride a unicorn? Was it by some Elven magic?"

"More like Spritely magic," explained Harold. "Our little friend, Loken, changed into a unicorn as my little Sassy was too small to carry me when the others felt a need to ride ahead. As a unicorn, Loken was even bigger than that grand warhorse you ride now. It was really quite remarkable, but it made for quite the hair-raisin' ride the way he charged through this forest."

"A unicorn that is really nothing more than a shape-shifting Pooka is not a unicorn at all," corrected Percy, with a disgruntle shake of his head. "I can only imagine though, the thrill of hunting a fine specimen in its prime!"

The smile on Percy's face vanished as Rainus Silverthorn abruptly turned his steed about, urging his mount toward him. The Prince sensed either the Elf Lord was going to insist on being the one to lead him on a hunting expedition or he was about to be the recipient of a severe tongue-lashing.

"Prince Percival, you do understand this forest is the domain of the Elfkind, do you not?"

"In all honesty, Lord Silverthorn, I am not certain exactly where the Enchanted Forest begins and ends, but yes, I am perfectly aware the forest is your domain."

"And tell me, does your father hold private hunting reserves in Axalon, parcels of land used exclusively by those of royal blood or those extended a personal invitation to hunt?"

"Of course, none are permitted to hunt, let alone enter, in these private reserves without our permission."

"And what happens to those unfortunate souls caught hunting in one of your reserves?" queried Rainus.

"It depends on the circumstance."

"Elaborate, please."

"If the hunter is caught with a kill, absolute proof he had been trespassing and hunting in this private reserve, the punishment doled out must fit the crime. A lowly boar, depending on its size, would cost the offending hunter a finger so he can no longer draw an arrow to hunt again," said Percy, raising his middle finger to the Elf to represent the offending digit to be amputated. "However, the killing of a majestic stag sporting full, 12-tine antlers is punishable by death. The guilty culprit is hanged by the neck until dead."

"You don't say!" exclaimed Rainus.

"Oh, I do! In fact, a public hanging serves well as a warning to all thinking of abusing this law. At the very least, it forces them to think twice before committing such a crime against the crown."

Harold blanched, the colour draining from his face as he thought on how often he had stumbled into private hunting reserves, not even being aware of it at the time.

"Do not look so surprised, my good man," said Percy, waving off Harold's look of horror. "It is a long-standing law and tradition that is common knowledge."

"But suppose the hunter didn't know he was intrudin' into one of these private reserves?" asked Harold. "Or suppose he was hungry and had a starvin' family at home and he was actin' out of desperation? Surely you'd show him some mercy."

"Mercy is for the weak! The citizens of Axalon are aware of this decree. They know exactly where these royal hunting reserves are. As for being hungry, that is still no excuse for committing a crime. Only a fool would dare break this law and the laws of the land decree that a criminal shall be punished as my father sees fit. It is the most efficient method to curb illegal activities and to control the criminal-minded."

"If that is the law of your lands, then does it not stand to reason that my realm, this domain under the stewardship of the Elfkind, be treated with the same respect and regard as your father's private hunting reserves?"

"I suppose it does make sense." Percy nodded in agreement.

"Then need I say more?"

"Not really, but I just want to be certain of your hunting policy, should I spy upon a worthy trophy."

"Then let me make this perfectly clear: no man, Elf or Dwarf is permitted to set foot in my domain for the purpose of hunting these creatures," stated Rainus.

"Yes, of course," agreed Percy. "However, you will make an exception for me."

The Elf's perfect brows arched up in surprise, and yet, inwardly, he somehow expected such an assumption from this mortal.

"Common courtesy requires that I ask for express permission from you, of course, to hunt a unicorn."

Rainus unleashed a dreary sigh, shaking his head in response to this hubris young man and his entitled ways.

"Come now, Lord Silverthorn, I would be an exception to the rule, being a royal and all."

"I am saying, Prince Percival, what remains of a once great and noble herd now seeks refuge from the human race. These creatures stand on the brink of extinction, no thanks to those hunting them for 'sport' or for the sole purpose of using their horns for fancy dagger and sword handles."

"So, you are telling me that you control the hunting of the unicorns in your domain and *you* would even refuse my father, the great King Maxmillian?" asked Percy. He looked aghast, paling at the mere thought that he had been denied a privilege that should be his by birthright.

Rainus reached over, seizing the horse's reins to make sure Percy's mount moved no further. When he was certain he had this young man's undivided attention, he made a final attempt to define his position on the matter.

"Allow me to make this absolutely clear so there is no misunderstanding while you are in my realm, Prince Percival: None, not even you, are permitted to kill a unicorn. These creatures are in the Enchanted Forest under the protection of my people. It will never happen again, not while I am on watch."

"Fair enough. But tell me, Lord Silverthorn, what does happen to a man caught hunting a unicorn in your forest, should that ever happen?" queried Percy. He wanted to weigh out the potential rewards against the possible punishment to be doled out, if he were to be caught in the act.

"As your father, the *great* King Maxmillian, sees fit to hang a man by his neck for hunting one of his stags, a common creature found throughout the lands, far and wide, I would say, at the very least, an equal punishment should suffice for such an offence."

Percy was momentarily stunned by the Elf's words.

"However, as the unicorn is *not* an ordinary creature, perhaps public humiliation and a vigorous lashing, followed by a very public beheading will serve as a better warning to the public wishing to commit such a heinous crime in my domain," continued Rainus. "Do you now comprehend what lengths I am willing to go to in order to protect this remnant herd?"

"Indeed," said Percy, as he nodded in understanding. "Of course, there is *always* an exception to the rule, say perhaps, in the way of a diplomatic gift."

"I make *no* exceptions!" Rainus responded tersely. "If a person chooses to kill one of my unicorns, I shall personally smite that fool. It is as simple as that."

"A *fool*, yes, but you would certainly make an exception for a *friend*, especially a royal one," insisted Percy, giving Rainus a sly wink.

"True, you are of royal blood, Prince Percival, however, your line of questioning, the assumptions you make, causes me to query just what kind of *friend* would make such a foolish demand in the first place."

It was obvious the Elf could not be swayed by these persuasive words, unwaveringly adhering to this decree.

"I was just curious," muttered Percy. His shoulders drooped; disappointed he would not have the opportunity to brag to his royal cohorts of hunting such a rare and exquisite creature.

"Let me make this clear, once and for all, there will be no hunting, not in this forest, and especially of unicorns," stated the Elf. "Am I understood?"

"Understood," conceded Percy.

"Huzzah!" cheered Harold, relieved that none of these magnificent creatures would now fall victim to a slew of arrows, all in the name of sport. "I like unicorns, especially when they're alive!"

"Oh, huzzah indeed!" grumbled Percy. Rolling his eyes in utter frustration over Harold's exuberance, he breathed a sigh of relief as the Elf released his horse's reins to return to the front of the procession where Tag and Myron awaited him.

"What a demanding prig of a prince," whispered Tag, as Rainus returned.

"The gall," added Myron, with a disapproving shake of his head. "How dare he ask you such a thing?"

"It was more a demand than asking for permission, as though that dolt feels he has a right to do whatever he pleases, whenever it pleases him," said Rainus.

"His sense of entitlement, the way he constantly uses his royal title for leverage, may one day be the death of him," whispered Myron. Glancing over his shoulder, he watched Percy. He rode alongside Princess Rose, but all the while casting an icy stare at the trio ahead for undoubtedly being in cahoots and for effectively putting the kibosh on his great hunting plans.

"I imagine the young sir is not used to being told what he can and cannot do, especially by one he views as being of lower status than him," determined Rainus.

"Perhaps a lesson is in order," said Tag, his eyes sparkled with mischief.

"And what? Be subjected to Princess Rose's wrath for subjecting her intended husband to this lesson?" asked Myron, shuddering involuntarily. "I think not!"

"As Lord Silverthorn pointed out, and it's pretty obvious to me, too," said Tag, "Prince Percival does not like being told what to do by any one of us. I can think of one lesson he can be made to learn to make him respect this forest, and we can do so without having to waste a single word on him."

"Whatever do you mean?" asked Rainus.

"Remember the first time we ventured into your domain?" asked Tag. "Do you recall how you found us and came to our rescue?"

"Yes, of course I do. You were in the midst of being pulled apart by a grand old willow tree that had the grave misfortune of being urinated against."

"Exactly! No one had warned me about that. I had to learn for myself exactly what *enchanted* meant in this forest."

"Hmph!" grunted Myron, as he mulled over this idea. "If Prince Percival takes certain displeasure on being told he cannot hunt a unicorn, I hardly think he will want to be told where he can or cannot take a piss."

"I think I get your meaning," said Rainus, giving his friends a thoughtful nod. "The young sir definitely does not like being told *anything*."

Loken ceased pushing against the bars of his prison as the Witch sauntered back into the cave. Resting her staff against the wall, she passed by the Sprite.

"I know what you were doing," muttered Sin. "Why do you waste your time?"

"It is not a waste, especially as there is nothing else to do with my time, but to attempt an escape."

Sin limped over to Loken's cage. Inspecting the circle of pink salt, it had now dried. She could make out where her prisoner had scratched and scraped to break the briny circle, but it remained intact. The runes she had initially inscribed with charcoal were either rubbed or washed away, but carving these runes into the wooden floor of this prison proved far more effective. Together with the salt, the spell to control the Sprite remained strong.

"It is an exercise in futility. You are trapped until you die, whether by my hands or you succumb to old age, either way you are my prisoner."

"And you reek," said Loken, tossing an insult her way. His nose wrinkled in disgust at the pungent fumes of acrid smoke lingering with curing candlefish wafting to his nose to assault his senses.

"And you are a pathetic, little Pooka," grunted Sin. Her good eye narrowed in contempt as she glared at Loken.

"I am proud to be a shape-shifter! And where I cannot change what I am, nor would I want to, you can certainly do something about that foul stink coming off your wretched carcass. Do us both a favour: Take a bath so we are not subjected to your rank odour."

"You exaggerate. I do not smell as badly as you claim."

"You reek probably a thousand times worse than you think," argued Loken. "Worse than a dead skunk ripe with decay. In fact, you smell so bad, a dead skunk would be resurrected from its perpetual slumber, only to die again from your stench."

"But I bathed recently."

"How recently?" Loken was highly sceptical.

"It was in the summer; at the height of the summer solstice to be exact!"

"That was months ago. No wonder you stink so badly."

"Well, I tell you what, you little vermin," hissed Sin, "as soon as I conjure up a spell that will make you my slave, I'll set you to work. You can be the one out there handling the fish and curing them over the heat and smoke. You can get your clothes reeking and when you're done with this task, you can draw me a bath. I will have time to luxuriate in a nice hot tub of water infused with lavender oil and scented with the attar of roses."

"Good luck trying to enslave me to do your bidding!" Loken snorted in derision. Her prior attempt failed, forcing her to cast an enchantment on her sock puppet in a bid to lure his friends into a trap. "And a good scrubbing will certainly do wonders for your smell, alas, it will do nothing to improve your looks. You will still be ugly as sin."

"Ha!" scoffed Sin. "Where you claim you would not change being a Pooka, but are now rendered powerless, I can certainly change my looks for the better, if I so desire."

"Right!" Loken shook his head in doubt. "If that were so, you would not cling to that disgusting husk of a body. You would have transformed yourself into something desirable and beautiful, than to be trapped in this hideous form."

"Perhaps I like this *'disgusting husk'*. At least as such, I am taken seriously where before, in my youth and beauty, my appearance had a way of winning over the hearts of the most discerning of men. But to be treated as nothing more than an empty-headed beauty rather than the powerful enchantress I truly am? I think not! This is the price to be paid so I am both feared and respected, rather than be ogled at for my seductive, good looks."

"Who would look at you?"

With her hands on her bony hips, Sin struck a provocative pose as she insisted, "At the height of my beauty, I turned many heads!"

"Yes, mainly the heads of those men you were twisting off to break their necks!"

"Tut, tut!" admonished the Witch. "You are an angry, bitter little creature."

"It is the company I am forced to keep. The more I am exposed to you and your hateful ways, the worse I become."

"Just keep up with those disparaging remarks. I shall twist off *your* little head."

"Sure! I dare you to stick your hands in here." Loken grimaced, bearing his teeth at her. "As bad as you reek, given the chance, I'd still bite you, if I could. I'd even spit in your wound, in hopes it'd get lethally infected."

"You vicious, little miscreant! I will prove my point to you. I will show you just how beautiful I can be."

"Do not bother trying to impress me. I will not be fooled by your ruse, and it will not change the person you are on the inside," grunted Loken.

"Oh, it is no bother at all! In fact, it will help to inspire me to prepare my next trap."

"Even if you attempted to regain your youth and beauty, you cannot fool my friends, especially Silas Agincor. He will know you on sight, striking you down where you stand."

"Of course he'd remember me if I assumed my former beauty!" snapped Sin. "That is why I plan to adopt a new form, one that none of your pesky friends will recognize. It will be a pleasing form that none of them can resist, being the weak-minded men that they are."

"You may be able to seduce my mortal comrades, but you will not entice the likes of Rainus Silverthorn. It will take a beauty that far exceeds that of the fairest Elf maiden to lure Lord Silverthorn."

"Who said I was going to adopt the form of a human or Elf?"

Loken pressed his worried face between the bars. "What do you mean by that? What are you up to?"

"You will see," answered Sin. A cruel smile curled her thin, cracked lips as she pulled out a knife from the folds of her cloak. Turning her back on Loken, she limped toward Elee as she muttered, "They will not even see me coming."

❖ ❖ ❖

"Thank goodness you had warned me about these blasted trees," Percy nodded in gratitude to Rose as he raised himself onto his steed's saddle after a much needed break. "Heaven forbid had I been attacked while relieving myself."

"I just want to make sure you remain safe in this forest," said Rose. "It was bad enough when Tag was accosted by an angry willow tree, but when that *thing* attacked Myron and me, dousing us with sticky sap when we attempted to rescue Tag, that was more than I could bear. And I shall rue the day when a nasty, old tree attacks my man and I had done nothing to prevent it."

"It was decent of you to warn me," praised Percy. "No man, not even that Yairet git, deserves to be assaulted in the midst of emptying his bladder."

"In my opinion, Tag had it coming. He was forewarned this forest was *enchanted* and not necessarily in a delightful way."

"You think that impudent sod would have taken the time to warn me, man to man, rather than leaving it up to you."

"He can be a bit forgetful at times. I am sure it was an oversight on his part," responded Rose.

"Well, I shall be mindful of where I conduct my *business* in the days to come while we are in Lord Silverthorn's domain," said Percy, glancing up to the high canopy.

"Excellent! No harm in taking precautions in unfamiliar lands."

"Unfamiliar, indeed," said Percy, his eyes taking in the enormous girth of the trees rising around them. "One thing is for sure, the trees in Axalon grow nowhere near as large as these beauties."

Percy's head tilted back, his eyes gazing skyward as they followed the length of the towering tree trunks rising around him. His mouth gaped as he stared in awe of the magnificence of this old growth forest.

"Even the largest in my country cannot compare, only to be overshadowed by the smallest tree in this forest," noted Percy. "Think of the possibilities!"

"What do you mean?" queried Rose.

"My dear Rose-alyn, you may see these towering columns as merely trees. I, on the other hand, with my brilliant mind for business, see potential! Just think of how mutually beneficial it would be if these giants were harvested for their timber!"

As if perturbed by this mortal's threatening words, the trees shuddered, groaning in response. Leaves made crisp by the first kiss of autumn frost fluttered restlessly as an ominous wind blustered by Percy to blow his flaxen hair across his face. Sputtering, he dragged his fingers across his porcelain skin to extricate the errant strands from his mouth. Percy scowled upon being the victim of this perceived invisible assault.

With a toss of his head, he flipped his locks back into place. Percy continued, "As I was saying, imagine the commerce and financial gains to be generated. Axalon, and the Elves of course, can benefit greatly, if we were to harvest these magnificent trees, cutting a clear swathe from here to where the real giants grow in the heart of Elfdom."

With a snort of disdain and a roll of his eyes, Rainus brought his steed to an abrupt halt.

"For pity's sake!" Percy grumbled beneath his breath, watching as Rainus shook his head and shot a baleful glance over his shoulder. With a look of consternation clearly etched across his face, the Elf wheeled his horse about, trotting toward him.

"I feel another lecture coming on," muttered Percy.

"Only because it is evident another lecture is in order, due to your words that continue to betray your clay-brained, self-serving motives where my forest is concerned," scolded Rainus.

"Good gracious, just how well do those pointy ears hear?" asked Percy.

He was stunned this Elf was able to listen in on a conversation he believed only Rose was privy to, as Lord Silverthorn was leading the party, riding in silence at the vanguard of this procession while Tag and Myron shared in conversation.

"My auditory senses are as sharp as a fox; acute enough to hear every word that comes out of your mouth, even discreet whispers."

"I have heard rumours of the Elfkind having exceptional eyesight, but I knew not of your ability to hear to this degree."

"Our senses are the envy of mankind. Unfortunately, it exposes us to hearing and seeing things we would rather not be privy to, however, we have a way of tuning out the ignorant and mundane. In this case, my selective hearing could no longer withstand listening to the drivel leaking forth from your mouth."

"You heard, even from way up there?" asked Percy, pointing with his chin to where Tag and Myron rode at least a good seven horse-lengths ahead of him and Rose.

"Believe me, Prince Percival, in this forest, your voice carries - far. If you are wise, you will heed my warning."

"Yes, yes! I am confident your warning that this forest is your domain, and any suggestion of harvesting these trees, even for mutual commercial gains, will result in *you* happily doling out some kind of punishment. Is that not so?"

The Elf shook his head. A knowing smile curled his lips as he addressed Percy's concerns. "Trust me when I say I will not be the one to dole out punishment for your stupidity, if you wish to continue with these foolish threats to cut down and harvest this forest primeval."

Percy glanced about nervously, peering up at the dense canopy that seemed to lean in over him to block out the sun's light as the Elf's foreboding words sent a chill through his veins.

"Are you saying the trees are truly enchanted, so much so they can do harm to me, if they wish to do so?"

"It is unwise to test or challenge these old souls," cautioned Rainus, glancing up at an old elm tree that crowded over menacingly, as though listening to this exchange. "Some of them are so old, ancient by human standards for sure. They have a will of their own that not even I, lord of this woodland realm, possess the power to control them, if they choose to *misbehave*."

Percy glanced over to Rose. He waited for her to downplay the Elf's warning. Instead, she nodded in agreement.

"It is unwise to even raise an axe in this forest," warned Rose, speaking with all certainty.

"So these trees are not so much enchanted as they are bewitched by dark magic," determined Percy. As he spoke, he stared anxiously at a great willow tree, its sinuous, vine-like branches twisting about like slender serpents, moving unnaturally against the breeze whispering through the forest.

"Trust me when I say that a little respect can go a long way in this place, whether this respect is extended to the animals or the plants, great and small. They are not here for your amusement nor are they to line your coffers to compound your wealth."

"Forgive me, Lord Silverthorn. I meant no offence. I was merely thinking aloud. I could not help but think of the riches timber of this size and quality would reap for your people, and mine, as a source of shared commerce between our nations."

"I am *not* interested in harvesting these trees."

"If it is a matter of ethics, because you believe these trees to be *alive*, complete with a *soul* and a *will* if that is even possible, then how do you justify cutting them down for your own benefit? I have heard great tales of the Elves renown for their woodwork. I hardly believe these trees would allow you to carve them up, if they are as *alive* as you claim."

"It is true we excel in the crafting of wood, creating elaborate and ornate furniture, homes and sculptures," admitted Rainus, nodding proudly of this inherent skill.

"You will be witness to some of the most exquisite pieces you will ever have the privilege of seeing, Prince Percy," added Rose.

"Aha! So, the cutting of trees is permitted, but only if *you* feel inclined to sacrifice them for your own benefit!" declared Percy, his tone was as accusing as the finger he thrust toward the Elf.

Rainus unleashed a dreary sigh as his eyes rolled in utter frustration. "These trees are indeed here for our benefit, but make no mistake, Prince Percival, we are all connected. We co-exist with the forest in a mutually beneficial partnership. Without this forest, my people would not exist. Without my people to guard this great forest from your axes, these trees will cease to exist. It is crime, a sin really, to carelessly plunder this resource."

"How can harvesting be considered plundering when you have so much? Of course, if we were given permission to log your forest, you'd be compensated fairly."

"It is not about the money," retorted the Elf.

"It is *always* about the money," insisted Percy.

"For you, perhaps, but I have seen the handiwork of greedy mortals! I have been witness to mountainsides stripped bare of trees for their timber. I have watched as winter rains washed away the earth to foul rivers and streams and to expose rocks so nothing can grow and the animals are left without a habitat."

"Come spring, after the winter snows melt away, these waters run clear once more. As for the animals, they just move on to live in new locations," dismissed Percy.

"Your ignorance and pathetic attitude is a truly frightening testimony to the fate of the natural world, if the wild lands are left in your stewardship," admonished Rainus. He shook his head in disgrace at this human being. "There will be nothing left for the generations to come."

"Oh, come now, Lord Silverthorn. Look around us! There are more trees here than you can shake a stick at, no pun intended. Even if we were allowed to harvest only the biggest trees, there would still be plenty left."

Rose pressed a finger to her lips, gesturing for Percy to lower his voice as the surrounding trees swayed, groaning in protest with his insistence to do harm.

"I find your words and lack of foresight truly appalling, Prince Percival," admonished Rainus.

"And I find your words filled with contradiction, Lord Silverthorn! You admitted the Elfkind are expert woodworkers. You implied you *do* harvest trees in order to undertake this task!"

"You are as blind as you are dim-witted! Look around you. Do you see dead and dying trees anywhere?"

Percy sat tall in his saddle as he scanned the forest. There was not one tree blown over by violent windstorms, its roots exposed, its crown shattered in the fall. Nor were there diseased or dying specimens to be seen.

"This forest appears healthy, unnaturally so," noted Percy, with a shrug of his shoulders.

"We cull the diseased and harvest only the trees damaged in lightning strikes, uprooted by powerful winds, or those coming to a natural end to their long life. And when we harvest these trees, we take great pains to plant new ones in their place. It is our way to ensure there will always be a vigorous, healthy forest for generations to come."

"This practice seems altruistic, unnecessarily complicated and costly, especially when you consider how time consuming it can be. As a commercial enterprise, one would go bankrupt in short order, than if a small army of men were allowed to come in to clear-cut a parcel of land than to hunt out these individuals trees that are dead or dying."

"Do I truly look like I am interested in a commercial enterprise, especially with you?" grunted Rainus.

"You say that now, but in the future, should you and your people decide to retire to wherever it is the Elves go when they decide they've had enough of this realm, do keep me in mind. If you wish to sell harvesting rights to this forest, it will be wise to consider my offer before all others," suggested Percy, giving Rainus a prudent nod. "After all, if you plan to retire, you may as well retire a wealthy Elf."

"You astound me, Prince Percival," said Rainus.

"Well, thank you!" He tipped his head in gratitude to the Elf

Sensing the futility of explaining or reasoning with this mortal, Rainus unleashed a dismal sigh. He turned his steed away to join Myron and Tag.

"Brilliant! The Elf Lord called me astounding!" exclaimed Percy, puffing out his chest. He nodded in approval to Rose, pleased that he was making progress in wheedling his way into this fellowship he inwardly maligned, but simultaneously wished to be included in. "I do believe I am winning over Lord Silverthorn."

"Just keep in mind, Prince Percy, Lord Silverthorn should be treated with a degree of respect, especially in his domain," whispered Rose.

She desperately wanted Percy to fit in, but she knew he was walking a razor's edge. Speaking out of turn or making presumptuous demands, even though he had every right to do so as a royal, would only serve to place a greater wedge between him and her comrades, if he were not careful.

"Yes, I know. He is *lord* and *master* of this woodland realm," muttered Percy. He spoke under his breath in a mocking tone.

"Lord Silverthorn is considered a king in the eyes of his people. It will serve you well to accord him the same respect you extend to your father," suggested Rose.

"I am a stranger in a strange land," admitted Percy. "I suppose it does no harm in tolerating the Elf's demands and expectations for the time being."

Percy sat upright, straining to hear Rainus' muted words as he regrouped with his friends who had been waiting patiently for him to lead the way. Percy's face flushed with resentment as a burst of laughter erupted from Myron and Tag.

"That canker-blossom of a being gives all mortals a bad name. I so desired to cuff him on the back of his big head for spouting such ignorant ideals to me," whispered Rainus.

"If that is the only way to get him to listen up, to heed your warning, perhaps a good knock on his noddle will not be such a bad thing," said Tag, hoping Rainus would act on this threat.

"I agree," said Myron. "It will definitely prove to him just how angry he is making you and just how annoying he truly is."

"And how angry do you believe I'd come across to that arrogant sod, scolding him, but doing so while I fight to keep from laughing aloud?"

"I never thought Prince Percival as being humorous," whispered Myron.

"He is not. However, every time I rebuked him, he'd momentarily fall silent, his brows arching up. I had to muster all my strength and will to keep from laughing aloud, for that silly bruise surrounding his lips made him look ridiculously surprised."

Rainus' mouth opened as though frozen in a dumbfounded expression of astonishment. His demonstration caused Myron and Tag to laugh aloud.

"I see your point," said Tag. Feeling Princess Rose's icy stare burning through the back of his head, he stifled this outburst before he became the victim of her accurate aim.

"Do not lose hope, my friend," urged Myron, giving Rainus a consoling smile. "There was a chance the young man will learn some respect, or even grow some common sense, before this quest is done."

"Better yet," said Tag, "there is a chance it will all prove too much for that prig. If we're lucky, he'll abandon us and the quest."

"One can always hope," sighed Rainus, putting his heels to his steed's flanks.

Percy glared at the backs of their heads as the three friends rode on ahead of him, sharing in a chuckle, undoubtedly at his expense.

Rose broke the awkward silence, taking the opportunity to change the subject in a bid to distract the brooding prince.

"Oh, look!" said Rose, as a large, azure butterfly floated lazily by them.

"Beautiful!" declared Harold. He beamed with delight to see the iridescent flashes of sapphire wings catching the sunlight. The butterfly circled around the pair, as though in royal salutation.

"Beautiful? It is an insect," snorted Percy. He waved his hand about, almost striking the winged creature to drive it away.

"But it's a *beautiful* insect," corrected Harold, watching as it fluttered away. It set off to find a tree hollow to hibernate in over the winter, as the last of the meadow flowers yielded a minimal offering of nectar, wilting with the onset of autumn.

"So you say, but pluck off its fancy wings and what are you left with?" grunted Percy, glad to see the pest float up and away into the high tree canopy.

"A wingless butterfly?" responded Harold. Inwardly, he was mortified Percy would even suggest doing such a cruel thing to a harmless creature.

"You are left with an *ugly* insect, nothing more, you dolt!" snapped Percy.

"No need for name-calling, my lord," rebuked Loftus. "Harold's answer is quite true."

"But my answer is *more* true," growled Percy. He was thoroughly vexed that his captain would come to the defence of this behemoth fool.

"Take no offence, Harold," urged Loftus, as he offered his new friend an affable grin. "You are both entitled to your opinions, as different as they are. Just know that Prince Percival comes by his scorn for insects honestly. He feels he has just reason to fear these creatures, no matter how beautiful, small or harmless the rest of us perceive them to be."

"I do not *fear* insects!" snapped Percy. He shot a malevolent stare festering of malice at Loftus for revealing this secret to all. "I *loathe* them, that is why I so dislike being out-of-doors to begin with."

"Hmph!' grunted Loftus, with a shake of his head. "I could have sworn it was fear. Absolute, unadulterated fear I had sensed when a tiny garden spider crawled across your hand. The way you screamed, jumping when that happened, and how, to this very day, you either run from, or stomp on, any insect that comes near you, I was certain you feared bugs of all ilk."

Surprised by this revelation, Rose stared wide-eyed at Percy.

"You exaggerate, Loftus. I was a child back then, and that was not a *tiny* spider that dared to accost my hand! It was an exceedingly large, hairy beast that wanted nothing more than to sink its fangs into my tender flesh to inject its venom."

To those in his immediate company Percy held up his hand. The tip of the index finger and thumb came together to demonstrate the great size of the arachnid that had dared to touch him. "It was yay big! An absolute monster I tell you!"

"Look out below!" A voice rang through the forest.

Percy glanced up, hearing the snapping of branches and rustling of leaves overhead. He shrieked in fright, the colour draining from his face as he fainted, toppling from his saddle as a creature from his nightmares grazed his arm.

"Oh, dear!" said Harold. Abandoning Sassy, he ran to Percy's side as he flopped to the ground. Using the toe of his boot, Harold pushed away the very large, very dead spider that was pierced by a single arrow. "You were right, Gilbert. He really is afraid of bugs."

9

Shut Your Liehole!

As silent as a woodland deer, Halen Ironwood emerged from the forest.

"I am terribly sorry," apologized the Elf. "I had only one clear shot at that beast. I was forced to take it, before the spider scurried off again."

"Your appearance was very timely, my friend," praised Rainus. With a respectful nod, he greeted the Elf captain. "It is fortunate the cursed spider finally met its demise. Unfortunately, it almost landed on the Prince of Axalon."

Halen glanced down at the unconscious mortal as Princess Rose gently cradled his head on her lap. "What is he doing here?"

"It is a long, convoluted tale of woe, Captain Ironwood," answered Myron. He sounded genuinely contrite he was unable to prevent this interloper from accompanying them. "I am sure you will *not* want to hear about it."

"Yes, why bore and punish the good captain when he did us a favour?" asked Tag, nodding in approval to Halen.

"I am sure it was nothing more than an accident," insisted Rose, glancing up at the Elf as he slung his bow over his shoulder.

"If my actions were deliberate, believe me when I say that behemoth of a spider would have landed squarely on his head, my lady," stated Halen.

"That monster could have killed Prince Percy when it struck him, knocking him from his horse," said Rose. "You really should be more careful, Captain Ironwood."

"Nonsense, my lady, you worry all for naught," assured Loftus, as he nodded in greeting to the Elf. "I saw that spider as it fell. At the very most, it grazed his arm. He merely fainted at the sight of the beast as it came down. As I said just prior to this little mishap, he has a dreadful fear of all manner of things that creep or crawl in this world, especially spiders."

"You weren't exaggeratin' at all," said Harold, helping Loftus to prop up this limp body.

Percy moaned. A flush of colour, no doubt rooted in his feelings of embarrassment, returned to his cheeks as he stirred from this unnatural slumber.

"Wha- what happened?" Percy's eye fluttered open to see a circle of curious faces hovering around him. To his regret, he was not safe in his warm bed, waking from a dreadful nightmare as these onlookers came into focus.

"You fainted," answered Loftus. With an open hand, he lightly slapped Percy's cheeks, more so to accost him for this embarrassing display than to help him come to his senses.

Percy slowly sat up on his own, pushing the captain's hand away from his face as he snapped, "I did *not* faint."

"Oh, you most certainly did, Prince Percival. You dropped right out of your saddle, hittin' the ground like a sack of potatoes fallin' off the back of a wagon!" insisted Harold. "We saw it happen with our own eyes when you glanced up on hearin' Captain Ironwood."

"Captain Ironwood?" repeated Percy, staring up in a daze.

"That would be me," said Halen, jabbing a thumb to his chest before pointing at the ebony carapace of the eight-legged monster. "When you glanced up, spying upon that giant spider, you screamed in fright, and then you fainted, falling from your horse."

"Oh, yes," muttered Percy. He recoiled at the sight of the dead creature near to him, and then he rubbed the side of his head where it met the hard ground. "I remember now. I shouted out in *pain*, just as I was knocked from my saddle when that hideous thing fell from above."

"A leg or two grazed your arm as that spider came down," corrected Loftus, "but we're all pretty sure you were *not* knocked from your mount as you claimed."

"Are you calling me a liar?" snapped Percy. He glared at Loftus.

"I am saying you are embellishing the truth," replied the captain.

"Well, being *'pretty sure'* is not the same as *knowing* for sure," insisted the sheepish prince. He wavered on his unsteady legs as Harold lifted him onto his feet.

"Riding before you, I saw nothing until you screamed and fell, but I do believe Captain Loftus and Harold know what they speak of," said Tag. Inwardly, he was so proud he had mustered enough self-control that his urge to burst out in laughter was stifled, muted to nothing more than a hysterical grin. "Based on where that spider landed, it definitely did not strike you off your horse."

"It would serve you well to believe in the words of a prince over the erroneous observations made by those two fools," snapped Percy, as he scowled in resentment at Harold and Loftus.

"That would depend on the prince, but in this case, I absolutely believe them over you," responded Myron.

Percy's normally fair complexion suddenly flushed with anger, adopting an unflattering shade of red. It temporarily diminished the purple bruising around his mouth.

Halen frowned, staring at the perfectly round contusion marring this mortal's slightly swollen lips that gave him a seemingly permanent pout. He pointed at Percy's face as he asked, "What is the meaning of this? Is it a fashion statement of sorts for the male mortals of your realm?"

"Of course it is not a fashion statement," answered Rose, scowling at the Elf captain for pointing out the still visible contusion on her man's face. "It was an accident."

"It must have been a very... odd accident," noted Halen, a small smile crept across his bemused face as various scenarios played out in his fecund imagination.

"It was not *odd*, it was horrific!" snapped Percy. "But enough about the cause of this terrible disfigurement that ruins my otherwise perfect face! You, you reckless Elf, could have been the death of me! You brought that spider down on me; doing so deliberately!"

"This *reckless* Elf you speak of in such an offensive tone is the captain of my military might," declared Rainus, thoroughly agitated by Percy's damning words. "If his intention was to kill you, he need not use a spider to do so. That arrow would have been strategically placed in a part of your anatomy that would prove fatal, had it been his intention in the first place."

"Well, Elf captain, no doubt with a reputation that speaks of your deadly aim, it would have served you well to use some common sense in my presence. Had you any, you would have known that downing that beast above my head could have proven deadly to me."

"That was never my intention, my lord," responded Halen, bowing his head in apology. "When I unleashed my arrow, it struck its mark spot on. Unfortunately, the spider did not die immediately. I failed to anticipate it would clamber away as it did before dying."

Percy shuddered in disgust, jumping back as Halen reached over, yanking his arrow free of its victim. The great arachnid was truly hideous. The smooth, shiny ebony body and its eight, gangly legs, now stiff and curling in to partially conceal the crimson, skull-shaped marking on its underbelly, made the spider shrink to about the size of his horse's head. Percy imagined this creature, in life, was probably much larger than the biggest serving platter in his father's castle. He grimaced in repulsion to watch the Elf as he wiped clean the shaft of his arrow with a handful of dead leaves, removing the greenish-yellow blood that had stopped oozing from the wound made by this projectile.

"Now that is one monstrous beast," declared Percy. "I know now this forest is truly bewitched by dark magic."

"This forest is *enchanted*," corrected Halen, placing the cleaned arrow into his quiver. "That spider was bewitched, conjured up by the forbidden arts, as were the other three we had hunted down and killed since returning to this forest."

"There are more?" gasped Percy. Ducking behind Rose, his eyes anxiously darted about, searching for possible danger lurking in the shadows.

"I believe we killed them all. Four in total and each as big as this one," answered Halen. "This was the last of them."

"Are you positive?" asked Percy.

"The webs were so massive, they were hard to miss when you know where and what to look for," explained Halen. "So, yes. We are confident we have done away with the giant spiders."

"That is a good start, but in my opinion *all* spiders should be killed," insisted Percy. His foot stomped down, his heel grinding into the earth in demonstration of how all arachnids should meet their end.

"Rest assured, Prince Percival, the giant ones cursed by dark magic have been killed, however, we shall do nothing to eradicate the others," said Rainus, pointing over to the agitated mortal, "like the one crawling down your shoulder."

Percy yelped in alarm, jumping about as he frantically brushed the tiny, black and white striped jumping spider from the trim of his fur-lined cloak while all the mortals, with the exception of Princess Rose, chuckled at his frenetic response.

"For pity's sake, it's just a tiny spider," stated Myron, attempting to calm Percy. "It is more afraid of you than you are of it."

"I'd say Prince Percival is more scared," determined Harold, watching as the jumping spider bounded away from the mortal's hand, sliding down to the ground on a silken line to escape.

"I have every right to be!" snapped Percy. His trembling finger pointed at the ebony carcass he could barely stand to look at. "For all you know, that tiny pest could well be the spawn of that horrible beast!"

"Fear not, Prince Percival," said Rainus. "If it is of any comfort to you, the giant spiders had a preference for birds and bats easily trapped in their web."

"And Sprites," chimed in Harold. "Loken got trapped in one of those webs the last time we were here."

"No!" gasped Percy, terrified at the thought of being entangled, unable to escape a horrific death.

"Oh, yes!" countered Tag. "In fact, it's likely this spider Captain Ironwood had dispatched was the one that nearly killed Loken. He managed to save himself, effectively tearing through the web to fall to safety."

"Ooh, and don't forget all of those mummified animals that rained down on us when Loken escaped," Harold added, wiggling his fingers as he moved his hands down for added effect.

Percy grimaced in disgust, shuddering at the thought of an animal carcass touching his royal person.

"Loken was very fortunate in his quick thinking, otherwise he would have suffered the same fate as those poor creatures."

"If that blasted Pooka had – "

"*Sprite,*" corrected Harold, waving an admonishing finger in Percy's face. "Loken prefers to be called a Sprite."

"Yes, well… Whatever that shape-shifting miscreant prefers to call himself," continued Percy, "if he had any scruples, he would have made short work of that monster spider. He should have killed it when he had the chance to do so, than to allow it to roam free to possibly attack and kill an innocent person."

"Easy enough to say now," responded Myron. "However, we had matters of far greater concern to contend with than to hunt down a grossly oversized spider. We were in a race to save lives."

"Speaking of lives," said Rainus, turning to Halen Ironwood, "how do the citizens of Driven Hill fare in my absence?"

"You will be pleased to know that all those who had fallen victim to that mysterious and deadly illness have recovered beautifully, thanks to our friends delivering the medicinal tincture," answered Halen. He nodded in gratitude to Myron, Tag, Harold and Rose for having made the mercy mission.

"Thank goodness for that!" exclaimed Rainus, smiling in approval upon hearing this wonderful news. "And my wife? How does Valara fare now?"

"Fully recovered! Lady Silverthorn is in high spirits. She eagerly awaits your return."

"Excellent! I could not be happier, my friend. Valara must grow bored and impatient with my absence."

"At this very moment, Lady Silverthorn is preoccupied."

"How so?"

"She plays host to a special guest," said Halen.

"A guest?" repeated Rainus, his brows furrowed in curiosity. "Whom do you speak of?"

"Master Agincor has returned after meeting with the Council of Wizards," informed Halen.

Before Rainus could ask another question, Percy stepped forward. Seizing Captain Ironwood by his shoulder, he abruptly spun the Elf about to speak to him.

Halen glared at the mortal, shrugging this grasping hand off his shoulder. "Do you mind?"

"Of course not, I just mean to ask you a question, Captain Ironweed."

"It is Iron*wood*. And you need not lay a hand on me to ask a question," grumbled the large Elf.

"Very well! No harm done. I was just overzealous upon hearing your news." Percy raised his hands in surrender. "Did I hear you correctly, Captain Ironwood? The Wizard, Silas Agincor, *the* Dream Merchant is here in this very forest?"

Immediately, Tag and Myron's nerves bristled upon seeing Percy's reaction to this news while Rose merely unleashed a dreary sigh on hearing that she was about to face this wily old Wizard once more.

"You heard me correctly, Prince Percival. Master Agincor is here to offer Lord Silverthorn and his comrades counsel on the murderous fiend we are in pursuit of."

"That is wonderful!" exclaimed Percy, beaming with delight on this confirmation.

"You seem very excited about this," noted Myron, bothered by this royal's sudden exuberance.

"Too excited," added Tag, his eyes narrowing in suspicion as he scrutinized this royal.

"Oh, come now!" responded Percy. "This is *the* Dream Merchant we are speaking of, a Wizard of legend! Who would not wish to have an audience with this magical being?"

"In hindsight, I regret it," sighed Rose.

"That is because you lacked the foresight to utilize the full potential of a Dreamstone," explained Percy, giving her a disappointed shake of his head. "It is a power that many, with the exception of those who are extremely intelligent like me, lack the ability to fully appreciate what such a magical crystal can do. In the hands of the right person, a Dreamstone can become the gateway to incredible possibilities."

"I used to believe that, too," said Rose. "I learned the hard way that pretty much every wish granted comes with a weighty price."

"True enough, my dear, simple-minded girl," agreed Percy. "The real trick is making sure the reward meets or exceeds the price called for."

"Well, the whole business of wishing is very messy," warned Rose, her hand resting over the Dreamstone hidden beneath her blouse. "As soon as this quest is done, I shall return this cursed thing to the Wizard."

"As I said, if you understood all the intricacies involved, you would not have such negative feelings about possessing that enchanting crystal."

"And you understand the intricacies?" snorted Tag, shaking his head in doubt.

"I am brilliant, so of course I do! Given the chance, a proper sit-down meeting with the Dream Merchant, allowing me to intervene on Princess Rose's behalf, so she has a better grasp of utilizing the magic crystal to its full potential, is all she requires to change her mind on this matter."

"Believe me, I found out too late the price I paid, squandering the love of my parents in exchange, was far too great," admitted Rose, hanging her head in sorrow.

"The solution is simple, my dear!" insisted Percy, his fingertips lifting Rose's chin so he can gaze into her troubled eyes. "A meeting with the clever Wizard, demanding he remove the daily quotas so the rewards outweigh this price you paid, that is all it will take. I will even do the honourable thing, stepping forward to speak on your behalf, if you wish. A moment of my time is all that Wizard will need to put things right."

"But I thought I was fixing –"

"Hush, now!" Percy pressed his index finger to Rose's lips. "Fear not, I shall make everything right in your little world. The Dream Merchant need only speak to me."

"Why all this interest in the Dreamstone and the Wizard?" questioned Myron. He hoped to force Percy's hand into revealing either his ulterior motive in joining this quest or to foolishly reveal his past encounter with Silas Agincor and the deadly price he was willing to pay to acquire a Dreamstone of his own.

"It is not so much interest, as it is old-fashioned curiosity and a need to alleviate the Princess' needless stress," replied Percy.

"And that's it?" asked Tag.

"Unlike you, I am human. I have a desire to help those whom I care for, plus, I possess a natural curiosity of all things strange and unusual, unless the strange and unusual deals with you."

"I believe you're confused," said Tag.

"On what matter?

"I am indeed human while *you* are the one that is strange and unusual."

Percy glared at the knight-in-training, then snorted in derision, waving off this insolent young man as he berated him. "You are quite humorous in your own odd way, Yairet."

"And you are strange, unusual *and* odd in *every* way," grunted Tag, puckering up his lips to mock Percy's bruised mouth.

Rose stepped in between the two young men as she issued a warning, "There is no need for animosity."

"Yes," added Harold. The badger pelt he wore on his head wobbled to and fro as he nodded in agreement. "Why can we not just get along?"

"Sure, we'd all get along just fine if Prince Percival can be honest enough to speak the truth for once," said Tag.

"Are you calling me a liar?"

"I am inviting you to be honest with the Princess. Tell her exactly why you're here on this quest!"

"What are you talking about?" asked Rose. She turned to Tag for answers.

"Why don't you ask your *wonderful* prince?"

Rose spun on her heels, facing Percy she asked, "What is the meaning of this? Are you lying about something?"

"You are a princess! Do members of your royal house make it a habit of lying?"

"Of course not... At least, not deliberately!"

"Are we not cut from the same noble cloth, my dear Rose-alyn? I would never lie to you!"

"Yes, but you'd certainly withhold information as you see fit!" declared Tag, shaking his head in disgust.

"What information?" asked Rose, her eyes darting between the two as they squared off once more. "What are you talking about?"

"Your demented friend is speaking absolute gibberish, my dear," insisted Percy. "He means to drive a wedge between us, being as jealous as he is!"

"Jealous? I'm not jealous! I just believe the Princess is entitled to the truth, where you're concerned."

"Will someone tell me what is going on?" demanded Rose.

"The truth is..." Percy's hands rested on her shoulders. He stared into her worried eyes, so Tag was no longer a distraction.

"Yes, go on," she urged him.

"The truth is, in the few, precious days we had journeyed together, something has been eating away at my heart and soul the more time passes between us."

"It's called a conscience," snipped Tag, "a *guilty* conscience, to be exact."

"Shut it!" ordered Rose. "Prince Percy has something important he wishes to share with me."

"Pray it is the truth," muttered Tag.

Rose ignored her friend, her amethyst eyes shining brightly as she waited for Percy to speak the words she longed to hear.

"The truth is, I must confess something to you that has been burdening me; weighing heavy on my mind and heart, the longer I keep this secret from you."

"Do tell," prompted Rose. She felt the sensation of a thousand butterflies launch, swirling through her stomach and causing her heart to palpitate as she gazed into his eyes.

"There is something you have that I desire more than anything in this world, my dear, sweet Rose-alyn."

Myron, Tag and Rainus were dumbfounded; surprised this conniving young man was willing to finally admit the truth to her. They waited in wide-eyed anticipation, as eager as Rose, to hear this confession he was prepared to declare before all.

"What is it you desire?" asked Rose, in barely a whisper.

"My dear, you have the one thing I have been searching for, wishing for, my entire life. I know now you are the only one who can give this to me. If I do not possess it, I know I will surely die!"

"Come on! Out with it," urged Tag, waving Percy on to confess. "Tell the Princess what you really want from her."

"Hush!" Rose snapped impatiently. Her friend was severely undermining this magical moment. She shoved Tag away, and then resumed staring into these pleading eyes. "Now, what is it, Prince Percy? What is this one thing you must have? Tell me now! If I can give it, I shall make it so."

"Not when you find out what it is he wants," grumbled Tag, as Myron motioned the young man to step back; allow destiny to take its right and proper course.

Percy dropped down onto his left knee before Rose, taking her hands into his. "When my father arranged our betrothal, at first I was resentful. Now, I know fate had brought us together for one reason. If you give me this one thing, I shall cherish it forever."

"Give you what?" asked Rose. Her breath hitched in the back of her throat as she held tightly to his hands. "What is this one thing?"

"Your heart, my dear Rose-alyn! I must have your heart, so I can love you forever. I was struck by this revelation that I now know I love you more than life itself."

Before he could seal this solemn pledge with a kiss, Percy was taken by surprise.

Tag charged, shouting, "Here's another *striking* revelation!"

Flying through the air, he tackled Percy, knocking him to the ground as Rose shrieked in horror.

Before Tag's balled fists could swing, delivering a swift and bruising punishment to Percy's eyes to match the one encircling his mouth, Myron and Rainus lunged forward. Subduing their angry, young friend, they pulled Tag from atop his victim, as Percy's hands came up to shield his precious face from the blows that were about to rain down with a vengeance.

In a dishevelled heap, Percy pointed a trembling, accusing finger at his foe as he shouted, "A madman, that is what you are!"

"Shut your liehole!" snapped Tag. "You're a liar, so fetch off!"

"An insolent, pugilistic dog like you should be whipped and muzzled for this treachery! You will be punished!"

"Enough!" shouted Myron. He and Rainus tightened their grip on Tag as he thrashed about, attempting to attack Percy again.

"I suggest – no! I *demand* that you remain here," ordered Rainus, raising a hand at Percy to come no further.

"Say again!" gasped Percy. He jumped to his feet, confronting the Elf. "How dare you order me about? I will not remain here in this wretched forest, alone, while the rest of you go gallivanting on your merry way. Suppose another giant spider is lurking about?"

"You will not be abandoned, for it is evident to me that you will not survive on your own for long," answered Rainus. "To allow calm to prevail and level heads to engage once more, I shall ride ahead with Myron and Tag, giving you both some distance and time to consider your rude and unruly conduct."

"He was the unruly one!" Percy pointed a damning finger at his foe, only to have Tag swat at it. "See! He attacked me again!"

"Oh, fetch off!" snapped Tag.

"Fine!" Myron snapped. He stepped in between the two adversaries, a hand on their chests to keep them apart. "Tag was *unruly* in his conduct and you were just plain *rude*."

Appalled by this knight's surly tone, Percy's mouth dropped open. This orifice looked strangely enlarged thanks to the bruise outlining his lips.

"Halen, please escort Harold, Captain Loftus, the royals to Driven Hill," ordered Rainus. "We shall meet there, once Prince Percy and Master Yairet have taken the opportunity to calm down and reflect on their words and actions."

"I protest!"

"Protest all you want, Prince Percival." Rainus' tone was indifferent. "I will hear none of it. I will see you again when your hot temper has had sufficient time to cool, so stand down. Get back on your horse, if you wish not to be left behind." The mortal stomped off, reclaiming his steed. Snatching the reins from Loftus' hands, with a grunt, he demanded his captain to give him a leg up onto his saddle.

Rainus turned to Halen, discreetly whispering to him so the agitated royal would not hear. "Do not hasten your trek, my friend. I desire some private time for consultation with the Wizard, before the poor soul is thrust into the presence of this petulant prig of a mortal."

Sensing Rainus' intense dislike for Prince Percival, Halen nodded in understanding. "I will take him on the *scenic* route."

"Thank you," said Rainus. With a polite nod, he bid farewell to Halen and those left in his care.

Percy scowled in resentment. Bitterness filled his heart, knowing that it was not him, but Tag, to be the one invited to ride off with the Elf Lord and Sir Kendall for an audience with the Dream Merchant. With eyes gleaming of vengeance, he glanced down at his captain. Percy snapped at the man, "Don't just stand there, Loftus, you fool! Mount up. If we ride now, we can catch up to them."

"Let them ride ahead. There is no need for us to rush," said Rose. With a leg up from Harold, she settled on her mare's back. Attempting to console Percy and quell his brooding anger, she reached over to gently touch his arm as she spoke, "What about us?"

Her words prickled at his shattered pride. Percy's eyes had an icy sheen, as cold as his demeanour. He yanked his arm away from her as he muttered like an angry child, "What about us?"

"Just a moment ago, you declared your love for me," reminded Rose. She was taken aback by the sharpness in his tone after making this heartfelt pledge to her. "Has this feeling for me suddenly waned?"

With forced affability, Percy smiled at her. "Of course not. The feeling remains, but the mood was lost when I was assaulted by that idiot you call a *friend*."

"I must apologize for Tag. I do not know what has gotten into him of late. His mood seems to change, shifting as quickly as the wind at times. Obviously, something vexes him."

"No need to apologize on behalf of that ruffian of a halfwit. I will make Yairet apologize in due time, and he shall be made to do so publicly."

Harold unleashed a great sigh as he spoke, "Those sound like fightin' words, my lord."

"There will be no fight, as long as that dolt apologizes without being coerced to do so and he is truly contrite," stated Percy.

"And if Tag doesn't, then what?" queried Harold.

"If that sorry sod refuses, then vengeance will be mine! He shall receive his comeuppance for attacking me without provocation."

"I strongly advise against taking the young man to task on this matter," urged Loftus, as he steered his horse toward Percy. "You may be taller than Tag, but without a doubt, he obviously has much more in the way of fighting skills, just the way he took you down so swiftly."

"He did *not* take me down. I tripped when that idiot came at me like a rabid dog!"

"So you say, but I fear even to engage him in even minor fisticuffs will see you soundly trounced," warned Loftus. "You are better to spare your body a beating and your pride a bruising by standing down."

"That is what you are for, Loftus!" declared Percy. "I will have you thrash the fool within an inch of his life, if he refuses to apologize to me before all!"

"That is not going to happen, my lord," stated Loftus.

"But I wish to salvage my wounded pride; restore my dignity. You will make it so."

"For pity's sake! You are not a child. You are an adult, and a prince to boot! Behave like one."

"And allow that insolent fool to get away with assaulting and insulting me? Think again, Loftus."

"I mean no disrespect, Prince Percival, but to retaliate all in the name of pride is a fool's errand. The best way to fix a battered ego is to do the gentlemanly thing and resolve the matter yourself, man-to-man," countered Loftus. "Go speak to the young sir. I am sure he will listen."

"A severe tongue-lashing will not do."

"I was not speaking of subjecting Tag to a *'tongue-lashing'*," said Loftus.

"So we agree on this matter?"

"Apparently so," said Loftus.

"Good! Then you will rough him up and tell him off," demanded Percy. The evil smile curling his mottled lips took on a sinister, yet comical appearance as he imagined his nemesis receiving a sound beating by the captain's hands.

"I was suggesting a *civil discussion*; working out your differences with words, rather than fists."

"I am no fool, Loftus! That impudent mutt was set off by mere words. He cannot be reasoned with."

"Perhaps I should intervene on your behalf then," suggested Loftus.

"Yes! I appoint you to do my bidding. Whether by fist or by sword, cut that knave down to size!"

"Without hesitation, I will champion you in a matter of life or death. As a knight upholding the law and shaped by the very meaning of chivalry, there is no dignity in taking on a boy, just to settle a childish feud on your behalf."

"Why are you even here?" snapped Percy. His face flushed with anger on being met with opposition yet again from a captain who was nothing more than his manservant, but doing a poor job of it. "You are a waste of air!"

"I am here to keep you safe, Prince Percival. At this moment, it is evident I must keep you safe from yourself. If you have intentions of physically retaliating against Tag Yairet, you will only regret it."

"Are you siding with that dolt?"

"I am siding with sanity, my lord."

"So, you are saying that I must take charge and teach him a lesson by mine own two fists?"

"It would be a grave mistake on your part to challenge the young sir to a physical test of strength, for it is obvious to me that you shall only lose in engaging him."

Percy mulled over the captain's warning. His eyes grew dark as he brooded, seething in his anger as this man dared to embarrass him with such a declaration, especially before his intended bride.

"Tag is quite the scrapper," warned Rose. "He will have no qualms about engaging in a bare-fisted brawl, if you challenge him. But I know you are smart enough not to be baited into a fight."

"Smart, indeed!" Percy nodded to her as he attempted to salvage his pride and bolster his ego. "In fact, that fool is quick to anger and eager to fight, all signs of one who is intellectually challenged."

"Say again!" said Rose.

"Tag Yairet will be challenged, but he will be made to use his wits, his feeble, little mind, against me! He may well be able to build his muscles to defeat me in a contest of strength, but he will never stand up to me in a contest of intellectual warfare!"

"Good gracious!" groaned Loftus, with a roll of his eyes. "I will give you that, my lord. *Nobody* has a mind quite like yours."

Percy sat tall and proud in his saddle as he beamed with demented delight. "It is settled then! I shall outwit and outsmart that rogue of a rapscallion. Put him in his place, once and for all."

"That would certainly do the trick," said Rose, nodding in approval. "If Tag refuses to apologize, it will serve him well to know he may have the upper hand when it comes to dealing in blows, but a wiser man need not resort to physical violence to deal a nasty blow to his ego."

"That knave will be cut down to size, and it will not require my sword, only my pointed wit and sharp mind," declared Percy, as he smiled grimly at Rose.

"Well, I have no doubt you will find out just how intellectually challenged the young master is," sighed Loftus, as he turned to the Elf. "Perhaps we should be on our way, before night falls."

"Yes," agreed Halen. "I doubt very much these young royals will want to spend more time than necessary in the forest."

"Do you wish to walk along with Harold? Or do you care to share a ride with me?" offered Loftus, looking to his fellow captain as he patted his horse's withers.

The Elf smiled in gratitude, "Thank you, but no, Captain Loftus. I have a horse of my own."

Percy snickered as he spoke in a mocking tone. "Is this a magical, invisible Elf steed you speak of? For I see none but our animals here, and I will be the first to say that I share my horse with no one, so you are best to take Loftus' offer to ride with him."

Halen's nerves bristled under this mortal's sardonic words. With a loud whistle, this summons echoed through the forest. It was answered by an eager whinny sounding through the stand of trees, followed by the steady thunder of hooves racing toward the Elf.

"There you are," said Halen, raising his hand in warm greetings to a great, white stallion dappled with grey that allowed it to blend in perfectly with the forest.

"I am duly impressed," confided Percy. His critical eyes scrutinized the magnificent steed that stood as many hands high as his warhorse, but sported an elegant, streamlined physique that spoke of this creature's speed and agility. "You called, and this horse came galloping, like a well-trained dog to his master. Well done, Captain Ironwood."

"Valyon is this beauty's name and it is not so much that he is *well-trained,* as he has genuine respect for me. Consider it a mutual respect, one that is the very foundation of our relationship."

"Mutual respect for a *pet?*" Percy frowned in bewilderment. "In my world, that is unheard of. I believe the master is the only one to expect and receive respect."

"Then yours is a petty, sad world, my lord," said Halen. "Valyon is his own master. If there was no respect between horse and rider, there is potential that it will be a ride fraught with danger."

"Truly?"

With a whispering of Elvish, Percy's warhorse reacted. The animal snorted, tossing its head as it pranced in tight circles as Percy struggled to control this steed.

"It is not so much a relationship of one having control over the other, but judging by your horse's response, he has no respect for you. Instead, that fine creature fears you," explained Halen, rubbing the warhorse's velvety muzzle while Valyon patiently waited for him.

"To be feared *is* to be respected!" retorted Percy, tightening his grip on the reins to steady his mount.

"If there truly is respect, a horse would not rear or bolt on you. These are the acts of a fearful creature wanting to run from you, than to please you."

As though on cue, the horse suddenly reared, forcing Percy to lean forward over this animal's powerful neck to remain in his saddle.

"You did that!" declared Percy, as he glared at Halen. "You made my horse try to unseat me with that foreign gibberish you spoke."

"I did no such thing. And I speak Elvish, I am not acquainted with *gibberish.*"

"Whatever you said, you made my horse rear up on me."

"You seem inclined to believe whatever you want to, even if you are wrong. Just know this horse is deserving of your respect, or one day, you will find yourself unseated from your saddle with no way home, but to walk. No amount of coaxing will lure this horse back to you, if your idea is to control and master his will through acts of cruelty or intimidation."

"That is ridiculous. I am a prince. My subjects know to bow down before me. This is nothing more than an animal, so of course it requires a cruel hand, from time to time, to show this stupid beast that I am the master."

Sensing his rage, the steed suddenly bucked, pitching Percy forward as Sassy brayed in excitement. The Prince cried out as the horse's hind legs slammed down, the percussion jarring him to his bones. Just as abruptly, its forelegs pushed upward as it reared. This time, Percy's nose struck hard against the horse's neck.

Halen took control of the reins as he spoke Elvish to the agitated creature. His soothing tone and gentle words immediately calmed the steed.

Percy slid down from his saddle, clutching his nose as he cursed beneath his breath.

"Are you hurt?" asked Rose, jumping down from her mount to

comfort her man.

"Of course I am hurt!" growled Percy. His voice was nasal sounding as the blood streamed from his nose and trickled down the back of his throat. "My nose is broken! Broken, I tell you!"

Rose froze, horrified by this latest spectacle that was Prince Percy, as Harold scrambled. He tore into his pack, searching for a clean rag to staunch the flow of blood. As animal pelt headpieces flew in all directions, Halen calmly approached the wounded royal.

"If you will permit me, I can alleviate your suffering; stop the cascade of blood," offered the Elf, watching as Percy's already pale complexion lost all colour, making the crimson rivulets look unnaturally dark against his pasty skin.

"What can you do?" muttered Percy, his eyes watering as he glanced up at Halen.

"I can help you."

"I will not be subjected to cures that invoke dark magic," insisted Percy, as he stepped away from the formidable Elf.

"I am not a Sorcerer. I do not delve in the forbidden arts," responded Halen, watching as this mortal shrank away.

"Please, Prince Percy, allow Captain Ironwood to help you," pleaded Rose. "The Elfkind possess the power to heal all manner of injuries, great and small."

"No dark magic involved?" queried Percy, as he stared suspiciously at Halen.

"Not at all, my lord. My people have the natural gift to heal what is broken, mend what is torn."

"Will it hurt?" Percy's words sounded ridiculously nasal as he breathed through his mouth as he spoke.

"Only if you keep moving about while I am trying to heal the damage," informed Halen, rubbing the palms of his hands together to summon his healing energy.

"Must you touch me?"

"Why?" asked Halen.

"Because protocol demands that a commoner is not to touch a royal," explained Percy.

"I have no interest or desire to touch you, my lord, but how well and how quickly you heal depends on how quickly I can get to work."

"And you are sure it will not cause me undue pain?"

"Only if someone should bump me from behind, causing me to squash your nose into your face," answered Halen.

"Very well, then," said Percy, waving the others to stand well away as he invited the Elf to proceed with this healing session.

Halen raised his left hand, holding it close to this mortal's face. It hovered just before Percy's broken nose. The Prince grimaced, trembling with fear as he felt a strange energy surging from the palm of the Elf's hand. It felt warm, becoming warmer still as it absorbed the pain in the form of heat rising from his broken nose.

"Will you stop shaking?" ordered Halen. He struggled not to touch this royal nose while administering his healing magic.

"I am not shaking," insisted Percy. He felt immediate relief as the pain dissipated and the blood stopped flowing. "I believe it is your hand that is trembling before my greatness."

"So you say," muttered Halen, removing his hand from the mortal's face. "This is the best I can do, considering I am not one to break with protocol by daring to touch a royal."

"Fair enough! I am just glad my nose is on the mend. I feel no pain now. And the bleeding, it has stopped." Percy gingerly touched his nose. He was pleasantly surprised it no longer throbbed in agony. It did not even feel tender after the terrible blow it endured.

"Thank you, Captain Ironwood," said Rose. She breathed a sigh of relief to see Percy was not condemned to heal with a permanently disfigured profile. "Do thank the captain for coming to your aid."

Percy frowned in annoyance. "He should be thanking me for allowing him to get this close to a genuine prince!"

Halen unleashed a disgruntled sigh, "Worry not, Princess Rose. It was my honour to aid Prince Percival."

"See! He feels honoured, and who in his right mind would not be?" said Percy. He wiped away the drying blood from his face on the small, silk handkerchief Rose handed to him.

Although Halen knew he did what he could to mend the break and reduce the swelling of Percy's accosted nose, he also knew that the by-product of such an injury was often two black eyes that can appear sometimes hours later. Just as he had to the power to heal the purple contusion around Percy's mouth, he also had the power to further the healing process to ensure purple bruises would not develop around his eyes. After careful consideration, Halen decided there must have been a valid reason that Rainus Silverthorn never bothered to rid this mortal of the ridiculous bruise around his mouth.

This wanting, ungrateful mortal made it all too easy for Halen to withdraw further assistance when it became apparent a simple thank you was not forthcoming.

"Perhaps I should change my soiled apparel; rid myself of all this blood," said Percy, "after all, I wish to make a positive first impression when we reach the heart of Elfdom."

"Those who care will be of no matter. Those who do matter will not care," said Halen.

"I suppose there is some truth to that," said Percy.

Though this Elf spoke with utmost honesty, Percy was more concerned rumours would fly in the wake of his arrival, no thanks to Tagius Yairet pre-empting his version of the truth by telling tales of beating him to bloody his clothing.

"I care not," said Rose. "I am not bothered at all. You look rather manly, all roughed up like this."

"Of course I do!" Percy puffed out his chest like a proud rooster. Glad he could breathe easy once more now that his nose was miraculously healed, he held it up high so she could admire his proud, flawless profile. "Let us move on."

"First, there is this," announced Halen, passing a burlap bag to him.

"What is it?" asked Percy. Inwardly, he was hoping it was a princely gift the Elf was about to bestow upon him. "It looks empty."

"It is for you, and it will not be empty for long."

Although this bag was intended to hold the pine mushrooms that Halen had planned to collect on his trek home, he now had a new and better use for this fabric container.

"For me? And just what am I to do with that tatty old thing?"

"You are to wear it."

Percy frowned, mystified by this order.

"Place it over your head. You must do so before we ride deeper into this forest," said Halen, tossing the bag to him.

"Are you mad? I am a prince! If this were a crown, I would be happy to comply, but a bag? I think not!"

"If you wish to be delivered to Driven Hill, our secret enclave must remain just that, a secret. As Master Murkins and Princess Rose have been to Driven Hill in the past, there is no need to blindfold them, for they are always welcome in our realm. You, however, have never been to our community and in light of the unfortunate events of late, we wish to keep the location of our community a secret."

"This is outrageous!" snapped Percy. "It is unheard of."

"I beg to differ, my lord," said Loftus, coming to the Elf's defence. "It is a common practice, used by many wishing to maintain a secret location."

"Indeed," said Halen, nodding to the captain.

"Then what about Loftus?"

"I will deal with Captain Loftus after I am done with you, but before we advance, I must take appropriate measures to safeguard the route to Driven Hill. Put that on."

"You cannot be serious," grumbled Percy. He stared with absolute disdain at this burlap bag, as though by wearing it, he was committing the ultimate crime against good taste and fashion.

"I am always serious. If you do not wish to spend the night here, where I killed that giant spider, then you will wear it." Halen pointed to the ebony carcass cast to the side of the trail.

"Fine!" Percy snapped in agitation. Feeling the coarse fabric he had to ask, "Would you have one made of silk, or perhaps a fine, velveteen one, by any chance?"

"I am afraid not. One size, one kind, to fit all," said Halen, trying his best to sound truly apologetic. "And as I am but a lowly Elf, perhaps Princess Rose would be so kind as to help you don the head covering to make sure you cannot see the way."

"Why can he not just promise to keep his eyes closed for the duration?" asked Rose.

"Prince Percival can promise, however, if the urge to peek is too great to resist, even a quick peek, enough to recognize landmarks and so on, it will force my hand."

"Force your hand to do what?" asked Percy.

"To kill you for foolishly stealing a peek," answered Halen.

"Even if it was by accident?"

"Yes, I will respectfully follow Lord Silverthorn's orders, a new edict put into place since evil infiltrated this forest. Consider it a matter of security, as we do not welcome the incursion of strangers into our domain."

"But I am no stranger, I travel in the company of Princess Rose and her companions."

"Before today did you know me? And I, you?" The Elf stared at this demanding mortal. "I think not! Therefore, logic dictates you are a stranger to me."

"I am a prince, Prince Percival Augustus Chadwick, heir apparent to the throne of Axalon, to be exact. I am no stranger; I am royalty. My name is known, far and wide."

"I do not know you from a hole in the ground," countered Halen.

"Well, you know me now! Logic dictates that we are no longer strangers. So there!"

"What is my middle name?" queried Halen, his voice taut with exasperation.

Percy frowned in response.

"When was I born?"

"How would I know?" grunted Percy.

"What is my favourite colour?"

Percy shrugged his shoulders. "Why all these irrelevant questions?"

"Your inability to answer even one of these *irrelevant* questions proves you know nothing about me, therefore, we *are* strangers," responded Halen. "And at the rate you prattle on, I have no desire to know you anymore than I do now."

"How – how dare you? You – you - " stammered Percy. Shaking the bag in Halen's face, his mind raced, scrambling to find the appropriate adjectives to soundly berate this captain.

"Elf. I am an Elf, the one appointed to deliver you to Lord Silverthorn's residence. If you do not wish to spend the night here, you will don that bag and do so now, for darkness falls quickly in this forest."

"Have it your way then," muttered Percy. As he begrudgingly placed the bag over his head, his angry sneer of resentment was finally hidden away from all.

"My lady, will you do the honours? Make sure the bag is placed securely over his head," said Halen.

Rose unleashed a disheartened sigh, but she had as much desire to spend the night out here as Percy did. She reached over; pulling down the edges of the burlap to make sure the bag did not come off, and if he did steal a peek, the most he would see was the ground as they travelled.

"Captain Ironwood, how am I to steer my horse if I cannot see the way?" asked Percy. He blindly fumbled about, grabbing a fistful of mane in his left hand as the right held tight to the reins.

"Your horse will follow, as will Captain Loftus' steed," answered Halen, as he lifted himself onto the white stallion's back.

"But how?" Percy demanded to know. "Are you going to *make* our horses listen? *Respectfully* order them to do so?"

"Yes, with some choice words of '*Elven gibberish*' I will make it so,*"* muttered Halen, as he reached into the folds of his cloak.

"A bag for me, Captain Ironwood?" asked Loftus, coaxing his horse next to the Elf's.

"Sorry, Captain Loftus, all I have is this." Halen passed to him a clean, white, silk handkerchief that was exquisitely embroidered with a delicate flourish of pale green ivy.

"It will do just fine," said Loftus. With an appreciative nod he was willing to play along with the Elf.

He was glad it was Percy made to bear the indignities of having his head 'bagged' like it was a giant root vegetable being delivered to market. With a congenial smile, he accepted the square of fabric. Folding it into a long, neat strip, he placed it over his closed eyes, knotting the two ends at the back of his head to secure the blindfold.

"We're all set," said Harold, taking up Sassy's reins. "Lead the way, Captain Ironwood."

Percy responded with a sigh of resentment.

"Just think of this great honour, Prince Percy," cooed Rose, in a bid to soothe his agitated nerves. "You will be one of the first in your royal house to be invited to Driven Hill!"

"No doubt that was a first for Prince Percival," said Myron, as he reined in his stallion, slowing his mount to an easy canter.

"First?" Tag asked absentmindedly. He was still seething in anger as he rode alongside his comrades. "First what?"

"I believe you were probably the first and only person to have the honour of telling that royal to *'fetch off'* to his face. Quite ballsy of you, my bellicose, young friend, but in the future, I do recommend being more mindful of your words and actions where he is concerned."

"It did not take balls to tell him off. That fool had it coming to him," grumbled Tag, his shoulders shrugging with indifference.

"Indeed, but I have never heard of that expression until this day," noted Rainus, as he glanced over to Tag.

"What do you speak of?" The grip on Tag's reins loosened, his anger melting away the greater the distance grew between him and the blustering Prince of Axalon. "I have given him an earful on this day, so you'll have to be specific."

"It was during your physical altercation with him. I have heard the expression 'shut your piehole' used before by mortals, but I believe you told Prince Percival to shut his *'liehole'*, if I remember correctly."

The last of the tension and anger festering in Tag's heart was finally dispelled as he chuckled. "Oh, that! It just blurted out. It seemed fitting in the heat of the moment, as that prig was blatantly lying and would not shut up."

"Fitting, indeed," Myron nodded as he warned his young friend, "however, it is necessary to keep your personal feelings in check where Prince Percival is concerned. Even though he was lying to Princess Rose about his personal agenda, I dread to think what would have followed, not so much from that dolt, but his father, had he been present to witness his son's public thrashing and humiliation."

"I care not. She deserves to know the truth," reasoned Tag. "I would have done it again; beat a confession from him, given the chance, so she'd know the truth about that snake."

"Rainus and I care. That is the only reason we felt compelled to intervene when we did," said Myron. "You already know how Princess Rose is so taken by that cad. Do you honestly believe she would have believed Prince Percival's words that he wants her Dreamstone, rather than her heart, if a confession was forced from him under extreme duress? Had those words been throttled out of him?"

"Myron is quite correct, my friend," said Rainus. "You mean well, however, Princess Rose will only come to despise you, blaming you should this budding, one-sided romance come to an abrupt end."

"We all agreed that until Prince Percival freely admits his desire to secure the Dreamstone from her, there is no point," reminded Myron. "If we force her to believe what she refuses to, it shall only drive her away from us and closer to him."

"So we must wait until he repels her, whether it is by revealing the truth or by hoping she comes to her senses, seeing him for the conniving, duplicitous rotter that he truly is," sighed Tag.

"As it stands now, it appears to be the *only* way she will accept the truth, not from us, but from him," surmised Rainus.

"It will crush her to hear him speak the truth," lamented Tag.

"But it is a truth she must hear," stated Myron. "Whatever her reaction will be, as her friends, we will shore up her spirits, should they founder. We can make her see that there are worse things in life than *not* being bound in wedlock to a self-serving, murderous rake of a prince. She will fare far better without him, in the long run."

"Speaking of reactions, I hate to see what Master Agincor's reaction will be when he finds out Prince Percival is here, heading to Driven Hill," said Rainus.

"I am quite eager to see exactly how the Wizard will respond, dealing with that impudent sod in his own, creative way," responded Tag. A small smile of anticipation curled his lips as his imagination ran wild.

10

Magic, Murder and Mayhem

Silas' eyes bulged. Rather than gag, the wine spewed from his mouth like a damaged fountain as he sputtered, "He is here? That deceitful, conniving twit of a prince is here? Say it isn't so!"

"It *is* so," responded Tag. Having ducked just in time, he had avoided the worst of the carmine liquid sprayed in his direction.

"I bet this is nothing more than a cruel prank!" The Dream Merchant's eyes narrowed in suspicion as he stared across the table at the young mortal. "If so, a pox upon you, on all of you!"

"Regrettably, it is not a prank, Master Agincor. Prince Percival is on his way as we speak," informed Rainus. He quickly wiped the table top of the misting of wine before passing this linen napkin on to the Wizard to blot dry his bearded chin before his silvery whiskers became stained. "We rode on ahead to forewarn you of this ill news. Captain Ironwood takes his time in delivering them to Driven Hill so we can have this conversation in complete privacy."

"Them?" queried the agitated Wizard, sulking as he sat upright in his chair.

"He does not come alone," said Myron.

"It better not be King Maxmillian! It is bad enough I will be made to suffer his arrogant, young progeny again. If he comes with the backing of his father, it will be more than I can bear. Undoubtedly, they will arrive with a party of many; knights, servants and cooks, all made to accompany them whenever they venture beyond the safety of their castle."

"Take comfort in knowing that Prince Percival is in the company of one," said Myron.

"One, you say?" Silas' wiry brows arched up in surprise. "I suppose there is some consolation in that, if it is not his father."

"Captain Gilbert Loftus acts as his personal bodyguard. They ride in the company of Princess Rose and Harold Murkins," answered Myron, as he replenished Silas' goblet with more wine to settle his rattled nerves.

"A man appointed to lead an army," groaned Silas. "It is with great trepidation I must undertake this quest with a mortal wanting nothing more than to take command, all for the glory of that prince. Do you three mean to kill me in disclosing this news?"

"No," assured Tag. "Mind you, the thought of throttling Prince Percival did occur to me for one, fleeting moment."

"Oh, my! I am intrigued. Tell me more!"

"I was about to teach the fool a lesson for lying to Princess Rose. I only got as far as tackling him to the ground when our dear friends intervened," confessed Tag, his eyes darting over to Rainus and Myron. Inwardly, he was still bitter he was denied this opportunity to pummel this pompous royal.

"You did plenty of damage to his oversized ego," said Myron. "I get the sense that what you dealt him, in Princess Rose's presence no less, was far worse for him to endure than any physical beating."

Silas snorted as he laughed aloud, slapping his thigh in delight. He imagined a lively brawl between this agitated knight-in-training and the pretentious royal would have been severely one-sided. Tag was quite capable, holding his own without a doubt, but Percy was another matter.

This was a self-righteous prig of a man whose greatest contribution to any fight was not in the swinging of his fists, but in the slinging of insults, before unleashing another to champion him. In all his privileged life, Percy had never been engaged in a real fight, except for the staged swordplay his opponents were *advised* to forfeit. It was a piece of advice heeded by all challengers wishing to remain in King Maxmillian's good graces, and now, this sheltered life could well prove to be Percy's undoing should he be faced with danger along the way.

"I take it, you had hoped to beat a confession from the fool?" determined Silas.

"Alas, he did confess, but it was not what we had hoped," sighed Rainus. "Instead of telling Princess Rose he wanted to acquire her Dreamstone for his own nefarious gains, he declared his love to her, claiming he wanted nothing more than to win her heart."

Silas groaned as his balled fists repeatedly rapped his forehead in utter frustration. "Curses! Prince Percival is like an evil serpent, slithering into her life. The more he speaks of his love for her, the deeper she will fall under his spell. Persuasive in his words and actions, and given time, it will be enough for her to ignore or overlook his treachery and deceitfulness."

"It is as you had warned us, Master Agincor," said Myron. "From the start, it was obvious she would do anything to shine a positive light on Prince Percival in a bid to have us embrace him in our fold. Instead, his arrogance and sense of entitlement wears thin on us."

"Yes," added Rainus. "In mortal terms, he can be likened to an infected canker sore that refuses to heal, and yet, she defends him, making excuses for his appalling conduct and abrasive nature."

"And somehow, it is always our fault when Prince *Prissy* makes a fool of himself," said Tag.

"Efforts to warn Princess Rose of his true intentions shall only fall on deaf ears or it is sure to raise her ire, if she even bothers to hear us out," said Myron.

"The young lady is besotted by love," declared Rainus. "It tugs at her heartstrings, serving to impair her judgement where he is concerned. In all certainty, Princess Rose will lash out at us, and our good counsel, because she will refuse to believe the one she is betrothed to is anything but her one true love."

"I fear to confront the Princess head-on," confessed Myron. "Warning her of all we know about Percival and his meeting with you long ago in his bid to acquire his own Dreamstone shall only drive her toward that deceitful fool, than to open her eyes to the truth."

"Well, I can truly empathize with Tag. I understand his desire to throttle a confession from that dolt, but it will only serve to undermine us in her eyes, than to expose that self-serving fiend and his true agenda," stated Silas. "Of course, you three did all you could to prevent him from coming along, I imagine."

"Absolutely!" averred Myron. "Why do you think his small army of personal attendants and his battalion of royal bodyguards, comprised of both knights and seasoned soldiers, were reduced to a party of one, namely the captain of his father's army?"

"I imagine if the rigours of enduring life in the wilds, with only the minimal comforts, were not enough to dissuade that demanding mortal from attending this quest, then you had done all you could to put him off."

"We did," said Tag.

"To be rid of that ignoble prince has proven to be about as difficult as scraping fresh cow dung from one's boots," stated Rainus. "The evidence may be gone, but a foul pong still lingers."

"It is clear he means to stay close to Princess Rose, or more so, to her Dreamstone," said Myron. "Either he will steal it from her, or he means to take advantage of its powers by manipulating her, if he is unable to persuade you to gift him with one of his own."

"Whatever the case, Prince Percival is intent on meeting with you," warned Rainus. He nodded his thanks as the Elf maiden Arissa delivered another decanter of wine to their table. She slipped out as quietly as she had arrived.

"He dared to admit that?" Silas was astounded by the mortal's audacious nature.

"Yes, he did. Of course, it was in the guise of doing Princess Rose a great favour," answered Rainus.

"So, now what?" asked Tag, pushing aside his oversized goblet of wine. "What is our next plan of action, Master Agincor?"

"I have been busy as well, my young friend."

"So you met with the Council of Wizards?" determined Myron. He leaned forward, eager to hear more.

"Indeed, I did as I had planned when we last parted company."

"And what news did the benevolent Wizards share with their brother?" queried Rainus.

"They shared plenty, but at the risk of sounding redundant and wasting my breath speaking than enjoying this fine wine, I shall wait until all in our party are here. All, especially Princess Rose, should be privy to this news as it greatly affects this quest."

"Even Prince Prissy will share in this news?" asked Tag, hoping against hope Silas would not include him on the details of this meeting.

"Yes, even that fool will be made privy to what I had learned from this Council. It is my hope that mortal will quail at the news; scurrying home with his tail between his legs like a cowardly dog, when he learns what we will be up against."

"Let us hope," sighed Tag.

"And hope, we shall, young man," said Silas, giving Tag a wry smile as he hoisted his goblet once more in good cheer to his comrades. "But before I allow myself another sip, is there more in the way of bad tidings you wish to impart on me?"

"The worst of it involves Prince Percival's insistence on accompanying us," replied Myron. "Other than that, we have nothing more to share, as we have yet to hear a single word about the fate of Loken."

"The royal brat's reputation precedes him, so you need not say more, but what is your opinion of this Captain Loftus the Prince drags along behind him?"

"Our first introduction happened when you delivered us to the courtyard of King Maxmillian's castle," answered Myron. "Our unorthodox mode of transportation took the captain and his men by surprise. Needless to say, he was distressed by our abrupt and mysterious arrival."

"He was a bit gruff at first," added Rainus, "but Princess Rose was quick to smooth things out so we were not housed in the bowels of the castle keep on that night."

"So, he can be rash in his actions, but he is one that can be reasoned with," determined Silas.

"He was much more civil once he came to understand our reason for appearing in the courtyard as we did," said Myron, "and of even greater import, we had earned his respect when he came to realize we were not about to put up with any nonsense from Prince Percival as we embarked on this quest."

"I quite like the man, much more than the Prince," admitted Tag. "I like his forthright nature, especially his directness in dealing with his lord and master when that pribbling prince presents Captain Loftus with an unreasonable demand or insists on being rude to us."

"In all honesty, I admire the captain and how he patiently tolerates the demands made by his royal charge," added Rainus, nodding in agreement with Tag. "His ability to tactfully handle situations with a degree of diplomacy puts Percival to shame."

"Yes, the good man even stood up for Tag, and got away with it, when the Prince demanded Captain Loftus assault our young friend for defying him," chuckled Myron. He thought back on how this knight crossed the border beyond the jurisdiction of Axalon, waiving his position that placed him at Percy's constant beck and call, to act in the best interest of the group than to cater to this one individual.

"He disobeyed Prince Percival?" gasped Silas. He was startled, but amused by this bit of news.

"Make no mistake, the captain outright *defied* him," answered Myron.

"Hmph!" grunted Silas. He gave his comrades a thoughtful nod. "If we are stuck with that fool of a prince, perhaps we should be grateful that Captain Loftus is in his company. He may well be the one person able to keep the young mortal in line and out of harm's way as this quest unfolds."

"I admire the captain's presence of mind, however, I do not envy his position," said Rainus. "If Prince Percival survives this quest, I have no doubt he shall report Loftus' conduct to his father. King Maxmillian's hand will be forced. He will be pressured to take what his son deems as appropriate action. The Prince will demand his father punish the man for insubordination, even if his actions were to preserve the idiot's life."

"Because of his integrity, we are willing to vouch for his good character before King Maxmillian, if it will help spare the captain some royal wrath that is sure to ensue," insisted Myron.

"In truth, Captain Loftus should be commended; be the recipient of an award even, for enduring that snivelling fool's never-ending demands and insults," said Tag.

"So, the man has little tolerance for the frivolous and the foolish," said Silas. In pensive thought, he scratched his bearded chin as he considered Gilbert Loftus' possible role in this mission.

"Very much so," answered Rainus, as he stood up from his great seat at the head of the table.

"What is it?" asked Tag, seeing the tips of his ears prick up as his gaze turned to the entrance of this royal residence.

"We have company," announced Rainus, as Arissa glided to the door to welcome the guests.

She nodded in greeting as Princess Rose stepped inside. Harold came next, and following close behind, Halen carefully guided Prince Percy and Captain Loftus through the door, escorting them behind the others as Arissa led the way into the dining hall that served now as a meeting room.

"Welcome, one and all," greeted Rainus. He was unmoved that the mortals guided to this table were deprived of their sight, while Myron, Tag and Silas were momentarily taken aback to see Percy with a burlap bag over his head while Captain Loftus donned a silk handkerchief as a blindfold.

"Salutations," responded Halen, with a polite nod. He positioned the two mortals at the head of the table before Rainus. "As you had requested, I delivered your guests and the location of our secret enclave remains secure in doing so."

In one fluid movement, Halen removed the blindfold from about Loftus' eyes while the other hand snatched away the bag concealing Percy's head.

"Good gracious!" gasped Rainus. "What happened to you?"

"What do you mean?" questioned Percy. He squinted as his eyes adjusted to the many candles burning brightly in the room.

"Your eyes!" said Rainus. "Did you anger Princess Rose, causing her to punch you, twice?"

"I had an accident. Struck my nose, breaking it against my horse's neck when it reared up," answered Percy. "But as you can see, Captain Ironwood did a fine job of healing it."

"Fine, indeed!" said Rainus. He frowned in bewilderment as he glanced at Halen, for he knew this Elf's healing powers were great, more than enough to heal a broken nose *and* to prevent the bruising around the eyes.

Halen merely shrugged as he answered, "I did the best I could, given the circumstances."

"I concur," said Percy. "He did well enough that the bleeding ceased. It no longer throbs in pain."

"That is a good thing." Silas nodded, his lips twisting into a wicked grin.

Frowning in confusion, Percy turned to face Rose. Thinking she would divulge what the Wizard would not, he asked, "So what is the cause of that ridiculous smirk on his face?"

Rose gasped! Clamping both hands over her mouth, she attempted to conceal this horrified, yet amused expression from her dear prince. Unfortunately, it was not enough to cover her eyes that felt as though they were bugging out.

Those already seated were silent, each with a similar expression of shock that matched the Prince's visage. The purple ring that encircled Percy's lips was now coupled with clownish, blackened eyes, effectively giving him the appearance of a deranged raccoon cursed with the permanent look of surprise.

"Good gracious! You – your -" sputtered Tag. Gasping for air between bursts of laughter, unable to speak, he pointed at Percy's face. Guffawing, Tag thumped his forehead on the table as he surrendered to the fit of laughter racking his body.

Compounded by Tag's mirth, Myron chuckled. He struggled to rein in his own laughter, as he shook his head at Percy.

Peering at the royal's now angry face, Harold stood rigid and tight-lipped, attempting to stifle his laughter for the sake of Percy's pride.

"What are they laughing at?" Percy scowled as he turned to Loftus. Glaring at the captain, he demanded an explanation, as no one else seemed willing or capable of doing so.

Loftus faced him, only to abruptly turn away from Percy. His broad shoulders quaked as he tried to silence his laughter, struggling to wipe the grin off his face before addressing his royal charge.

"My lord… I'm afraid you suffer from the unfortunate aftermath of breaking your nose. You look rather like a… a startled raccoon caught in the midst of making off with some ill-gotten food."

"Say again!" snapped Percy. His balled fist, in bitter retaliation, struck Loftus on his arm.

Instead of the captain being bowled over by the assault, Loftus snorted loudly as he doubled over in laughter.

This response caused the Wizard to lose the last vestiges of propriety. As though his spine had suddenly melted, Silas slid from his chair. Snorting, gasping and hooting with gay abandon, he surrendered, unable to resist the overwhelming power of a great belly laugh. In the most undignified manner imaginable, he rolled about on the floor as the unbecoming and silly sight of Percy's strangely bruised face worked its magic.

"So much for showing a measure of decorum," sighed Rainus, with a shake of his head. He lifted his legs, making room as Silas rolled about at his feet like a dog suffering a terrible itch smack dab in the middle of its back that could not be reached by neither teeth nor paws.

Rose knelt down, peeking beneath the table as she admonished the Wizard. Her tone was muted, but her words were stern as she scolded Silas. "This is most unbecoming! Stop it, I say! You are the Dream Merchant! You must behave accordingly before royalty."

Silas wrapped his arms around his aching ribs and violently jiggling belly, gasping as he tried in vain to contain his laughter. When he was composed enough to finally speak, his retort was choked out between surging tides of mirth: "You for... forget, Princess. I abandoned that vocation. I am... I am a writer, a teller of tales! And this young man has just added fodder to the stories yet to be shared."

As he roared with laughter once more, Rose reached under the table, slapping Silas on his shoulder in a desperate bid to make him stop.

"Get up!" demanded Rose. "Do you not know this is the Prince of Axalon you so rudely disrespect with this childish display?"

"Forgive me, Princess!" Silas drew in a deep breath to regain his composure. "I am indeed aware of whom this young man is, however, the last time we met, Prince Percival certainly did not look like... *that*."

Silas blotted away the tears rolling down his rosy cheeks as his index fingers circled around his eyes and mouth to remind her of the Prince's dark contusions, in case she was too in love to take notice of the deep bruises marring his otherwise perfect visage.

Rose frowned in confusion at Silas as she asked, "You know Prince Percival?"

"You, my dear girl, are not the only royal in this world to wish for a Dreamstone," confided Silas, as he crawled back into his chair. With a deep exhalation, he released the last of the merriment from his body as he took his place next to Rainus once more.

Rose turned, staring in bewilderment at Percy, and then to Silas. "You know this Wizard?"

"We met *once*, many years ago when I was a just wee child." He was quick to confess, speaking up before Silas had a chance to steer the course of this conversation.

"Say again!" gasped Rose. The colour drained from her cheeks as she stared in disbelief at Percy. "You had summoned the Dream Merchant?"

"It was long ago, but yes, we had met when I was little." Percy's tone was dismissive as his shoulders shrugged with indifference. "But worry not, my dear Rose-alyn. Practically every child I know, at one time or another, has summoned this illustrious Wizard, even if it was to fulfil a foolish, childhood wish or did so on a childish dare."

"You lied to me!"

"I never *lied* to you," gasped Percy. He looked appalled, but instead, he resembled a startled raccoon. "It is better to say I did not bother to divulge this one, small detail from my past."

"But you said you were in want of nothing, therefore you had no desire to own a Dreamstone," reminded Rose, flummoxed by his sudden admission.

"In my *adult* life, that is very true!" He placed his left hand over his heart in solemn promise to her. "But as a young, foolish child, with no true appreciation for what I had, nor the ability to know the difference between want and need, I gave in to temptation, calling upon this powerful Wizard."

"Why did you not tell me this before?"

Rose's eyes darkened into a deep shade of amethyst that was rarely seen as she glared at Percy. Her mind raced, her emotions riding a stormy tempest of both anger and confusion. Where others would break down in a fit of giggles to see his mottled face as he stared with pleading eyes, Rose's eyes were like daggers as she searched his face for the truth.

"Yes, Prince Percival! Why did you not disclose this news before?" asked Tag. His arms crossed his chest as he waited for an explosive admission sure to result in an equally explosive response from the Princess.

She raised one hand to Tag, motioning him to cease talking as the other pointed accusingly at Percy. Incipient tears glazed her eyes as she confronted him. "Why did you not tell me this from the start?"

"For this very reason, my love! I did not want to upset you more than you already were. Being in possession of that cursed stone, it seemed to fill you with unreasonable dread. I did not wish to burden you more than necessary."

"You could have said *something* to me." Her eyes narrowed in suspicion as she scrutinized his remorseful face.

"In hindsight, I should have been forthright, but my love for you prevented me from speaking about this. And as I said before, because of the act of a silly child, one who came to his senses in due time, I felt there was no need to dredge up the past. The last thing I would ever want is to cause you needless grief in sharing old, forgotten memories that have no relevance to me in the here and now."

Rose turned to interrogate the Wizard, raising a hand for Percy not to interrupt. "Is it true? Did you gift him with a Dreamstone?"

"I am no fool! In the end, I did not, nor did – " Before Silas could divulge more to her, Percy seized her by the shoulders. Turning her away from the Wizard so they were now eye-to-eye, he quickly jockeyed to control the conversation.

"Nor would I have taken it, for the price was too great," stated Percy, pressing her hands into his in a bid to steal away and hold her undivided attention.

"Did the Wizard trick you into forfeiting the love of your parents for a Dreamstone?" queried Rose. Empathizing with him, she squeezed his hands, offering an understanding smile to ease this confession from him. "There is no shame in admitting you had been tricked."

"I did not *trick* Prince Percival! Nor did I trick you!" declared Silas. He was offended by her choice of words, but he went ignored.

"Alas, he asked that I trade my mother's *life*, never mind her love, in exchange for one of his damned crystals," confessed Percy. He held her hands to his heart as he managed to squeeze out a single, pathetic tear from one of his raccoon eyes to entrench himself deep in her sympathy.

Silas' mouth dropped open, dumbstruck by this mortal's twisted version of the truth.

"That is terrible! It is no wonder you had declined!" said Rose. Her heart soared, ecstatic that her fears had been allayed and her man's intentions in not revealing this small detail in his life were indeed honest.

"And rightly so," said Percy. His eyes misted over as he gazed into Rose's face, searching for forgiveness. "Sadly, my mother passed away shortly after that unpleasant encounter with this Wizard."

"You poor dear!" exclaimed Rose, as she blotted away this tear he mustered from his left eye.

Tag unleashed a disgruntled sigh as he snapped impatiently at Percy. "Go on! Tell Princess Rose how your mother died. She deserves to know the truth."

Rose scowled in disapproval at Tag, hugging Percy as she whispered to him, "I know your mother passed long ago. There is no need to say more."

"Oh, no!" exclaimed Tag, waving his hands about to encourage Percy to speak. "There is plenty more to say. Tell her how your mother died. Tell Princess Rose the truth! You owe her that much."

Before Rose could admonish her friend again, Percy spoke up. "You do deserve the truth, my love."

Tag and his comrades waited with bated breath, eager to see if indeed the truth was about to be told.

"Sadly, my beloved mother died, I believe it was on the fortnight after my first encounter with this Wizard," said Percy, pointing an accusing finger at Silas. "My mother was found dead in her bedchamber, stricken by an illness that stole away with her life. As a wee lad, I had the grave misfortune of finding her, cold and lifeless."

Percy suddenly wailed in hysterical grief, dropping to his knees before her.

"Say no more!" cried Rose, pressing his head to her heart as she consoled him.

"But he –"

Rose shot a threatening glance at Tag as she rebuked him. "For shame, Tagius Yairet, for shame! Where is your sense of decency? Can you not see Prince Percy's grief is still raw?"

"But – "

"He need not say another word! And neither should you!" snapped Rose. "Prince Percy has suffered enough. There is no need to dredge up the past, especially as it has nothing to do with rescuing Loken or capturing the murderous fiend we seek now."

Tag jumped up from his seat, his balled fist smashing down on the table as he shouted, "He ki – "

Percy suddenly wailed. This heart-wrenching cry drowned out anything else Tag could say. This dramatic display also caused Rose's heart to swell with sympathy.

Captain Loftus shook his head in disgust as he hoisted Percy onto his feet. "Come now, my lord! Though your grief is great, even with the passing of all these years, for the sake of your dignity, a little composure will go a long ways."

"It would also serve my friends well to mind their words and be mindful of their attacks on my husband-to-be!" added Rose. Her angry scowl travelled up one side of the table and down the other to make sure all present would cease with their teasing of her sad prince.

In the most dramatic fashion, Percy pressed the back of his hand to his forehead as he shuddered, unleashing a final sob to make sure Rose's comrades knew that he will be the one to ultimately control the conversation where that fateful night was concerned. He knew for certain now that to manipulate Rose's emotions, soliciting her sympathy, he'd win out over the innuendos and suggestions Tag and his friends were likely to throw her way to undermine him.

"That is quite enough," muttered Rainus. "Please, join us at the table. There is much to discuss."

Without doing the gentlemanly thing by seating Princess Rose first, Percy simply abandoned her. He made a mad dash to claim the great chair at the other end of the table just to be seated directly across Rainus Silverthorn, a position that surely represented one of respect and power.

"Here you go, my lady," said Harold, pulling out the chair next to Myron.

Rose pretended she did not expect Percy to do the chivalrous thing, especially with a lackey like Harold present to tend to her. At least with Percy seated at the end of the table, she can sit to his left, while Captain Loftus can assume the chair to the Prince's right.

"Ahem!" Rainus cleared his throat, garnering Percy's attention. "Prince Percival, I must insist you remove yourself from that chair. It is reserved for another. I invite you to take the one next to Master Agincor."

Percy frowned. He was both annoyed and embarrassed he was now being denied this coveted seat he perceived as one of privilege and power over the others.

"Why so? Is it reserved for one of greater status than a prince?"

"It is reserved for one of greater import to *me* than a mere title can bestow," answered Rainus. He nodded to Halen to replace this presumptuous mortal's position at the table. "And you forget, in my eyes it is not one's status that defines character, it is one's character that defines one's status."

"I suppose that makes sense," responded Percy. He sheepishly removed himself from this great, carved chair to make room for Halen. "It will be easier for this Elf to leave this table should you need him to deliver food and refreshment to us."

Rainus' eyes grew icy, stabbing through this mortal as he corrected him. "This *Elf* is the respected captain of my legion of warriors. Let it be known, the only thing Captain Ironwood has proven any good at delivering is a deadly hail of arrows."

With forced affability, Percy sheepishly nodded his head in feigned respect to the great Elf commandeering *his* chair. He waved at Captain Loftus to pull out the chair tucked against the table so he may be seated next to the Dream Merchant.

"I will accept this honoured place next to the great Wizard," said

Percy, convincing the others sharing this table that he was in a position of respect with his proximity to the Elf Lord and the Dream Merchant. "Loftus, do join me by my side, as I may need you to run errands for me during the course of this meeting."

Captain Loftus rolled his eyes in silent protest, swallowing his pride as his royal charge made it known to all that he had absolute control over him. Loftus also knew this strategic seating was to deliberately block Harold Murkins, a man Percy detested, from sitting so close to one of his royal pedigree.

"If Lord Silverthorn does not oppose," said Loftus, looking to the Elf for permission first.

"Absolutely, Captain Loftus! You are welcome to join us, as is Harold," invited Rainus. He pointed to a vacant chair, directing the large mortal to take his place between Halen and Captain Loftus.

Harold nodded in gratitude, respectfully removing the badger pelt from his head as he made himself comfortable at this table.

Once all were seated, Arissa glided into the room. She returned with a silver tray carrying a large decanter of red wine and more crystal goblets, one for each of the new guests sharing the table.

Filling the empty goblets and topping up those in need of replenishing, she quietly slipped out of the room for the meeting to commence.

Rainus lifted his goblet in good cheer to those gathered before him. "Welcome, one and all, to Driven Hill, the last great enclave in Elfdom. Let us raise our glasses to honour this esteemed company."

"Oh, my!" exclaimed Percy. He wrapped his hands around the bowl of his goblet as he marvelled at its size. "This is a two-fister; larger than any wine goblet I have in my castle."

Rainus peered over the rim as he sipped, staring intently at his royal guest to hear what he would say next.

"A small fish can easily live in a goblet of this size! This is a wine-lover's dream come true."

"My people do enjoy a full-bodied, robust wine. There is no denying that," said Rainus.

"Oh, yes! I have heard tales the Elves are quite the lush; as fond of drinking wine as my father is fond of indulging in that Troll-crafted cheese!"

A profound and awkward silence filled the room as Rose's eyes opened wide in astonishment. Placing her goblet down loudly, she tried to capture Percy's attention to warn him to stop with his comments. She knew the words he spoke could be taken out of context or as an insult, but it was apparent he did not clue in to this, even with all eyes staring at him.

"And he's at it again! Making friends everywhere he goes," muttered Tag, shaking his head in disgust.

"You are so silly, Prince Percy," said Rose, in a teasing voice. "The Elves do enjoy their wine, but they can hold their drink far better than any mortal. And do not forget, a large bowl allows the wine to breathe, permitting its most subtle notes to rise to the surface."

Percy tipped the goblet to his lips, taking a loud sip. In an audacious display, he closed his blackened eyes to fully appreciate its flavour, swishing the carmine liquid about in his mouth to wash over his fussy palate. Allowing every discriminating taste bud to sample the fruitiness and spicy undertones, in his own pretentious way, he noisily sucked air in between clenched teeth, allowing the oxygen to mix and mingle with the wine to enhance its flavour. Having determined the quality of this wine, he swallowed the mouthful.

"Full-bodied and sophisticated!" announced Percy, nodding in approval to his host as he finally set his goblet down. "Your people are as talented with the craft of winemaking as they are with their woodwork. Both very exceptional!"

Rose breathed a sigh of relief that his insult was finally followed by words of praise. She smiled in approval at Percy and he smiled back. With the bruising around his mouth now faded compared to his freshly blackened eyes, the wine that should have stained the skin on his upper lip with a purple moustache just blended in with the contusion so no one noticed.

Rose hoped all would appreciate Percy's sincere compliment more than remember his earlier insult. Then, to her horror and embarrassment, he raised his right hand, loudly snapping his fingers. He glanced about, searching for Arissa, as he demanded: "More! I want more of this sumptuous wine!"

All fell silent once again, appalled by this tasteless display in a bid to summon Arissa to serve him, even though the decanter was easily within his grasp, centred on the table.

Just as Arissa rushed into the room, alarmed by the incessant and urgent sounds of finger snapping, Captain Loftus stood up. Bowing to the maiden, he sounded sincerely contrite as he apologized to her, "Worry not, my lady. We are quite capable of pouring our own wine, thank you."

Loftus reached over for the great decanter. He replenished the goblet only to have Percy gesture for more.

"Come now, Loftus, do not be stingy!" scolded Percy, his fingertip tapping the rim. "Fill it right up."

"If I fill your goblet any more, you will not be able to lift it. And if you do succeed in drinking it all, then you will be the one all shall be calling a *lush*," muttered Loftus. He raised the decanter to the others to see if they required a top-up. When all declined the offer, the captain set the decanter down upon the silver tray.

Taking his seat, Loftus nodded respectfully to Rainus, inviting him to speak. "My sincere apologies, Lord Silverthorn. Let there be no further distractions. I believe you have news you wish to share."

Percy suddenly yelped in pain, rubbing his right arm as he turned to the Wizard. "What was that for?"

Silas made no apology for sharply pinching the mortal. "I had to make sure you are indeed for real; not just a terrible symptom of too much libation. Now that I have determined you are indeed here, I now have an overwhelming desire to drink all the more."

"Ha!" snorted Percy. "You are as humorous as ever, Wizard."

"And you are as grating – " Silas' sentence was cut short.

"Great!" interjected Rose, shooting a mincing stare at Silas. "He means to say you are as *great* as always, Prince Percy."

"I am!" He proudly puffed out his chest, nodding in approval to Rose.

"I say, we stay the course," suggested Loftus, pressing a finger to his lips for Percy to stop talking so Rainus may resume.

"Do not hush me!" grumbled Percy. His left elbow came up, jabbing the captain's right arm.

"Indeed, I do wish to continue," said Rainus, glancing at Percy, and then to Silas to determine if they were going to keep their feelings in check. "If there are no further outbursts, Master Agincor is here to speak to us. He comes with tidings from the Council of Wizards."

"Bad tidings, I assume," responded Myron.

"I come with ill news, my friends. There will be no glad tidings on this day," announced Silas. With a dismal shake of his head, he studied the faces of those gathered around this table. "What I learned from my brethren left me with more questions that remain unanswered."

"Tell us what you do know," invited Myron.

"I know the culprit we seek is shielded by dark magic, one that made it difficult for the members of the Council to precisely determine the Witch's whereabouts."

"Whoa, whoa, whoa! A *Witch*, you say?" gasped Percy, his brows furrowing in confusion over his blackened eyes. Raising his hands, he motioned for Silas to stop talking. "What is the meaning of this? I was led to believe we are in pursuit of a dangerous necromancer, not some lowly, old hag concocting potions and hexes!"

"Not once did we tell you we were on the hunt for a rogue Wizard," reminded Myron, his words terse as he addressed this royal interloper. "It was an assumption you had made all on your own."

"When you spoke of dark magic, murder and mayhem on such a grand scale, I had every reason to believe you were in pursuit of that demented Sorcerer, Parru St. Mime Dragonite, not some pathetic old biddy cooking up nasty potions in a cauldron."

Outwardly, by his stance and demeanour, Percy seemed offended he was made to waste his time on a manhunt for a lowly woman. Inwardly, his heart was overjoyed. He breathed a sigh of relief knowing that this dangerous quest promised to be less than deadly now, in light of this criminal's gender.

"I am astounded by the true level of your ignorance, Prince Percival," rebuked Silas. "There are Witches that walk this realm wielding great and terrible magic; some are as powerful as my brethren Wizards."

"I have never known a Witch to be powerful," sniffed Percy, quick to dismiss this warning.

"At least you are willing to embrace your ignorance," said Silas. "And you should know, my lord, what makes these Witches truly frightening is that some are more than willing to abuse their powers for personal gains, if you get my meaning?"

"Yes, with a hex here, a spell there," giggled Percy, as he pretended to wield an invisible wand. In a comical display, he pretended to dispense this magic to downplay the Wizard's concern.

"Do not underestimate these women because you perceive them to be the weaker sex," cautioned Silas.

"So true, Master Agincor!" exclaimed Harold. Nodding in agreement, he leaned over the table so he would not be speaking through Captain Loftus in order to warn Percy. "We've seen this crazy Witch in action, Prince Percival. She's to be feared, and rightly so! She conjured up a terrible dragon from a tatty, old sock puppet; usin' this phantom dragon to attack us and to drop Tag into a river of lava."

"A dragon from a sock puppet? I think not! Besides, if it were so, that dragon could not have been so terrible. The evidence is right there," argued Percy, as he glared across the table at his nemesis. "Yairet is still alive, after all!"

A collective gasp sounded around the table as Percy waved off their concern. "Good gracious, people! Do not get your knickers in a twist! I was speaking in jest."

"The point being, this particular Witch is extremely dangerous, unpredictable and worse, she is insane and bent on revenge," cautioned Silas. "Our saving grace is that Harold bravely wrestled the

Dreamstone away from her before she vanished."

"Thank goodness for that!" exclaimed Rose. She nodded in gratitude to Harold as her hand rested over the crystal hanging from about her neck.

"Yes, we have managed to declaw the bear, but this old sow still has her teeth," said Tag.

"I suppose a powerful Witch bent on revenge can be somewhat troublesome," said Percy, contemplating the level of threat this woman can potentially pose. "And here, I thought I was helping you all to capture the maniacal, mime-loving Sorcerer; a worthy foe to add another feather to my cap of accomplishments, so to speak, if I were to have a hand in capturing this villain."

"Another feather?" Tag snorted in derision as he glared at him. "What other feather is there? Whom have you captured?"

Percy sneered at Tag, and then smiled coyly at Rose as he spoke, "I have captured the heart of this delightful, young lady! Truly, the greatest accomplishment of my life to date! But do not distract us from the matter at hand. We were discussing this bothersome Witch."

"Bothersome?" snapped Myron, his voice tightened with annoyance at Percy's cavalier attitude. "You have no idea, my lord."

"All I am saying is this foe you seem to dread so much is nothing but a lowly woman! No doubt an ugly hag of a female specimen, but she is a woman, nonetheless. Surely you exaggerate the level of danger she poses."

"If it boosts your ego to know this Witch we hunt is truly dangerous, suppose I told you that she is bent of revenge because we had a hand in doing away with her brother," revealed Rainus.

"I suppose she would be more motivated to retaliate; seeking vengeance for the loss of a sibling, but really? How dangerous can she be?"

"Her *sibling* was the infamous Parru St. Mime Dragonite," answered Silas. "And she had vowed to kill all, but only after she harvests the blood of the one responsible for killing her brother."

"And just who was the brave soul responsible for killing that despicable fiend?" questioned Percy. Glancing up and down the table in search of the hero to congratulate, he deliberately overlooked Tag.

"I killed Dragonite," answered Tag. The admission was made with no boastful words, just a solemn declaration of the truth.

"Well then, here is an easy solution that can potentially spare many lives. Sacrifice this braggart!" said Percy, pointing across the table to Tag. "The Witch gets what she wants and we walk away unscathed! Problem solved!"

Percy yelped more in surprise than pain as the palm of Captain Loftus' right hand reached up, smacking him on the back of his head.

"You struck me!" snarled Percy. Though the sting was fleeting, the humiliation of his captain's very public action was forever seared into his heart and mind. He glared at him with utter contempt. "How dare you touch me?"

"How dare you make such an asinine suggestion?" countered Loftus, embarrassed by his royal charge. "Do you not understand the goal of a quest undertaken by a fellowship such as this is to accomplish the deed as a unified front? To work together for the benefit of all?"

"Of course I do!"

"Well then, somehow the meaning eludes you, for it does not mean sacrificing one member of the group for the benefit of the others, namely you."

"Fine!" snapped Percy, as he rubbed the back of his head. "But how dare you assault me? Before the end, I will make you pay for your insolence, Loftus."

"Pay for what?" asked Tag. "I saw nothing. Did any of you see Captain Loftus assault Prince Percival?"

"I am sitting directly across from the good captain," said Myron, with a shrug of indifference. "I did not see a thing."

"From where I sit, positioned at the head of this table, I saw nothing of this said assault," added Rainus, as he glanced down to the opposite end. "How about you, Halen? From your vantage point, did you see Captain Loftus attack Prince Percival?"

"With all certainty, I did not, my lord," answered Halen. The Elf shamelessly lied to spare Loftus from royal retaliation.

"You, Harold Murkins, surely you saw what happened?" queried Percy. He pushed Loftus against the backrest of his chair to confront the large man seated between the captain and Halen Ironwood. "You are sitting right next to this insufferable brute. Surely you witnessed him reaching over to strike me?"

"I was lookin' across the table when you cried out. I was starin' at Tag's face when you insulted him, sayin' that we should offer him up to the Witch," answered Harold. "I didn't see anythin', but I hardly think Captain Loftus would do such a thing in the first place, my lord."

"I did *not* cry out, you big buffoon!" Percy fumed. His face burned as he shouted at Harold, "Now, stop lying to cover up for the captain's atrocious actions."

"I'm not coverin' anythin' up," insisted Harold. "And I certainly don't lie."

"Well, I know there is no point in asking him or his scallywag of an apprentice what they observed," grumbled Percy, turning his nose up at Myron and Tag before looking to Rose. "Obviously, my dear, you witnessed this assault, did you not?"

He cast a threatening stare her way, hoping his non-verbal cue would steer Rose to lie, if she must, just to stay in his good graces.

"In all honesty, Prince Percy, when I heard you, I was in the midst of imbibing. My view was obscured by the bowl of this very large goblet," answered Rose.

Like a spoiled child, Percy jumped to his feet, his balled fists slamming down on the table as he raged. "You all conspire against me!"

"But I did not say it didn't happen," explained Rose, in a bid to pacify him. "All I am saying is that I did not bear witness to what you claimed had happened."

Percy glared at Rose as he scolded her, "Even had you not witnessed this sordid event, you, as my intended bride, should know your place. I am always right! And you are always to agree with me, otherwise, what is the point of being my consort, if not to stand by my side to prove your loyalty to me?"

Rose looked aghast, dumbstruck by his accusing words.

"No need for such ugliness when we are already graced by your ugly face at this table," admonished Tag.

"I should have Captain Loftus cut out your tongue for speaking to me with such disrespect," growled Percy, "but being the mutinous dog that he has proven to be, it shall be nothing more than a hollow threat. You have all managed to turn my captain against me!"

"They have done no such thing," protested Loftus. "I am solely responsible for my words and actions."

"If you feel that we all conspire against you, perhaps you are better to abandon the quest," said Silas, as he motioned for Percy to settle down. "Return to the safety of your father's castle. Leave us to do the work of bringing the Witch to justice."

Percy glared at the Wizard, pointing an accusing finger in Silas' face. "That is exactly what you want!"

"Yes!" whooped Tag, his fist pumping the air in victory. "Finally, the Prince gets it!"

"And just to spite you, I will continue on with this quest," scoffed Percy, as he sneered at his nemesis. "I shall endure! I have more fortitude than all of you combined. I refuse to be brow-beaten or humiliated into quitting!"

"That is a foolish reason to endanger your life on this quest," admonished Rainus. "This pride of yours may well be your end, if you are not careful."

"My pride?" snorted Percy, his tone dismissive as he engaged the Elf. "My pride and good sense prevents me from allowing this lovely young lady to venture on a dangerous mission with a motley crew of undisciplined ruffians! I will journey on, but only to ensure the safety of my ladylove and to prove my loyalty to her."

His words oozed of charm as he smiled at Rose. He was delighted to see her face glow as she beamed with adoration for him and his bold claim for resuming this quest in her honour.

Tag flopped against the backrest of his chair, feeling defeated that every effort to reveal Percy as the deceitful, conniving weasel he truly is was thwarted by this royal's fast-talking skills of manipulation.

"If you intend to continue on this mission, then you best brace yourself for what is in store," cautioned Silas, motioning Percy to sit down and listen up.

"I have endured the company of your friends thus far, I am more than certain I will handle the dangers of this quest splendidly!" Percy reluctantly took his seat, glancing over to Loftus first, and then to Silas, as he muttered a warning, "I am watching you both, so do not even think of accosting me again!"

"We have more important things to do than to find ways to antagonize you," assured Loftus, as he urged the Wizard to resume speaking.

Silas nodded in agreement. "The news the Council of Wizards shared was a testament to the dangers Cinyah Morningstar, as she was once called, is sure to cast our way in our efforts to capture her and to rescue Loken."

"Cinyah Morningstar…" repeated Percy, as he pondered this unfamiliar name. "You say she is a crazy Witch, and yet, her name sounds rather enchanting."

"She goes by *Sin Mourningstar* now, or just plain old *Sin*," explained Silas.

"Sin? Now she sounds more *naughty* than dangerous," mused Percy, snickering as he imagined just what kind of magic this Witch was capable of conjuring up.

"Trust me, she is extremely dangerous," averred Rose. "Even without the Dreamstone in her clutches, if she succeeds in resurrecting Dragonite to steal away his powers, she will truly be a force to reckon with."

Percy's bruised lips pursed together, making his mouth look almost normal as he mulled over Rose's foreboding words.

"If you question Sin's might in terms of power as she delves into the forbidden arts, then do not question her resourcefulness, Prince Percival," warned Silas. "This Witch had found a way to capture and hold Loken. This is no easy feat. Our little friend is a shape-shifting Sprite with tremendous powers of his own, but even his skills were no match for her."

"Well, I suppose I shall have to see for myself just how powerful this woman is," said Percy. "But you had stated the Council of Wizards do not know where she had fled to?"

"I said they were unable to determine her *exact* location," answered Silas. "Just know that in her travels, Sin has been meeting with the various covens, all in a bid to gain their backing and to consolidate the far-flung groups; bringing them under her leadership so she may defy with impunity the Council of Wizards."

"Then how are we to find her, if your powerful brotherhood could not?" asked Percy.

"They had gathered information from reliable sources that the Witch has journeyed to the north."

"Reliable sources? Then I assume it was gleaned from credible folks of good repute? Barons and earls across the lands have no doubt banded together to gather intelligence on this villainess."

"The barons and earls I am acquainted with do not wish to partake in matters that concern Wizards and Witches," answered Silas.

"Then I question the integrity of the Council's *reliable* sources," contested Percy.

"If you must know, the details of Sin's movements were gathered from the very Witches she had approached."

"Hmph!" grunted Percy. "I thought as much! How are we to trust in the words of Witches about a fellow Witch?"

Myron leaned across the table, staring at the Wizard. "No disrespect, Master Agincor, but I must agree with Prince Percival. Why would the Witches turn on one of their own? It makes no sense."

"I understand your concern, however, consider this, my friend. Through the course of her long life, Sin's actions in the past had served to splinter the most powerful of covens in her quest for notoriety and power. They have little trust for one who delves so deeply into dark magic."

"So, she has made no lasting bonds with the existing covens?" queried Rainus.

"Being the sister of Dragonite has done nothing to curry favour or respect from her sisterhood," answered Silas. "She is considered a menace and a rogue, bringing ruin to the reputation of the various covens she wished to control."

"Oh, my!" said Harold. "She is as power hungry as she is powerful."

"That is why it is so important to not just rescue Loken, but to put a halt to this Witch before she becomes an unstoppable danger to all," reminded Tag. "I'm sure for as many Witches to reject her, there will be just as many who will side with her, either through greed or intimidation."

"So, how far north does she flee?" questioned Rainus.

"Rumour has it, she hides in the lands beyond the Fire Rim Mountain Range," answered Silas. "We shall head north to the world's end; where land is no more and the Sea of Shadows begins."

"Good gracious," moaned Rose, her eyes grew dark with worry. "So we are forced to venture through dragon territory once more?"

"If you know she hides out somewhere along the Sea of Shadows, then why not use your powers to transport us directly to that place, than to go traipsing through dangerous, dragon infested lands?" asked Percy. "In doing so, it is sure to save us time and potential grief."

"The country to the north facing this sea is as vast as it is barren," warned Silas. "We have a vague idea where she is, so we are forced to follow the clues across the lands to determine the exact location of her secret lair."

"You are not saying this to prolong my misery or to dissuade me from proceeding on this quest, are you?" questioned Percy, staring through suspicious eyes at the Wizard.

"I say this so you, all of you, are well aware of what potential dangers await us."

"Frigid climates, strange lands, deadly dragons a-plenty!" exclaimed Tag. He shrugged his shoulders as though this was a daily occurrence in his life, while he smiled at Percy. "I would not want you missing out on this little adventure."

"You only say that because you hope I get eaten by a dragon, or worse!" snapped Percy, waving an admonishing finger at Tag.

"Worse, actually! But if that should happen, it will only occur because of your own stupidity or cowardice," responded Tag.

"This is shaping up to be a truly exciting quest," said Harold. "Aside from that phantom dragon the Witch conjured up, I've never seen a real dragon before. Mind you, Loken did turn into a strange lookin' one to dig us out of the Mines of Euphoria, but he doesn't actually count for a real dragon."

"You are a fool to wish for such a thing! Big or small, they are dangerous, nasty creatures!" said Rose, shaking her head at the large man. "It will be dangerous enough pursuing this crazed Witch. Trust me when I say you will not want to meet up with one of those reptiles along the way."

"You're right, Princess," agreed Harold. "I just got swept up in the excitement of it all."

"Sounds more dangerous than exciting," commented Loftus, with a thoughtful nod.

"Are you backing out?" asked Percy, hoping against hope he was about to find a way to return to Axalon without losing face. "If so, I know with all certainty my father will prevent me from venturing forth without a personal bodyguard by my side."

"I said nothing about backing out," answered Loftus. "It is obvious our new friends can use as much help as can be afforded them. And just think, my lord, it means you will indeed be able to carry on, venturing forth to keep Princess Rose safe as you had vowed!"

"Oh, huzzah!" Percy cheered with feigned enthusiasm.

Whether she ignored or did not hear the sarcasm in his tone, Rose's heart swelled with joy just knowing he was not planning on abandoning her on this quest. She fervently applauded his bold words and his passion to prove to her comrades that he is truly a man of action.

"I will make it clear to all, this quest will be fraught with danger as we hunt this Witch down," warned Silas. "There is also a possibility that wretched soul has torn down Loken's resistance, either by magic, torture or threat to use his powers against us to prevent her capture and to ensure our demise."

"So, we are up against a demented Witch *and* a dangerous Pooka?" asked Percy, as he pondered the risks.

"Are you getting scared?" asked Tag, searching for that shadow of fear to flicker in this royal's eyes.

"Me? Never! I just want to be certain of what I will be up against," said Percy. He was thoroughly agitated by Tag's mocking tone.

"If those two possibilities are not a cause for alarum, do not forget, Prince Percival," added Loftus, "as we venture farther to the north there will be dragons and adverse weather for sure."

"Winter comes early to the lands beyond the Fire Rim Mountain Range," cautioned Silas. "More than the dragons, the weather poses a far greater threat to our lives."

Percy shook his head as he addressed the Wizard. "I beg to differ! As far as I am concerned we are better able to endure the cold, if we are dressed properly for the weather, than to withstand the claws and teeth, and not to forget, the torrent of fire many dragons expel."

"You will be relieved to know that with the impending cold, dragons tend to fall into a state of torpor. They find refuge, seeking the warmth provided by the caves in the many, still active volcanoes to the north," said Silas.

Percy seemed to melt with relief, sinking against the backrest of his chair upon hearing this news.

Rose perked up, sitting upright as her eyes shone with anticipation. "No dragons? Truly?"

"I kid you not, my dear Princess," answered Silas.

"Does that mean we can ride our horses north, across those wretched lands?" asked Rose.

"With no need to avoid dragons, yes, we can ride, at least as far as the furthest mountains to the north, if that is where the clues direct us," replied Silas.

"I am so happy!" exclaimed Rose.

It was bad enough being made to go on another quest, and even worse that they were heading north as winter encroached upon the lands skirted by the Sea of Shadows, but this bit of news lessened the blow. Rose was so grateful she would not be made to walk the distance as she did when the search for the Sorcerer delivered them deep into dragon country.

"I am pleased you are eager to proceed, Princess," praised Rainus, "but night settles with haste upon the lands as our world surrenders to the chill of autumn. I recommend a hearty dinner and a good night's rest."

"We venture out in the morning?" asked Rose.

"At first light," confirmed Rainus. "For now, I shall have Arissa deliver you to your rooms. The four of you can use this time to freshen up for dinner, as Myron and Tag already had the opportunity to do so."

"Excellent!" said Percy, using both hands to lift his wine goblet from the table to take with him. "There is no point in allowing this to go to waste."

"And there will be more served with dinner," promised Rainus. "On this night, we shall speak no more of Witches and dragons. Instead, we shall enjoy in a shared meal and pleasant company, for it may well be a long time before we dine again in such civilized surroundings after tomorrow."

As though Arissa heard Rainus' every word, she swept into the dining room, ready to deliver his guests to their appointed bedchamber.

"I am confident you will approve of the accommodations, Prince Percy," assured Rose. "They are quaint, but tastefully appointed."

Percy sighed, for in his opinion, that could only mean small in size and sparse in lavish furnishings.

As Princess Rose, Prince Percival, Harold and Captain Loftus followed Arissa down a long corridor, the others remained at the table.

"Do join us once you are ready," Rainus called to his guests.

"But no need to rush," added Tag, for he was in no hurry to see Percy's mottled face any time soon.

No sooner than Arissa delivered Percy to his room, a mortified shriek echoed from his bedchamber. It was his first glimpse of his freshly bruised face staring back at him from a mirror.

11
Game of Crones

"Are you positive these cloaks will keep us warm?" asked Percy. "Warmer than the luxurious one I am being made to abandon?"

Twisting about in his saddle, he addressed Rainus, as this Elf and Tag were taking up the rear. He motioned for Harold, now riding a large, grey dappled horse and travelling alongside Captain Loftus, to get out of his line of vision so he may address his concerns to the Elf.

"Yes, I am positive," said Rainus.

"Well, that's insulting!" snapped Tag. With a disgruntled shake of his head, he scolded Percy. "Do you honestly believe Lady Silverthorn would gift us with these fine Elven cloaks, if they were not weather and season appropriate?"

"I only ask because this fabric feels so light. Although it feels adequately warm for now, how can I be sure I will not freeze to death as the weather grows progressively worse the farther north we travel?"

"My wife is not a cruel prankster," grunted Rainus. "If she were, and *you* were to be the recipient of a cruel trick, why would she provide the identical apparel to *all* my friends?"

Percy pondered his words. "That is a valid point, Lord Silverthorn. I suppose it would defeat the purpose of this quest, if we were all to die of exposure before the deed was done."

"There will be no freezing! I promise you, we will be fine," said Rose, coaxing her mare next to Percy's warhorse. "Though this colour is not particularly flattering for one of my delicate skin tone, over my leather riding jacket, this special cloak is comfortable and more importantly, it is form flattering! It does not make me look big and bulky, like a fat, little bear that is ready for hibernation."

"Form flattering indeed," agreed Percy, throwing his shoulders back, "but as there is none I must impress at this moment, function is my greatest concern."

"I assure you, Prince Percival, these cloaks were created from the finest worsted wool," disclosed Rainus. "It has been woven together with a special plant fibre, of which I dare not divulge to you, lest you get it in your head to harvest it for financial gains. The outer layer has been treated with a special wax and oil mixture that will effectively repel moisture should there be rain or snow. With some Elven *ingenuity* the inner layers have been designed to insulate while wicking away perspiration, as I know how you human beings can sweat profusely. These features will help to keep you adequately warm and dry during the worst of inclement weather."

"And don't forget about the colour," reminded Tag.

"What about it?" asked Percy. With a sneer of disdain he stared down at this new cloak that ensconced his body with the generous warmth Rainus had promised. "I find this colour nothing short of dreary. It does nothing for my complexion, nor does it enhance the blue undertones of these captivating, steel grey eyes."

"These sylvan colours will allow us to seamlessly blend into our surroundings," explained Rainus. "That pretentious, purple cloak with its white ermine trim you wore stuck out like those ghastly bruises against your fair skin. As we journey northward, especially against the open countryside, you promise to stand out in your royal attire. I hardly think you will want to be a visible target for annihilation."

"But I had heard rumours that dragons cannot distinguish between the various colours," said Percy.

"Do you really want to chance your life to unsubstantiated rumours?" queried Rainus, staring with raised eyebrows at the mortal. "What I do know for sure is that movement is certain to draw the attention of a hungry dragon, more so than any particular colour."

"Really?" Percy's brows furrowed in doubt.

"Yes," added Tag. "First one to flee in terror will be the first to be devoured. You won't be long for the dragon lands, if you run for your life."

"A prince does not run like a coward. I shall stand my ground; slay the dragon before I become fodder for one of those beasts!"

"So you say," said Tag. "Even if dragons were not able to distinguish between colours, that squirrelly-eyed Witch certainly can. If she spots you, she will definitely try to kill you."

"What does he mean by *squirrelly-eyed*? The Witch has rodent-like qualities?" questioned Percy, turning to Rose for an explanation.

"Tag meant to say that the crazy, old Witch is blind in one eye, so the other functioning one is constantly darting about, as though doing the work of two eyes," answered Rose. Her eyes rattled to and fro in demonstration. "It is most unsettling!"

"Ewww! I can only imagine!" Percy shuddered at the thought of this Troll-of-a-one-eyed Witch staring him down.

"Just be grateful it will be much harder for that woman to pick you out against the landscape as we advance," said Rainus. "In this cloak, you will be far warmer *and* safer than had you elected to wear that audacious purple monstrosity."

"I suppose, on this occasion, it is wise to forsake my tasteful fashion sense for the sake of safety," responded Percy, nodding over his shoulder to the Elf.

"It is," said Rainus. "Now, pick up your pace. Keep up with the others."

Percy turned about, glancing forward. With Rose by his side, ahead of them were Halen, with Myron and Silas riding close behind. This Elf had not slowed down while he was conversing with Rainus Silverthorn. The trio had put greater distance between them and were now a good nine horse-lengths in front of him.

Clucking his tongue against the roof of his mouth, Percy's warhorse snorted in response. With the prodding of heels to its flanks the animal broke into an easy canter. Rose's mare reacted instinctively, along with the other horses following behind them. The animals hastened to catch up to those in the lead.

Tag watched as Harold sat proudly on the mighty steed Rainus had provided him on this occasion. This fine specimen was large enough to comfortably handle his weight, allowing Harold to ride instead of running alongside his little donkey.

Now, this mortal was bestowed with the responsibility of leading two packhorses to join the one Captain Loftus led on behalf of his royal charge. With the amount of supplies, especially equipment needed to survive harsh winter conditions, Sassy would not have fared well. As much as Harold was already missing his petulant, little companion, he knew the distance and encroaching winter weather could prove deadly to Sassy. He had to be content in knowing she was in the care of the Elves. He also found satisfaction in the fact Rainus Silverthorn trusted him with this fine mount and the care of these two packhorses and all they carried. The added responsibility promised to keep him busy, so there would be little time to miss his equine companion.

As Percy's mount caught up to Silas and Myron's steeds, he called out to the Wizard. "How do you know we are on the right trail to begin with, when your brother Wizards were so vague in sharing details?"

"They were vague in providing the exact route the Witch had travelled, but they were precise in the intelligence they had gathered. There is no mistake she had escaped to the north."

As Rose coaxed her mare next to Percy's mount, she said, "I believe Prince Percy means to say that in pointing us to the *north*, it is a such a vast land. How do we find Sin, once we get there, based on what little your brethren had shared with you?"

Percy literally deflated, unleashing a frustrated sigh as he scolded Rose, "Do not speak for me! I am perfectly capable of doing so myself!"

"I am sorry." Rose's face flushed with embarrassment as she pursed her lips to keep from offending him further.

Percy raised a hand to her, motioning for silence as he spoke. "So, how do we find the Witch, once we get there, based on what little the Council of Wizards had shared with you?"

"We do what we had done in the past. We shall hunt her down in the conventional manner, just as we hunted down her brother," answered Silas.

"But what is this conventional manner you speak of?" asked Percy.

"We travel to the location of her last confirmed sighting, and then we must be patient and observant; meticulous in our search for clues to guide us on."

"Clues, as in her footprints?" assumed Percy.

"Yes, but clues, more than just footprints, can tell us more than just the direction she travelled."

"Like what?" questioned Percy, having never been part of a hunt unless it was for sport to chase down a fox, boar or stag and under the directions of a skilled huntsman.

"Lord Silverthorn will vouch that Captain Ironwood possesses exceptional skills," responded Silas. "He is second to none when it comes to tracking, whether the object of his pursuit moves on two legs or four."

"Yes," agreed Myron. He nodded in approval to the Elf leading the way. "It does not matter if the one Captain Ironwood is searching for moves across a rocky escarpment, a carpet of leaves or a dry riverbed, his keen senses allow him to see even the tiniest details others do not."

"Even if Captain Ironwood is an excellent tracker, how will he even distinguish her footprints from the myriad of others? I am confident even the remote forests to the north have hunters, trappers and travellers traipsing about in all directions."

"Fear not, my lord," said Halen, "I will know the steps left behind by that Witch."

"But how?" queried Percy.

"From what we have been witness to, Sin has a very distinct, loping gait exaggerated by a limp," answered Halen. "She also uses

Dragonite's staff as a walking stick. The hexagonal tip of this staff leaves a unique impression in the ground at very specific intervals."

"I see. But what are these other things that can be revealed by these clues, other than the direction travelled?" queried Percy.

"By the length of the stride, I can tell if our quarry is walking or sprinting away. Careful determination can reveal to me just how quickly and how far she travels. Also, by the freshness of these impressions, I can determine approximately when she had passed by."

"And what else?" Percy was now genuinely intrigued.

"By the footprints, I can tell if there is an exaggeration to her limp. It can be indicative of a new injury. Sometimes, even the type of wound can be determined," said Halen. "But it is more than just the obvious footprints I seek when I search for clues."

"Such as?"

"Such as those indicating what our quarry, in this case, that demented Witch has eaten and when, where she slept, even what she wears, and so on, if you know exactly what to look for," answered Halen.

"And you are that good?" Percy was astounded by this Elf's claims of expertise.

"I do not wish to sound like I am boasting, but I do possess innate abilities that have been honed over many hundreds of years. My skills and experience combine to serve me well," replied Halen, his words matter-of-fact. "So, yes. I am '*that good*', at least, better at this task than the most highly trained mortal."

"Oh, yes!" called Harold, overhearing this conversation. "As good as I am at trackin' all sorts of critters, I'll tell you right now, Captain Ironwood is far better than I'll ever be. If anyone can hunt down that villainess, it'll be this great Elf!"

"Thank you for the glowing endorsement, my friend." Halen glanced over his shoulder to nod in gratitude to Harold, "But I recommend that you reserve such high praise until the quest is done and that Witch is captured."

"I have high hopes," said Silas. "Not only do we advance with the blessings of my Wizardly council, but even the Fairies offered to do their part, if it means saving Loken from harm."

"Speaking of the Fairies, how did Pancecelia Feldspar take the news of Loken's disappearance?" queried Myron.

"As you can imagine, she was distraught when I delivered the news to her," answered Silas.

"Understandably so," agreed Myron, feeling great sympathy for this Fairy.

"The poor dear! To be separated from her true love yet again after being reunited after all these years," lamented Rose, with a sad shake of her head. "Theirs is a love story that is so very tragic."

"This is the Queen of the Tooth Fairies you speak of, correct?" asked Percy.

"Yes," answered Rose. "Where Loken and Pancecelia Feldspar are concerned, fate has been fickle and the powers that be have been less than kind. It is as though they conspire to tear asunder this union between Sprite and Fairy."

"In my way of thinking they are not meant to be together," stated Percy.

"How can that be so?" asked Rose. "Their love has survived, not only intense scrutiny from their own people, but to unite their races. It has endured through the hardships of separation, dark magic, even murder. Theirs is a love that is truly meant to be."

"You are such a romantic, my dear Rose-alyn. Your generous heart blinds you to the obvious, making you oblivious to what others know and see," responded Percy.

"Blind, indeed!" chirped up Tag.

"Fetch off, you knave!" snapped Percy. "I was speaking to the Princess, not to you."

Rose frowned in confusion as she spoke, "What do you mean that I am blind to the obvious?"

"Your gentle heart is somewhat gullible. You want to believe in love so much, it blinds you to the fact that some things are just not meant to be, my dear."

"And you believe this is one of them?" asked Rose. "That Loken and Pancecelia are not meant to be together?"

"Absolutely!"

"Explain," ordered Rose. Her nerves prickled with an undercurrent of agitation, as much from his condescending, know-it-all tone as it was from his efforts to strike down the validity of her absolute belief in the power of true love.

"Yes, do explain!" invited Tag, hoping his words would force Rose to finally see Percy in all his true, sordid colours.

Percy sneered at the young man, clamping together the fingers and thumb of his left hand in a gesture for Tag to shut up. As quickly as the sneer on his face appeared, it was smoothed over by a disarming smile as he turned his attention back to Rose.

"Take no offence, my dear, but the whole, childish notion of *true love* muddles your mind."

"So, you do not believe in love?" Rose gasped. "Are you trying to tell me there is no love between us?"

"We are different from *them*," explained Percy, raising his hand for silence so he may continue uninterrupted. "Just think on this: How can the union between a Pooka and a Fairy be natural?"

"Loken prefers to be called a Sprite, albeit a shape-shiftin' one," corrected Harold.

Percy peered over his shoulder. He shot a baleful glance at the large man, letting him know he was not invited to comment.

Under this threatening stare, Harold seemed to shrink, withering beneath Percy's hostile gaze.

"As I was saying, before I was so rudely interrupted, it is like condoning the union between a monarch and a commoner, diluting the royal bloodline and demeaning the very essence of what it means to be of royal lineage."

"But Loken, in his own right, can be considered a royal," said Rose. "He is one of the last of his kind. Pancecelia Feldspar holds him in highest esteem and with the greatest respect, for he is both noble and gallant in his loyalty to her."

"My dear, sweet, gullible princess! A village may have but one idiot, and if he were to save a child from drowning in the village well, his deed may be deemed noble, earning the momentary respect of the townsfolk, but he still remains the village idiot."

"So, in your mind, the Queen of the Tooth Fairy lowers her standards in embracing Loken as her consort?" queried Rose.

"Yes! But it is worse than that, for they are not even of the same race."

"But true love knows no bounds," argued Rose. She held on fiercely to what she had always believed in.

"You are such a romantic! The truth is so obvious even a blind man can see this to be so," averred Percy. "The point being, when the obstacles are many and the road to love is pocked with ruts and insurmountable barriers along the way, these are the very forces of nature itself condemning such an unnatural union!"

"So, you do not believe in the power of love?"

"I believe in love that is grounded in substance, not some silly, adolescent notion of *romantic* love. The love I offer is real, unwavering even, but it is founded on three cornerstones that will ensure a lasting union."

"And these cornerstones, what are they?" questioned Rose.

"An enduring, untainted royal bloodline, greater power, and a mutually beneficial relationship based on *real* admiration are what will allow us to weather all the uncertainties of life, once we are joined in matrimony."

"It sounds so very… practical," gulped Rose, as she digested this revelation.

"Sound, practical *and* mutually beneficial," stated Percy, flashing her a knowing smile.

"So, I suspect by your words and attitude, helping us to rescue Loken is low on your list of priorities?" determined Myron.

"It did not even make it onto my list." Percy nodded to the knight. "As far as I am concerned, my sole purpose is to keep Princess Rose safe, should you and that ruffian, Tag Yairet, fall short of your duties. If I have a hand in helping to capture the old crone, then bully for me, but I am indifferent to the outcome of the Pooka's life."

"How can you say such a terrible thing?" admonished Tag. He struggled to contain his urge to throw something at the back of Percy's head.

"Easy! To capture the Witch can change the tides of fortune for many, maybe even save the world, if the threat you all claim she poses is genuine. It shall mean returning a hero and being the recipient of many grand accolades. Now, should the Witch escape and we manage to rescue the shape-shifting miscreant, so what? Who will care? It will make no difference to the world at large, but we can still be in peril while the Witch remains on the loose."

"Pancecelia Feldspar will care," insisted Tag. "In fact, we all care, even if you don't."

"So you say, but just remember, I am not like poor, lowly *you*, living with a mind burgeoning with grand ideals that bear little relevance to real life matters and what truly counts in the big scheme of things," muttered Percy. He sneered with disdain at the knight-in-training. "I shall rue the day when I endanger my life, and the life of my future wife, to rescue that Pooka. Loken's life, or death, will not mark a significant change in this world, however, that Witch? That is another matter altogether. If she were to be captured, her momentum to garner greater power will be put to an end."

"I do not know this Sprite, but I still have compassion for Loken," confided Loftus. "Knowing what he had done to save the lives of those he cares for speaks of his true character. Surely, my lord, in all your wisdom you can show some compassion, too, for our comrades' missing friend?"

"To show compassion to the undeserving is a show of weakness," grunted Percy.

"To show compassion to those who need it the most is the greatest show of one's strength and character," argued Silas.

"And this is how you manipulate others to do your will," said Percy.

"You gnaw at their conscience, filling them with guilt or you motivate them with false aspiration to achieve greatness through their actions. It is so pathetic! Manipulation at its worst!"

"What is truly pathetic is your apathy," rebuked Silas. "It is this indifference that shall mark the beginning of the end for all humanity."

"Good gracious!" gasped Harold, his brows arching up in surprise as he considered Silas' warning. "Wouldn't that make Prince Percival more dangerous than the Witch, if this is so?"

"Bite your tongue, you big oaf!" scolded Percy, shaking a clenched fist at Harold. "I may be dangerous with a sword or with my fists, but I am not a crazy, evil entity bent on world domination."

"Yes, you would prefer to accomplish this on the backs and sweat of others, so they would look like the crazy ones," mocked Tag.

"Not so! I would never associate with those deemed as crazy, with the exception of you, whom I have no choice in the matter," exclaimed Percy. "At least I am genuine in my intentions of embarking on this quest; to keep my dear Rose-alyn safe and to stop this supposedly dangerous Witch!"

"Ha!" scoffed Tag.

"Unlike you!" Percy snapped. "You uphold the guise of venturing on this quest for the sake of honour and nobility, of doing the right thing, but you cannot fool me!"

"Keep this up, my lord! Speak a little louder," rebuked Myron, his voice tightened in frustration. "At the rate you bluster on we will have no need to hunt down that Witch. The old crone will find us instead, once she hears you ranting and raving as you do now."

"Make no mistake, Sir Kendall, I do not rant, nor do I rave," argued Percy. He trembled as he struggled to regain his composure and stifle his anger so he would not be branded a lunatic. "I am merely stating a valid point none of you wish to consider because you are too close to the truth. Just know that this impudent whelp, this orphan you had taken under your wings, has a hidden agenda. Why else would Yairet be here now?"

"Hidden agenda?" snapped Tag. His eyes blazed. His face reddened with these accusing words. "I'm not the one – "

"Stop, my friend." Rainus reached over, resting a consoling hand on the young man's shoulder. This calming touch and his soothing tone immediately caused the anger boiling in Tag's heart to melt away. "Your words are wasted on Prince Percival, and on us. As your trusted friends, we know what is in your heart and what keeps you in our company after all we had endured together. You need not say a word to defend your honour. We gladly do that for you."

"Thank you, Lord Silverthorn," said Tag. He beamed with delight, his smile annoying Percy to no end.

"Of course you would side with this dolt!" Percy shook his head in disgust.

"You call this young sir a dolt, but we know him as a *friend*. It is an honoured title we do not take lightly," said Myron. "Unlike you, Tag has earned a rightful place in our group."

"Given time, I, too, will earn a respected place amongst your comrades!" insisted Percy. "Mark my words! As this quest progresses and dangerous situations arise, I shall prove to all that I am worthy of an honoured place in your circle. I am even willing to bet I shall oust this ruffian from his respected roost within your inner sanctum, should the opportunity arise to show my true qualities."

"You are welcome to try," said Tag, offering Percy a smug grin along with this invitation. "At least your efforts can potentially make you a more likeable person, if you prove to be of help, rather than a hindrance, to us."

"What a bunch of malarkey! My title alone makes me likeable. In fact, I am downright loveable in the eyes of my people, especially those of the fairer sex!"

These boastful words sent pangs of envy rattling through Rose's bones. Her eyes narrowed in resentment as she scowled at Percy for speaking these words.

"Of course, I am adored by many, but I only have eyes for you, my dear Rose-alyn!" He gave her a winsome smile and playful wink to end her jealousy and to circumvent potential wrath.

"Whatever you believe, rest assured, this quest is certain to test your mettle to the extreme," promised Silas.

"I will be ready for whatever danger comes our way," vowed Percy. Puffing out his chest in pride, he was poised for action.

"Well, if danger should strike, at least you will look the part of a hero rather than a frightened raccoon," teased Silas, as the others, with the exception of Rose, shared in a chuckle at Percy's expense. "It was rather difficult to take you seriously looking as you did last night when Captain Ironwood delivered you to Lord Silverthorn's residence."

Percy pretended to be unmoved by this snickering. He joined in by laughing heartily while he shaped his mouth into an expression of surprise to mimic the now vanquished bruise that had encircled his lips.

Having received further healing, this time from Rainus Silverthorn just prior to departing Driven Hill, it made it easier to make fun of himself even as his mind replayed the horror. The memory of seeing his bruised mouth and blackened eyes reflected in the mirror of his bedchamber was now indelibly etched into his mind forever.

Rose smiled proudly at her man, pleased he did not respond to this good-natured ribbing with a show of anger.

"Well, there will be no teasing now, thanks to Lord Silverthorn's handiwork." Rose nodded to Rainus in gratitude, and then glanced over to Percy, indicating that he should do the same.

"I am grateful Captain Ironwood had the decency to heal my nose when it was broken, but why did he not further the process by healing my bruises? This mystery continues to vex me," whined Percy, speaking louder so Halen would hear these words of ridicule. "Does he lack the power to do so because he is not a high Elf?"

"My greatest concern was your most grievous injury," answered Halen. "It was not that I lacked the power to do further healing, I merely lacked the interest in doing so. Need I say more?"

The large Elf promptly whinged and whined, mimicking this mortal's actions of that day.

In protest, Percy snapped, "I told you at the time it was against protocol for a commoner to touch one of royal blood. Lord Silverthorn is another matter though, being the high Elf that he is."

Rainus shook his head in disapproval. He knew the truth. This mortal feared Halen's powers to heal, believing it might hurt him on initial contact.

"If that is so, I would say it was your pride that prevented Captain Ironwood from continuing with the healing session," said Rainus. "And you should know, Prince Percival, even though he is not a *high* Elf, he may well be the one to save your life as this quest takes us deeper into dangerous lands. I recommend showing him a measure of respect, if you have it in you."

"So you say, but there will be no need to save me. You will come to see I can be quite capable with my sword in a contest of skills."

"Trust me when I say, there will be no *contest*, only a fight to the death should we come across Sin." Rainus spoke with all certainty.

"Against a decrepit woman probably older than time? I think not," snorted Percy. He laughed like a braying donkey as he quickly dismissed Rainus' warning.

"Lord Silverthorn is very serious," cautioned Rose. "Sin is powerful *and* crazy; a deadly combination for sure!"

"Just because you and your friends feel threatened by this hag, until she gives me reason to fear her, I will boldly confront that Witch, should I be challenged."

"This is a *hag* with the powers of the forbidden arts on her side," reminded Myron.

"With the implementation of shrewd strategy even the most clever of foes can be taken by surprise," countered the hubris, young man, spouting off as though he was speaking from personal experience.

"Prince Percy is quite correct," agreed Rose. "In fact, all of you at one time or another have sung the praises of good strategy and the importance of the element of surprise."

"Yes, but rather than living vicariously through the pages of a book, we have firsthand experience in real battles and in dealing with those dispensing dark magic," reminded Myron.

"Well, I am a firm believer in knowledge," argued Percy, his index finger tapping against his forehead. "Knowledge and wisdom combine to arm one with poise, an essential quality if one is to weather misfortune, should calamity strike."

"You talk a good game, Prince Percival," said Silas, in mock praise. "Let us hope this knowledge and wisdom serves you well when needed the most."

"Where one can lose the keen edge of a blade and the tip of a sword can be dulled over time, the sharpness of my mind will never be lost *or* dulled!"

"I beg to differ." Tag spoke with all seriousness. "Your mind is far from sharp and it can be lost, quite easily, from what I've seen so far."

"Har, har! You are a funny one!" Percy snorted in feigned laughter. "If I did not know better, I'd say you are more suited to be a court jester than a knight."

"The joke is on him," teased Rose, attempting to divert this negative attention from Percy. "Tag was once appointed as my personal court jester. Unfortunately, he never was that funny!"

"Truly?" Percy gasped in surprise. His healed lips twisted into a smirk of a grin as he cast a condescending stare over his shoulder at the embarrassed young man.

"Sad, but true," admitted Tag. "Care to reveal why I was appointed to such an onerous vocation to begin with, Princess?"

"Do tell!" exclaimed Percy, eager to hear of Tag's tale of humiliation.

"There is nothing to tell," answered Rose. "And what there is to tell shall only bore you to death. Such mundane details of Tag's sorry life are sure to put you to sleep."

"Then I shall trust you on this," said Percy, waving dismissively over his shoulder to motion to Tag to say no more on this matter. "If anything, my fecund imagination can conjure up a dozen and one droll reasons for that pathetic appointment and just as many amusing ones that will serve to explain his presence here now!"

"Believe what you want," grunted Tag. "At least I will not be taken by surprise should that Witch show her ugly face. Mind you, had she seen *your* face prior to Lord Silverthorn's healing session, Sin would have been so busy rolling about on the ground in a fit of laughter, she'd be unable to retaliate with magic."

"Brilliant! Now that's a grand idea!" exclaimed Harold, with a snap of his fingers. "If that were to happen, we'd be able to swoop in and capture her, just like that!"

"You idiot!" growled Percy. "If you think I am going to disfigure my perfect face just to make it easy for you and your comrades to capture that Witch, then think again!"

"But you won't need to endure a beatin' this time, neither by bottle nor horse," said Harold. "We can just smear the juice of some berries around your mouth and eyes for the same effect. It'll look just as hilarious and sure to render that Witch helpless, so we can move in and nab her."

"Fetch off, you big buffoon!" demanded Percy, twisting about in his saddle to shake an angry fist at him.

"Better not to poke the bear, Harold," said Loftus, offering the mortified man a consoling smile. "He does not realize you were speaking in jest, my friend."

"Jest or not, we have more important things to discuss," said Percy. He was eager to steer the conversation on to other matters that had nothing to do with the unflattering appearance that was the cause of so much humiliation for him. "If we are able to pick up this Witch's trail, that indeed would be most fortuitous. However, what happens if she is able to evade capture, using magic to cover her tracks?"

"If all physical evidence of her is no more, then I shall have to rely on the continued help and wisdom of my brotherhood," answered Silas, prodding his horse on to keep up with Halen's mount. "Failing that, then Pancecelia Feldspar and her people will do what they can to help us."

"And just what can those puny beings do?" asked Percy, his brows furrowing with doubt.

"Do not assume that just because the Fairies are small in size, they are powerless to aid us," rebuked Silas.

"Fine! I shall keep an open mind on this subject. So tell me, just how can the Queen of the Tooth Fairies and her subjects be of any help to us?"

"How well acquainted are you with the Fairies?" queried Silas. He glanced over his shoulder to level a scrutinizing gaze at this mortal.

"I remember when I was a child, they would steal into my

bedchamber in the dead of night, whenever I had lost a tooth. My teeth were always pristine, and yet, those little beings were as stingy as they were tiny. They would leave a single copper for a perfect molar or incisor, but still, you'd think they'd offer up a piece of gold, knowing that the tooth came from the mouth of a genuine prince."

"The Fairies do not care about the source of the teeth, only the quality," informed Silas. "Other than that, what else do you know? Have you ever had the chance to meet one? Ever speak to one of these fascinating beings?"

"I might have squashed one, thinking it was a moth, but no. I have never met a Fairy. Even when I was young and had set a trap, using a tooth as bait in a bid to capture one, they proved to be elusive quarries."

"Good gracious! What is it about you royals and this need to capture Fairies?" muttered Tag, shaking his head in disapproval as he glanced at Percy, and then the Princess.

"Never mind that," urged Rose, motioning for Tag to cease talking. "Master Agincor was addressing Prince Percy's concerns when you so rudely interrupted."

Tag rolled his eyes in response, annoyed she did not want Percy to know that she had done the same, and her foolish action had incurred the wrath of Pancecelia Feldspar to initiate this quest in the first place.

"Yes, Master Wizard," said Percy, "you were going to explain to me how the Fairies can be helpful to this quest."

"The Fairies roam far and wide during their nocturnal forays. Their small size and discreet nature make them perfect for gathering intelligence, usually going unnoticed as they go about their business of harvesting teeth."

"So they eavesdrop on the conversations of others," said Percy, with a shrug of indifference. "Even if they gleaned some valuable information that is pertinent to this quest, how will they, or even their Queen, locate us while we are on the move, if they have vital news to share?"

Silas rummaged through the great folds of his cloak. Finding what he was looking for, he held up for all to see a tiny, red velvet pouch with a gold drawstring holding it closed.

"What is it?" asked Percy.

"See for yourself." Silas tossed the little bag to him.

Percy caught it with his left hand. Using his teeth, he tugged at the drawstring. He widened the opening of this pouch, tipping it into the palm of his right hand. His brows furrowed with curiosity as he asked, "Is this what I think it is?"

"What is it?" called Harold.

"It is nothing but a disgusting, little tooth!" answered Percy, grimacing in repulsion. "Is this joke?"

"The joke appears to be on you," determined Silas, "for it is obvious you do not know what that tooth is for."

Just as Percy was about to toss it away, Rose reached over, seizing him by his wrist to stop him.

"It is no ordinary tooth! I am sure of it," insisted Rose.

"Quite correct, Princess," said Silas.

"Care to explain?" Percy took it up between his index finger and thumb, holding it up for better scrutiny. He searched for signs that made this gleaming white molar as special as the Wizard claimed it to be.

"Think of it as a beacon of sorts," replied Silas. "All the Fairies specializing in the gathering of teeth for Queen Pancecelia have an innate ability to find a tooth that has been shed by natural means or lost through accident. However, this tooth has a special enchantment cast upon it."

"What kind of enchantment?" queried Percy. He placed the tooth back into the velvet pouch for safekeeping.

"It will be easy enough for Pance, as she prefers to be called, to find us if she has news to share on the Witch or Loken's whereabouts. However, with this enchantment, should we need to share news or must summon her for whatever reason, this tooth will be used for this specific purpose."

"I am intrigued," said Percy, tossing the pouch back to the Wizard. "How does it work?"

"The concept is simple, really! All I must do to summon Pance is to place the tooth under my head as I sleep. As soon as I nod off, the tooth will work its magic, beckoning for her to come when she is needed."

"Seems a bit unorthodox, but I suppose if it works, that is all that really matters," said Percy.

"Can't be anymore odd than how we mortals sometimes light great bonfires as beacons to summon a call to arms," responded Tag.

"When you think about it, what else would a Tooth Fairy use?" said Harold, his shoulders rolling in a shrug. "Makes perfect sense to me!"

"Well, it seems the uncouth or the unorthodox makes sense to your simple mind," responded Percy.

Halen suddenly raised his left hand, clenching it into a fist to motion for silence.

"I did not mean it as an insult. I was just speaking the truth," insisted Percy, unmoved that he may have hurt Harold's feelings.

"Quiet!" ordered Myron, flashing an angry glance over his shoulder to Percy.

"Why? Does the captain see a sock puppet lurking ahead, waiting to attack us?" muttered Percy, as he snickered under his breath.

"Shut it," ordered Myron, drawing an index finger across his throat to make it clear to Percy that he was to cease talking. He watched as Halen sat tall on his mount that he had slowed to a stop.

"What is it?" asked Silas, seeing all the telltale signs this Elf had spotted something that caused him concern.

"I thought I saw someone up yonder," whispered Halen, pointing in the direction with his chin as he removed the bow from over his shoulder.

"I see nothing," said Silas, staring ahead to see what Halen had detected. "Mind you, your eyes are much sharper than mine."

"Whoever he is, he seems to be watching us," cautioned Halen. He nocked an arrow onto his bow just as Rainus guided his mount up next to his.

"Do you believe it is the Witch?" Rainus' words were hushed as he stared in the direction Halen's eyes were fixed on. He strained to see beyond the bend of the trail where it wound through a thick stand of trees. Their ears pricked up as they listened intently.

"If what my brother Wizards say is true, Sin ventures northward," answered Silas. "Unless she has doubled back, I doubt it is her."

As the breeze shifted, blowing in from the north, Rainus and Halen detected the slightest of movement in the deepening shadows.

"There is a foul stink in the air," whispered Halen, as his nostrils flared.

"I smell it, too," said Rainus.

"I smell nothing," said Percy. Like a hound scenting out a fox he loudly sniffed the air to smell what the Elves detected on the breeze.

"Of course you wouldn't smell your own stink. You're used to it," teased Tag, as he eased his gelding next to Percy's steed.

Rose reached over, squeezing Percy's arm with one hand as the other pressed an index to her lips, motioning for him to be silent.

"Can you make out who it is?" whispered Myron.

"Whether that person is friend or foe, it is impossible to tell from here," answered Halen. "He neither flees nor does he advance. It is as though he, or she, waits for our approach."

The evening breeze swelled, causing the tree branches to sway in its wake.

"I smell that stink now," whispered Myron. He grimaced in disgust as a faint, sickly sweet odour of decay laced the air. "It smells of death."

"We should investigate," said Silas. "Find out who that is before we proceed."

"I agree," said Rainus, "but let us be discreet in our advance."

"Who goes there?" Percy shouted as he brandished his ceremonial sword in threat. "Make yourself known or we shall attack!"

"Good gracious," admonished Tag, shaking his head at Percy. "There is nothing subtle at all about your approach."

Halen and Rainus sat tall, staring at the shadow within the shadows as it stirred ever so slightly in response to Percy's demand.

"He does not answer," noted Rainus.

"Perhaps he is mute or deaf, or both even," said Harold.

"And just what would a mute, deaf person be doing here, in the middle of nowhere?" asked Percy.

"Maybe he's huntin' for food?" answered Harold.

Halen scanned the forest, searching for other signs of danger. "I see no one else. He seems to be alone."

"Maybe he is frightened and cannot answer," said Rose. "Perhaps he is mute, fearing that if he runs, he will be killed or if he advances, we will perceive him as a threat."

"Well, he is certainly not retreating," assessed Rainus.

"We cannot stay here forever, waiting for that fool to get out of our way," insisted Percy. "I say we advance; trample him down, if we must."

"There will be no need for that!" snapped Silas. "Perhaps it is someone who had spotted the Witch. There is a chance he can point us on our way."

"Remain here," said Halen. "I shall ride ahead; investigate the nature of this person's business."

"We advance together," suggested Myron.

"I have a feeling a procession such as ours will only serve to intimidate this soul," said Halen. "Allow me to advance alone. I will warn you if there is something untoward about this character."

"Go, but keep your bow at the ready," cautioned Rainus. "We shall wait here."

"I will not be long," promised Halen, prodding his horse on.

As he galloped off, Captain Loftus steered his mount ahead as he called to the others, "I will follow. I have a bad feeling about this."

Halen glanced over his shoulder to see the knight galloping behind him.

Just as the Elf turned his eyes back to the trail rolling out before him, Halen gasped in surprise and pain. An invisible force caught him high across his chest and shoulders to send the Elf crashing from his mount to the unforgiving ground.

Loftus' horse skidded to a stop as the captain leapt from his saddle, dashing to Halen's side as he shouted, "Help! Captain Ironwood is down!"

He propped the Elf's head up as Halen gasped, catching his breath again after having the wind knocked out of him.

"How do you fare?" asked Loftus, his eyes searching for signs of blood or broken bones.

Halen peered up to see his comrades hovering over him, concern clearly etched upon their faces.

Rainus knelt by his side. With his hands hovering just over Halen's body, he sensed there was no disruption in his life force. "You seem unhurt."

"I am more surprised than hurt. I was unseated from my horse," groaned Halen, sitting up with Loftus' help.

"By what?" asked Myron. Drawing his sword, he glanced about, searching for potential danger.

"I do not know. I remember glancing behind to see Captain Loftus riding up. When I turned forward, a powerful force hit me. I did not see it, but it was strong enough to knock me clear off my horse. I am sure had I not been wearing this vest of Elven mail, I would have been cut in two!"

"Can you stand?" asked Silas, motioning for Halen to rise.

Harold rushed in, helping Loftus hoist the Elf onto his feet.

Halen wavered slightly, taking a deep breath to clear his mind and calm his rattled nerves.

"A powerful, invisible force, you say?" Percy glanced about nervously. "Was it the Witch? Did she attack you?"

Halen shook his head. "I did not see a bolt of light, like the one she used on us in previous attacks. All I know is that I did not see what hit me. It happened suddenly.

"Look!" said Myron, pointing over some shrubs to the mysterious figure. "He continues to watch, but still refuses to advance."

"This is all very creepy," gulped Harold, staring nervously at the shadowy figure lurking in the shadows of the trees.

"If that is not a Witch, then I do not know what is!" declared Percy, hoisting his fancy sword once more.

"Over here!" called Tag. "It's a trap!"

His fingertip traced the thin, near-invisible line that was stretched taut across the trail.

"Silk… Spider's silk," determined Silas. Touching the tip of his staff to the line, with an utterance of a spell and a crackle of energy surging from his crystal, the line snapped. Taking up the end of the line, he gave it a tug. It was strong enough that it could be used as a hangman's noose.

"I thought you killed all the monster spiders," gasped Percy. His skin crawled at the mere thought of these detestable creatures.

"I killed those we found in the Enchanted Forest," answered Halen.

"We are no longer in your forest?" asked Percy.

"We left my domain a good four leagues ago," answered Rainus. "Be mindful of large webs and equally large spiders."

"This was definitely not laid out by a spider," said Silas, giving the line another hard pull.

Knowing now what to look for, Rainus' eyes followed this line as it created a wide circle around the mysterious person Halen attempted to approach.

"This was meant to decapitate," said Myron. "Had it been one of us, anyone sitting lower than Halen on his great steed, at a full gallop, one of us would be minus a head."

Silas' eyes narrowed as he stared at the figure that remained unmoved in all this time. "Who are you? What do you want from us?"

"It's that crazy Witch, I tell you!" insisted Percy, as he left Rose's side to duck behind Loftus.

"No," said Silas. "If that is Sin, she would not have hesitated to kill us."

"And yet, that figure remains unmoved, seeming to hover in the most unnatural manner," stated Tag.

The Wizard raised his new staff, now made of white oak, to replace the one that was broken by Sin during their last violent encounter. The glow of his crystal mounted atop the staff remained dormant as a show he was prepared not to use his powers.

"We come in peace," called Silas. He crept closer to this shadowy figure stirring in the wind. "We mean you no harm. Now, speak up! Who are you? What is your business here?"

"There will be no answers forthcoming from this one," said Rainus. From where he stood, he could now see the same silken cord wrapped around this person's neck, dangling this body from a tree branch.

The others gathered their horses, following behind the Elf and Wizard as they cautiously approached the dead.

"It is no wonder we thought he was hovering," noted Percy. "That silken cord is nigh on impossible to see."

"Who is he? And why was he hanged?" Rose wondered aloud as she stared at the body; the head shroud in a black cloth to shield his identity.

"Cut him down, Halen," ordered Rainus, as Loftus wrapped his arms around the legs of this dead body so it could be lowered to the ground.

Halen called to his steed. Climbing on to the stallion's back, he urged his mount to sidle up next to the corpse. Reaching up with his dagger he cut through the tenacious line.

The body flopped over Loftus' shoulder, Myron catching it before it hit the ground. By the stench and the limpness of the corpse, rigor mortis had long passed, and this person had to have died a good three or four days prior.

As the others stood back, Silas reached down, loosening the silken noose wrapped around the neck. He drew back the black cloth, freeing the head.

"Who is he?" asked Rose.

"*He* is a *she*," announced Rainus. He was inwardly stunned by this revelation.

"I know this woman!" grasped Silas. He brushed the tangled shock of white hair from the face now frozen in a permanent grimace of pain.

"You do? Who is she?" asked Myron.

"Her name was Malis... Malis Ravensee. She was the leader of a Witches' coven that dwells in a sleepy little hollow on the outskirts of a village called Home."

"Home? That sounds familiar," said Rose.

"That's where we first met Rupert and Molly Cottle," reminded Tag, thinking back on how Rose insulted Molly's 'peasant' style of cooking, only to devour her venison stew after that first taste.

"Oh, yes! I remember now," said Rose. More than this couple, she remembered Tag's ill-fated purchase in this village. The Gnome Positioning Service, or G.P.S. as he called it, that proved to be less than stellar.

"Never mind that," grunted Percy, as he addressed the Wizard. "Malice Ravensee, you say? That sounds like an appropriate name for a Witch, if ever there was one."

"I said, *Mah-lis,* you fool, not malice! She was a respected leader amongst her people. She practiced in healing spells and herbal remedies and such that ails mankind."

"Who would do this to her, if she was one of the good ones?" asked Rose.

Peeling the hair matted by dried blood off her forehead, Silas reveals the mark of a serpent devouring its tail crudely carved onto her forehead. Within this circle was an equally crude star. "This is the mark of Sin Mourningstar. She did this to Malis."

"We shall return her body to her people," said Rainus. "Perhaps if they did not meet the same fate, they will be eager to share news that will help to capture Sin and avenge their leader's death."

"That is a worthy idea." Silas nodded in agreement. "We shall return her body to her people, so they may grieve her death and celebrate her life."

"Carry her back? That stinking corpse?" gasped Percy. His face screwed up in utter disgust. "I may have the largest and strongest horse of all, but there is no room on my mount for that dead body!"

"Fear not, Prince Percival," said Halen. "I will construct a litter for this purpose."

"I will help you," offered Loftus. "If it helps to speed us on our way, I will be glad to give you a hand, Captain Ironwood."

"I'll cut some of this spider silk," said Tag, pulling out his dagger. "I think it's more than strong enough to tie the branches we'll need to make this carrier."

"Good thinking," praised Silas. "The faster we can be done, the sooner we can move on."

"What can we do to help?" asked Harold, turning to Rainus for instruction.

"While Myron and I scout on ahead to make sure there are no other traps lying in wait, you and Rose shall tend to the horses, take them down to that creek over yonder. Water them now while there is time."

"Consider it done, Lord Silverthorn," said Harold, as he and Rose gathered their mounts.

"Well then, looks like everyone has something to do," said Percy. "No point in me getting in the way."

"You have a job to do, too, Prince Percival," said Silas, as he marched over to one of the packhorses.

"What is that?"

"You will help me."

"With what?"

The Wizard removed a rolled up tarp from his saddle. "You will help me wrap the body in this, to transport poor Malis back to her kin."

The colour drained from Percy's face as the mere thought of handling this rotting corpse made his stomach churn.

Silas led the way, escorting his comrades toward the small village of Raven's Hollow with Percy's great warhorse taking up the rear. Much to the Prince's chagrin a litter carrying Malis' body was lashed to his mount. A gasp rippled through the party as an ephemeral mist hugging the ground took on the acrid smell of smoke. It swirled, rolling away in their wake as they entered the village. Against the twilight they spied upon a scattering of simple huts that lay in ruin. What was not destroyed by an incredible force was consumed by fire; wisps of smoke continued to drift lazily into the deepening sky.

"It is strangely quiet," whispered Rose, appalled by the destruction to greet their eyes.

"Unnaturally so," agreed Silas. He brought his horse to a stop.

"It does not look at all promising," noted Halen, searching about for signs of life. "If there were any to survive this carnage, I am sure they have moved on."

"Well then, let us just dump this body; be on our way," suggested Percy, wanting nothing more than to be done with this onerous task. "Allow nature to take its course."

"Malis Ravensee was an honourable woman," said Silas. "She was respected by her kinfolk and by the mortals of Home and beyond, for she opened up her apothecary to all needing her help. She did not reserve her kindness to only her people. If there is no one left to give her a decent burial, then we will do so."

"We will?" said Percy.

"Quiet!" ordered Rainus, pressing an index finger to his lips as he motioned for silence.

"Why am I always the one being told to be quiet?" muttered Percy, unleashing a disgruntled sigh.

"Shut it," demanded Rainus. He cocked his head as he stared at one of the huts. The damage was extensive: fallen walls leaned to one side; its roof collapsed and imploded on the structure; the door and window shutters ripped from its hinges by an incredible force.

"You hear that too?" asked Halen, gazing at the ruined cottage Rainus was scrutinizing.

He and Rainus dismounted, sprinting over to the demolished home.

With light, quick steps, Halen scrambled over the toppled remains of one of the walls to peer through a dark opening ripped into the roof. He jumped back as a hand burst through this hole, reaching out to him.

"There is someone trapped inside!" shouted Halen, motioning for the others to come to his aid.

All, with the exception of Percy, were quick to dismount. They abandoned their horses, dashing over to the Elves to lend a hand.

Working swiftly, they lifted the layers and chunks of heavy sod roofing and the shattered beams that once supported it.

Calling upon the powers of his crystal, Silas held it aloft, allowing its radiant glow to shine down on what was left of this crumpled abode.

"There! In the corner," cried the Wizard, spying movement through the settling dust as the sounds of a sobbing child caught his attention.

"Salvation!" cried a woman's voice, even as the smaller of the two children huddled in this tight corner, clung to her in fear of these strangers.

"Worry not, child," said Silas, in a soothing voice. "You are safe now. We are here to help."

"Thank you! Thank you for rescuing us!" cried the woman. "We've been trapped in here going on to three days now, I think."

Silas lowered the crystal to illuminate three tear-streaked, dirt-smudged faces staring up at him, squinting in the glare of his light.

"Meerah Ravensee? Is that you?" asked Silas, reaching his hand down to the woman.

"Silas Agincor?"

"Indeed!" answered the Wizard, pleased to see a familiar face.

"I've never been so happy to see you," exclaimed Meerah. Instead of taking his hand, she lifted up the weeping child, the younger of the two girls, in her company. "Take her first, and then her sister."

When the three survivors were safely removed from the collapsed shell of a cottage, they joined in the search for others. For as many burned remains they discovered in the homes that were razed, they found almost as many trapped in the ones that were destroyed by magic.

After gathering the living, while Rainus and Halen helped to heal the injuries of the survivors, the others set up their tents as temporary shelters for the worst of the wounded. Harold and Rose were kept busy passing around ladles of water to the thirsty. When this was done, the pair began scavenging for whatever foods they could find from the demolished pantries and root cellars. They gathered enough provisions for Harold to create a simple venison stew to serve with the loaves of stale bread they found. It was enough to feed Meerah and the twelve survivors, as well as their rescue party.

Still reeling from the devastation of their homes, the villagers slowly came to their senses. They sat huddled around a great bonfire, eating their meal in silence, struggling to make sense of the harrowing events of late. There was barely a sound to be heard as the wounded now rested peacefully, recovering quickly with the aid of the Elves' healing powers.

Silas stared at all the distraught faces, many still caked with dirt streaked by tears that fell from eyes still haunted by the violence that led to the demise of more than half their people. However, the one the Wizard hoped to speak to could not be found amongst this small crowd.

He glanced over to where the horses had been picketed for the night. There she was. Meerah Ravensee was standing next to the litter still carrying the tarp-wrapped corpse.

"That's her, isn't it?" asked Meerah. She sensed Silas' presence without even looking to see. "That's my sister."

Silas nodded. "Yes, that is Malis."

"Thank you for returning her home, not that there's a home to return to now."

"What happened here?" asked Silas.

"*Sin* is what happened."

"She was here?"

"That monster appeared out of nowhere, demanding that our coven be hers; that we denounce Malis as our leader; accepting Sin Mourningstar as the Grand Witch, one to unite all the covens."

"And Malis declined," said Silas.

"Yes… we all did, but she paid with her life, standing up to Sin to defy her."

"Is that what happened here? All this death and destruction?"

"Sin was far more powerful than Malis had anticipated, even with our combined powers," said Meerah, resting a comforting hand gently on her sister's shoulder. "We should have anticipated the worst when she came with her brother's damned crystal."

"It would hardly have been a fair fight," said Silas.

"She knew the dangers when that old hag wielded the powers of a Sorcerer's crystal, but it was more than that. Sin conjured the powers of the forbidden arts, one that any decent Witch in her right mind would steer clear off."

"That would certainly explain the level of destruction," said Silas, glancing over to what little remained of their village. "As great as Malis was, she did not stand a chance against one so powerful."

"My sister was more skilled than most of her years, but that bitch of a Witch... Sin challenged her, treating the whole thing like it was a game to her; a test of skills and magic: winner takes all."

"In this deadly game of crones, Malis was the loser," said Silas.

"My sister lost her life protecting us, but her nemesis *did not* win. Sin defeated Malis, but when she realized we would still not side with her in this war she plans to wage against you and the Council of Wizards. We were ready to choose death than to join her. In the end, Sin came away with nothing."

"So she made off with Malis' body to punish you, and to use as a warning to all the Witches, far and wide, to expect terrible retribution for denying her," determined Silas.

"Yes," Meerah said with a nod of confirmation. "Sin made it clear that even if we refused to join in her efforts, the other covens will come to fear her once she was done with us."

"No wonder the coven leaders were so willing to funnel details of Sin's whereabouts to my brotherhood."

"We all know that Witch is insane. She will not stop at half measures to get what she wants. Sin is not satisfied with just ruling over the covens. Ultimately, she wants to destroy the Wizards, you included, once she attains greater powers through dark magic."

"There is no doubt she is single-minded in her approach, but this obsessive determination driven by an insane mind is proving to be a deadly combination."

"Before Sin vanished with my dear sister, she declared that she would make an example of Malis, a stern and terrible warning to all, of what they can expect, if they refuse to take a knee before her."

"That would explain the very public display and the clever trap that would likely decapitate anyone rushing in to investigate or take Malis' body down for burial.

"Sin did warn us that anyone wishing to foolishly touch Malis' body would likely lose their heads in doing so. Now we know from you her words were true."

"What will you do now, Meerah Ravensee?"

"I shall take over for my sister. I will lead our people."

"And your first order of business?" asked Silas, watching as Meerah removed the tarp to look upon her dead sister's face, now frozen in anguish.

"Revenge," said Meerah. This word was spoken with unsettling calm, as she stared at Sin's mark of the serpent and star carved into Malis' forehead. "I will have my revenge."

12

An Eye for an Eye

Against the glare of the morning sun Rainus spied upon Captain Ironwood as he made final preparations. "Are we set to go, Halen?"

"Yes, the horses are ready. All we require had been packed. With the others lending a hand, I even had time to do a final healing session for those unfortunate souls still requiring it."

"Very good," Rainus nodded in gratitude to Halen. "Now, all we need to do is gather our comrades; resume our hunt for that crazy Witch."

"As we speak, our friends are breaking their morning fast, but our problematic prince is running behind, as usual."

"How so?" Rainus glanced over to where Percy was sitting next to Rose by the campfire.

The young man was complaining loudly about eating porridge instead of a hot and hearty meal of sausages, perfectly poached eggs served with buttered toast for dipping into warm, velvety yolk.

"I thought he woke with the others," said Rainus.

"He did, but he was in a foul mood to start with, for having been made by Silas to give up his private tent last night. Even though it was used as a place of healing for the most injured, the Prince was rather incensed he was ousted from his home away from home."

"So he complains because he was made to sleep under the stars, like the rest of us?" questioned Rainus.

"Yes, but worse than that, he made a terrible fuss this morning when he discovered he had an unwelcome visitor as he slept."

"Do tell!" Rainus' brows arched up in surprise. He was eager to hear more of Percy's latest tale of woe. "I was awake for most of last night, but I saw none intruding on our camp."

"It was not a person."

Rainus frowned in bewilderment upon hearing Halen's words.

"That mortal had the misfortune of having a slug crawl across his head as he slept."

"Interesting!"

"Yes, and this was no ordinary slug. It was one of those woodland species that grow yay big," announced Halen, holding his hand open to indicate the slimy gastropod was longer than the span of his palm.

"That would make for one snotty mess in his perfect head of hair."

"That was not the worst of it," confided Halen.

"What can be worse than that?"

"You will see for yourself," answered Halen.

"See?"

"Oh, yes, for it is hard to miss. That slug left more than a trail of slime as it crawled to and fro across those golden tresses."

"No!" gasped Rainus.

"Yes! The giant slug became impossibly tangled as the heat emanating from that mortal's noggin as he slept caused the trapped animal to shrivel up and die."

"On his head?"

"It was dried to the consistency of shoe leather, matting to his head just so." Halen demonstrated by scrunching up a fistful of his perfect hair.

"Disgusting!" declared Rainus.

"Yes, so much so that he shrieked like a child when he made the discovery, begging Princess Rose to remove it!"

"So that was the hideous sound I heard this morning," said Rainus, thinking he had heard a frightened child. "And knowing the Princess, she refused to touch it. Is that not so?"

"Yes. She was so repulsed, refusing to detangle the slug from his hair that Captain Loftus felt it necessary to intervene on her behalf."

"He took the time to *pick* the slug out of his tresses?"

"Captain Loftus took the opportunity to remove the slug, but he did not believe in wasting time. He took his hunting knife, using it to cut free the dead slug, and all the hair matted to it."

"And that was the second cry of anguish I heard this morning," determined Rainus.

"Indeed," said Halen. "After practically begging for someone, *anyone*, to remove the slug, Prince Percival was just as horrified by the aftermath. When he was done threatening Captain Loftus, and he could not find you during your inspection of the village perimeter, the Prince came to me. He demanded I use my healing powers to regrow that missing clump of hair Captain Loftus had unceremoniously hacked off."

"The young mortal is as vain as he is pompous," declared Rainus. "Of course, I told him that neither his head nor his hair was injured. A bad haircut is something that will remedy itself over time, but he basically accused me of denying him; of refusing to come to his aid during his darkest hour."

"Oh, my! He is quite the dramatic prig."

"To call him a prig is an insult to all the other prigs of the world," laughed Halen. "In the meantime, I strongly recommend *not* bursting out in a fit of laughter when you see the back of his head."

"It is that bad?"

"Captain Loftus was not gentle with his blade. It looks as though his head was attacked and mauled upon by a deranged goat."

"That is very descriptive."

"My words do this abomination no justice. In time, you will see for yourself," said Halen. "As mortified as Prince Percival was by this whole ordeal, I do believe it to be divine justice. This is his comeuppance for making such a fuss about relinquishing his tent for those who needed it more."

"Perhaps you are right, my friend," said Rainus. "It seems a fitting punishment for one so self-centred and egotistical."

Halen glanced over to those gathered around the fire, watching as his comrades rose onto their feet, while Percy remained stubbornly seated. With the bowl of now cold, congealing porridge in hand, even with the cream and dollop of honey to make it more palatable, he continued to complain.

"I believe Master Agincor and the others are ready to proceed," announced Halen.

"Let us join them in bidding farewell to our unfortunate hosts," suggested Rainus, motioning for Halen to come along.

"I see the horses are ready," said Silas. He nodded in greeting to the Elves as they joined him by the dwindling campfire.

"Yes, we should leave now," said Rainus, "take advantage of the light of day."

"You heard Lord Silverthorn," announced Silas. He clapped his hands, motioning his friends on to their mounts. "We make ready."

"But I have not yet finished eating this slop," protested Percy. "Had I a proper silver spoon, I would have been done by now. This wooden one is much too cumbersome to eat with, never mind the risk of slivers."

"Did you eat at least half of it?" asked Silas.

"I believe I choked down about that much. Why?"

Silas raised the end of his staff, knocking the bowl from Percy's grip. It hit the ground, dumping what was left to splatter his fine riding boots in the process.

Percy's mouth fell open in rage, while Tag's eyes opened wide in surprise as he watched this interaction.

Picking up the bowl, the impatient Wizard placed it back in Percy's hands. "Well, it looks empty now, my lord. You are done. Now we leave."

"But- but- " stammered Percy, his face turning many shades of red as his anger began to boil over.

"Worry not," urged Rose. She spoke gently in a bid to quiet his temper. "You already said how much you hated porridge. I have some dried fruit you can nibble on, should you get hungry before our next meal. Now, come along. We have a quest to undertake."

"Hurry!" ordered Silas, ushering them to their horses. "Our quarry waits for no one. We leave while the day is young."

As Percy tossed the empty bowl and spoon over his shoulder, he jumped to his feet. Like an ill-tempered child having a tantrum, he pushed by the Wizard. Stomping angrily by the Elves, he marched away to claim his horse.

Rainus' eyes opened wide as he slapped a hand over his mouth to stifle his laughter. True to Halen's words the back of Percy's head looked as bad as he had claimed. It was as though a blind barber equipped with dull shears had massacred his scalp.

"Not a word," muttered Silas, pressing an index finger to his lips as he addressed the surprised Elf. "We can ill afford another delay should Prince Percival demand time to preen."

"Yes," agreed Halen. "And it shall take a whole lot of preening to undo that atrocity of a hairdo."

"He has not seen the extent of the damage to his glorious head of hair?" whispered Rainus.

"Not yet, but who cares?" answered Silas. "Even Princess Rose downplays the extent of Captain Loftus' handiwork, all in a bid to spare his ego."

"Well, as we venture north and the winds begin to blow, I am sure he will find out when his *ego* gets cold from that missing clump of hair," said Rainus.

As the companions mounted up, Meerah shouted out, "Wait! Wait, Silas! I have something for you!"

"It better not be more of that disgusting porridge," grumbled Percy.

"I have a gift for you, to aid you on this quest!"

Silas raised his hand, motioning for Percy's silence as Meerah approached, followed by her people joining in to bid farewell to this fellowship.

"There is no need to repay us for doing what common sense and compassion dictates, Meerah," said Silas, bowing his head in respect to the Witch.

"No need to be hasty, old man!" ordered Percy. "It could be gold or jewels she offers."

Silas shot a baleful glance in his direction.

"I know! I know! Shut up, right?" Percy grumbled as his eyes rolled in frustration.

"What gift, my dear woman?" asked the Wizard. He stared at the small ceramic container cupped in Meerah's hands. A cork seal covered the mouth of this jar she presented to him.

"While you and your comrades broke your fast this morn, my sister Witches and I had been hard at work. We gathered what supplies we could salvage to conjure up a special potion and enchantment that will aid you in your search for Sin Mourningstar."

"Ooh! I'm intrigued," said Harold. He hovered over Silas' shoulder to take a peek. "What's in there?"

Meerah placed the container into the palm of the Wizard's hand as she spoke. "Open it, Silas, for this will help you see the way when you need it the most."

Passing his staff on to Harold to free up this hand, the Wizard pried off the cork seal.

Peering inside, he recoiled. A pungent odour wafted out to assault his senses. Bobbing to the surface of this briny solution was a single, round, bloodstained object.

Harold jumped back, yelping in horror as a bloodshot eye of cloudy green stared up at him.

"What the heck is that?" gasped Harold.

"It's an eye, of course," answered Meerah. Rubbing her gnarled hands in glee, she was pleased to present this gift to the Dream Merchant.

"We can see that, no pun intended," said Rose. She glanced at the faces of the survivors clustered around Meerah, searching for the one that had donated an eyeball. "But I am afraid to ask who it belonged to."

"This is Malis' eye." Silas spoke with all certainty as he glanced up at Meerah.

"Indeed!" The Witch nodded.

"You removed her eye?" gasped Myron.

"Malis is in a wonderland of her own making now," responded Meerah, with a shrug of her bony shoulders. "It's not like she needs this anymore."

"And just what are we to do with that disgusting thing?" asked

Percy, grimacing in repulsion. "We are in no need of a memento of your late sister on our travels."

Silas raised his hand for silence.

"Yes, yes! I know… Shut up," muttered Percy, speaking up before the Wizard could issue an order.

"Please ignore Prince Percival's rudeness, Meerah," apologized Silas. "I know this is more than a memento, but what am I do with this?"

"As I said, we were able to salvage some of our supplies from the ruins of our homes. After removing my sister's left eye –"

"Her better seeing eye," chirped up one of the survivors.

"Yes," said Meerah. "We bathed it in a special brine solution that included some secret ingredients."

"That sounds rather dubious. What kind of *secret* ingredients?" questioned Percy.

"The kind that'll get you killed, if you pry," answered Meerah. "Just know this brine will not only keep it preserved, but with a magical spell, it will be the perfect aid to help you locate my sister's killer."

"So, it has been imbued with magic?" asked Myron, staring back at the eyeball that bobbed about in the jar.

"That is correct, Sir Kendall," responded Meerah.

"But how does it work?" asked Tag.

"A very good question, young sir! What do you think is the last thing my sister saw as her life was stolen from her?"

"I imagine it had to be her killer," answered Tag.

"Yes," said Meerah, with a nod. "The image of Sin Mourningstar has been forever burned into this eye. Because we use the powers of the natural forces, whether it is by moonlight or sunlight, just ask it: Where is Sin? This eye will show you the way to that vile murderess."

"It is like a divinin' rod, but to find an evil Witch, instead of water," assessed Harold. He was barely able to look at this eye that stared up at him.

"Well said!" praised Meerah, nodding to the large mortal.

"And it works?" asked Rainus.

"Test it now," urged the Witch.

Silas changed his angle, holding up the jar so the morning sun shone upon it. In a clear, steady voice he asked, "Where is Sin?"

He and his comrades watched in morbid fascination as the eyeball suddenly rolled onto its side. The torn optic nerve that once kept it anchored into the eye socket began to sweep back and forth, like the tail of a tadpole. In an eerie, supernatural display, the eyeball bumped against the side of the jar. It repeatedly and stubbornly bounced and pressed against the container.

"Hey! It does work!" exclaimed Harold.

Rainus glanced up to the sun, and then gazed over to the distant mountains. "The eye is *looking* to the north."

"Excellent!" cheered Rose. "I get the feeling this will work much better than that silly G.P.S. Tag tried to use during our first trek to those dreadful lands."

"What's a G.P.S.?" asked Harold, as he stared quizzically at her.

"It stands for Gnome Positioning Service," explained Tag. "We hired a Gnome, one familiar with the lay of the land to the north, to show us the way. It worked just fine!"

"Yes, as long as you had plenty of root vegetables to feed him in exchange for directions," reminded Rose.

"What happens should you run out?" asked Percy.

"I imagine he would have conveniently stopped showing us the way, but an eagle swooped down, plucking up the little fellow before we reached our destination," said Rose.

"That's horrible!" gasped Harold.

"Lucky for him, Lord Silverthorn and his men were not far behind, saving the Gnome before he became food for a nest of eaglets," added Tag.

"Yes, I get the sense this enchanted eyeball will work much better," said Silas, as he nodded in thanks to Meerah. "Already, it shows the way and it will not make demands upon us."

"Hogwash!" Percy grunted as he gave the Wizard and the Witch a dismissive wave of his hand. "I believe it was mere coincidence that dreadful thing turned in the direction we were already heading."

To challenge Percy's scepticism, Silas held forth this jar for him to see. He slowly turned away from the sun so his back was facing the north. Gradually, this eyeball continued to stare northward, its optic nerve of a tail wiggling about, swimming to correct its direction no matter which way Silas turned.

"I'll be damned!" exclaimed Loftus, watching with keen interest. "Look, my lord! You were wrong once again. And consider yourself lucky when the Wizard asked *where is Sin*, that it did not turn to you!"

"Keep up with this demonstration of insolence and you'll be *damned* all right!" snapped Percy, shaking an angry fist at the captain.

"You've got to admit, Prince Percival, this really does work!" declared Harold. He pointed at the magical eyeball wilfully directing them to head to the north. "Look at that little thing go! If it wasn't so ugly, it'd almost be cute!"

"Yes, yes!" Percy waved off Harold's enthusiasm. "I am both

amazed and repulsed, much like when I first set eyes on you."

"So you agree it works?" asked Silas, placing the lid over the mouth of the jar.

"Whether I do, or do not, what difference does it make?" muttered Percy. He rolled his shoulders with obvious indifference. "Even if I said I wholeheartedly believed this was nothing more than a cheap parlour trick, it would hardly matter. You and your loyal cohorts will do whatever you want, even if common sense dictates this whole magic eyeball thing is just a bunch of malarkey."

"This eye will guide us, telling us exactly where we must go." Silas patted the jar. "If you do not wish to follow, then I invite you to find your own way home from here."

"I will not leave my beloved in the company of a bunch of witless rabble-rousers!" snapped Percy. "I will journey on, but only to keep her safe from harm."

"We shall see how long you last," grumbled Silas. "If you thought a lowly slug was dreadful to deal with, wait until you see what deadly creatures lurk far to the north."

"Ha!" snorted Percy, with a shake of his head. "Do not issue hollow threats to dissuade me, Wizard. I am no fool. I remember you stating that the great dragons of the Fire Rim Mountains are in the throes of hibernation, immersed in a deep slumber as the chill of autumn settles upon the lands and winter's icy embrace threatens to come early in those places to the north."

"Nice try, Master Agincor," said Tag, giving Silas a consoling pat on his shoulder. "I suppose there are some details that were better not shared with this dolt of a coward."

"If I was such a '*dolt*', then why did I remember this important detail?" argued Percy, as he glared menacingly at Tag.

"Oh, I don't know… Maybe because cowards tend to remember what frightens them the most," mocked Tag.

"Stop it!" cried Rose. "I have no desire to venture to the north in pursuit of the Witch, but I have no choice, if we are to stop that vile soul. If you do not wish to proceed, I understand, Prince Percy. Before we journey too far for you to travel safely on your own, perhaps it is better for you to turn back."

"Fear not, my dear Rose-alyn," insisted Percy. "I have endured far worse things than dragons."

"Like what? Cold porridge?" snorted Tag. "What can be worse than dragons?"

"You and your cohorts, that's what!" snapped Percy. "All of you, perhaps with the exception of the Elves in present company and

Princess Rose-alyn, of course, have been insufferable to the extreme."

"*We're* insufferable?" gasped Tag.

"Incredibly so, but it has made me even more determined to carry on, just to spite you all!"

"Now there's a fine motivator, if ever there was one," grumbled Loftus, shaking his head in embarrassment at his bombastic charge.

"Well, Captain Loftus, we shall test your prince's fortitude as we journey on," responded Silas.

"I wish you well," bade Meerah. "May you be protected on your journey; find success on this quest; and return safely to your respective homes."

"Thank you, my friend," said Silas. "This gift will help speed up the search for Sin."

"Yes, my sister's eye will be your guide when the way is lost," promised Meerah. "I pray you catch that one-eyed crone, and when you do, show her no mercy."

"Though she is not worthy of mercy, I will not be the one to dispense punishment on her," said Silas, glancing at the solemn faces of the survivors. "She will be made to answer for her crimes before my brotherhood. They shall decide her fate."

"So you say, but if Sin should die by *accident*, by your hands or another, she is deserving of death, where my sister was not," growled Meerah. She waved farewell to Silas and his party as her foreboding words chased behind them. "An eye for an eye, Silas! Do you hear me? An eye for an eye! Remember that!"

Harold frowned upon hearing this Witch's ominous words. He leaned over, whispering to the Wizard, "Was that a pun? Or was she serious?"

"She was being serious, my friend," assured Silas, "deadly serious."

"Why do we not stick to the trails?" grumbled Percy. His impatience swelled. He was forced to duck beneath yet another low-hanging bough as his steed followed the others plodding along behind Silas' horse as it wove between the trees. "It would make for easier travel, that is for sure."

When Percy's griping went ignored by Silas, Rose felt compelled to placate his mounting agitation.

"I am sure Master Agincor will say it is because, according to the hexed eyeball, this is most direct route to deliver us to Sin," explained Rose.

"That may be so, but I firmly believe if we had stuck to the well-travelled roads and trails, even if it took us farther out of the way, it would still make for a faster journey than to negotiate these dense forests," complained Percy. He shuddered in repulsion as he ducked in time to avoid riding into a wisp of a tattered spider web.

"You are welcome to take to those well-used trails you think so highly of," invited Rainus. "Just be warned though, if the trap we encountered where we found Malis' body is any indication, there may well be others set along the way, possibly even more deadly and elaborate than the first."

"So, you are saying we should be safer going out of our way to avoid established trails and roads?" asked Percy.

"That is our intention," answered Rainus. "It is a plan I continue to agree with."

"But even I know the best laid plans can go awry," countered Percy. His smug tone served to reflect his know-it-all attitude.

"True enough, but we are confident we lessen the chances of encountering one of Sin's traps in taking a route seldom, if ever, travelled."

"A safer route, even if it is more arduous, makes sense to us, even if it makes little sense to you," said Tag. "But what do you know about the perils of such a quest?"

Percy chose to ignore Tag's snide tone, instead, addressing Rainus once more. "Will we be stopping for the night any time soon?"

"Are you getting weary?"

"Of course I am not tired! I can go on well into the night, if that is what I desire."

"Then perhaps we should keep riding until the moon is high?" responded Rainus. "It promises to be a clear night. We can go far."

"I have the stamina of an Elf! I can last as long as you can, if I must. However, I am worried Princess Rose-alyn is growing weary with all the hours and leagues we have travelled on this day."

"It is so kind of you to think of me," said Rose. Touched by Percy's concern, she offered him a grateful smile.

"As your intended husband, it is my sworn duty to think *of* you and *for* you," said Percy, sounding like a gallant knight. He flashed her a dashing smile, all the while, inwardly praying that she would not insist on riding late into the night for the sake of the others. "A delicate flower must be cared for, not subjected to all manner of neglect and abuse, if it is to flourish."

"Delicate flower! The Princess? I think not!" scoffed Tag. His eyes rolled in ridicule. "In fact, I'm pretty confident she can beat the snot out of you, if you get her riled enough."

"Never mind him," urged Rose. She scowled at Tag as she glanced over her shoulder. "It has been a long day, and in this deep forest, it will be dark very soon."

Silas reined in his mount as Halen raised his left hand, motioning for all to stop. Without question, the procession came to a halt as the Wizard pried the cork seal off the jar. Holding it before him, he asked the enchanted eyeball, "Where is Sin?"

In response, the ghastly orb that was staring up at the Wizard suddenly rolled onto its side. The optic nerve, serving as both a rudder and propeller, wiggled to and fro in response. This time, instead of staring directly north, the eye veered slightly to the northeast. And then just as suddenly, it switched course, circling about before staring to the northwest.

"This is odd," commented Silas. He watched the eyeball as it repeatedly bumped against the side of the jar, swimming about as though it had momentarily lost its bearings.

Halen glanced in the direction the eye was staring to now, and then he gazed over to the westering sun. "By my estimation, the eye is staring off to the northwest."

"Apparently not," said Silas. He watched as the stringy *tail* whipped about, adjusting its course so it stared directly to the north once more.

"What is going on up there?" shouted Percy.

Silas unleashed a disgruntled sigh. As he placed the cork lid back into place, Malis' eye rolled up, staring vacantly at its dark surroundings once again.

"In need of a break to relieve yourself again, Wizard?" asked Percy, with a snort of derision.

"Why do you not *relieve* me of your silly questions, Prince Percival? Do you mean to test my patience?" snapped Silas.

"No need to get testy, old man," muttered Percy. "I was just curious as to why we had come to a stop in the middle of nowhere."

"I merely wished to ascertain that we are still heading in the right direction."

"Well?" Percy's voice tightened with his mounting impatience.

"Well, what?" grumbled the Wizard.

"Are we still on the hag's trail?" asked Percy.

Silas dismounted as he answered, "It appears so, but as you are so sceptical where Meerah's powers are concerned, perhaps that eye is not enchanted at all. It could just be bobbing about haphazardly, pointing northward consistently, but only by coincidence."

"Do not be so quick to discount my scepticism just because I am a man of science, one driven by logic, while you are hindered by beliefs steeped in age-old superstition and stupid, antiquated beliefs supported by dodgy magic."

"Age-old superstition?" muttered Silas. "Stupid beliefs?"

"Yes, it is *stupidstition* to believe in and base your actions on such foolish things in this day and age," insisted Percy.

"That is not even a real word," grumbled Silas.

"As a real prince, I have the power to create new words as I see fit."

"More like the audacity, than the power, to corrupt the common speech as we know it," countered the Wizard.

"So you say, but in the end, mine may well be the voice of reason to keep us alive," stated Percy.

Silas shrugged with indifference as he passed the jar to Halen for safekeeping. He then turned, walking away from his party.

"Where are you going now?" Percy demanded to know.

"I am going to relieve myself."

"Of my silly questions?"

"I wish! I am going to take a piss, not that it is any of your business," muttered the Wizard. He wandered off, ducking behind a great pine tree for some much-needed privacy, but most of all, to get away from this mortal's incessant nattering.

While Silas answered the call of nature, Rainus stared at the sun sinking low on the horizon. He then glanced up through the tree canopy to the deepening sky.

"This is as good a place as any to set up camp for the night," decided Rainus, glancing over to a small clearing to his right.

"Well, huzzah!" said Percy, in mock cheer. He hopped down from his mount before the Elf could change his mind. "It is about bloody time."

"I thought you said you could ride on through the night," said Rainus.

"So I did, but I was only thinking of my lovely bride-to-be. Princess Rose-alyn has spent more time riding on the back of a horse than humanly possible for a lady of her fine pedigree. Any longer and I would consider it a brand of torture."

"It is kind of you to say," said Rose. She smiled in approval to her prince as she waited for Harold to help lift her down from her mare as she learned it was a task Percy considered menial and would repeatedly pass on to others. "I agree with Lord Silverthorn that we should make ready for the coming of night, while we have the waning light of day to work by."

"I shall help Harold ready our horses for the night," offered Loftus. Eager to be free of his royal charge, he hopped down, gathering up the reins of her mare and Percy's steed.

"I shall assist Halen with erecting your tent," said Rainus. He was quick to pick a task that would not pair him with Percy.

"I'll give you hand," offered Myron, as he turned to Tag, Rose and Percy. "The three of you can get to work on preparing a fire pit and collecting wood to last us through the night."

"It will be done," promised Tag.

Throwing his pack over his shoulder, Tag marched off to a sizeable clearing as Rose followed him. Glancing about, he searched for the ideal location to scrape out a fire pit.

Tag made sure there was adequate clearance so the flames would not set overhanging tree branches ablaze. He also checked that there was an opening in the canopy directly above to allow the smoke to rise unimpeded, than to be trapped, building up around them at ground level.

As Tag began to scrape away at the dried leaves and pine needles to expose bare ground, Rose offered to collect rocks to place around the pit to keep the fire contained.

"Good idea." Tag nodded to Rose. Peering up, he spied on Percy picking at his teeth, still standing where they had left him. "While we do this, why don't you start gathering firewood?"

"Me?" asked Percy. He looked momentarily gobsmacked; appalled this twit of a pauper would see fit to appoint a menial task to him.

"No!" snapped Tag. His voice bristled with sarcasm as his eyes rolled in frustration. "I was speaking to that squirrel right next to you."

Percy jumped. He glanced down, searching for this rodent as he yelped in surprise.

"I was speaking in jest. And why are you so scared of a harmless, little squirrel, anyway?" queried Tag, as he used a broad, flat piece of tree bark to clear the ground of debris.

"It carries parasites, possesses sharp, nasty teeth, and quivers with nervous energy," answered Percy. "It is most disgusting!"

"Are you speaking of yourself?" asked Tag.

"Of course not! I was speaking of squirrels, in general."

"If you're scared that a squirrel will attack you, fear not, Prince Percival." Tag grinned with mischief. "A squirrel will only attack if you have nuts. Thus far, you have proven to have none."

"Do not mock me!" As Percy turned, stomping away from them, he shook an angry fist at his nemesis.

"Hey! Where do you think you're going?" hollered Tag, standing up to confront him. "There's work to be done."

"Yes, and I shall get to it when I am good and ready." Percy kept on walking.

"Get to work now!" demanded Tag.

"I will when I am done."

"Done what?"

"If you must know, I wish to go relieve myself first. And as I value my privacy, I am going to find a secluded place. One that is well away from *you* and your constant harping, where I can conduct my business in peace."

"Fine, then! Just don't wander off too far," ordered Tag. "Do you hear me?"

"I hear you, but I am not listening!" scoffed Percy.

"You better not wander away!"

"Are you worried I will get lost?"

"Personally, I wouldn't mind if you did. The only thing I am worried about is wasting valuable time searching for you."

"You are too funny!" Percy waved him off.

"I was being serious," stated Tag.

"Well, do not worry that ugly, little head of yours," grumbled Percy, as he stomped away. "I will return, and I shall do so with a great armload of firewood to last through the night."

"I'll believe it when I see it!" Tag hollered back, wishing for nothing more than to throw the piece of wood in his hand at Percy's head. Using the ugly patch of roughly shorn hair from where the tangled slug was removed, it would have made the perfect target to aim at.

With an indignant sigh, Percy marched off, heading in the opposite direction the Wizard had taken. Weaving through the stand of trees he searched for a secluded spot on the pretence of relieving himself. In reality, he wanted to find a quiet place to hide away while the others toiled.

Glancing over his shoulder, Tag and Rose had resumed preparing a place for their campfire. Looking toward the horses, Harold and Loftus were busy removing saddles and attaching feedbags of oats to each horse's head. Under the trees near to where Rose and Tag worked, Myron, Halen and Rainus readied his tent as Silas wandered back, stretching and yawning under this twilight sky.

Satisfied that all were too preoccupied to notice his absence, Percy ducked behind a towering fir tree. Settling down upon the carpet of dried needles, he was cradled between the gnarled tentacles of roots that formed the great buttress supporting this massive fir. Here, he would not be easy to spot. This was the perfect place to steal away for a quick nap. Once the fire was blazing and until the smell of dinner roasting over the flames wafted through the air to summon him, he planned to remain here, away from the prying eyes and the menial tasks he was never meant to undertake.

Percy unleashed a sigh of relief. Relaxing in the shadow of this towering tree, he wrapped his Elven cloak around his body. Swaddling himself in comfortable warmth, even against the chill of autumn hanging in the air, he marvelled at the ingenuity of this apparel. Though it made no statement of one's wealth or power like his regal, ermine and sable-lined cloak did, it was always perfectly warm, never too hot or too cool. Magically, it was constantly adjusting to his body heat and the ambient temperature no matter the time of day.

He closed his eyes, eager for sleep to whisk him far away from these primitive surroundings. Drifting off into a peaceful slumber, Percy's eyes snapped open. He bolted upright to a loud baritone accosting his senses.

"Prince Percival! Come out, come out, wherever you are!" Harold's voice boomed through the forest.

"Prince Percy, where are you?" hollered Rose. Her heart raced with the realization he was nowhere to be seen. "Come here right now!"

By the urgency in her voice he could tell she was on the verge of hysterics.

"I'm pretty sure he buggered off this way," called Tag. Jabbing his thumb over his shoulder to where he last saw Percy, as he waved Harold and Rose on to follow him.

Percy unleashed a groan of disappointment. Hearing Tag's voice, he knew his loathsome foe was closing in on his hiding place.

"Well, what do you know?" said Tag. He came around the tree to spy upon Percy struggling to sit upright.

"Were you asleep?" gasped Rose. She was appalled to find him swathed in his cloak and looking so comfy.

Percy shook off his drowsiness while trying his best to sound aghast. "What are you talking about?"

"You were here, sitting on your laurels; slacking off while the rest of us were busy setting up camp," admonished Tag.

"For shame, Prince Percival, for shame!" scolded Harold. Peering upon this young royal in his hiding place, he shook his head in disappointment, his badger headpiece shaking in agreement. "If you didn't want to help us, you should've just said so, instead of havin' us search for you, worryin' as we did."

"You are an inconsiderate idiot, that's what you are!" rebuked Tag, pointing an accusing finger at Percy. "Princess Rose was worried sick. She thought you had gotten yourself lost, or worse."

"Well, as you can see, I am *not* lost."

"Yes, you were just being lazy! So much for helping to gather firewood."

"I had started to."

"Really?" grunted Tag.

Percy held up a single stick he conveniently found by his side as he pretended to struggle to stand up.

"I was gathering wood, but this forest was dark to begin with and getting darker still. On this uneven terrain I had twisted my ankle. I was just resting, waiting for the pain to subside so I can return to camp on my own, than to bother any of you."

"You *are* a bother and a pain, and I'm not just speaking of that ankle of yours!" snorted Tag, doubting Percy's every word.

"Why didn't you just call for help?" asked Harold, watching as Percy gingerly stood up. Balancing on his left foot, he leaned against the tree trunk to lessen the weight on his right ankle.

"This is terrible," groaned Rose. "If the injury is severe, we will have to leave you behind, for your own safety, if Lord Silverthorn cannot help you."

"You will not wait until I'm fully healed?"

"We are on a mission. We wait for no one, especially for you!" snapped Tag.

"Perhaps Captain Loftus can be convinced to remain behind; escort you back to Axalon," said Rose. Her heart dropped to the pit of her stomach knowing that she and Percy were about to be separated by both fate and distance.

"I assure you, my dear, it is only a light sprain," lied Percy. "Wisely, I have been resting here, keeping my weight off it. I only feel twinges of pain every now and then, but luckily, because of my fast actions to prevent further aggravation to the injury, my ankle is not even swollen."

"That is wonderful, but instead of sitting out here all on your own, you really should have called for help," insisted Rose.

"Why? So this idiot friend of yours can harass me? Make light that I needed assistance? I think not! I would rather gouge out my eyes with a splintery, wooden spoon than to ask for his help."

"You are much too proud for your own good," stated Tag. "I can help *and* provide you with that dull spoon, if you like."

"You are a scoundrel of the worst kind," muttered Percy. "I do not need your help."

"Excellent!" said Tag. With a loud whistle, he alerted his comrades who had spread out. It was their signal to end the search; that their wayward interloper had been found.

"You!" called Percy, as he pointed at Harold. "Do be a lamb. Carry me back to our camp, will you?"

"I thought you said the sprain wasn't severe?" responded Tag. He watched in stunned disbelief as Harold willingly complied, easily scooping Percy into his arms like he was an overgrown baby.

"It is not severe at all. I just do not wish to put unnecessary stress on my ankle when I have this horse of a man to carry me about."

"Harold is not some beast of burden," argued Tag.

"I beg to differ!" sniffed Percy. He lay like a helpless child in Harold's large arms, his legs swinging to and fro in time to this man's rolling gait as they headed back to the inviting glow of the campfire. "He is a beast of a man and he can be a burden at times, so there!"

"That was not a nice thing to say," scolded Rose. She was taken aback by his condescending words directed toward their friend, even though Harold seemed oblivious to the insult.

"It was, if I meant it as a compliment," countered Percy. "Now, my big, beastly man, do be careful. Try not to bump my injured foot against any of these trees."

As Harold arrived with his passenger, Silas frowned upon their approach.

"What is the meaning of this?" asked the Wizard. "How dare you waste our time on a search for you?"

"Prince Percy cannot even take a piss without getting hurt," teased Tag, laughing as he sat down next to Myron.

"What happened?" asked Rainus, watching as Harold carefully seated Percy upon his saddle that now doubled for a chair before the campfire.

"Before this ruffian lies or exaggerates the truth, after I found a secluded place to relieve myself, I took on the task of helping to gather firewood."

"You were crippled by the weight of your armload?" questioned Silas.

"Yes!" declared Tag. "One measly twig of a stick almost broke his back when he tried to pick it up!"

"Fetch off!" demanded Percy. To lend emphasis to his imagined injury he gingerly rubbed his right ankle. "I will have you know, I had just begun collecting wood when I stumbled on the uneven ground in this dimming light."

"Truly?" responded Myron. His brows furrowed with doubt as he watched Percy favouring his foot.

"It can happen," said Harold. He knelt down before the fire, feeding it more wood. "I'm always stumblin' about, even when the ground is flat with nary a dip or hole in it."

"How badly hurt are you?" queried Myron.

"No thanks to Tag's harassing ways, my pride is now more wounded than my ankle," grumbled Percy. "Luckily, it is not that bad."

"Still, I should take a look," offered Rainus, rising from his place by the fire to come to his aid. "I can use my healing powers to lessen your pain, if nothing else."

Percy raised his hand to the Elf, motioning him to sit back down.

"It is kind of you to offer, Lord Silverthorn, but I assure you, it is not that bad at all. There is no swelling and even as we speak, the twinges of pain are beginning to subside."

"So, you will not be staying behind to recuperate while the rest of us move on at first light?" asked Myron.

"No, I shall journey on; finish what I had started."

"Damn!" muttered Tag, his fingers snapping in regret upon hearing Percy's declaration.

"If only to spite you," taunted Percy, as he sneered at Tag. "But I am a bigger man than you will ever be. I am determined to keep Princess Rose-alyn safe, as your incompetence continues to astound me."

"Suppose I astound you with a sound beating for being such a prig?" offered Tag, shaking a balled fist in his direction.

"It makes sense you would threaten me with blows when I am wounded and at my most vulnerable."

"I don't believe in lopsided fights," stated Tag. "I'd be fair and let you have the first few swings before I level you out."

"So you say, but I'm beginning to believe that old Witch. '*An eye for an eye,*' she said. If I had my way, I'd gouge out your eyes, throw them into that jar with the pickled eyeball, and then I'd abandon you in this forest, for good measure."

"Good gracious!" cried Harold. "I hardly think that's what Meerah meant when she said that."

"Oh, it was!" blustered Percy. "And this fool of a knave will get what he deserves."

"Stop it!" cried Rose. "We are heading toward danger. We do not need to be burdened by animosity."

"I agree," said Harold, as he sat down next to Halen. "It's goin' to be tough enough, but when friends are bickerin' amongst friends? It'll be worse!"

"Take comfort in this, my big man," said Percy, as he pointed at Tag, "that idiot is no friend of mine!"

"And I'd be an idiot indeed to ever consider the likes of you as a friend!" snapped Tag.

"I hate you!" growled Percy.

Rose glared at Tag. Her eyes flashed in anger, as though to warn him not to declare this hate was mutual.

"And I dislike you intensely," responded Tag.

"As far as I'm concerned, you two can hate each other all you want," said Loftus, pulling a bottle of wine from Percy's not-so-private stock. "I will not stand in your way, if you want to go at each other. Just know that if your animosity jeopardizes the rest of us, I'll gladly thump your heads together, in hopes it'll knock some sense into you both."

"Good plan!" praised Silas, nodding in gratitude to the captain. "I like your no-nonsense attitude."

Loftus nodded to the Wizard, passing the bottle of wine to him first to partake in a shared drink.

Silas happily accepted, taking a swig before passing it on to Tag.

"Here you go, my bellicose, young friend," said Silas. "Take the edge off your temper so calmer heads can prevail once more."

"Gladly!" said Tag. He gulped down a mouthful. Using the back of his hand to wipe away the dribble of wine from his chin, he held the bottle toward Percy. "Here you go, if you dare."

Percy glared at Tag. "I know what you are insinuating."

"You are so bloody paranoid! I'm not insinuating a thing. I'm just offering you a drink... from this lovely bottle." Tag shook the container at Percy as he goaded him on. "If anything, I'd just advise you to be careful."

With that said, Tag's lips protruded like a duck's bill, but swollen and distorted to boot.

"You dare mock me?" cried Percy.

"It cannot be a dare when it is so easy to do."

"Oh, my! This wine only serves to fuel your anger," muttered Silas. Snatching the bottle from Tag's grasp, the Wizard took another swig. "I anticipate a long and painful quest ahead of us."

Rose's hands clapped together to garner the attention of all.

Her anxiety mounted upon seeing the two people she cared for the most continue to clash. It would not be long before punches, instead of insults, would be thrown at one another.

"Master Agincor is quite correct. We have a long journey before us," stated Rose. "Perhaps you would be so kind as to tell us what we should expect, if our travels take us far north to the Sea of Shadows?"

Silas' demeanour changed as he passed the wine bottle to Myron. Leaning forward, even with the light of the campfire, his face became pensive; lined and shadowed as dark imaginings filled his mind. Immediately the mood of the camp was tempered, the anger gave way as they waited with bated breath for what the Wizard was about to reveal.

"Rarely does man or Elf survive, venturing that far to the north, let alone set foot in the lands surrounded by the Fire Rim Mountains," said Silas, his tone strangely foreboding.

"But why? Is it because they die before they get there?" asked Harold. His eyes widened as he hung on the Wizard's every word. "I mean, I know there's those big, nasty dragons between here and there, but is that the only reason those lands are rarely travelled?"

"When the Fire Rim Mountains are lashed by the cruel winds of winter, indeed, the dragons are of no concern, but when these reptiles are up and about, they pose a deadly threat indeed."

Rainus nodded to Harold as he spoke, "Trust me when I say the mere thought of these treacherous beasts roaming about poses a serious deterrent to all with any common sense daring to enter those lands."

"This does not speak well of the company you keep, Lord Silverthorn," commented Percy. With a shake of his head, he gazed over to Myron and Tag. "Still, luck was obviously on their side when common sense failed them, for they are still alive."

"Do you know what makes for great dragon fodder?" questioned Myron, staring intently at the royal.

"No," said Percy.

"Well, it is still early on in the fall, so there is a chance you'll find out on your own, if what common sense *you* possess does not tell you to remain behind," averred Myron.

"Are you threatening to feed me to the dragons?" asked Percy. His tone was indignant knowing this knight was openly commiserating with Tag to make his life miserable.

"I was merely posing a question to you," said Myron, his shoulders rolling in a shrug of indifference. "Mind you, I refuse to be held responsible if you do get in the way of one of those voracious beasts."

"I am no fool, Sir Kendall. You mean to dissuade me from continuing on with this quest."

"Did it work?" Myron looked hopeful as he glanced over at Percy.

"I will have you know, wherever Princess Rose-alyn goes, I will follow. Besides, if Tag and Harold, never mind Loftus, possess the courage to venture north on this mission, then I have just as much, if not more, than all three of them combined."

"Just be warned this great courage you claim to possess can be the death of you," cautioned Rainus.

"I'll help to keep an eye on Prince Percival while he keeps a watchful eye on Princess Rose," promised Harold. "But tell me, Master Agincor, what's beyond the Fire Rim Mountains?"

"North of that towering mountain range, of which many of those mountains are active volcanoes, if we survive the trek, the land beyond is surrounded by the deadly Sea of Shadows. It is entrenched in great mysteries."

"How so?" asked Harold. He leaned forward, eager to learn more.
"Though it is barren and desolate, it is also a place of extraordinary beauty."
"Tell me more!" demanded Harold.
"Have you ever heard of the Northern Lights?" asked Silas.
"No, but I take it, they're some kind of light from way up north," assumed the big man.
"Indeed, but these are no ordinary lights."
"Go on!" urged Harold, taking a gulp of wine before passing it on to Loftus. "Do tell."
"I've heard of this strange phenomenon," said Loftus. With a nod, he accepted the bottle. "I was told this great show of eerie light is the spirits of the dead; those forever trapped in this realm. Some believe the lights Master Agincor speaks of are souls trying to escape into the netherworld."
"Spirits of the dead?" squeaked Harold. Fear manifested as a lump catching in the back of his throat. The hairs on his arms and the back of his neck stood upright as ghostly phantoms floated through his rampant imagination.
"Some who have witnessed this night-time display have indeed described it as eerie, Captain Loftus," acknowledged Silas. "However, having seen them with mine own eyes through the ages, I believe this spectacle to be quite amazing! Depending upon the time of the year, on a cloudless night an incredible show of light, ranging from pale yellow and emerald green to a dazzling magenta, dances across the northerly skies."
"Oh, my! That does sound spectacular!" gasped Harold, as he glanced hopefully at the deepening sky. "Is it like a magical rainbow runnin' wild?"
"The display is far more spectacular than even a double rainbow, my friend!"
"Did you not say this show of light is the dead?" asked Rose, waiting for Captain Loftus to elaborate on what he knew.
"I did, my lady. Tales of old claim that's what those mysterious lights are," answered Loftus. "On rare occasions I've seen faint glimmers in the winter skies to the north while I stood guard on the ramparts of the castle. However, I am sure to see them up close as this Wizard has, it can be quite fantastic."
"But is that true, Master Agincor? These are ghosts that remain trapped in our world?" gasped Harold, listening in awe. He was as frightened as he was amazed by this news.
"These are not the souls of ordinary folks I speak of," explained

Silas. "Legends of yore tell of great Wizards, my kinfolk, from days gone by is the cause of these lights. Those who had died in historic battles, their souls forever bound to this realm, stretch high into the heavens seeking respite from this world. It is said this great show of light is their collective souls attempting to break the shackles that bind them to this earthly realm."

"Is that so?" asked Tag, intrigued by his words.

"If you believe in the legends, it is," answered Silas. "Personally, I quite like the whole notion behind these tales, that there is life beyond what we know here in this physical realm."

"Is there?" asked Rose.

"It comes down to what you believe in your heart. In the end, the lights to the north could be nothing more than some strange interaction between our world and the sun or the moon, but who can say with any certainty."

"My forebears shared tales of how the souls of benevolent Wizards continue to haunt the northern most reaches of our world," said Halen. "I quite like those tales. Through the ages, for the Elfkind, it has been a fine reminder of the powerful Wizards that had made selfless sacrifices to spare us from evil."

"Oooh! I tend to agree with you, Captain Ironwood." Harold nodded in approval. "If I'm fortunate enough to see these magical lights, I'd much prefer them to be goodly souls of great Wizards than evil spirits of wicked men, that's for sure."

"Hold on!" demanded Percy, motioning for Harold to cease talking. "If these phantom lights are the souls of the dead, how do we know they will not harm us as we venture north?"

"We don't," responded Silas, offering the others a sly wink.

"So we dare journey on toward the Sea of Shadows to capture a Witch, with no guarantee that we will be safe?"

"Prince Percival, even to live a life that is not bound to a monumental quest does not come without risks. You can be bowled over by a runaway wagon setting foot outside your castle," responded Silas. "As we said before, you are welcome to stay behind. In fact, I *urge* you to stay."

"You are trying to trick me!" snapped Percy, his feet stamping the ground in defiance.

Tag and the others stared down at his feet that ground into the earth as he fumed like an angry child.

"I see your ankle is feeling better," noted Tag.

Percy's face reddened with embarrassment, having forgotten his feigned injury.

"Yes, it is feeling much better." He rubbed his left ankle, pretending to dispel the nagging twinges of pain.

"Hey... Wasn't it your other ankle that was hurt?" questioned Harold, rubbing his stubbly chin in pensive thought.

Percy's face burned a deeper shade of red as he snapped at Harold. "So it was. I happened to jar this ankle right now, but overall, I am fine."

"Well, that is mighty convenient," noted Rainus. "Good thing I did not waste my healing powers on an injury that was basically non-existent."

"Yes, well... I heal quickly," said Percy. "My royal blood makes me much more resilient than any of you give me credit for. My ankle is fine now."

"Perfect!" exclaimed Tag. "It will make it easier for you to run for your life should those phantom lights attack."

"You are still not funny," grumbled Percy, as he sneered at Tag. "But never you mind. What else can we expect to encounter up north, Wizard?"

"Yes, what about the Sea of Shadows?" asked Harold. "That's a foreboding name, if ever there was one. Is it because the sea is dark and shadowy?"

"Yes, where the waters run deep, it is as dark as squid ink," answered Silas. "But there are *things* that dwell in this deep, dark sea that create the shadows in this body of water."

"Like?" asked Percy.

"There are all manners of beasts, great and small, that reside in the depths, rarely seen by mortal eyes."

"Oh, and what about Mermaids?" asked Harold, his eyes shone with excitement. "I heard those fish-folk reside in this particular sea."

"They are folk, but they are not fish," corrected Silas.

"But I heard they live and breathe in water and they have the tail and scales of a fish."

"Yes, Harold, but it does not make a Mermaid a fish. It is like saying a unicorn is a horse with a horn," explained Silas. "Or an Elf is a human being with pointed ears."

"And not to forget: acute hearing, keen eyesight, as well as being aesthetically perfect in every way," added Rainus.

"I see where Harold is coming from, but if Mermaids are not fish, or at least half-fish, then what are they?" asked Percy. "To me, if they act like a fish and look like a fish, then they are a fish."

"For one who claims to be so well-read, you are so bloody ignorant," snorted Tag. "Someone, please, set him straight on this matter."

Silas motioned Tag for silence. "Allow me, my young friend."

"Oh, great! I feel another long-winded lecture coming on," grumbled Percy, slouching in his makeshift chair.

"Don't know about lectures, but I do *love* stories!" declared Harold, as he motioned for the Wizard to continue. "Do tell, Master Agincor!"

"Since you insist, many centuries ago, well before I came to be, there was a beautiful maiden, but she was no ordinary maiden."

"She was more beautiful than Princess Rose?" asked Harold, wondering if this was even possible.

"I meant she was not ordinary, as in she was not a mortal. Instead, she was a Naiad."

"Naiad?" repeated Percy. "This is a type of Water Nymph, is that not so?"

"*Was* a Water Nymph," corrected Silas. "The Naiads are no more in this world. When they did exist, they presided over bodies of fresh water; usually fountains, wells, and springs. Sadly, because of the tragic mistake made by the queen of the Naiads, her kind was condemned to suffer a terrible fate."

"What happened to this beautiful Water Nymph?" asked Harold.

"Hers was a tragic tale of love and jealousy, deceit and murder," continued Silas. "Long ago, Cyrene, this beautiful Naiad I speak of now, had spied upon a farmer's son as he came to a tranquil pool in a westerly forest to water his horse after a long ride. For Cyrene, it was love at first sight. She desired this young man. I will call him Jon, as his name has slipped from my mind over the ages. Anyway, Cyrene lured Jon with an enchanting song that carried on the evening breeze. She ensnared this mortal, beguiling him with her beauty and her captivating voice. They fell in love, but it was a forbidden love, for the boy's father would never approve of such a union."

"So they killed each other so they could be together, forever, in the afterlife," muttered Percy. With a roll of his eyes, his hands flapped about, motioning for Silas to speed up the telling of this tale.

"Hush!" ordered Harold, pressing a finger to his lips. He was eager to hear more. "Allow Master Agincor to finish this story."

"Yes, well, theirs was an affair doomed from the start. As much as Cyrene was an ethereal beauty, she was also bitterly jealous. One evening when her lover failed to meet her at the appointed time, she crept to the young man's farm. There, she saw him with a young lady, beautiful and fair, but a mortal. Cyrene was sure Jon's father would approve of this maiden, while she was to be shunned, cast aside and forgotten.

In a jealous rage, the following night, she called with song to her love, luring him to the pool where they first met. She accused him of being unfaithful, of spurning her for a mortal girl. In a fit of envy and rage, before he could explain, she dove into the water, taking the young man with her."

"She drowned him?" gasped Harold.

"Yes, she held him down in the water until he was dead," said Silas. "She murdered her one true love."

"But how did she become a fish?" asked Percy. "You have yet to answer that."

"A *Mermaid*," corrected Silas. "After she killed the young man, Cyrene dragged his body onto land, hoping to punish this girl for coming between them. She wanted her rival to find Jon's body. She wanted to see and hear her anguish, to revel in this girl's grief.

The maiden did happen upon the young man's lifeless body, but to Cyrene's horror, this girl she believed Jon was courting turned out to be his sister. In her grief, Cyrene fled. In her despair and sorrow, she hurled herself into the sea where the briny waters would spell her doom. There, she prayed for release from this world, praying to be united with her true love in the afterlife.

Rather than drowning in the sea, fate intervened. Some believe her life was spared, but only to punish her for murdering in the name of love. Her Naiad form was changed forever. Her legs became fused like that of a fish's tail, covered in scales to endure a watery existence from which she would never be able to leave, developing the ability to survive in the salty sea, than to perish in it."

"And this gave rise to the Mermaids," said Myron.

"That is how the legend goes," said the Wizard. "In this way, it was hoped that mankind would be repelled by the Mermaid's form and these maidens, in turn, would not be able to venture onto land to seduce mortal men. Unfortunately, fate never took into account the Mermaid's enchanting song."

"I have seen tapestries depicting the Mermaids you speak of, but I do not know of one person who has seen a live one," said Rose.

"They must still exist. How else would Sin have gathered the pink salt that Captain Ironwood had discovered?" responded Tag.

"I heard that for decades the Mermaids were persecuted by sailors and fishermen that plied the seas," said Myron. "Though these sea maidens were always described as being beautiful, they were also believed to be dangerous because of Cyrene's jealous, murdering way to demonstrate the power of her love."

"Sailors and fishermen alike, lured by the seductive song of the Mermaid, had dashed their ships upon rocks and reefs," said Silas.

"Many lost their lives, falling under the enchantment of these beautiful creatures."

"These seafaring men must have been as drunk as a skunk to believe a fish-like woman can be beautiful," said Percy, grimacing in repulsion at the thought of kissing a female covered with slimy scales and possessing gills to breathe underwater.

"Might we be seein' a Mermaid or two, if we make it to the Sea of Shadows?" asked Harold.

"It is a possibility." Silas nodded. "But overall, they are as shy and elusive as the unicorn."

"I suppose if Sin holds a Mermaid prisoner to harvest her tears, then there is a chance we will see one, maybe even free her, when we rescue Loken," said Myron.

"I am hoping the Mermaid has returned to the sea and Loken has found a way to escape from his prison," said Rainus.

"I hope so too, my friend," said Silas. "However, I am confident had our little friend found his way home by now, then we would have heard from Pancecelia Feldspar, or surely from one of her Fairies."

"How about another story?" asked Harold.

"How about retiring for the night after we finish eating?" suggested Silas. "We have another long day before us when tomorrow comes."

"An excellent plan." Myron nodded as he passed around the loaf of bread and cheese to share with his comrades. "We eat, and then we sleep. And Tag, before the fur flies and nobody gets any sleep should you plant yourself in Prince Percival's tent, I will play the part of chaperone on this night. I shall present a formidable barrier for any prince or princess to overcome in those close quarters."

"That is good news to me," said Tag, nodding in agreement. "The way Prince Percival snores, at least I'll be able to get some sleep on this night."

"I do not snore!"

"Oh, you do! You're worse than a pig with a bad cold," argued Tag.

Myron raised his hand, motioning for silence. "Let us eat in peace for what remains of the night."

Tag and Percy fell silent. Their eyes burned of malice as they glared across the campfire at each other. They tore into their bread as though they were biting and tearing into each other.

Halen glanced up to the deepening sky, as he finally broke the uneasy silence that boiled with tension, "I shall take the first watch."

"It is still early," said Percy.

"It is never too early to steer clear of your constant nattering to find some solitude," responded Halen, as he gathered his bow and quiver."

"Never had truer words been spoken! I'll join you, my friend," offered Loftus. Stuffing the piece of bread and cheese into his mouth, he freed his hands to snatch up his sword.

"Myron and I shall replace you in a few hours," Rainus called behind them. "Keep a watchful eye for potential danger."

"Will do." Halen nodded politely before turning away.

As Elf and mortal settled down for a long night of sentry duty, Halen stared off into the blackness that smothered this forest. He stood erect, shoulders back and his squared jaw tilted up as he listened and watched. He was absolutely motionless as he searched for signs of life beyond the glow of the campfire.

Loftus observed uneasily, noticing how the tips of this Elf's ears twitched ever so slightly, listening intently for what he could not see.

"What is it?" asked Loftus, squinting to see what the Elf saw. "What do you see out there?"

"It is not what I see, it is what I hear," whispered Halen, as he stared into the growing darkness. "There is something evil in the wind on this night."

"Is it near?" asked Loftus, his eyes darting about.

"It is everywhere," answered Halen.

13

Ruffians and Scallywags

After several days of travel, to Percy's relief, the trek had been strangely uneventful.

Silas, with his gruesome, optical compass in hand, escorted the party ever northward. The horses trotted along, single file by the lake where Myron had first taught Rose how to fish during their initial adventure that steered them toward the Fire Rim Mountains.

"Do we have much further to go?" Percy called to the Wizard, as he spied between the stand of trees the mountains that loomed ever closer.

"It will be a two-day's ride to cross the dragon-infested lands to reach the mountain pass that will deliver us to the Sea of Shadows," estimated Silas.

"Two days!" groaned Percy. He shifted restlessly on his saddle. "In this cursed weather?"

"Be grateful it will be two days of travel unimpeded by deadly dragons. It will be this *'cursed'* weather to keep those creatures at bay, forcing them to seek refuge in the great caves riddling those mountains," stated Silas.

"Chin up, my lord," urged Loftus. "The great Wizard speaks the truth! For now, you should be glad we have been blessed, for there is nothing worse than riding in the cold, blowing winds of winter than being chased by dragons."

"I suppose," muttered Percy, shivering involuntarily at the mere thought of enduring such harsh conditions and formidable beasts.

"If it is of any consolation, we shall stop for the night," said Silas. He stood tall in his stirrups to search the area for a suitable clearing near the lake.

"Are we not going to ride on?" questioned Percy. He stared suspiciously at the Wizard.

"There is adequate cover along the shoreline and plenty of fresh water for us and our horses," answered Silas, pointing to the placid lake.

"And plenty of trout to be caught here, too," added Myron, as he thought about fresh, pan-fried fish for dinner, rather than chewing on dried strips of smoked venison.

"I thought we were going to ride until dusk, as we had all the other nights," said Percy.

"We are close to the dragon lands," answered Silas. "It is safer to cross during the light of day so we can spot and head toward an area that will provide us with cover for the night than to blindly wander about, falling into possible danger."

"But you said the dragons will be hibernating with the cold," said Percy.

"There are other dangers to be wary of as we venture across those dreaded lands," assured Silas.

"Like what?"

"If I tell you, you are sure to turn tail and flee for home."

"For pity's sake, tell him, Master Agincor!" urged Tag. "It is never too late for him to return to his castle, leaving us to do what must be done without him to impede our progress."

Percy raised his hand, motioning Silas and Tag for silence. "Say no more. This is just another feeble ploy to trick me into abandoning my princess and this quest!"

"You will continue to believe what you want," said Silas, his tone dismissive. "Do not say you were not forewarned should misfortune strike."

"Yes, yes! I have heard this all before," grunted Percy.

"This quest will not be easy, but it is fair to say Prince Percy is here to stay," stated Rose, as she smiled in adoration. "My charming prince will not abandon me."

"It is obvious he has no intentions of abandoning you, but there's nothing to say fate will intervene to disrupt his *chivalrous* plans," responded Silas, giving Tag a knowing wink that irritated Percy to no end.

"Oh, yes! And fate can be a real bitch," laughed Tag.

"You are so rude," scolded Rose, shaking an admonishing finger at her friend.

"Say what you like, Princess," said Tag, with an irreverent shrug. "You know better than all of us, especially this royal pain of a prince, that anything can happen along the way."

Rose dismounted. Wandering over to the shore of the lake, she shielded her eyes from the glare of the sun shimmering off the glass-like surface.

"Why does this place look familiar to me?" she wondered aloud.

"We've been here before," answered Tag, as he stood next her. His eyes searched about for signs of trout leaping from the water to feed on the late season hatch of insects.

"We have?" Rose frowned, searching her memories for this very place.

"Absolutely!" declared Tag, a mischievous grin creasing his face. "Do you not remember? This is where you were busy gawking at me from afar as I bathed! You'd think you would recall something as memorable as that."

"No! Not so!" protested Rose, embarrassed Tag would say such a thing in front of Percy. "If anything, I just happened upon you! There was nothing memorable about that situation at all and I was definitely not gawking!"

"Please!" scoffed Tag. "Your eyes were practically bugging out of your head as you stared. Plus, you certainly made no effort to immediately remove yourself after you '*happened upon me*'. You liked what you saw!"

"You boorish lout!" cursed Percy. "How dare you speak of my ladylove like she is nothing more than a wanton trollop?"

To the astonishment of all, like a delicate frog leaping from a burning hot rock, Percy sprang into action, lunging at Tag. His slender fingers knotted around fistfuls of cloak and shirt, but all attempts to hoist his foe into the air, or at the very least, onto his toes, failed. Even with anger and adrenalin to fuel Percy's physical act of retribution, his lean body lacked the muscles, weight and strength to lift Tag's well-muscled frame.

Laughing in Percy's face, Tag merely thrust his forearms straight up against the wrists to break his hold.

"Do you really want to do this?" grunted Tag, staring with amusement as the royal adopted a defensive posture before him.

"I must champion Princess Rose-alyn; defend my woman's honour!"

With his arms tucked against his chest to block any punches Tag could throw at his body, Percy's clenched fists suddenly came up to protect his face. Trembling with as much fear as nervous energy, they rolled in tight circles, one in front of the other before his chin, as he waited for an opportunity to take a jab at his opponent's smug visage.

Unruffled by this pugilistic display, Tag merely stood before him. With his hands on his hips, the knight-in-training exuded an air of self-assured indifference to a potential attack.

"As Loftus has proven utterly useless to me for this purpose, I will be the one to teach you a lesson!"

"In humility?" asked Tag.

"And then some!" growled Percy. He skittered side to side like a nervous crab; his quaking fists waiting to unleash a wrath unlike anything this rapscallion had ever been subjected to. "In the name of my beloved, you shall receive the thrashing of your life!"

"Instead of her honour, perhaps you should prepare to defend your pride and ego when I do this," said Tag.

"Do what?" Percy peered over his balled fists to glare at his nemesis.

Tag's hand popped up, smacking against the Prince's right fist. This balled fist flew back, striking against his left hand that hovered just before his face, clipping Percy smack dab on the chin.

Though the pain was fleeting; almost non-existent really, it was the bitter sting of humiliation, the resounding slap to his pride that caused Percy to erupt.

"I will smite you!" Percy shrieked in rage. He bodily flung himself at Tag.

"Enough!" shouted Myron, pushing the two apart. "Save this anger and energy to unleash upon the Witch."

"But he was the instigator!" pouted Percy. He pointed an accusing finger at Tag.

He lunged forward once more, only to come to a jerking halt. He gagged like a dog strung up at the end of its tether, as Halen reached over, seizing Percy. Snagging him by the scruff of his neck, he caught him at mid-stride, sparing him from further physical injury or greater humiliation.

"I care not who started this altercation. This foolishness ends now!" demanded Myron. He motioned for both to stand down.

"Yes, this is an utter waste of time," muttered Rainus, shaking his head in disgrace.

"Here, here!" cheered Loftus, as he grinned at his red-faced charge. "As valiant as your effort was, there is no sport in watching you beat yourself up with Master Yairet's help."

Loftus pretended to bop himself on the chin with his own fist to re-enact Percy's self-inflicted abuse.

"Fetch off, Loftus!" snarled Percy. With his blood boiling, he shook a trembling, balled fist at the captain. "Do not force me to teach you a lesson in respect! If I am made to vent my wrath upon you, you will be reduced to a useless, quivering heap of gristle and bones to be scraped off the ground."

Accosted by these belligerent words of threat, Loftus collapsed onto his knees. Instead of begging for mercy, he clenched his ribs, falling to his side as his body convulsed in a fit of laughter. Any words of apology, or ridicule, to roll out of his mouth was a garbled mess as he snorted and sniggered between roars of laughter as he lost the battle to regain his composure.

Another unrepentant wave of mirth erupted from the captain when Percy kicked him in retaliation. Without mercy, the tip of his boot struck Loftus on his shin, both of which were protected by steel greaves that were padded by a layer of double-boiled leather and cushioned by a wool liner. This act of vengeance left the captain physically unscathed, but rewarded Percy with a painfully stubbed toe.

Harold jumped in, making a futile bid to dampen Percy's rage. "Looks like you needn't use your fists to take the captain down, my lord. He's lookin' pretty helpless right about now."

Harold grabbed Percy by his left shoulder, attempting to hold him steady as he wavered and hopped about on one foot, cursing beneath his breath while the dumbfounded Princess watched this spectacle that was her beloved prince.

"Get away from me, you oaf!" snapped Percy, as he shrugged off Harold's hand. Sensing all eyes were on him, he growled, "Look away! Stop staring at me!"

"Gladly!" said Tag. He snatched up the coil of fishing line and hooks from his pack. "I've got more important things to do than waste my time on you and your pathetic threats."

"Pathetic threats, you say?" Percy snorted, shaking an angry fist at the back of Tag's head. "If they are so pathetic, then why do you run away like the cowardly cur that you are?"

Tag spun on his heels. Waving the fishing gear in Percy's face, he came dangerously close to snagging a royal nostril on one of the hooks as he growled, "I mean to catch us some dinner, but if you wish to carry on like a blustering coward, I'd be happy to use you as bait, being the spineless worm that you are."

"Look at you, resorting to insults in a feeble bid to cut me down," mocked Percy.

"Insults are not needed to cut you down to size," responded Tag. "In fact, you will be the first."

"First what?"

"The first person to die because of his own stupidity, that's what!"

"I am *not* stupid!" declared Percy.

"You are so stupid, you are likely to trip and impale yourself on your own stupidity!" rebuked Tag.

"You would both be wise to watch your words," warned Silas, raising his hands for silence.

"I am a prince! I can say whatever I want!"

"True, you are royalty, but words are the one weapon we all have the power to wield," rebuked the Wizard. "I find it is only the wise who can wield it effectively and for a higher purpose than just name-calling."

"So true," added Loftus. "Words are cheap, but it's the ones spoken carelessly that can cost you dearly."

"So take that!" shouted Percy. Electing to believe this warning was directed specifically at his foe, in a childish display, he thumbed his nose at Tag.

In response, Tag grabbed onto this offending digit, twisting it painfully so Percy yelped, prancing about on the tips of his toes in a desperate bid to alleviate the agony.

"Stop it!" cried Rose. She pushed Tag off of Percy to end this assault. "Stop it right now!"

"You heard her!" muttered Tag.

"You are such a bully, Tag!" scolded Rose. In pity, she clutched Percy's aching hand to her heart to console him.

Tag's heart fell into the pit of his stomach. He stood there, flabbergasted by Rose's scornful words.

The Prince sneered in contempt at his nemesis while joy filled his heart in knowing Rose was turning against her dear friend. Each time her eyes met his, Percy's scowling expression abruptly changed to that of a wounded puppy.

"I'm the bully?" gasped Tag. His eyes were wide in surprise as Rose glared at him.

"For pity's sake! Are you the one who is hurt here?" She gently patted her beloved's hand to soothe away the pain.

"I can't help it if he foolishly stuck his thumb in my face," grumbled Tag. "I reacted instinctively."

"But you should know better!" snapped Rose.

"Yes, *you* should know better!" crowed Percy. His scornful sneer directed at Tag suddenly morphed into a sad frown again as Rose gazed upon his face.

Before Tag could retaliate, Myron seized him by the shoulders, directing him toward the lake. "Time for you to catch some fish, catch your breath, and cool that hot head of yours, my friend."

"Yes, stick your head in the lake until your breath expires," shouted Percy. "That should permanently cool that foul disposition of yours!"

"You wish!" snapped Tag.

He stormed off, crashing through the shrubs to get away from the fool of a prince. Tag's heart thundered as his mind raced. His soul was wounded; angry and disappointed that Rose would side with Percy, sympathizing with this pretender than to believe in a lifelong friend.

Standing alone on the edge of the lake, Tag brooded in his misery, festering in pensive thought as he listened.

Behind him, Percy's shrill, taunting voice carried into the impending night as the Prince brayed, shouting loud enough for him to hear, "What a baby! If my words could score his pride so easily, can you imagine what would have happened had I resorted to physical violence, putting my fists to that dolt?"

"You would have broken both hands?" replied Harold. His matter-of-fact tone was delivered with a level of innocence that served to inflame Percy's already foul demeanour.

Tag felt some consolation in hearing Loftus, Myron and the Elves erupt into laughter as Percy shouted angrily at the large man, telling Harold to shut his big mouth. He could also hear Princess Rose's sharp voice ordering all in her company to help ready for the night. It was her attempt to spare her husband-to-be from further humiliation by turning attention to the work that was yet to be done before darkness encroached upon the lands.

Staring across the placid lake, its glassy surface served to calm Tag's rattled nerves. His resentful scowl and feelings of bitterness melted away as he entertained ideas of how to be rid of this pest of a prince. Drawing a cleansing breath, Tag then exhaled deeply as he unsheathed his dagger. Kneeling down, as though he was stabbing at a body, the earth became the object of his redirected anger. This exercise to dig up worms to bait his hooks became an effective way to vent his frustration and diffuse his rage as the blade sank mercilessly into the damp soil, repeatedly savaging the earth.

"Are you practicing?"

Tag glanced up to see Silas standing before him. The Wizard was staring quizzically at the dagger gripped in his hands; the blade caked in soil.

"Practicing what?" questioned Tag, rising to his feet to answer Silas.

"To murder that fool, that's what."

"If there were not so many witnesses on hand, it'd be so bloody easy to do," laughed Tag, as he threw the dagger. Landing with a dull 'thud', the blade sank deep into the disturbed earth at his feet. "I'd just toss his carcass into this lake; feed the fishes and be rid of him, once and for all."

"Going against my better judgement, I'd aid you with that onerous task, if I could!" declared Silas, offering Tag a sympathetic smile.

"Perhaps when everyone is asleep," whispered Tag. A mischievous grin stretched across his face as he pretended to concoct a foolproof plan.

"As tempting as it is, do not allow that young whelp to get the better of you, my friend," urged Silas.

"He already has. And it doesn't help that Princess Rose continues to side with that arrogant prig no matter how wrong or obnoxious he is."

"All the more reason for you to be patient with her while we wait for Prince Percival to trip up; revealing his true character and intentions."

"She is falling for him; hook, line and sinker!" snapped Tag. He waved before Silas' troubled face the fishing gear in case he needed reminding. "The longer we wait, the deeper she falls under his spell."

"Whatever it is she feels for him, when she falls out of love or infatuation, that is when she will need you the most."

"To say *I told you so* to her face?"

"You are a bigger man than that, Tagius Yairet. Just know it is not always the *fall* that hurts. More often, it is the *push* that landed you there."

"If you say so, but that means Prince Prissy will have to push her hard to make her see what he is truly capable of. And at this moment, she is stupidly blind to all he says and does; embracing only what she perceives to be his finest points, even if they are few and far between."

"Even a blind man knows when he has stepped off a cliff. It is obvious Princess Rose has yet to experience this fall we speak of. A simple nudge from the high pedestal she has placed him on will do the trick, but when she does fall, mark my words, Tag, it will not be pretty."

"So, you still believe she will accept the truth, but only if Percy reveals it to her?"

"Yes, and that is what will make it hurt all the more," responded Silas. "The illusion of her perfect prince, shattered beyond repair, is sure to break her heart, but it is a truth she must bear witness to, if she is to come to her senses where that cad of a royal is concerned."

"As her friend, I will catch her, should she fall, but we are waging a losing battle where Percy is concerned. He continues to ingratiate and insinuate himself into her life, so much so, I doubt she will find that sod guilty of having a hand in his mother's death, even if he confessed to killing her in cold blood."

"Do not lose faith in Princess Rose," urged Silas, giving Tag a consoling pat on his shoulder. "Given the proper circumstances and a *heart-felt* confession from Percival, she will come to her senses."

"I do hope so, but what is wrong with them?" grumbled Tag. He glowered in the direction of the camp where Percy's voice carried to the shoreline to grate on his nerves. His annoyance was compounded by the girlish twitter of Rose's laughter as she giggled at Percy's comment that no one else seemed to find humorous.

"Other than their royal attitudes, the fact that they are both quite self-absorbed, if not in themselves, then in each other, there is nothing wrong," answered Silas.

"Nothing?" gasped Tag. "If anything, I believed the Princess would have seen through that fool by now. There is something wrong in that!"

"Consider this, my young friend: Though we may all experience the same thing at a given time, what and how we perceive it can differ greatly. In the end, the greatest truth is the one you choose to cling to," explained Silas.

"You are speaking in riddles again, Wizard."

"Trust me when I say she will eventually come around to accept the truth."

"And if she doesn't?" queried Tag.

"Let us not even consider that for now," said Silas, with a sad shake of his head. "It is better to believe she will."

"Easy for you to say. I cannot help but think of how that snake is poisoning her against us, even as we speak."

"Then let us return to camp; keep that snake from whispering sweet nothings to her."

Tag unleashed a dreary sigh, but his heart continued to hammer angrily in his chest as his mind raced with a million thoughts of what would have happened if his friends had not intervened, allowing him to vent his frustrations on the mealy-mouthed Prince of Axalon.

"Are you ready to return with me?" asked Silas.

"I'm still too angry. If *Prissy* says one more stupid thing to me, I know I'm going to throttle that idiot." Tag's hands came up, wringing the air as though he was strangling Percy.

"I understand. There is no point in subjecting yourself to his annoying presence, if it only works to grate on your nerves all the more."

"Fishing will give me some peace of mind. Plus, it'll help to keep that fool away from me, as I know he'll fear that I'll ask him to gut and clean what I catch for dinner. I think my time is better spent doing something productive while keeping my distance from him."

"A smart decision, my young friend," praised Silas. "Just do not linger here for too long. Return to the safety of our campfire as soon as you can."

"I'll be back before the sun sets completely. The fish stop biting when darkness falls."

"Very good! In the meantime, I shall put that useless twit to work. It should keep him from underfoot, although it will probably serve to compound his whining," said Silas, as he turned away to help the others set up camp. "I shall see you soon. I do hope you catch a boast-worthy specimen of a trout."

"I hope so, too," said Tag. He knelt down to collect the worms that were frantically writhing about in the disturbed clumps of earth. "I think a hot, fresh meal will do us some good."

As the Wizard disappeared through the riparian shrubs a loud splash broke the tranquil surface of the lake. Tag glanced up, but only in time to see the surging ripples expanding out in broadening rings from where the fish had leapt before disappearing into the depths. By the size of these ripples, Tag estimated it had to be a very large lake trout, at least one-and-a-half stones or more in weight.

"That would feed us all, and then some," Tag spoke in a whisper as he hurried to bait his hooks. If he managed to catch this fish, it'd be a silent testimony to Prince Percival that he earned his rightful place in their fellowship by proving to be a contributing member, instead of using a royal title to finagle his way in.

If this trout turned out to be as big as Tag had estimated, and he was successful at landing this fish, it would become the largest one he ever had the good fortune of catching. And what better way to show up the obnoxious dolt, than to have him dine on food caught by his archenemy!

As Tag arranged the three hooks so they wouldn't snag onto the line once they hit the water, he imagined a humiliated Percy subjected to eating the fish dinner while made to listen to his comrades sing his praises for catching such a fine trout. If he were lucky, perhaps the Prince will even choke on a fishbone or two. This was motivation enough as Tag took aim, casting out. He watched as the small, lead weight delivered the fishing line just short of where the monster-sized trout had dove back into the lake.

"Excellent!" exclaimed Tag.

He was pleased his throw was spot-on. He assumed it landed close to where the fish undoubtedly still lurked about in the clearing free of water lilies. One of the baited hooks probably dangled before its hungry mouth.

No sooner than the weight sank from his sight, taking the baited hooks down with it, Tag felt the line pull taut, and then relax. He wound the line several times around his hand, waiting anxiously for the precise moment to set the hook.

If the fish were just nibbling at the worm, a premature attempt promised to frighten it away. Tag had to be patient, waiting until the trout took the bait, hook and all, into its mouth.

As the line grew slack in his hands, Tag's hope sank along with the weight. Suddenly, the fishing line snapped taut, almost yanking him into the lake. With his heart racing, Tag set his heels into the earth, bracing for a fight. He pulled hard, winding the thin line around his left hand each time it grew slack.

"Feels like I've hooked a whale," he said.

The line tightened around his hand, turning his fingers purple from the lack of circulation. Pulling on the line with his right hand, Tag leaned back, almost in a sitting position. He was determined to land his quarry. Clutching the line against his chest, he wrestled the fish closer to shore. Just as Tag thought he was winning this tug-o-war, his arms were yanked straight before him.

The fish was much larger and stronger than he had anticipated. It was determined to either snap this line or drown him, if he didn't let go.

Struggling to be free, Tag fought to unravel the tangled line while he was dragged toward the water's edge.

Frantically unwinding the line cutting into his hand, his feet sank deeper into the muddy bottom of the lake. The cold water spilled over the tops of his boots, sending a chill to his bones, as he was pulled deeper into the lake. Before he could cry for help, Tag swallowed a great gulp of air. He was hauled head first into the water.

"He is a better braggart than he is a fisherman," scoffed Percy. He warmed his hands over the flames of the campfire. The autumn air had taken on a distinct chill as dusk surrendered to the coming of night.

"Getting hungry, are we?" asked Myron.

"Well, Yairet did boast to all that he was going to catch some dinner, did he not?" Percy's response was smug as his stomach rumbled. "If he is as capable as he claims, he would have been back by now with a sizeable catch to boot!"

"Myron taught me how to fish at this very lake, and I will tell you now, it was not an easy task," said Rose.

"You toss in a hook. You wait for a fish. How hard can it be?" sniffed Percy, his tone haughty.

"Even if it were a difficult task to undertake, it is evident you would lack the patience required," noted Rainus.

"I will have you know, Elf Lord, I am plenty patient!" Percy shook an admonishing finger at Rainus. "If I were not, I would have lost patience with you and your infantile friends long ago."

"Oh, my!" gasped Harold. "That's not nice! Not at all!"

"If you cannot handle the truth, perhaps you should make camp elsewhere," grunted Percy, waving a dismissive hand toward Harold.

"And if you wish to be fed on this eve and not be ousted from *this* camp, I strongly recommend you learn to steady that tongue of yours, my lord," scolded Loftus.

"Of course you would side with these no-good ruffians and scallywags," grumbled Percy, as he scowled in contempt at the captain. "You are no better than the company you keep!"

"I take that as a compliment, my lord," said Loftus, hoisting a wine bottle in good cheer to honour those in his presence. "Just be mindful of what you say, for we *ruffians* and *scallywags* are many. You are but one."

"So you say, but at least Princess Rose-alyn sides with me! Just keep in mind that two royals win out over a handful of commoners and a useless Wizard."

Rose's mouth fell open, but words failed to form. She was caught between duty to her husband-to-be and loyalty to her friends.

Loftus erupted in hearty laughter; his broad hand smacking Percy on his back as he spoke with a guffaw, "Look at you, my lord! Making friends wherever you go. Make another disparaging remark, especially about Master Agincor and I'm sure this *useless* Wizard will be happy to demonstrate his powers for your benefit!"

Silas smiled slyly as he spoke, "I would not think of it, Captain Loftus! My magic would be wasted on Prince Percival. There is no point in him dying. The lesson would be lost on him; an exercise in futility, and ultimately, a tragic waste of my time."

"Are you threatening my life?" Percy's eyes burned; pinpoints of fire as he glowered at the Wizard.

"Unlike some, I do not make it my business to harm others just to get what I want," answered Silas. His eyes narrowed in contempt as he cast an accusing gaze at the mortal. His tone and words forced Percy's hand.

"It is a pity this fellowship lacks a sense of humour," sighed Percy, raising his hands in feigned surrender. "Of course I was speaking in jest! Only a fool would ramble on like this without considering the consequences."

"And yet, you do," noted Halen.

"It is not my fault none of you were perceptive enough to detect the hint of sarcasm in my tone or the air of comedy with which I speak. Perhaps, royals and commoners appreciate humour on differing levels?" offered Percy, in a pathetic bid to pacify his agitated companions.

"I heard it," said Rose, hoping this would sway the others to leave her man alone. "It was just a simple misunderstanding."

Percy patted Rose's hand, smiling at her in gratitude as he spoke, "I suppose it would have been better had I just admitted I was getting hungry waiting for Tag to return with our dinner as he had promised, and just left it at that."

"Yes, saying less would have been the prudent thing to do," agreed Loftus, passing the wine bottle to him. "Drink more. Talk less."

Percy waved off this offer even though he had finally mastered the art of drinking from a bottle without accosting his face or dribbling wine down his chin to stain his apparel.

Silas stood up, staring to the west to see the last fingers of waning sunlight burn stubbornly through the raft of clouds hanging low on the horizon. His worried eyes turned from the setting sun toward the dark lake that now reflected the faint glow of the first stars twinkling in the deepening sky.

"This is odd," said Silas.

"Indeed! Tag Yairet is exactly that!" Percy nodded in agreement.

"I was speaking of Tag's absence."

"I was not, but he did say he was going to catch us some fish to dine on."

"True, but when I left him, he said he would return before sunset."

"You know how stubborn Tag can be," said Rose. "Perhaps the fish are slow to take the bait, but he is just as determined not to return empty-handed."

"Even if that is so, Tag stated the fish do not bite after the sun goes down."

"The fish grow large in this lake," said Myron, standing up to peer over the shrubs hugging this body of water. "Perhaps Tag is having problems landing a monster trout."

"You think?" asked Harold. His badger headpiece dipped low over his brows as he frowned with concern.

"That would certainly explain his long absence, if he did indeed snag a fish, even one of modest proportions can pose a real challenge for him," insisted Percy, demonstrating how one with little strength would struggle to land a trout.

"The young sir is no weakling," stated Rainus, dismissing Percy's comment. "I sense something is wrong."

"I hope not," said Silas, picking up his staff to use as a walking stick. Passing his hand before the crystal mounted atop, it glowed, lighting the path he had taken to the lakeshore.

The others followed the Wizard, hurrying behind him. And Percy, not wishing to be left alone in these strange lands, was forced to abandon the warm glow of the campfire. He pushed his way in front of Harold so the large man would be made to take up the rear, just in case the Witch or some demented soul should leap out to attack them.

As the last of the sun's light was leached away to envelope the land in a velvety darkness, Silas stood before the water's edge. The light glowing from his crystal danced across the placid lake, obliterating the stars reflected on the surface.

"Tag, where are you?" called Rose.

Rainus scanned the shoreline, searching for their friend. "I see no signs of him."

"Where did you last see him?" asked Myron.

"Here… right over here," said Silas. He pointed to where Tag had used the blade of his dagger to dig for earthworms.

"Come!" called Halen, spying on some footprints. "This is where he cast his line."

With further scrutiny, Halen assessed the signs left behind. Noting the deep impressions of a pair of boot heels, he spoke, "And this is where he braced himself, presumably to land his catch."

"And?" asked Rose, staring at the clues the Elf pointed out. "What else do you see?"

"Give him a moment," urged Myron, motioning for silence so Halen could focus on the task at hand.

All were silent as Halen's eyes followed the signs that were indicative of heels braced against the earth. It furrowed like Tag's boots ploughed the ground, tilling the soil straight into the lake.

"Well?" asked Rose.

"This is where Tag was dragged into the lake," announced Halen, his eyes desperately searching the surface for signs of life, "but I see no evidence of him."

"Bloody hell!" cursed Percy, speaking with feigned disappointment. "So the fool got himself drowned."

Percy suddenly reeled. His eyes rolled into his head as the stars that danced before his eyes became one with those in the sky. In an instant, his world turned black.

14
Misery Loves Company

"Was that necessary?" Rose glared at Myron as she lifted Percy's head onto her lap. "Look at him! I believe you broke his jaw!"

"The other option in silencing him was to throttle the fool until he was dead," growled Myron. Having lost all patience for the obnoxious royal, he stood unrepentant. Hovering over the dishevelled heap that was Percy, this unconscious prince now lay on the cold, damp ground.

"He bloody well had it coming to him," averred Silas, nodding in empathy to the knight.

Myron brooded, rubbing his aching fist that smashed hard against Percy's smug face. A sense of tranquillity seeped back into his soul as Rainus' hand squeezed his shoulder. It was both a silent warning not to vent further wrath upon the defenceless young man, while at the same time, it served to restore a feeling of calm in Myron's worried mind.

"I will have you apologize to Prince Percy this instant!" demanded Rose.

"I think not!" grunted Myron.

"You will do so right now!" demanded Rose.

"Methinks it's rather pointless at this time, bein' that he won't hear a word of it," stated Harold. He stared at this body sprawled out before them.

"You speak the truth, Harold. An apology, if it were indeed warranted, will mean nothing to him at the moment," assured Loftus, helping Rose to prop up this raggedy form.

"How can you say that?" scolded Rose.

"Unfortunately, once again Prince Percival demonstrated this unique ability of putting his foot in his mouth," replied Loftus. "What he said was both cruel and foolish, Princess Rose. I can't rightly say I blame Sir Kendall for lashing out as he did. My lord's thoughtlessness tends to invoke a visceral and immediate response from most, but rarely is it acted on."

Watching as Percy's chin lolled on his chest like his neck now lacked the bones and muscles to support his head, she spoke in his defence. "Of course he did not mean to say that Tag had drowned."

"Yes," agreed Myron. "He meant to say he only *wished* that Tag had done so."

It suddenly dawned on Rose that her friend was truly missing. Fear seized her by the heart. Her mind raced in panic. She jumped to her feet, dumping Percy's limp body onto the ground as she stared out over the lake.

"Tag is an excellent swimmer! There is no way he could have drowned," declared Rose. She hastily erected a formidable wall of denial. Searching the dark body of water, she called to him. "Tag! Where are you?"

For the longest moment, she waited for his answer. Her call was followed by an ominous hush as every creature in and around the lake fell silent as her words evaporated into the velvety night.

Silas hoisted his staff on high, the glow of his crystal shining bright to push against the darkness.

Halen and Rainus quickly scanned the lake and the surrounding shoreline, searching for signs of their missing friend.

"I see nothing," said Halen.

"We should split up; conduct a thorough search," suggested Rainus. "Halen, you take Silas, Captain Loftus and Princess Rose. Scour the south end of the lake. I shall take Myron and Harold. We shall search the shoreline and surrounding forest to the north, meeting at the opposite end of here."

"What about Prince Percy?" asked Rose. "You should heal and revive him first."

"There is no time to lose," answered Rainus. "His whining and complaining will only slow us down should he wake and be made to search for Tag with the rest of us."

"We cannot just leave him here!" protested Rose.

"He's out cold," stated Myron. "It is not as though he can get into any trouble in this condition. He is safer like this."

"He can probably use some extra sleep anyway, my lady," added Loftus, as he stepped over Percy's prostrate body to join in the search.

"I agree," said Halen. "Let us waste no more time. We must search for Tag while the clues are fresh."

❦ ❦ ❦

Whether it was the icy breath of a draft swirling around him or the sharp crackling of firewood set ablaze, Tag finally came to. He shivered in his wet clothes clinging to his clammy skin. Forcing his bleary eyes open, he winced as the cold splash of water dripped from his hair into his right eye as it opened. Blinking it away, he squinted at a blur of light. Tag peered through narrowed eyes as they focused on a great campfire glowing brightly. It roared, but at twenty paces from where he sat, the heat exuded did little to warm him up.

"You finally wake."

This sweet voice whispered, helping to lift the gloom. There was a lyrical quality to this lilting voice. These words tinkled like a wind chime, echoing like a fading dream in his waking mind.

Tag felt soft fingertips gently caress his face, lifting his chin so he can gaze upon a beautiful maiden.

"Who are you?" asked Tag, blinking hard to vanquish this lovely mirage.

"I was the one to bring you here. You are mine now," she whispered seductively.

Kneeling, a waterfall of wavy, flaxen hair tumbled down to frame this comely face. There was something ethereal about this flawless, porcelain skin that made her azure eyes shine like dazzling gemstones of perfect sapphire. He stared dreamily into this vision of loveliness, mesmerized by these alluring eyes as the girl leaned in close to his face, whispering to him, "You are mine."

Tag struggled to sit up as her dewy, rosebud lips teasingly grazed his; her warm breath thawed his chilled body as she lifted his chin to kiss him. The mysterious, young lady straddled his legs, pressing her lips against his.

Just as Tag kissed her back, he heard a distant voice cry out to him, "Stop! Don't do it!"

Tag's eyes snapped open as this warning raked at his mind.

He gasped as this cascade of golden tresses suddenly greyed, turning wiry before his eyes.

Pulling his face away from hers, Tag writhed about, struggling to dump her from his lap. Instead, the girl remained seated. The horrifying realization his arms were lashed to his sides by a rusted length of chain winding around his body sent his heart racing. Thumping the back of his head against a solid surface as he turned his face away from hers, he knew he was bound to a pillar of rock.

Her giggle turned into an ear blistering cackle as Tag shrank away from her touch as these delicate hands with slender fingers morphed. Long, pointed nails more like claws erupted from the fingertips as these digits became twisted by knotted joints, while dark liver spots and webs of blue blood vessels protruded at the skin's thin surface. These aged talons grabbed Tag by his chin, wrenching his face forward to kiss him again.

"Who are you?" he demanded to know, as she hovered ever closer to his angry face.

Instead of an answer, she kissed Tag hard on his lips. He gagged as her slimy tongue, like a powerful slug, wormed its way into his mouth as he fought in vain to be free of her.

Feelings of disgust changed to horror and confusion, watching as a thin veil of mist swirled over the girl's left eyeball. This sapphire eye clouded over, turning to white like sour, clotted milk. Tag recoiled in horror, sputtering and gagging as the lovely face aged before his eyes. The perfect skin became sallow as it drooped, bagged and wrinkled while hairy moles erupted forth as the youthful body shrivelled into a bony husk.

"It's you!" shouted Tag. He struggled to wrench his face free from her gnarled hands.

"Of course it's me!" Sin cackled in glee as she leaned in for another kiss.

"He cannot be dead!" sobbed Rose.

Exhausted, she slumped down before the now cold campfire as the deep cobalt sky surrendered to the coming of dawn.

"Well, if that impudent sod had not drowned, at this point, even if my show of force last eve overwhelmed him to the point of cowardice and humiliation, I hardly think he ran off," said Percy. He held up for all to see Tag's sword that was resting on his pack. "Yairet hardly seems the type to abandon his precious weapon, especially as it was the only way he measured his manliness."

"That is a cruel thing to say!" snapped Rose. Without thought of the consequences, her hand flashed out, slapping Percy's face.

"I am a prince! You cannot strike me!" His hand rubbed away the sting of her assault that left a red handprint on his fair complexion.

"I am a princess, so *yes*, I can!"

This time, her balled fist punched his arm, striking him harder than the slap she delivered to his startled face.

"Now, now, my friends, nothin' gets resolved this way!" said Harold. "Though it's not lookin' good, as far as I'm concerned, as long as there's no dead body, then there's no real proof that Tag is truly dead."

Percy motioned for Harold to be silent as he scolded the big man. "It is a repugnant thing you do!"

"Huh?" responded Harold.

"How dare you give Princess Rose-alyn hope when there is none? In my opinion, Yairet is dead! Dead and gone! It will only be a matter of time before his stinking, bloated corpse bobs up from the depths of that lake to the disgust of all. Not even the fishes will make a meal of him."

In response, Rose unleashed a long, pitiful wail of despair as Halen and Rainus, lunged forward, seizing Myron. They restrained the angry knight, preventing him from assaulting Percy once again.

"Yes! Control that madman before he attacks again!" ordered Percy, waving at Loftus to come to his aid. He ducked behind Rose, should the Elves lose their grip on the bellicose knight. "Though you all deny it, I am positive he assaulted me last night."

"The tree branch you walked into was what *assaulted* you," insisted Loftus, deliberately modifying the truth to spare them all from Percy's ranting. "You really should be more careful walking about in the dark."

"You are a liar, Loftus! And a bad one at that!" rebuked Percy. "I swear it was Kendall's fist that laid me out last night."

"I willingly accept the blame, as you are so willing to admit to all, Princess Rose included, that I was strong enough to knock you senseless with a single blow," growled Myron.

Percy heaved a disgruntled sigh. He considered these damning words and the ramifications should he admit that one, measly punch had been enough to knock him out cold.

"Though my recollection of events are vague at best, then I swear this knight was the one wielding the sturdy tree branch like it was a club, if indeed that was what knocked me out."

"At the rate your mouth prattled on, to be rendered unconscious served us well. You had never been so helpful as you were last eve, oblivious to all and out of our way!" snapped Myron.

"You dare attack my good character?" growled Percy. Assuming a bold stance, he shook a balled fist at Myron even as he continued to use Rose as a human shield.

"You dare test my patience with your stupidity and asinine comments?" retorted Myron. He struggled against Halen and Rainus' tenacious grasp as the desire to throttle Percy rose to the forefront of his mind, causing his hands to ache with pent up frustration.

"Whoa! Hold on here!" ordered Harold. "This isn't gettin' us anywhere. I know we're all tired and upset, but if our friend is out there, hurt and lost, shouldn't we be usin' this time to find Tag, instead of arguin' like this?"

"Harold, you are the voice of reason in all this madness!" declared Rose. "You are absolutely correct! Other than the fact Tag is missing, there has been nothing definitive to say he had indeed drowned."

"If he did not drown, then what happened to him?" queried Rainus.

"Tag was wearing an Elven cloak. That, and he, would have floated to the surface by now, even if he had drowned."

"I do not mean to be morbid, but I am betting he was devoured by a great serpent like he was nothing more than a rotten piece of bait unfit for the hook," said Percy, daring to verbalize his greatest desire. "Swallowed whole, cloak and all, that is why he is completely and utterly gone."

"This is a fresh water lake, not the deep, dark Sea of Shadows, you fool!" Silas grunted in a dismissive tone.

"So none exist in this lake?" asked Percy.

"Shall we throw you in to find out?" responded Loftus.

"Fetch off, you dolt! I was speaking to the Wizard!" snapped Percy, as he pondered the possibilities. "So, the serpents of legend exist only in that northerly sea?"

"There are many great mysteries in this world yet to be discovered by mortal man," answered Silas. "Perhaps you will see for yourself, if you survive the trek."

"If I should encounter a monstrous serpent, what a grand topic of conversation that would be! A harrowing tale to regale my subjects with of how I bravely slaughtered such a horribly magnificent beast!" Percy puffed out his thin chest. "I would become the stuff of legends."

"What is it with you and this propensity to kill?" asked Rainus. He scowled in disgust at the mortal.

"Kill or be killed, that is what I say!" Percy's tone was haughty as he raised his nose in the air in the most arrogant fashion. "The larger and more cunning the quarry, the greater the admiration for the hunter's skills. I shall go down in the annals of Axalon's history for my prowess as the greatest hunter in this realm."

"A bold declaration, Prince Percival," said Myron. "But mark my words, that pompous attitude of yours will only see the hunter become the hunted, if you are not careful."

"How pathetic! I am not easy to scare, no matter how foreboding your tone, Sir Kendall! I am always careful. I can sense danger before it even strikes."

"Yes, like you sensed Princess Rose was going to slap and punch you," snorted Loftus, with a thoughtful nod.

"I was being a gentleman," countered Percy. "I was allowing her to vent her grief on me."

"We digress!" interjected Rose. She wanted nothing more than to steer the conversation away from her earlier actions and back to her missing friend. "Suppose Tag had an accident last night? There is a chance he is just hurt and lost, wandering aimlessly in a daze as we argue."

"I suppose there is a chance he ran into the same tree branch I hit last night," conceded Percy. "He could be dazed and confused more so than usual; his mind so addled he believed he was the fish he was trying to catch."

"There is always a chance the young man did not meet a watery death, although the footprints seemed to indicate otherwise," admitted Halen. "An accident to cause some kind of trauma to his head would certainly create a level of confusion, causing him to wander away, lost."

"Yes," agreed Myron. His hand rubbed the scars on his scalp hidden beneath his thick thatch of hair. "Such a trauma can even cause him to forget who he is, even who we are, hence fleeing than coming to our campfire last night."

"Here is something we have yet to consider," offered Silas, after pondering the limited possibilities.

"What is that?" asked Rose.

"Suppose Tag had been captured? Spirited away by dark magic from this very place?"

"Is that even possible?" questioned Rainus.

"If Sin is behind Tag's disappearance, anything is possible," answered Silas.

"How can that be?" argued Percy. "That damned bewitched eyeball you have so much trust in indicated that she was to the north of us."

"True enough," admitted the Wizard, "but just how far north she is away from this place is anyone's guess."

"If Sin is behind this, she may only be a stone's throw away," said Halen, glancing about for signs of danger.

"A few nights ago, you mentioned you had sensed something evil adrift on the night air as we took the first watch," reminded Loftus.

"You did?" gasped Rose. She stared in disbelief at Halen Ironwood. "And yet, you said nothing to us?"

"What was there to say?" Halen shrugged his broad shoulders. "I was not about to cause unnecessary alarum based on a hunch or sense of foreboding I was unable to substantiate."

"But suppose it was that crazy Witch you had sensed?" asked Rose.

"At the time, I did not know that with any certainty," replied Halen. "Whatever set my nerves on edge that night had passed quickly."

"But still, you should have warned us," scolded Rose.

"Do not be so hard on Captain Ironwood," urged Loftus. "When I was on watch with him, I detected nothing evil. If this good Elf sensed something, and it was quick to pass as he said, it may have been nothing more than Prince Percival breaking wind, which unto itself, is evil *and* vile."

"Quiet, you mangy cur!" Percy snarled as he shook an angry fist at Loftus. "I am of royal blood, not some common commoner. I do not partake in such acts of vulgarity."

"Oh, come now, my lord!" scoffed Loftus, dismissing Percy's rant with a wave of his hand. "You eat, drink, and shit like the rest of us."

Percy's mouth fell open as his face burned with embarrassment, glowing like a blacksmith's furnace.

"Did you know the words *evil* and *vile* are the same, but different?" interjected Harold, in a bid to diffuse the growing animosity threatening this fellowship. "They have the same letters, just arranged differently."

"Fetch off, you big buffoon!" fumed Percy.

"The point being," said Myron, "if Sin is behind Tag's disappearance, we should act with haste; strike down this camp and resume our search."

Rainus glanced to the east. "I recommend you all get some rest for now. At daybreak we shall conduct a final search when the light is good. While you sleep, Halen and I shall keep ourselves busy."

"And what will you be doing as we sleep?" asked Percy. "Indulging in my supply of wine?"

"While you sleep, Captain Ironwood and I plan to continue our hunt, this time, searching for signs of the Witch," answered Rainus.

"Get off me, you lecherous bag of bones!" cursed Tag.

Fighting against the chain securing him to a jagged pillar, Tag thrashed about. He managed to dump the Witch from his lap.

Sin scrambled onto her feet. This insult, compounded by his abrupt rejection, caused her heart to fester with malice. It was enough to break the waning powers of the magical potion and spell. The remnants of her sun-spun tresses deteriorated into a tangled nest of black and grey hairs as the deepest of wrinkles creased her ugly face. Crouching down in front of her prisoner, she leaned in to kiss him again, only to have Tag violently resist this attention.

"A moment ago you found me to be irresistible," she hissed. "Had this enchantment lasted a little longer, I would have had my way with you, and you would have been a willing partner, eager to indulge in a little sin."

"Say no more!" Tag paled. He retched, grimacing in disgust as he turned his face away from hers. "I just got sick in my mouth."

"You're merely feeling pangs of hunger or thirst, or perhaps both," muttered Sin, smacking him on the head in retribution for refusing her advances.

"More like waves of revulsion!"

"Shut it! You best be nice to me. I am the only one able to give you any kind of salvation from your suffering."

"What I want is to be free of you!" snapped Tag.

"Think again! I have plans. I will not release you, but if you test my patience, I will have you begging for death before the end."

"You don't plan to kill me?"

"Of course I will kill you, but I plan to make you suffer before I finish you off."

"Not if I escape first!"

Sin's mouth fell open in dismay, and then she began to cackle hysterically as she sputtered, "*Escape?* There is no escape! And if you try, then you will die."

"Death is a better option than being held captive by you!" snapped Tag. He spat at her feet.

"You ungrateful dog!" growled Sin.

"I have nothing to be grateful for, where you're concerned."

"You should be grateful I did not kill you and your cohorts when I had the chance."

"And you did not chance it because you knew we would have overwhelmed you, had you tried," said Tag. "You would not have stood a chance against us, that's why you must take us on one at a time."

"You are here for good reason. As for your foolish friends, they will die, but there is a time and place for everything. I will be the one to control their destiny, right down to when and how they shall meet their end."

"If you think using me to lure them into your lair will work, think again," grunted Tag.

"You are a fool! Using the Sprite as my hostage was enough to set you and your cohorts on this rescue mission. I can only imagine how motivated they will be now that I've captured you. They will risk all to rescue you, and if not to save you, to prevent me from executing my plans of which you are a crucial element."

"You are the bigger fool to believe I am going to cooperate!" snapped Tag.

"You say that now, but in time, you will be at my beck and call."

"Never! I will never be enslaved by you!"

"Hunger and thirst have a way of changing one's perspective; destroying one's will. You'll have a change of heart, once you're made to suffer."

"You know nothing about me. I'm more resilient than you know."

"Everyone has a breaking point."

"Bring it on!" snapped Tag. "Test me, if you dare!"

Laughing at this bold declaration, she taunted him. "I will! But the punishment I shall dole out for your insolence must wait, for at this moment the tide is in my favour to harvest from the sea."

"Perhaps the tide will work in *my* favour; sweeping you out to sea to be lost forever."

Instead of a clever retort, Sin's wretched face leaned in close to his. Tag shuddered, turning away from her. The sour stench of her breath made his skin crawl as she dragged her pasty tongue across his cheek.

His stomach churned. The thought this hideous hag had kissed him was bad, but he had unwittingly kissed her back. This was worse!

"You are such a tease! If you're lucky we'll pick up where we left off," said Sin, as she leered at Tag. The black crystal glowed as she used the end of this staff to snag the handle of the bucket containing her fishing net, lifting it off the ground. Before she limped out of the cave, she tossed a hefty piece of driftwood onto the fire as she spoke aloud to no one in particular. "That should keep it burning for a good long while."

Stealing a parting glance, Sin scrutinized Tag through her one good eye. She determined her prisoner was well secured. There would be no escape for him.

"Try not to miss me too much, lover!" chortled Sin. The glow of the obsidian crystal distorted her haggard face, casting it in a haunting blend of light and shadow as she ambled toward the tunnel. "Though misery loves company, there will be no making merry while I am out! Instead, we shall all indulge in my brand of fun when I return."

"Tell me, Witch, does the night still hold? Is it dark out there?" called Tag.

"It is as black as my heart, if you must know."

"Excellent! Perhaps if the sea does not claim you, you will take a tumble off a cliff in the dark instead."

"If I should meet an untimely demise, then so shall you," grunted Sin. "But for you, it promises to be a lingering death as you succumb to thirst and starvation. It can take days, but in the end, you will die nonetheless. For now, make yourself at home. I will be back sooner than you think."

"And much sooner than I'd like, no matter how long you take!" Tag shouted behind her. He watched as Sin disappeared into the darkness of the adjoining tunnel, her shadow cast by the black crystal shrinking away as she ventured into the night.

For the longest moment, Tag listened. Above the steady beating of his heart, he could hear Sin's limping gait punctuated by the dull 'thud' of her staff doubling as her walking stick as these echoes faded away. Unleashing a sigh of relief, he glanced about his dreary surroundings. Aside from the haphazard campfire blazing away in the centre of this cave, the only other sound was the gentle lapping of waves rolling in with the receding tide. By the damp, salty air that rushed through this chamber each time a wave rolled in, Tag knew he was far from the lake. He had to be by a sea, but which one?

"Psst! Tag! How do you fare?"

"Loken?" Tag struggled to sit upright. His eyes searched about for his little friend. "Where are you?"

Loken stood up, pressing his face between the bars as he called, "Up here! In this prison."

Tag followed the sound of Loken's voice, spying upon a small iron cage suspended from the sconce where a torch burned bright.

"I knew you were still alive!" exclaimed Tag. He was glad to see the Sprite, and now knew what Sin meant when she mockingly spoke of misery loving company.

"And here, I thought you were dead when that Witch reappeared in her lair with you in her clutches."

"You thought I was dead?" said Tag.

"What else could I think? You were as limp and lively as a dead, spineless fish. It wasn't until she began chaining you up did I realize you were still alive otherwise, she would not have bothered."

"She means to keep me alive for now," said Tag. He shook the lingering fog from his mind as he struggled to remember what had happened to land him here. "As soon as I can figure out how to break free of these chains, I'll rescue you and we shall both make good our escape, together."

"A noble thought, my friend, but how do you plan to do that?" questioned Loken.

"I take it, you've already tried," determined Tag.

"Numerous times, and the last attempt almost got me killed," responded Loken, his bound hands rattling the bars of his prison.

"You're unable to transform?"

"I've been rendered utterly powerless as long as this cage holds me."

"The Wizard had warned us that if you were not already dead, then

Sin probably uses a spell to imprison you, otherwise you would have escaped by now."

"A spell," confirmed Loken, the sole of his boot scuffing the carved runes on the floor of his cage, "as well as one of the most potent elements known in the realm of magic to reinforce it."

"The salt from the tears of a Mermaid?"

"Exactly that!" confirmed Loken.

"But where would that Witch obtain such a thing, if it is as rare as Silas claimed?"

"From me," answered a meek voice.

"Who said that?" gasped Tag. He struggled, twisting about in search of the source of these two small words.

"I did."

This response was followed by the sounds of splashing water coming from directly behind where Tag was chained and immobilized.

"Allow me to make the introductions," offered Loken. "Tagius Yairet, it is my pleasure to introduce you to the lovely Elee, maiden of the Sea of Shadows. Elee, this is my dear friend, Tag."

"You're a Mermaid?" Tag struggled to peer over his shoulder, but the most he could see was a shock of dark hair, dulled by drying salt and the glow of her shoulder's pale skin peeking through the cascade of tresses tumbling down to her waist.

"I am indeed a maiden of the sea," whimpered Elee. Her soft voice drifted through the salty air.

"The Witch has proven more dangerous and clever than I first believed," said Tag. "How did we come to this sorry state?"

"She obviously employed both the forbidden arts and cunning to capture us," answered Loken.

"No doubt," said Tag. "But how? All I remember with any certainty is almost drowning in a lake, and then suddenly, I woke up here."

"Elee and I witnessed the Witch concoct a potion. She conjured up a spell to transform into a beautiful Naiad," replied Loken. "I believe she used this form to trick you, luring you away from our friends."

"But the Naiads are no more," said Tag, as he suddenly recalled the vision of loveliness that freed his hand that was ensnared by the fishing line. Trapped in the depths of the lake, his lungs ready to burst, Tag thought this dying memory of the beautiful maiden was nothing more than his imagination as he surrendered to a watery demise.

"That is true, but Elee and her kind still carry the blood of the Naiad," informed Loken. "The Witch created a magic potion using her blood."

"But why not just change into a Mermaid?" asked Tag.

"Because a Mermaid would not survive long in fresh water,"

answered Loken.

"But a Naiad can," determined Tag. "That makes sense."

"Yes, and whether it was a Naiad or a Mermaid, throughout history, mortal men have been enchanted by both," reminded the Sprite.

"That explains much, but what about you, Loken? When I last saw after we escaped from the Mines of Euphoria, you said you were going to follow Sin, promising to keep a safe distance from her in a bid to go undetected in order to locate her secret lair. What happened to you?"

"I was tricked by that hag! I watched as she disappeared into the side of a mountain. I was about to return, reporting on her whereabouts, when I heard a familiar voice calling to me, crying for help. It was a cry of distress I could not ignore."

"Sin was calling for help?" questioned Tag. He was momentarily baffled as to why Loken would feel compelled to rush to her aid, knowing that the Witch had every intention of destroying or capturing him.

"No, had it been Sin, I would have left her to rot. Instead, I heard my beloved Celia calling out to me from the dark of the cave."

"So you had to go rescue her," said Tag.

"Of course I did, just as you would have, had it been Princess Rose. I feared for her life, so I had no choice."

"It was that bewitched sock puppet, wasn't it?" asked Tag.

"When I followed the sounds of Celia's voice into the mountainside, I came upon this very cage that holds me now. It was suspended in a beam of light that shone through from a small hole to the outside world into a cave, and inside the cage was my beloved! She begged me to set her free. Without hesitation, I flew to her prison. Just as I opened the door to free her, there was Sin. You can imagine my surprise when Celia abruptly slumped over, only to transform into that damned sock puppet!"

"And before you could morph or escape, Sin set the spell into motion."

"Indeed! So here I am now, trapped since that fateful night. But how did you know it was her puppet, and how did she lure all of you to that particular lair when I was detained; unable to report on her whereabouts?"

"Like you, we were all tricked! She used dark magic to transform her sock puppet into you."

"*Me?*" Loken gasped in astonishment. He stared in disbelief at Tag as the young man elaborated.

"That *thing* was your spitting-image, Loken. The likeness was so uncanny it had fooled us all. We followed as it guided us into the cave where that foul thing flew into this beam of sunlight you spoke of. It fell to the ground, taking on its regular form as it tried to crawl away."

"Did you kill it?"

"Not that a sock can be killed, but the Princess tried to. She was giving it a sound trouncing, but in the process, stomped straight through the cave floor. She almost died when she fell through the hole, along with that sock puppet."

"But you saved her, correct?"

"We did, and just when we believed the bane of our existence was no more, that creepy thing reappeared out of nowhere! At one point, it followed us into the huge chamber where we eventually saw you in that cage. I had crushed that horrid thing under a great rock. Princess Rose even packed earth around it to make sure it could not follow us."

"And then Sin used her powers to change it into that great dragon of shadow and sand," said Loken, as he recalled that frightening moment he was forced to witness, helpless to forewarn his friends or come to their aid as the monster erupted from under this rock.

"Yes."

"Did all manage to survive that attack?" questioned Loken.

"Much to the Witch's chagrin, we were unscathed in that battle. Harold had come to our rescue in the nick of time," answered Tag. "He tried to rescue you, too, but that hag disappeared with you in her clutches."

"And the nasty sock puppet, what happened to it? I have not seen it since then."

"When Sin disappeared from the cave, her magical bond with that phantom dragon was broken. It disintegrated, falling to the ground as a harmless sock puppet once more. When it did, I threw that ghastly thing into the river of lava."

"It was destroyed?" asked Loken.

"Utterly," answered Tag. "We watched as that hexed plaything burned until nothing remained."

"What is a sock puppet?" asked Elee.

"Say again," responded Tag. Perplexed by her question, he struggled to peer over his shoulder at her.

"A sock puppet... What is it? It sounds to be a powerful, magical weapon."

Loken was quick to explain to Tag, "Her people do not wear clothes, so she does not know what a sock puppet is, let alone a sock."

"Wait... She is naked?" gulped Tag. His cheeks burned red. He suddenly felt uncomfortably warm as he abruptly averted his eyes so he could not be accused of sneaking a peek over his shoulder at her nude form.

"Of course Elee is naked," said Loken, his words matter-of-fact. "She has no need for clothing."

"But are you not cold, Elee?" asked Tag.

"I feel the chill of the air, but not when I am in the sea."

Before Tag could question her lack of modesty, Loken added, "In the sea, there is no need to wear clothes. It will only get wet and is sure to impede swimming."

"I suppose that makes sense," said Tag.

"Of course it does," averred the Sprite.

"But what is this sock puppet you both speak of?" asked Elee. "It sounds truly dangerous."

"Only if it is imbued with dark magic," responded Tag. "A sock is a piece of apparel that human beings wear on our feet to keep them warm before donning shoes or boots to protect our feet from rough terrain."

"I understand now," said Elee, thinking back on the footwear she had seen on drowned sailors swallowed up by the seas after their ship had capsized or struck a reef.

"In this case, a sock puppet is a child's plaything," continued Tag. "An old sock is adorned to look like an animal or person, then worn on one's hand to manipulate it, to pretend it is alive to play with."

"I think I understand what you mean," said Elee.

"I take it, she used the bewitched sock puppet to capture you as well," said Tag.

"No," answered the Mermaid, as she stared over at her seal. Flotsam had remained still, as much entrenched in her misery as she was by the net holding her hostage from the beckoning sea. "That wretched woman had captured my pet seal, using Flotsam to lure me into a trap to remove me from my home and away from my family."

"The sea is right there. Have you tried calling for help?" asked Tag, hearing the rush of water being drawn away with the receding tide.

"Like you, I am chained to this rock. My cries can only be carried afar when underwater," answered Elee.

"But it sounds to me that you are already in water," said Tag.

"I am trapped, confined to this tidal pool. It is just enough seawater to keep me alive to prolong my suffering, but it is not deep enough or connected directly to the sea to allow me to call to my sisters for help. At this point, I believe they have given me up for dead. We shall languish in our shared misery, doomed to die in this wretched place."

"Do not lose hope, Elee," urged Tag. "I know my friends. It will only be a matter of time before they arrive to rescue us, if I don't find a way to escape first."

"You are sounding mighty optimistic, Tag," said Loken. "Do they come with an army of Elves to do battle against the Witch?"

"No, we were moving in secret, so travelling with Lord Silverthorn's army would prove difficult. Just know that we have extra hands." Loken's aura grew bright as he thought on his ladylove. "Celia travels with them?"

"No. Silas ordered her to remain behind to protect her realm, should Sin return to attack. Pancecelia tends to her subjects' safety while sending out her nightly brigade to discreetly gather information pertinent to Sin, and your whereabouts."

Loken's aura dimmed, but he agreed, "It is better for my beloved to stay far from harm's way, but you spoke of *extra hands*."

"Four to be exact," responded Tag. "Mind you, one pair has proven completely inept and more of a hindrance than help."

"By your foreboding words, there is cause to worry. Care to elaborate?"

"To make a long and sordid tale short, upon your disappearance we were forced to regroup in Axalon while Silas headed off to meet with the Council of Wizards. Part of the reason was to allow Princess Rose to explain to King Maxmillian that the quest had taken on a new wrinkle, thereby postponing plans for announcing her betrothal to Prince Percival."

Loken paled upon hearing this. "Say it is not so! That ne'er-do-well of a prince came along to steal away with the Dreamstone or to coerce the Wizard into giving him one."

"Pretty much," said Tag, heaving a dreary sigh. "The only positive news is that his man, Captain Gilbert Loftus, has proven very useful. He even takes it upon himself to keep Prince Percival in line when that dolt has one of his many tantrums."

"Brilliant!" said Loken. "At least help is imminent. Where are they now?"

"Before I was captured, I last saw our friends by the lake in the forest bordering the Fire Rim Mountain Range."

Loken unleashed a troubled sigh. He slid down the bars of his prison, sitting in a dejected heap on the floor of the cage upon learning this news. "There is a chance we will be dead before they get here."

"I know it sounds like they are so very far away, but they will come," promised Tag. "When you think about it, with the dragons taking refuge from the cold weather, the trek should be quick and easy."

"True," agreed Loken, "but do they know the location of Sin's secret lair? Do they know exactly where she holds us? I think not!"

"No, but they know in which general direction to travel, and the closer they get to here, the easier it will be to locate us."

"I'm intrigued," said Loken, sitting up to learn more. "How is this possible? Does the Wizard use magic?"

"In a way, yes! Before this magic though, Captain Ironwood was leading the way, following the clues. Now, Master Agincor has the perfect tool showing them the way, leading them to that murderous Witch."

"What is this perfect tool?" Loken's brows furrowed with curiosity.

"It was gifted to Silas by a Witch."

"Wait… Sin gifted Silas with a tool to find her? That makes no sense."

"I meant to say the Witch in question is the sister of Malis Ravensee, the leader of the coven just outside the village of Home."

"Malis of Raven's Hollow?" asked Loken.

"Yes! Malis was murdered by Sin," explained Tag. "Her sister removed one of the eyes from Malis' body, casting an enchantment upon it. As the last person she saw was her killer, the spell allows this eye to show us in which direction Sin moves."

"Morbid, but ingenious!" said Loken. "Using a Witch to find a Witch may be just the thing to deliver them here."

"Even as we speak, that bewitched eyeball is leading them to this very place," said Tag. "I'm sure of it."

"Where is Sin?" asked Silas.

He held the small, squat jar up toward the first light of the morning sun. As though using this brilliant orb to set its bearings, the eyeball twitched about. Suddenly, the stringy optic nerve whipped to and fro, propelling this eye in circles until it abruptly stopped. It bumped repeatedly against one side of the jar.

The Wizard lowered the container, peering at the eyeball as it enthusiastically showed the way. It literally set its unblinking sight to the northern expanse of land rolling out before them as they stood at the edge of the forest.

"Well?" asked Rose. Though she stood next to the Wizard, she had no desire to look upon this morbid directional indicator. There was something unsettling when that thing stared back at her. "Where do we go from here?"

Silas scrutinized the broad, flat valley rimmed by great mountains along the north, west and eastern perimeter and lined by a great forest along the south where the Wizard and his comrades now stood. This vast expanse, composed mostly of volcanic ash blanketing earth and rocks, was barren except for the scattered islands of trees hugging pockets of fertile soil along the ribbons of creeks and rivers flowing through it.

"We head that way," answered Silas, as he pointed across the desolate valley.

Percy guided his steed to the river, allowing it to drink with the other horses. Standing next to Silas, he ascertained the eyeball's direction as he had little trust in the words of a Wizard.

"And what place is this?" asked Percy, as he stared across the bland landscape.

"Behold! Before you are the formidable Fire Rim Mountains!" announced Silas. "This is the valley we must cross."

"Well, this is rather unspectacular," grumbled Percy. His eyes narrowed, scrutinizing the sprawling terrain before them. "I had imagined a lost world of prehistoric plants and molten rivers of lava. I had pictured fire and brimstone spewing forth into a dark, brooding sky roiling with great clouds of ash over a land choked by poisonous gases to reduce it to a barren wasteland."

"Do not be fooled by the seemingly tranquil landscape," cautioned Silas. He pointed to where several thin plumes of ash and steam vented to become one with the low-hanging clouds hugging the shoulders of these mountains. "They are quiet now, but many are still highly active volcanoes. They wait for unseen forces to awaken them."

"Can you tell when they will erupt?" asked Percy.

"It usually begins with tremors rising from deep within the bowels of the earth," answered Silas, "but there is no sense in worrying about it now."

"Of course there is cause for worry!" snapped Percy. "Such tremors are a sign to run for our lives so we are not swallowed up by molten lava or suffocated by putrid ash or poisonous gases."

"One cannot simply outrun the wrath of a volcano should it rumble to life with a vengeance."

"I would be highly motivated," insisted Percy, "enough to speed away on my great warhorse."

"It is like saying you can outrun the wind. It is a feat you cannot accomplish, not even on the swiftest steed."

"Your words are rather ominous, Wizard," noted Percy. "So we shall do the prudent thing; find another way to avoid these lands to get to our destination."

"You wish! We shall now begin our trek across this land ruled by the dragons, but this time in a north-northwest direction as this enchanted eyeball indicates."

"Fine! So, do we follow this river?" Percy's eyes traced the fast-flowing water that began as a small creek at the lake of Tag's disappearance. Fed by other forest streams, it grew and continued northward as an ever widening, but shallow river.

"It meanders through this valley, twisting to and fro like it was carved out by the thrashing tail of a great dragon," said Rainus. "If the eyeball directs us to head toward those distant mountains, then the fastest route is to take the straightest possible course. We shall cross the river here where it is shallow enough for our horses to safely wade through. And then we head that way, toward the mountain pass to the Sea of Storms."

"You heard Lord Silverthorn," said Halen. "While the light holds, we ride. Mount up!"

Percy seized the pommel of his saddle. Slipping his foot into the stirrup, he prepared to mount his horse. He hopped, pushing off the ground several times, trying to gain the momentum he needed to launch himself up.

"Here, my lord, let me help you," offered Harold, reaching over to give Percy a leg up onto his horse.

"Get off me, you big dolt!" snarled Percy. He shoved Harold as he finally swung his leg over his steed's rump, nearly kicking the large man on his chin in the process.

Harold stumbled back, bumping into Silas just as the Wizard was about to fix the lid back onto the jar containing Malis' eye.

"*Oof!*" grunted Silas. The force knocked his body forward to send the eye flying out of the open jar.

Everyone, except Percy, dashed toward the eye as it reached the zenith of its arc, almost hovering in the air for a split second before swiftly plummeting down toward the rushing waters.

"No!" cried out Myron.

He launched himself bodily in an attempt to catch the eye before it was too late. Groaning in pain and frustration, his body slammed onto the rocky ground at the river's edge, his hands empty. The eye stared at Myron briefly as it landed with a *'plop'* into the coursing river. Quickly, it was swept downstream and out of sight.

"Brilliant! Absolutely brilliant!" snapped Silas, as he scowled in anger at Percy. "There goes our only way of pinpointing Sin's location."

"I swear you did that on purpose!" admonished Myron.

"I did not even touch the Wizard! It was you, you clumsy oaf!" scolded Percy. He swatted at Harold's head to knock the snout of his badger headpiece low over his pudgy nose. "Look what you did! It is all your fault."

"It was an accident," cried Harold. "I was only tryin' to help you."

"Yes, it was an accident that could have been avoided, had you not pushed Harold aside to begin with," scolded Loftus.

"Maybe all is not lost. That eyeball's still headin' in a northerly direction," stated Harold. "I'm sure of it."

"I believe the natural flow of this river has everything to do with where that eyeball is heading now," determined Myron.

"What do you think will happen to it?" asked Rose, as she lost sight of the gruesome Witch finder.

"If it doesn't get snapped up by a fish or a hungry raven, and the currents do not wash it out to sea to be lost forever, I sense that enchanted orb will continue on to seek out Sin," answered Silas, as he tossed the worthless container over his shoulder. "But it matters not at this point, for it is now lost to us."

"Too bad we cannot just catch up to it," lamented Harold.

"The water flows too swiftly," said Rainus, his keen ears detecting the sounds of distant rapids as the volume and velocity of the river being fed by other streams caused it to grow as it stretched northward. "We shall never catch up to it now."

"Well then, I suppose if Tag and the Sprite are indeed in the evil Witch's grasp, we must learn to accept our losses; be grateful that the casualties were kept to a minimum as we return home," said Percy, his spirit buoyed by the possibility of ending this quest here and now.

"We cannot abandon them!" cried Rose. She was mortified that he would even suggest such a thing. "And I will be damned if I leave Tag at Sin's mercy."

Appalled by her level of commitment and concern for this missing ruffian, Percy's mouth fell open.

"Tag may have been your *friend*, but I am the one destined to be your *husband*," reminded Percy. His face reddened, twitching in jealousy. He was thoroughly incensed she continued to place so much value on her relationship with Tag, even now that he was gone. "You should be grateful it was not me the Witch had absconded with, for *that* would be truly traumatic for you, my dear Rose-alyn. Had it been me, it would have been a loss you would never recover from."

"You are an egotistical fool!" declared Myron. With a condemning finger he jabbed Percy's chest as though to puncture and deflate his pride. "Had it been you to disappear, save for Princess Rose, we'd be more inclined to abandon this search. But as this is Tag we speak of, we must rescue him before it is too late."

"Too late?" grumbled Percy. "In truth, it may be too late now. In all likelihood, the fool is already dead. So why bother?"

"Then it is still up to us to stop that Witch," answered Silas.

"Stop her from what? We shall risk our lives, but to what end?"

"Whether we capture her or she is killed in the process, she must be stopped," said Silas.

"You want her dead? So be it! She retreats north, to the end of the world," reminded Percy. His slight shoulders shrugged with indifference. "If anything, she will freeze to death with the coming of winter or she will be killed by a dragon in the warmer months of spring. Either way, the Witch is dead. Problem solved!"

"You know nothing! If Sin kills Tag, it promises to be the start of great and terrible evil," warned Silas, "the likes of which you cannot even begin to imagine."

"Oh, blah, blah, blah!" muttered Percy, as he scornfully mocked the Wizard. "Whether Tag is dead or he is to be killed by that Witch, if she did indeed abduct him in the first place, I hardly think our combined efforts, no matter how heroic, will make a difference in sparing his life, even if we raced our horses until they dropped dead from exhaustion. Because of Harold's careless blunder, I hardly think we'll find the Witch's location now."

"Should Tag be killed by her, it will be to harvest his blood," stated Myron.

"So the Witch will be reduced to cannibalism due to limited resources as winter sets in. What do I care if she takes to drinking his blood and gnawing on his bones?" said Percy, unmoved by the pallor of Rose's appalled face. "She is a Witch. She is crazy. It is what crazy Witches do when they have nothing to eat."

"She will not cannibalize Tag," said Silas. "Sin needs the blood of her brother's killer for a potion to resurrect that necromancer. Should she succeed, then woe to all who stand in her way. She will become a destructive force none can reckon with."

15

In the Company of Fools

Sheer desperation forced her hand. Rose removed the Dreamstone hidden beneath her blouse. "Suppose I try to wish that dreadful eyeball back into our possession? That should be easy enough to do."

Silas gestured for her to put away the magic crystal as he explained, "A worthy suggestion, Princess, but it will be all for naught. That eyeball is under a powerful enchantment. You can wish for it back, and the very likeness of Malis' missing eye will reappear, but it will not be infused with Meerah's magic. It is a power that a wish, no matter how exacting, cannot replicate unless you are a Witch. It would be like wishing for another Dreamstone, and though another will appear in its likeness, it will be rather impotent when it comes to making wishes come true."

A mere glimpse of the Dreamstone sent Percy's heart racing with avarice driven anticipation. With eyes wide in wonder he motioned for Rose to not yet hide away the object of his desire. "If we cannot wish for that wretched eyeball, then why can Princess Rose-alyn not just wish us to where that vile Witch hides now, based on what that eye saw? If Tag's life does indeed hang in the balance, it is sure to spare us a great deal of travelling time."

"You ninny!" snapped Silas. "For her to wish us to appear in Sin's lair, it will require Princess Rose to form an exact image of this place in her mind's eye. It is an impossible task, if she knows not where it is or how it looks."

"She must be that exacting?" questioned Percy.

"Of course!" grunted Silas.

"So, if she wanted to, Princess Rose-alyn can wish us back to my father's throne room because she has been there before?" questioned Percy. This was more to better understand the workings of this crystal than to actually wish to be delivered back to Axalon in order to forego the misery of an arduous trek home.

"Yes," responded Silas. "Do tell me you wish for this! I am positive Princess Rose will be happy to grant you this immediate trip back to your castle."

"You mean to trick me! I will not endanger my beloved by leaving her to suffer in the company of fools!" Percy's lips curled into a sneer of contempt. "You could not even keep one of your own safe. I'd be an idiot to entrust you with her precious life."

"So, we will *not* be parting company?" queried Myron, as he glanced over hopefully at Percy.

"Of course not! But if it is a question of Princess Rose-alyn conjuring up an exact image of what she wishes for, then why does she not just wish for Yairet to appear before us. As forgettable as he is to me, I am sure his ugly face, right down to his smug grin, is indelibly etched in her mind."

"I *can* wish Tag back to us!" exclaimed Rose. Her eyes gleamed with hope as she considered Percy's suggestion.

"Think again, Princess," said Silas. "If Tag is Sin's prisoner, she will shield him with dark magic, preventing all from readily finding or wishing him away to safety. Just as you could not wish for Loken's return, it will be the same for Tag."

"However, if Tag is only injured and lost, there is a chance Princess Rose can do just that," said Myron.

"True enough." Silas nodded in agreement. "Then wish away, my dear girl. Return our young friend back to our fold."

Rose hoped she was not too late. Clutching the Dreamstone to her heart, she closed her eyes. Clearing her troubled mind, she conjured up an image of Tag as he appeared to her prior to his disappearance. With his form perfected in her mind's eye, Rose wished for Tag to appear before them.

When Rose finally opened her eyes. Her heart dropped into the pit of her stomach as she glanced about. Tag was nowhere to be seen.

"Well?" asked Harold, staring hopefully at her. "Where is he?"

"It did not work," groaned Rose.

"Very true, but I do not consider it a wasted wish, Princess," said Rainus. "At least we know for certain that Sin holds Tag captive and she does indeed shield him from us with dark magic."

Percy unleashed a dreary sigh as he turned to the Wizard. "So, we journey on."

"There is no time to waste," said Silas. "We must find Tag before Sin does the unthinkable."

"That was disgusting!" Tag shuddered at the thought of the lecherous, old Witch. "I can't believe she kissed me."

"Worse yet, I cannot believe you kissed her back," reminded Loken, as he grimaced in revulsion.

"As a friend, you should have said something to stop me."

"I tried to warn you! I tried to stop you from kissing her, but you either did not hear me or refused to listen. Whatever the case, it was truly repulsive."

"Hey, I'm the one who's repulsed!" retorted Tag. "How could it be so for you?"

"Unfortunately, I was made witness to the unthinkable. I cannot un-see it. It is now indelibly etched in my mind."

"Before you make me sick, can we change the subject?" asked Tag. His eyes focused in the gloom of this chamber as the angle of the waning moon allowed its light to reflect, dancing on the waves rolling in through the mouth of cave that was now fully exposed thanks to the low tide.

"The only subject that comes to the forefront of my mind is how we escape from here," replied Loken. In utter frustration, his bound hands rattled the unyielding bars of his prison.

"What about you, Elee?" asked Tag, speaking over his shoulder to address her. "Any ideas?"

"The thought of escape has long abandoned me. I wish I could hold the tide at bay; allow this pool to drain away so I may die before that Witch tries to harvest more of my tears."

"Now that is a dreadful thought," said Tag.

"True, but if I pass from this world, she will have no reason to hold my dear little Flotsam any longer. At least my seal will be set free."

"What do you think Sin is doing at this very moment?" asked Tag.

"I believe she is taking advantage of the moonlight and tide to fish," said Elee.

"I tend to believe Sin is harvesting the sea for ingredients she can use in potions," said Loken.

"Well, whatever it is that preoccupies her now, let us hope she is distracted for a good long time," sighed Tag, as he studied the rusted length of chain looped around his body.

The encroaching tide and rising sun brought with it Sin's return to her lair. She was in a dour mood, muttering and grumbling, as though speaking to an invisible friend. Propping her staff against the wall, Sin tossed aside the wooden bucket that contained nothing more than a sea perch she kept for herself and several spiny sculpins she flung at the seal.

Flotsam eagerly pushed her snout through the netting, her teeth crunching down on the fishes' big heads before quickly gulping down this meagre offering.

For Sin, it was not a show of mercy, but more a matter of practicality. In keeping the animal alive, it would allow to further her torment on the seal, thereby getting what she most wanted from Elee.

"I see you avoided being swallowed up by the sea, or you did fall in, but being so detestable, the sea spat you back out," mocked Tag, watching as she stoked the stubborn embers that continued to glow before placing more driftwood onto the growing flames as the fire sputtered back to life.

Sin's only response to his derogatory comment was an odd, nerve-rattling cackle. She squatted before the fire, warming her bony hands as the frosty dew glazing her hooded cloak began to thaw.

From where Tag sat, the hag looked like a massive heap of steaming, fresh manure on a cold winter's morning. The evaporating moisture wafted from her crouched form; the heat swelling from the fire warmed her bones, drying her apparel.

Too weary to make a breakfast of the perch, Sin reached over to the wooden drying rack she had mounted near to the fire. The thin slices of clam meat she had carefully spaced to allow heat and smoke to dry and cure this delicacy would provide an adequate meal for now.

Removing several strips, Sin's narrow, pointed chin bobbed, moving in slow, deliberate circles as she chewed while staring into the heart of the fire. Her decaying molars pulverized the food into a saliva-moistened pulp that she washed down with a swig of water. Tearing off manageable pieces of cured clam, she focused on this task, ignoring Loken's taunting and Tag's snide commentaries as she ate. Each salty bite was like chewing on the toughest pieces of boiled shoe leather that had been left out in the summer sun to dry. It was not hard to imagine that the energy she hoped to gain in eating this food was probably expended on trying to work each mouthful into a masticated wad she could swallow.

Snorting in a deep breath, Sin's weary jaw muscles were beginning to ache.

"Hey! What about us?" called Tag. "How about sharing some of that food?"

In defiant response, Sin thrust the entire strip of clam into her mouth. The hard edges of this desiccated food bulged as sharp angles against her hollow cheeks to further distort her features. She deliberately brushed off her hands to show they were now empty and she had no intention of feeding any one of them after her exhausting and fruitless night. Like a ruminating cow working its cud, Sin's jaws continued chewing on this tough piece of food. She suddenly cried out, her ugly face grimacing in pain. Using the tip of her tongue, she pried the offending clam free. Digging it out with her fingers, her mouth was agape as her good eye narrowed. She stared at the partially chewed clam that was now streaked with blood.

"Thought so," she muttered as a talon-like fingernail picked out a shattered tooth that had become embedded in the food.

A quick examination revealed a good chunk of a rotting molar had indeed snapped off. She carelessly tossed this tooth over her shoulder as she used her tongue to probe about. She felt the gap created by this missing tooth as well as the sharp, jagged remains of what was still anchored in the gum. Flicking the offending piece of clam into the fire, she then rammed her hand into her mouth.

Sin reached in.

She grunted in pain as she yanked free what was left of the broken tooth. The pronged roots, now caked in blood and stringy bits of tissue, was indicative that she was able to remove it all than to be subjected to the misery of a never-ending toothache, if the nerves remained exposed.

Tossing this bloodied tooth into the fire, Sin rose to her feet. Limping over to the bucket she had abandoned, she removed the net and the perch to find a puddle of seawater had collected at the bottom of this container. Picking it up, she tipped the water into her mouth. Looking like a bullfrog puffing up its throat pouch, Sin swished the brine about in her mouth, rinsing out the bloody cavity where the tooth was once rooted. Her gaunt cheeks ballooned as she forced this water from side to side. Spitting out the nasty mixture of seawater, saliva and blood, Sin used the tattered sleeve of her frock to wipe away the trail of spittle from her chin.

She threw the bucket down. Tossing the perch back inside, she piled the cold, wet netting over top to keep the fish fresh until she was ready to make a meal of it.

Sin then searched the rickety old shelf for a tiny bottle. "Ha! There you are!"

Wrenching off the cork seal, she dipped the tip of her index finger into the oil of cloves. She gingerly dabbed it onto the wound made by the missing tooth. Instantly, the aromatic oil helped to numb the throbbing pain.

"That's better," she muttered as she resealed the bottle before returning it to the shelf.

Limping over to the furthest corner of the chamber, Sin removed her cloak, spreading it over the wool blanket and a threadbare patchwork quilt that was thrown haphazardly over a wobbly cot. Here, the rhythmic echoing of waves rolling into this sea cave promised to lull her to sleep. With a great yawn, the Witch crawled beneath the bedding. Seeking respite from the disappointment of a wasted night, until the setting sun and the retreating tide beckoned her once more, Sin closed her eyes and shut her mind to the waking world.

Percy squinted, shielding his eyes from the sun as it continued its steady ascent into the pale blue sky. A gauzy raft of stray clouds drifted lazily across the face of this radiant orb, its brilliance piercing through the wispy patches. Shafts of golden beams shone down, serving to accentuate the desolate nature of his surroundings.

He pointed ahead as he announced with an air of sarcasm to all, "In case Captain Ironwood's *far-seeing* eyes failed to notice, just up yonder I see signs of someone's passing through these parts."

"You do?" Rose followed the direction of Percy's finger.

"Yes! In my opinion, it looks to be a prominent landmark of sorts, no doubt to indicate the halfway point of this valley."

"Rest assured, Prince Percival, I did see it, but it is *not* a landmark," stated Halen, urging his mount directly toward Percy's object in question.

"Of course it is," argued Percy. "Even from here I can see there are two adjacent rows of tall markers of graduating size, punctuated by a huge boulder. You cannot tell me this is an accident of nature! It is too perfect to be a natural occurrence."

"I'd say you are the accident of nature and that indeed is a natural occurrence," countered Silas.

"I shall ignore your insult, for only an aged and feeble mind such as yours cannot see the obvious," snorted Percy.

"Master Agincor and Halen Ironwood are quite correct. Those are nothing more than bones," explained Rainus.

"*Bones?* I think not!" Percy's voice was strained with annoyance that the Wizard and Elves were so quick to contradict him before Rose.

"We have already encountered a multitude of bones scattered about on our trek, both of dragon and deer, not to mention the odd livestock those murderous, thieving beasts have killed and dined on. I will bet Loftus' life those are anything but bones! They are much too big. And note their arrangement. It is all too precise!"

"Then what are they?" asked Loftus.

"I am more inclined to believe they are strategically placed monoliths of stone or tree trunks devoid of branches to make that marker obvious to all."

"Oh! So you believe the single, massive *boulder* at the far end of those tall, skinny '*monoliths*' was somehow transported down from one of the mountains to that very place for this purpose?" queried Loftus. Annoyed this royal would so eagerly gamble away his life in a bet, especially when he was so wrong; the captain readily sided with the Elf Lord.

"I am willing to concede that the Wizard is partly right about it being a natural occurrence," decided Percy. "That boulder's placement is most likely due to a volcano."

"Truly?" said Loftus. His eyebrows arched up as he waited for a logical explanation to substantiate this claim.

"Yes. I believe it was deposited there when one of those volcanoes erupted, blowing that massive rock off like the cork from a badly fermented bottle of wine. Whoever erected that landmark merely took advantage of that boulder's placement, incorporating it as a permanent marker should those taller pieces of stone or timber topple over with the passing of time."

"I'm thinkin' that sounds pretty logical," said Harold, nodding to Percy. He watched as a crow or a raven, as it was difficult for his mortal eyes to ascertain from this distance, alighted upon the tallest of the erect formations.

"Of course it is logical," snapped Percy, "but I am in no need of the words of a fool to lend credence to mine."

"Then you are the real fool to believe in your own words," insisted Myron. "Those are indeed bones – very big dragon bones to be exact."

"What a bunch of malarkey!" declared Percy. "Dragons of that size do not exist. They never did and I shall prove it!"

Before Rose could tell him about the size of the monstrous dragons they had encountered when they were last here, Percy was off. Digging his heels vigorously against his steed's flanks, he charged ahead of the others.

"Bombastic twit!" Silas muttered. He shook his head in disgust as he waved his comrades on to follow Percy before the hubris mortal found himself in trouble.

"Bombastic?" repeated Harold. He glanced over to Loftus for an explanation.

"Pompous, pretentious, overbearing, verbose," answered Loftus, his words matter-of-fact. "Take your pick, my friend, for they all apply where Prince Percival is concerned."

When the party caught up to Percy, he had already dismounted from his horse to investigate his find. His arrival was greeted by the scolding cries of a raven taking flight when he and his warhorse came too close for comfort. Now, standing in the middle of what he had assumed was a man-made landmark, the young man was absolutely gobsmacked. He stared up in slack-jawed awe at the skeletal remains so large, it could only be that of a once gargantuan dragon. The ribcage he now stood in could easily house his father's largest carriage as well as the horses to draw it. The towering formations of sun-bleached rib bones dwarfed him, the tops curving over his body like they were two rows of teeth waiting to clamp together to swallow him whole. It was obvious this beast had toppled over onto its back when it died.

Between these two rows of rib bones, rising up from the ground and protruding just above the earth like a crudely constructed path of cobblestones, was a single line of bones that once formed the spine of this great dragon. Shattered remains of what had to be the creature's hipbone transitioned to a long, tapered tail that snaked to one side. This appendage was represented by a long string of bones that gradually shrank in size. It terminated abruptly where predatory animals, most likely smaller dragons, made off with the scraps of meat clinging to these smaller, easy to manage bones where the tail was the thinnest. On the opposite end of the massive ribcage where Percy now stood, the backbones that continued on to form the neck that once supported the dragon's head were much larger and relatively intact. This column of cervical vertebrae, most buried in layers of volcanic ash, came to an end, crowned by the largest skull he had ever seen or could possibly imagine.

The lower jawbone, still armed with many sharp, serrated teeth, lay shattered and twisted to one side of this skull. Percy's hands could easily fit into one of the holes that patterned the top of the skull bone just behind the eye sockets. These two hollows, long devoid of eyeballs, were big enough for a man as large as Harold to climb into and sit comfortably.

The puncture wounds to the dragon's skull indicated one much stronger and larger killed this creature. Once the belly had been ripped open and the internal organs were devoured, evidence of razor-sharp teeth that had slashed through skin and muscle left long, linear scrapes on these vertical stands of rib bones.

"As you can see, Prince Percival, you were wrong once again," said Myron, "It is just as Lord Silverthorn and Captain Ironwood had stated: *dragon bones*."

"Yes, yes! But from where I first spied upon this skeleton, my earlier declaration must be counted as an honest mistake. Besides, never have I seen tapestries nor have I read of documentation representing dragons of this monstrous proportion. If anything, I am sure this creature was an anomaly; a freak of nature, to be sure," grunted Percy.

To emphasize the abnormally large size of this skull, he peered into one of the puncture wounds, sticking his entire head into where the dragon's brain was once housed.

"*ARGHHHH!*" shrieked Percy.

In fright, his head jerked free from this dark cavity. Tumbling to the ground, he watched as a small, dark cyclone of bats erupted from this hole in a clamour of flapping, leathery wings. These creatures took flight, emptying into the sky. They were just as frightened by this mortal's intrusion into their artificial cave as he was by their unexpected presence in the dome of this great skull.

As Silas unleashed a great belly laugh that sent the bats scattering in confused flight into the light of day, Rose ran to Percy's side. In angry embarrassment, the Prince shrugged off her hands as she tried to help him onto his feet.

"Well, just know this *anomaly* was killed by another *freak of nature*," stated Myron. He pointed to the radius of the bite mark left on the dragon's skull where long blades of teeth undoubtedly stabbed into the creature's brain, killing it instantly before twisting this head to break the victim's neck.

"Yes, by the evidence left behind, this dragon did not stand a chance. Its killer was easily twice its size," added Rainus, as he stared to the west. "I have a feeling death was dispensed by the great beast that tried to kill us when we where hunting for Dragonite at the Devil's Tears east of here."

"I have no doubt," said Halen. "That was easily the largest creature we had seen in these parts."

"Largest and undoubtedly the most foul-tempered dragon we had the ill fortune of encountering," added Rainus. He recalled how they barely escaped with their lives when they were forced to dive off the cliff, rather than climb down the ropes, to avoid the beast's snapping maw.

"Well then, it is a bloody good thing you had killed that dragon," said Percy. "It will not be giving us any grief!"

"Kill it?" said Rainus. "We could not even think of a way to do away with a beast of that great size."

"It lives?" Percy's eyes opened wide in fear.

"Indeed!" answered Halen. "As we speak, it probably takes refuge from the cold, seeking warmth in one of the many great caves riddling these mountains."

Percy brushed away the traces of dust and embarrassment as he confronted their audacious claims. "I know you both say this to frighten me, all in the hopes that I abandon this quest!"

"If frightened bats taking flight is enough to incite this level of horror from you, I can only imagine what even a small dragon will do to test your courage," chuckled Silas, as he snorted in laughter.

"I was only *startled* by them!" corrected Percy. "Those detestable creatures were the ones that were horrified of me!"

"So you say! Just know that you will be no good to us if you are unable to fight or even run for your life," stated Myron. "We tell you this now because we are in the very heart of dragon country. You should be fully aware of what creatures dwell here."

"Well, then!" snapped Percy. "It is a bloody good thing the dragons are deep in their hibernaculum, waiting for the return of spring weather to draw them out again."

"True," said Rainus. "The colder it is, the deeper their sleep, but just because they sleep, it does not mean they cannot be roused."

"For pity's sake!" snapped Percy. He scowled in disapproval at Rose. "See how your friends attempt to scare me off? I shall rue the day when I allow their words to drive me from your side!"

"It is not their intention to scare you," assured Rose. "They only mean to keep you safe by alerting you to the possible perils along the way. The better prepared you are, the better you will be able to respond to danger, no matter the size."

"Bah! For too long you have been in their company!" protested Percy, shaking an admonishing finger in her face. "I am no fool! As long as we are out *here* and those dragons remain in *there*, deep inside those mountain caves, there will be no danger, other than that hag we seek now."

"Bold words, my lord, bold words!" chided Loftus.

"Bold, indeed! But mark these words, for they are true!" insisted Percy. He turned away from the captain to confront the Wizard as he pointed to the north. "You intend to lead us through that mountain pass, is that not so?"

"That is correct," responded Silas.

"So, there is no plan to lead us *into* one of those mountains to reach the lands beyond, is that not so?"

"Correct, again," assured Silas.

"There you go, Loftus!" Percy snorted at the captain. "The plan is for us to stay out, and for those dragons to stay in. There will be no such encounter between man and beast on this quest."

"Plans can change abruptly, my lord," said Loftus, with a shrug of his shoulders. "Though you are a prince, you have no control over the outcome of the future. It is best not to mock or tempt fate."

"What do you know?" snapped Percy. "I swear, I get the sense you wish for something bad to unfold, just to see me suffer!"

"I would never dream of it," stated Loftus.

"You are lying!"

"Think on this, my lord. If you are made to suffer, then I know you will make sure we all suffer twice as much."

"And rightly so," declared Percy.

"Though my powers of divination are limited, I predict you will cease with this tiresome rambling immediately, my lord." Halen cast a stern look of reproach at this mortal.

Percy was momentarily dumbfounded by the Elf's candid words. His mouth drooped open, but a witty retort did not follow.

"Let us waste no more time on useless chatter. There is a Witch to be captured and friends to be rescued," reminded Halen. "Mount up. We shall journey on."

After enduring many more leagues of travel, Halen raised his left hand, signalling to his comrades. Slowing the horses from a gallop to an easy canter, and then a leisurely walk, he sat tall on his steed. Searching about for footprints, a shred of clothing or signs of a struggle, he hunted about for anything to indicate if Tag or Sin had come by this way. By the length of his shadow stretching out long and lean before him, without even glancing behind, this Elf knew the westering sun would allow approximately two short hours of light.

"We have stayed true to this course, travelling this far, my friend," said Myron, as he steered his horse next to Halen's. By his reckoning, they had covered well over half the width of this valley since setting out early in the morning. "What do you see?"

The Elf issued a troubled sigh. He scanned the featureless terrain rolling out before them as a restless wind constantly shifted the powdery volcanic ash studded with chunks of pumice that were easily shattered, crushed beneath the weight of the horses' hooves.

"I see neither the passing of the Witch nor signs of our missing friend," replied Halen.

"More importantly, I see no dragons," chirped Percy. He revelled in the fact he was neither burdened by Tag's presence nor threatened by rampaging reptiles as they ventured on. "And it is an unfortunate thing, for I am in the mood to slay a dragon or two."

"Considering that you now know the size these creatures can attain, you only say that because none have yet to make an appearance," retorted Silas.

"Not so!" gasped Percy, appalled by the Wizard's condescending words. "Any dragon meaning to harm my beloved shall die regretting it! The beast will meet with a hasty end by the edge of my sword, I can promise you that."

Rose's heart was sent a-flutter with Percy's vow to keep her safe. Though her soul was burdened by Tag's absence and the profound sense of safety he provided was no more, there was certain comfort in knowing Percy was more than willing to assume this responsibility, promising to do so with utmost zeal.

"That is right, my dear Rose-alyn! I am more than ready and willing to protect you should one of those treacherous monsters attack."

"Like Master Agincor said before, these lands are empty now," reminded Myron. "The unseasonable chill forces the dragons to take refuge."

"Well, that is beside the point!" grumbled Percy. He was thoroughly vexed this knight had no issue with daring to steal his thunder.

"If anythin', we ought to be grateful the trek's been pretty easy so far," said Harold. "I'm thinkin' we can be through that mountain pass by nightfall, at the rate we're travellin'."

"We move with speed through this cursed land, but we shall set up camp at the foot of the pass, in the shadow of those great mountains, even if the sun's light continues to hold once we arrive," announced Silas.

"Why stop? Are you scared of the dark, old man?" Percy snorted in derision.

"Night comes quickly to the north. Do you really want to chance crossing a treacherous mountain pass as the sun goes down?" queried Silas, staring to the northerly range where a mantle of snow permanently capped the tallest of these mountains. "Unless you've suddenly developed the keen sight of an Elf and the light of the moon shines brightly, you shall be tempting fate. When all is blanketed in white, it is difficult to know if your footing is sound."

"Are you concerned I will take a tumble over a precipice?" asked Percy, astounded that Silas would actually care to issue such a warning.

"If that happened, I would be more unsympathetic than I would be concerned for your plight, for you'd be justly rewarded for your stupidity," answered Silas. "I would be more worried that your foolish actions will bring the mountains crashing down upon the rest of us."

"You say that now, Wizard," grunted Percy, "but I will have you know I am not some incompetent, bumbling fool like Harold or Loftus. Plus, without Yairet here to carelessly place us in danger, I highly doubt we will be faced with such grave misfortune."

"Famous last words, Prince Percival," cautioned Rainus. "You have no idea what is in store as we cross into the land to nowhere."

"Do not take me for a fool, Lord Silverthorn. Every land leads to *somewhere*," argued Percy.

"Not if it takes you to the very edge of the world and there is nowhere else to go," countered Rainus, his words were devoid of emotion as he scrutinized Percy.

"Hey, I wonder if you peeked over that edge, if there's a chance you'd fall into nothingness?" Harold pondered this mystery aloud.

"I suppose anything is possible. Should we stand at the edge of the world, I will gladly take my boot to your backside to see what transpires," offered Percy, his lips contorting into a smirk of a grin.

"That is hardly a courteous thing to say," admonished Rose. She was inwardly appalled that Percy could be so gallant one moment, and then just as quickly, reveal glimpses of a moodier, darker persona he was quick to stow away.

"Worry not, my lady," said Loftus, flashing a wicked smile her way. "Should the Prince see fit to do such a heinous thing to Harold, I shall be the one to gladly put *my boot* to *his backside*, sending him over the edge to retrieve our friend."

"All I am saying is, if this is indeed the edge of the world, and beyond these mountains is a *land that leads to nowhere*, as the Elf Lord claims, it will be interesting to see if one can actually fall off the world or simply drift away into oblivion."

"It is the world's end, as in, it is the very edge of this land mass and it takes you to nowhere," explained Silas, "for beyond the shores, it is a deep and forbidding sea that appears to go on forever."

"I suppose the high point in knowing this is that if the lands run out for us, it does so for the Witch as well," noted Myron. "There will be only so many places Sin will be able to hide from us."

"That is my hope, now that we no longer possess the bewitched eyeball to show us the way," said Silas, his heels prodding his steed on. "For now, we ride while we are blessed with the sun's light and this fair weather."

❧ ❧ ❧

"Fair weather, indeed!" Percy's voice was raked with sarcasm as he snapped at the Wizard. He drew the hood of his cloak low over his brows as billowy clots of snowflakes danced and twirled around them, shrouding their world in a ghostly twilight. "Where the hell did these damned clouds blow in from?"

"I had warned you before of having no idea what is in store as we journey north," reminded Rainus. He took to the rear to make sure none of the horses strayed, becoming lost in this blinding flurry.

"But this is – " Percy's whining was cut short.

"There will be no complaining from you, Prince Percival. I know for a fact I had cautioned you about the unpredictable nature of the weather," shouted Silas.

"How much farther to go?" hollered Myron, calling to Halen as he pressed his mount on into the face of the howling winds driving down from the north.

"Half a league, if that. We shall find shelter in the grove of trees nestled at the base of that mountain before we lose the sun completely!" Halen shouted to be heard as he pointed in the direction the Wizard had set them on. He glanced over his shoulder to see the dull glow of the sun. Sinking ever lower on the horizon, its light barely penetrated the thick flurry threatening to swallow them up. "We shall be near to the mountain pass, but protected from the worst of this wind and blowing snow."

"Why can we not stop here?" questioned Percy. He squinted through eyelashes encrusted with crystalized flakes of snow. "It promises only to get worse the farther we travel. We shall freeze to death, if we delay setting up camp."

"No moaning, whining, or whinging, my lord," admonished Loftus. "We ride until Captain Ironwood tells us we ride no more."

"If this cold proves to be my death, so help me, Loftus, I will personally kill you!" snarled Percy.

"Are you saying that royal blood is not as robust as the blood of the common man?" questioned Loftus. He stared with an equal measure of disdain and ridicule at Percy. "For Harold and I have no issues with riding on, if that's what is required of us."

"It is only because you are both better insulated with generous layers of fat to protect your bodies. And if anything, I was only thinking of Princess Rose-alyn's safety. It will only be a matter of time before this delicate blossom shrivels up to die in this freezing weather, and if she does, I shall blame you both for that, too!"

Rose peered over to Percy, offering him a reassuring smile as she spoke. "Fear not, my love. I am adequately warm for now. I am sure

I can endure until Captain Ironwood delivers us to our destination."

"Rest assured that on a night like this, we shall definitely not tackle negotiating the mountain pass," stated Silas, prodding his mount on to keep up with Halen's steed.

As the horses plodded through the deepening snow into the small thicket of fir trees and gangly shrubs hugging the base of the mountain, the wind had picked up speed, funnelling through the pass to blast horses and riders with its ferocious speed and biting cold. Frozen snowflakes whipped around them, lashing abrasively against exposed skin.

Loftus helped Halen to picket the horses under the branches of the largest tree they could find, but there was little relief from the harsh elements. The horses huddled next to each other, turning their rumps to the wind as snow piled upon them.

"Never mind the horses! Pitch my tent!" demanded Percy. Instead of helping the others, he stood there with his cloak wrapped tightly around his body as he shouted. "Do so immediately!"

Loftus removed the tent from the packhorse. Harold helped him to unfurl the canvas only to have it ripped from their hands by the force of the gusting winds.

"This is impossible!" declared Loftus, as Rainus and Halen dashed to his side. They struggled to control the flapping tent that slapped mercilessly at Harold. "We shall freeze before we even get this tent sorted out."

"Captain Ironwood and I can endure this cold better than most, but even this wind is testing our mettle," admitted Rainus.

"Perhaps this is an appropriate time to call upon a wish," suggested Silas, looking over to the Princess.

"I am not opposed to that." Clutching the Dreamstone to her chest, Rose spoke through now-chattering teeth as the icy winds tugged at her cloak.

"Princess, can you wish for us to be shielded from this foul weather?" asked Myron. "Perhaps wish for us, and our horses, to be protected by a great bubble that is impermeable to the snow and wind; one that will hold up until the worst of this storm has passed?"

Rose glanced about, shielding her eyes from the blowing snow as she considered a suitable refuge from this snowstorm.

"I can do better than that," she said.

"Then go to it, my lady! Just make sure it is an encompassing, grand wish that will accommodate us all, for after this, you will only have one left for the remainder of the day," reminded Myron. "Do you think you can do that?"

"I will try," promised Rose. Being deep in dangerous territory and close on the Witch's heels, she understood the perils of squandering this wish, leaving them with none, should she be forced to make adjustments to this one by using the last wish.

"Gather around," ordered Silas, motioning for his comrades to come closer. "She will be better able to concentrate, if she is protected from the worst of these winds."

Everyone, with the exception of Percy, nodded in understanding as they crowded around Rose, their bodies now acting as a physical barrier. She smiled in appreciation as her friends withstood the brunt of the wind's terrible force.

Grasping the Dreamstone in her hands, Rose closed her eyes, attempting to block out any external distractions. All the while, Percy stared intently at his bride-to-be, not wanting to waste this opportunity to observe as she conjured up her wish.

Exhaling, Rose understood this would now be a race against time. It would take too long to imagine a new shelter from scratch, so she delved into her memories, settling upon an abode to accommodate everyone. Her mind worked quickly to picture each piece of stone and wood in their proper place. An abundance of kindling and chopped wood sat by a roaring fire. The popping and crackling filling her ears as the smoke wafted up and out through the chimney. A cot appeared in her mind's eye with freshly laundered linens before she diverted her attention to the table. She reimagined the solid oak table, this time with room enough for each member of her party. The chairs were outfitted with plush, velvet cushions for added comfort and formal place settings of the finest china, crystal wine goblets and silverware glowed in the light of a beautiful candelabra positioned perfectly on the centre of the table.

Rose then quickly turned her attention to the food itself, envisioning each dishes in vivid detail, down to the herbs used and the steam sending delicious aromas wafting into the air. Her mouth watered as she pictured the desserts, her stomach rumbling at the thought of the delectable sweetness to tease her fussy palate.

One of the horses suddenly whinnied as snow spilled down from an overhead branch. It reminded Rose that they, too, needed shelter. She worked swiftly to conjure up suitable food and lodging for their equine friends.

Satisfied, Rose completed her wish. She whispered, "Make it so."

Opening her eyes, she smiled to spy against the snowy landscape a humble cottage, its windows emanating a warm and inviting glow that beckoned to them.

"This is truly amazing!" gasped Percy. He pushed by Harold to be the first to enter. As he opened the door he was met by golden candlelight and a blast of warm air. Rushing inside, he reached out, his fingertips tracing the mantle of the fireplace to make sure it was real and not some dream conjured up by his rising sense of panic. "It is hardly even quaint, but at least it is warm and more civilized than languishing outside in this desolate hinterland."

Loftus responded by swatting Percy on the back of his head as he chided him, "Is that any way to say thank you to Princess Rose? It was hardly complimentary!"

"I said it was *civilized*, did I not?" grunted Percy, as he rubbed the back of his smarting head.

"This place looks strangely familiar," noted Myron. He glanced about at her creation as the others filed in and Silas quickly shut the door on the world outside.

"Welcome home," said Rose, looking to the knight for his approval as she ushered them inside.

"This shall work nicely," praised Myron. "Just don't tell me my property is now devoid of its cottage, should I survive this quest and require a home to return to."

"Fear not! I only wished to replicate the likeness of your cottage, as Pepperton Palace was far too grand, requiring too much work to reimagine it in light of our precarious situation." She shook the snow from her cloak before hanging it on one of the wooden pegs on the front door. "As we speak, even the horses are housed in a warm barn. They have been watered, fed and groomed for the night."

"Well done, my lady!" praised Myron, smiling in approval of Rose's efforts to protect their horses, too.

"Oh, my! This is a whole, new world of deliciousness!" exclaimed Harold. His eyes bulged at the sight of the awaiting feast as his mouth watered, seduced by the delectable aromas wafting around him. "We'll be eatin' like royalty on this night, my friends!"

"As we should," said Rose. "If this is to be our last meal together, then let it be a truly memorable one shared amongst friends."

"Unlike most in present company, I possess discriminating taste, but this will suffice for now," said Percy, giving her a judicious nod.

With an air of snootiness that was now his hallmark, he stared down his perfect nose to scrutinize the magnificent spread on the table. Whipping off his cloak, he tossed it over his shoulder to land over Loftus' head. Abandoning the others, Percy made a mad dash for the dinner table.

He was the first to grab a seat, claiming the chair he deemed to be at the head of the table. Without first offering a drink to his comrades, Percy eagerly poured enough wine to fill his goblet to the brim. His eyes feasted on the succulent piglet roasted to perfection, the herbed rack of lamb and the fire-grilled pheasants served with a side of savoury gravy waiting to be sopped up by generous slices of freshly baked bread. And holding true to her proclivity for desserts, there were more sweets to dine on than vegetable dishes to serve with the main course.

"Well?" said Rose. She looked expectantly at her prince, waiting for him to seat her by his side.

Instead, Percy guzzled down his wine, barely taking notice of her. He motioned for Harold to seat Rose as he began filling his plate, not even waiting for the others to join him.

"He must be famished," decided Harold. Inwardly, he was appalled by Percy's rudeness as he seated Rose, pushing her chair closer to the table for her dining comfort.

Just as Harold was about to occupy the chair to Percy's left, the Prince shooed him away like he was nothing more than a stray mongrel sniffing about for scraps of food.

"That seat is reserved for one of honour," stated Percy, not wanting this commoner to sit close to him.

"It is?" Harold's face reddened with embarrassment. He glanced down to the opposite end that could have just as easily been designated as the head of the table where the Wizard prepared to sit.

"I can remedy that," grunted Silas. He was thoroughly incensed by Percy's arrogance and insensitivity. Touching the crystal mounted atop his staff to the table, it glowed with resplendent light as the Wizard closed his eyes, setting his powers in motion.

To the surprise of all, and much to Percy's chagrin, Silas' magic transformed the rectangular table into a round one. "There you go! Problem solved. There is no head of the table for you to be concerned about, so sit wherever you please, Harold."

"Brilliant!" praised Rainus, as he motioned for Harold to occupy the seat next to Percy. "Now we are truly equal as we partake in this shared meal."

"Brilliant, indeed," grumbled Percy. He issued a disgruntled sigh as he moved his arm to make room for the large man to be seated by his side.

As bowls and platters were passed around the table and wine was poured to fill the goblets, Myron stood up to address his comrades.

"On this night, let us offer a toast to honour our missing friends," said the knight.

While everyone picked up their goblets, Percy chose to reach across the table for another slice of bread. In response, Loftus smacked his hand, admonishing him: "Show some respect, my lord."

Percy's face reddened. Sheepishly, his hand withdrew as he spoke, "I was just about to do that, had you given me the chance!"

Hoisting his goblet with far less enthusiasm than the others, Percy gestured for Myron to continue on.

"Here is to Tag and Loken," said Myron, raising his goblet on high. "May they be kept safe from harm until we meet again."

"Here, here!" cheered all sharing this table.

Even Percy toasted the missing comrades, but Myron was confident it was to spare him from further retribution, as Captain Loftus seemed eager to correct any behaviour he deemed inappropriate from his royal charge.

As they settled into their meal, dinner was shared in relative silence, made unnaturally quiet by Tag's conspicuous absence. As Percy eagerly stuffed his face, taking certain joy in eating decent food in a civilized manner now that he was armed with a full set of silver cutlery, Rose nibbled on her meal. Even her favourite desserts were not devoured with her usual zeal as thoughts of Tag dogged her.

Was he hurt and alone? Was he cold and hungry? Was he even alive? These troubling questions weighed heavy on her mind.

"You have barely touched your meal," noted Percy. "You must eat; do so while the food is fresh."

"My appetite wanes," admitted Rose, her fork pushing the fruit tartlets around her dessert plate until it became lodged in the quagmire of sticky bread pudding.

"Is something troubling you?" Percy glanced over at her as he helped himself to another serving of tender pheasant.

"Of course I am troubled! I cannot help but wonder about Tag and how he fares."

"I understand you are concerned, my dear, but it is all for naught," insisted Percy.

"How can you say that?"

"Now, now, my love! All I am saying is that it is a waste of energy to worry about him. It is quite pointless, to say the least!"

Rose's pouting lip began to quiver as she digested Percy's foreboding words delivered with obvious indifference.

"There is no point in crying either," groaned Percy. His eyes rolled in exasperation upon sensing a geyser of tears were about to erupt from her. "There is nothing more wretched than to see a pretty maiden in the throes of misery brought on by a bout of the ugly cry, especially when she is blubbering over nothing."

"This is Tag you speak of!" scolded Rose. Her eyes glistened with incipient tears. "He is my best friend."

"Yes, well... consider yourself fortunate that I shall be taking his place as your dearest friend, should the worst happen to that bugger," assured Percy. He pressed her linen napkin into her hand, motioning for her to blot away those tears.

"It is not as though his friendship can be so easily replaced," protested Rose.

"Of course it can, you silly girl! That scoundrel of a rapscallion is quite expendable when you think about it."

"Say again!" gasped Rose.

"I will, as you obviously need reminding! I am everything he is, only better! I am taller, more handsome, smarter and far wealthier."

"And scrawnier, dim-witted, cowardly, and pretentious," whispered Rainus to Myron, as Percy continued to boast.

"Plus, and here's the real boon, my dear Rose-alyn, I have a royal title and a kingdom that is destined to be mine on my father's passing. Actually, two kingdoms, if all should unfold as we hope!"

Percy capped his statement by flashing Rose a knowing smile and a wink that only served to exacerbate her melancholy mood.

"As your fair prince lacks the sensitivity to offer you sincere words of solace, just know that we, your *expendable* friends, are all concerned about Tag's welfare, my lady," stated Myron. "We will make every effort to save him."

"Thank you so much," said Rose, nodding in gratitude to the knight.

"For now, let us share in this wonderful meal," urged Silas. "Gather your strength, and then find some rest on this night, for tomorrow is another day. A new adventure awaits with the coming of dawn."

Percy smiled at Rose, but he could feel a distinct chill emanating from her and this party of rabbles.

"Though I felt it necessary to bolster Princess Rose-alyn's courage with words spoken in truth, than to allow her to wallow in a false sense of hope, perhaps I could have done better," admitted Percy.

"Can't argue with that, my lord," said Loftus.

"Well, it is about time you stopped arguing with me, you impudent sod," grumbled Percy. "As I was saying, it is better to not think of our missing comrade and that Sprite, not because they do not matter, but only because there is nothing we can do at this very moment. Instead, it is time to forget about our woes; share in this humble meal while engaged in sparkling conversation that is not so emotionally taxing on the Princess, therefore draining on me, should she carry on lamenting

Tag's absence."

"In Prince Percival's eloquent way, he means to say: let us change the subject," deciphered Loftus.

"Eloquent, indeed!" agreed Percy, as he motioned for the captain to shut up. "And I will be the one to choose the topic of conversation."

"I suppose it will not hurt to take my mind off of Tag for the time being," conceded Rose.

"Trust me, it will do us all some good to not think about him as we try to enjoy this meal," assured Percy.

"We can talk about Sassy and how she's probably missin' me somethin' fierce," offered Harold.

"There shall be no talk about your ass at this dinner table," demanded Percy.

"Yes, as we already share the table with one," Silas muttered beneath his breath.

"Say again," demanded Percy. He shot a baleful glance upon hearing these muted words as Myron, seated next to the Wizard, chuckled in response.

"It was nothing of importance," answered Silas.

"I thought as much, but this brings to mind, Master Agincor," continued Percy, "I had read the latest story you had penned."

"And did you enjoy it?" asked Silas.

"The plot was thin, the characters were shallow and the outcome was predictable, but overall, it was a jolly good romp of an adventure, if that is something one is into."

Silas' frowned in curiosity, "That was a backhanded compliment, if ever there was one."

"It is what it is," responded Percy. "Just be grateful I did not say it was a dreary tome best suited for kindling to start a fire, for a scathing review by one of my status can quickly put an end to your writing career."

Silas' nerves bristled.

"But this begs the question," continued Percy. "Why would a mighty Wizard forsake his true calling to become a lowly writer – a teller of tales? It makes no sense to me!"

"I have my reasons, most of which I hardly believe you have the mental capacity to truly grasp."

"I believe I know at least one of these reasons," said Percy, giving Silas a shrewd smile.

"Truly?" The Wizard's brows furrowed with curiosity.

"I believe you chose to abandon the whole business of magic to escape."

"Interesting. Pray tell, just what would I be escaping from?"

"I believe you use your imagination to escape this mundane reality that is your life."

"That is the furthest thing from the truth," retorted Silas. "The imagination is a powerful tool, a magical gift, really. I use my imagination to create new realities, not to escape this one."

Percy frowned at the Wizard, and then he alone burst out in a fit of laughter.

Rose jabbed him with her elbow, as he seemed oblivious to all those staring at him.

"Where is your sense of decorum?" whispered Rose, as her friends ceased their staring, electing to ignore Percy. They resumed with their meal as his laughter languished, muted by the noises of shared conversation and the clatter of cutlery as they ate.

"Yes, well... Let us dine now, and then we shall sleep," said Percy. Eyeing the only bed in the cottage, he made his claim. "I call dibs on the cot!"

☙ ☙ ☙

The change in the weather was abrupt.

Even before Sin ventured out of her lair to investigate, she felt it in her bones – in the aching of her joints and the gnawing pain radiating through her thin muscles.

After stoking the flames and sacrificing more driftwood to the growing fire, she made a quick meal that was chased down with a swig of a magical tincture she had concocted the week before, in preparation for the impending cold to settle on the lands. This bitter potion eased the pain in her joints and would also help to protect her from the deathly chill that awaited her as she endured her nocturnal foray.

After last night's failed bid to secure a much-needed ingredient, Sin was in no mood to cater to the needs of her prisoners. Instead, of offering scraps of food and water, she dispensed ugly sneers and words of contempt as she inspected their restraints and Loken's cage to make sure they would remain secured while she was out and about.

For the longest moment, Tag and Loken watched as she disappeared into the adjoining tunnel, hoping she would vanish into the night so they can plot their escape, taking advantage of her absence to undergo this task without fear of retribution. Instead, Sin returned. She had limped off into an adjacent chamber that acted as her larder and where she stored driftwood so this fuel could dry out well enough for her to use as firewood.

Sin grumbled as she returned to the chamber, dragging along a large branch from a fallen cottonwood tree. Snapping off the boughs to break the tree branch into manageable pieces, she tossed it over the smouldering embers of last night's fire. The resinous buds and the dried leaves that clung to it exploded into flames as the rapacious fire devoured this fuel. For a moment, from where Tag was bound, he could feel the heat it exuded, filling this gloomy chamber with great warmth and light, albeit temporary.

Without either a word of farewell or a threat of abuse, Sin took another swig of the warming potion to steel her body against the cold. Picking up her staff and bucket loaded with the fishing net, she limped away, shuffling down the length of the tunnel. Tag and Loken watched, her shadow shrinking as the light from the obsidian crystal faded away until the tunnel was black.

Peering through the bare branches of the shrubs that kept this opening concealed during the warmer months when the foliage grew thick, Sin's eyes were greeted by a world turned a ghostly white and a leaden sky devoid of a single star on this night. She believed the lands this far north knew only two seasons: summer and winter. There seemed to be no gradual change in the weather, as was evident by the sudden arrival of snow.

Stepping beyond the mouth of the tunnel, Sin's cloak barely rippled in the gentle breeze. The cruel north wind ceased to blow. Instead, the air was thick and silent, insulated by the soft flakes floating down from the brooding sky where heavy clouds scudded across the infinite darkness. With a dreary sigh, Sin wrapped her cloak around her bony frame. She picked her way through the mantle of snow, making her way to the rock-strewn shores that hugged the shoal where the receding tide exposed a dark, sandy beach too wet for the snow to accumulate.

Between the biting cold and a moonless night, these were not the ideal conditions to catch a very special kind of fish, but she had no choice. She needed to harvest the spiny puffer fish for its liver. Even one of modest size would suffice. This organ was filled with toxins so deadly it would normally be used for a potion meant to kill. Whether ingested raw or dried, ground, and then inhaled into the body, this powerful toxin worked quickly to paralyze the diaphragm, resulting in catastrophic respiratory failure. But when prepared and administered just so, it can also be used to bring on a death-like state rather than outright kill her victim. This fish's liver was the missing ingredient she needed to resurrect her dead brother, now that she had managed to secure the mortal responsible for his untimely demise.

But time was of the essence. Now, she was forced to work with speed. In her heart, Sin knew a rescue party was on its way to save Tag, and possibly the Sprite, too. She had to secure the liver of one large, or several small puffer fish, and harvest the boy's blood while it was fresh. Of course, this had to be accomplished before his cohorts arrived to meddle in her affairs. If many nights of failed fishing attempts worked against her, Sin was aware this mortal could die from hunger, sickness or, if she were driven to madness, killing him out of sheer spite.

Standing on the tip of one of the long, flat boulders that formed a natural jetty at the mouth of the shoal, here the land dropped off into deep waters. In the cold months, this was one of the favourite breeding grounds in the Sea of Shadows where the spiny puffer fish gathered. When the moon was full and the celestial lights danced on the surface of the water, this was when schools of puffer fish rose up from the deep. They would rise to the surface to form a flotilla of fish that ballooned into spiny balls of gills and fins when accosted by predators lurking overhead or when the males of the species inflated themselves to bloated proportions to impress a potential mate.

With a whisper of an incantation, the obsidian crystal glowed brightly, shining like an artificial moon on the restless sea.

Studying the dark depths, Sin could see no promising signs that these fish were swimming below the surface. Without the Dreamstone in her grasp to simply wish for a full net, she had no choice but to cast it into the sea and hope for her wish to be parlayed into a successful night of fishing.

"She is gone for now," whispered Loken. He peered through the bars of his cage as he listened for a long while after the Witch disappeared from his sight.

"How long this time?" questioned Tag.

"If our luck holds, and hers does not, I'd say she'll be gone until dawn," answered Loken.

"How do you fare, Elee?" Tag asked over his shoulder.

"I will live for another day," sighed the Mermaid, rejuvenated by the surge of seawater rolling in with the high tide. Using the end of her tail, she splashed water onto her seal in a bid to offer Flotsam some relief with the cooling comfort of the sea that refilled the tidal pool.

Tag sensed a hint of disappointment in her voice that her life in captivity had merely been prolonged.

"How about you, Loken?" asked Tag.

"I'd be better if I were free." He rattled the unyielding bars of his prison.

"Are you any closer to escaping?" questioned Tag.

"While the hag slept I had been trying to scrape away at this ring of salt," said Loken. "My hands ache and my fingertips sting. They have been worn raw as this salt has dried as hard as a rock. How about you? Are you any closer to freedom?"

"I was just as busy," said Tag. The clatter of iron chains echoed through the chamber as he shifted about. "I've been filing away at this rusted chain, working on what looks to be the weakest link."

"Are you making progress?"

"About as much as you are," answered Tag. "It's slow going, but I am not about to give up."

"I have been saying that very thing since I was first captured," sighed Loken. "If it were not for the hope of being reunited with my beloved Celia, I would have given up long ago."

"And yet?" said Tag, sensing apprehension in the Sprite's voice.

"And yet, that nagging doubt I will not be rescued or be able to facilitate my own escape gnaws at the back of my mind."

"Do not lose hope just yet, Loken. Now that Sin is away, I can really get to work."

Tag reached down with his left hand, picking up a flat, palm-sized rock that lay next to him. Struggling about, he managed to tuck it between his belly and the segment of rusted chain he had been attempting to file away while Sin slept. Taking up the sharp-edged stone he had been using to wear away at the layers of rust and metal, Tag began to steel his nerves and his stomach muscles. He used the surface of the flat rock as an anvil as he did his best to hammer through the piece of chain.

With the approach of the midnight hour, Tag's work was slowed. Dogged by both thirst and hunger, his efforts waned as the bruise on his stomach grew with each strike.

"Any luck yet?" asked Loken, staring hopefully to the mortal.

"Do I look like I'm free?" muttered Tag, unleashing a disgruntled sigh as the flat rock slipped onto his lap. His arms ached from contorting them in an effort to break this chain and his growing weariness made his attempts all the more feeble.

"Do not lose heart, my friend," said Loken. "It is just taking longer than you had anticipated."

"Much longer, but I'm not about to give up."

"You are far more motivated than I am," commented Elee. She was impressed this mortal had been working continuously since the Witch had drifted off to sleep, and now that she was gone, he had taken to this task with renewed zeal, until the hours of toil finally wore him down.

"Take some time to rest, Tag," urged Loken. "Get some sleep for now, and then start fresh. There is no point in toiling as you do now, if you are not getting the results you desire."

"You're right," agreed Tag. "I'm exhausted. Perhaps if I nap, waking before Sin returns, I'll have the strength to resume this task."

"Then sleep, you will," said Loken. He rested his back against the bars of his prison, closing his eyes to dream of Celia and his life of contentment in the Fairy's Vale.

The gentle swell of waves lapping against the shore quickly lulled Tag to sleep. He didn't even wake when his right hand slipped from his lap, the sharp stone tumbling to his side.

As the midnight hour approached, the fire was reduced to a dwindling pile of cinder. Aside from the waves steadily rolling into this sea cave, the occasional, defiant crackle of firewood and Tag's deep, regular breaths as his chin lolled on his chest while he slept, all was quiet.

In a dull throb of light tempered by the glow of the dying embers in the fire pit a Tooth Fairy appeared. Aster glanced about, spying upon the sleeping mortal slumped against a pillar of stone. Immediately upon hearing that long, steady, telltale breath, she knew it was safe for her to proceed. Tiptoeing about, she found the item that first drew her here: a tooth.

Picking up the specimen, Aster examined it. Her tiny face screwed up in disgust as she unleashed a sigh of disappointment. It was only half of a molar, and terribly decayed to boot. A quick assessment and she determined this tooth was only suitable to line the palace dungeon. It proved to be a substandard find, but a find nonetheless. The little Fairy reached into her pouch to leave a ha'penny in return.

Just as she used her powers to shrink the tooth and enlarge the copper piece, with no pillow to slip it under, she searched about. The creak of a cage hanging from one of the torch sconce caused her to panic. The piece of copper she clutched *'pinged'* as it fell, striking against a stone.

Aster's heart raced in fear as the mortal suddenly stirred. In a flash, she vanished just as Loken cried out to her, "Wait! Aster, come back!"

16

Nowhere to Hide

"Come back!" pleaded Loken. He pressed his face between the bars of his prison as the Fairy's aura faded away; taking with her the last trace of hope he had left.

"What happened?" Tag asked through a great yawn. He watched as Loken dropped to his knees in utter despair.

"She was here!"

"Sin?"

"No! A Tooth Fairy - Aster Lumenia to be exact."

"Are you sure you weren't just dreaming you saw her?" asked Tag, shaking the fog of sleep from his head.

"I swear it to be so! I caught a fleeting glimpse of her just as she vanished," insisted Loken.

"Do you think she was sent by Pance?"

"Who is Pance?" asked Elee, the chain tightened around Tag as she twisted about to speak to him.

"Pancecelia Feldspar is the Queen of the Tooth Fairies. He is her royal consort," answered Tag, using his chin to point at the Sprite. "So, tell us what happened, Loken."

"She was here! Aster Lumenia was here! I was not imagining it. She must have been drawn to the broken tooth Sin had cast aside earlier. But now, Aster is gone."

"Will she come back?" questioned Tag.

"I doubt it. She got what she came for. I hardly think she heard me. If she did, she may not have recognized my voice when I called out. If anything, you are the one she saw and wished to avoid. When you stirred, she vanished."

"But there's still a chance she will come back," said Tag.

"Like any good Tooth Fairy diligent in her duties, her primary goal is to collect teeth, leave money in exchange, and to do so unnoticed. Mission accomplished. Hence, no reason to return."

Silas woke with a start. His eyes flew open to spy upon a menacing form looming over him. This shadow stretched across the room, gliding silently up the far wall. The Wizard bolted upright from his bedroll, seizing his staff to fend off this intruder.

"Fear not, Silas Agincor! I come with glad tidings!"

Having alighted upon the dining table, and now, backlit by the flames of the logs crackling in the fireplace, Pancecelia Feldspar's tiny form cast a great shadow. She launched into the air, her aura glowing brightly with her growing excitement as she hovered before the Wizard's surprised face.

"What brings you here?" asked Silas.

"I come with news!" announced Pance. She buzzed about the cottage, unable to contain her elation. The thrum of her wings and her radiant aura stirred the others from their slumber.

All were jolted awake as a dark form burst into the cottage. Sword in hand and a whirlwind of snowflakes in his wake, he threw the door open, prepared to attack.

"What is happening?" gasped Rose.

She sat upright in her bedroll that was spread out on the floor at the foot of Percy's cot.

"Worry not," said Rainus. Breathing a sigh of relief, he lowered his sword. "It is friend, not foe, we are faced with."

Rubbing the sleep from her eyes, Rose made out the great, shadowy figure that was Halen Ironwood as a golden orb of light floated about the room.

"I was checking on our horses when I saw through the window an unnatural show of light," stated Halen. "I rushed in, fearing the Witch was on the prowl."

"This is no Witch, Captain Ironwood," assured Silas, as he used his staff to stand onto his feet.

"I can see that now," said Halen, bowing his head in respect to Pancecelia.

"Hush up, people! I am trying to sleep! It is much too early to partake in conversation, mundane or otherwise," grumbled Percy, as he pulled a pillow over his head to mute their words.

"What gives?" queried Loftus. "Normally, to rouse you before your time is like waking the dead."

"And rightfully so, for the dead and creatures of the night are the only things active right now, so let me sleep," demanded Percy. "And shut that blasted door, for pity's sake! You're letting all the heat out."

Halen hastily shut the door behind him as the snowflakes that blew in with him floated down onto the floor, melting into tiny, gleaming droplets that shone in the firelight.

"Look! It's the Queen of the Tooth Fairies," announced Harold. His pudgy hands rubbed the sleep from his eyes as they fixed on the sphere of light.

"Well, I'll be!" gasped Myron, standing to greet the diminutive being. "What brings you here, Your Majesty?"

"Huh?" muttered Percy. He lifted his head from under his pillow to squint at the radiant aura hovering in the centre of the room. "Did someone say *Fairy*?"

"Indeed," said Rainus, bowing his head in respectful greeting. "We are graced with the presence of Her Majesty, Pancecelia Feldspar of the Fairy's Vale."

Percy was suddenly wide-awake. He bolted up from his cot, leaping over Rose as he dashed to the table. Snatching up an empty wine goblet, he turned his attention to the Tooth Fairy. "Quick! Catch her before she escapes!"

"No!" cried Rose, motioning for him to stop before he irreparably offended this being. "Stop it!"

Before Percy could use the crystal goblet to capture the Fairy, in a resplendent show of light, Pance morphed before his startled eyes. Percy was absolutely gobsmacked. He stumbled over Harold's jumbled bedroll, falling against the large man.

"For shame, young man!" chided Pance, waving an admonishing finger in his face as she glared in resentment at the mortal.

Percy's eyes bulged as he stared at this regal being now towering before him, larger than life and much larger than he could ever imagine. Her gossamer wings trembled with anger as she addressed him. "What is it with you royals always wanting to capture me?"

"I know I exude princely qualities and my reputation undoubtedly precedes me, but I am curious, Your Majesty, you speak as though we have met before," said Percy.

"It is better to say I know of you, as we have never been formally introduced," responded the Fairy.

"You know of me?" repeated Percy, his perfect brows furrowing in curiosity.

"Yes, I tend to remember all the mortals I have personally gathered teeth from, royal or not, if that mortal happens to make my task a treacherous undertaking by staying up late into the night in hopes of catching more than just a glimpse of me at work."

"Well, you are not the first to sing my praises. I have been told by many I am quite memorable," said Percy, hoping to take the edge of her sharp tone by offering her one of his charming smiles.

"I take it, you wanted to capture me for wishes in exchange for my freedom," grunted Pance, unmoved by his snake of a grin.

"Me? I think not!" said Percy. He discreetly placed the wine goblet back onto the table. "I merely wished to meet the great Fairy I had heard so much about. I hoped to greet you with a welcoming glass of wine, for it is the courteous thing to do."

"Yes... I just bet you did," sniffed Pance, as she turned her attention back to the Wizard.

"You said you come with news," reminded Silas.

"Exciting news, indeed!" exclaimed Pance.

"Tag! He's alive!" cried Rose.

"Rejoice, Princess! I was surprised to hear that your friend had been captured, but seeing that Tag is not in your company now, I assume that was indeed his fate."

"And Loken?" asked Myron. "Does he live?"

"Are they together?" asked Harold.

"And where are they now?" asked Rose, eager to learn more.

Rainus raised his hands, motioning for calm. "The Queen is over-whelmed with questions. All will be revealed in good time."

Pancecelia sat upon the chair Myron pulled out from the table for her.

She drew a deep breath, gathering her thoughts as she prepared to share the information she had gathered.

"As you know, I had sent forth my workers on their nightly forays with the additional task of keeping their eyes and ears open for any news pertaining to my dear Loken."

"So, one of your Fairies had chanced upon words of Loken's possible whereabouts?" queried Rainus.

"It was more than hearsay," assured Pance.

"Do tell!" Silas motioned her speak.

"On this very night, Aster Lumenia, one of my most productive workers, returned with her collection of teeth as well as an eyewitness account of the events that bring me here tonight!" Pance held her hand before all in her company to present them with a broken molar.

Percy grimaced in disgust as he sneered at the tiny object in the palm of the Fairy's hand. "Who would have thought your consort would be plagued by such poor dental hygiene?"

"Of course this did not belong to Loken," snapped Pance. "This is from the one holding him prisoner."

"Sin Mourningstar?" asked Silas. Taking the tooth from her hand, he held it up to his nostrils, sniffing it.

Percy's nose wrinkled in repugnance as he commented, "Your odd habits leave much to be desired, Wizard."

"This tooth is old, broken and decayed," stated Silas, as he dropped the molar back into her hand. "It does indeed reek of the Witch."

"So Tag is with Loken?" asked Rose.

"Apparently, Aster spied upon a young man sleeping. He fits Tag's description perfectly," answered Pance.

"And she saw Loken?" queried Myron.

"When the mortal stirred, Aster departed immediately, but just as she did so, she heard Loken cry out to her. She stated that there was no doubt in her mind it was Loken's voice she heard."

"If she was there, why did Aster not facilitate their rescue?" queried Silas.

"Because Sin is a vengeful, dangerous creature. I ordered all my Fairies to report back to me, if they chanced upon her lair. They were not to take action on their own."

"That makes good sense," said Silas, accepting that a regular Fairy had little chance of surviving a confrontation with a demented Witch immersed in the forbidden arts. "It is safer to rally the forces to oppose Sin, than to go it alone."

"And where does she hold them?" asked Myron.

"According to Aster, they are being held captive in a sea cave hidden in the white cliffs facing the Sea of Shadows."

Touching her wand to the crystal atop the Wizard's staff an image of these steeps cliffs pummelled by the foaming waves of an angry sea appeared within his crystal. Silas studied this image as an entrance to a cave at the foot of one of these cliffs came into focus. Sparse shrubs, denuded of leaves and now, encrusted with a glistened layer of frozen snow partially obscured this opening. On the ground, a single pair of footprints along with the small impressions made by a staff or walking stick left at regular intervals were evident. These prints led away from this cave.

"Oh, my! That's as north as one can get," said Harold. "So that bewitched eyeball had been steerin' us in the right direction all along."

"I know nothing about a bewitched eyeball, but Aster knows what she saw and heard. She returned to the Fairy's Vale immediately to report her findings to me."

"Excellent!" said Silas.

"We can leave immediately," said Pance. "Take that Witch by surprise."

"No. Instead, you shall leave immediately for your realm," ordered Silas.

"I can help win their freedom," insisted Pance, holding up her wand for all to see as it throbbed with magical light and power.

"I have no doubt you can," averred Silas. "But as you said, Sin is a vengeful, dangerous creature. You cannot chance her launching an attack on your people, should she elude us and you are not there to protect them."

"You must place your trust in us once more," urged Rainus. "We will do all we can to see both Loken and Tag freed of Sin."

"Yes, keep the Fairy's Vale safe in our absence," said Myron.

"But Loken needs me," said Pance.

"Your people need you more," reminded Silas. "Loken knows this. He will never forgive us if harm should come to you during his rescue, nor will it sit well with him if your subjects are harmed in your absence during efforts to rescue him."

Pance drew a deep breath, and then she nodded in understanding. "You speak the truth, my friend."

"Of course I do!" Silas gave her a knowing smile. "Make haste! Return to the Fairy's Vale. Prepare for war, should Sin elude capture. She is sure to strike with a vengeance, but come what may, we shall see to Loken and Tag's safe return."

"Very well." Pance bowed in gratitude. "Allay my fears; see to Loken's rescue and I shall tend to my people. I will pray for your safe return and success on this mission."

In a blinding show of light, the Queen vanished.

"Please tell me we are not embarking on the quest right now," groaned Percy. "It is darker than dark out there, and though that blasted wind has died down, the snow still falls."

"Worry not, Prince Percival," responded Silas. "I am no fool. It is unwise to venture forth at this late hour. The quest will be doomed to fail should we meet with disaster blindly clambering about in such treacherous terrain in this darkness."

"Phew!" exclaimed Percy, as he pushed by Harold to reclaim his warm cot. "It puts my mind at ease to know I will be able to meet the new day well rested."

"Yes," said Silas. "Sleep now, my friends, for we leave at dawn."

🥀🥀🥀

"What are you doing?" asked Loken, as he peered over to where Tag was chained.

"As you had so clearly pointed out that your fleeting encounter with the Fairy maiden has proven fruitless, I resolved that this is not the time for sleep. Instead, I think I've discovered a way to escape."

"Did you manage to weaken the links, enough to break that chain?" asked Loken.

"No, but there may still be a way out of this. Elee, do as I do," instructed Tag.

"But I cannot reach the lock to open it," said Elee. "Even though it is not rusted by saltwater like the one that secures this chain that holds me, the lock that secures the length of chain the Witch wound around us both is out of my reach."

"True, but just listen to me," ordered Tag. "Sit up as tall as you can against this pillar and I will do the same."

"And then what?" asked Loken. He watched as the two prisoners worked together.

"Then I shall attempt an escape."

"But how?" asked Loken.

"When I arrived here, you said I looked dead at first glance, is that not so?"

"Indeed!" Loken nodded.

"Is it fair to say Sin struggled to wrap this chain around us while I was unconscious?"

"She struggled, all right. Sin was cursing up a storm; you kept flopping forward or to one side or the other."

"And Elee, did you struggle about as she attempted to secure me to this rock, winding this chain around you, too?"

"I certainly did not make it easy for her."

"Perfect!" exclaimed Tag.

"Perfect?" repeated Loken. He frowned in bewilderment on hearing this. "Perfect for what? I mean no disrespect, Tag, but I hardly think you possess the strength required to break free."

"True enough, but thirst and hunger works in my favour this time."

"Say again," said Loken.

"I believe I am thinner than when I first arrived here. Now, Elee, do as I say: Sit up, straight and tall against this pillar."

She did as Tag instructed, throwing her shoulders back while pressing her spine against the barnacle-encrusted formation.

Tag dug his heels into the ground, using it for traction as he straightened up, pushing his back firmly against this pillar. He smiled as the chain encircling him suddenly lost its tautness.

"Now, Elee, on the count of three, exhale; force all the air from your lungs, then hold it. Do not take in another breath. We will both do this at the same time. Do you understand?"

"Yes," she answered. "I believe I do."

"Good! Now… One… Two… Three!"

Elee and Tag exhaled loudly. Once their lungs were empty, they both held their breath. Tag worked with speed, squirming and writhing about. It was enough to work the highest loop of chain up his arms, almost to his shoulders. With a gasp, both mortal and Mermaid gulped down some fresh air. Filling their lungs, the chain now felt tighter than ever.

"I see what you're doing," said Loken. "If you can work the chain up, over your shoulders to your neck, it will be loose enough for you to slip them off!"

"That's the plan," said Tag, as he took a deep, replenishing breath. "And as soon as I'm free, I can break the chain holding Elee and smash that cage imprisoning you."

"Well then, go to it, my friend," urged Loken. "Be quick about it, for there is no telling when the Witch will return."

"Are you ready, Elee?" asked Tag.

She drew a deep breath before answering, "Yes."

"One… Two… Three!" counted Tag.

He and Elee exhaled, and then both held their breath as Tag resumed manipulating the loosened coils of iron. Squirming and raising his arms ever higher, with that final shrug the top loop of chain clinked as it popped over the top of his shoulders. It dangled loosely around his neck.

"You did it!" cheered Loken. He was ecstatic as he hopped about in his prison.

Elee breathed easier, feeling the slack in the length of chain.

This time, Tag wriggled down, twisting about to slip his head from this loop.

"You did it!" gasped Elee, feeling this coil of chains suddenly loosen around her, dropping away from the original one that still imprisoned her.

Working the last two loops of iron down from around his waist, Tag slowly stood up, rubbing his numb legs that prickled with pins and needles from sitting in one position for so long.

"Free Elee first," ordered Loken. "The Witch has held her captive for longer than I have been her prisoner."

Tag limped over to the table, looking for his dagger in hopes of using the blade to break or manipulate the padlock holding Elee's chain. Searching through the assortment of dirty dishes, pots and wooden utensils, his only weapon was gone.

"Your dagger," called Loken, pointing overhead, "I saw her place it on that shelf, just in front of you."

"There it is!" said Tag, snatching it up from where it was hidden between two ceramic jars.

"Oh, no!" cried Elee. Glancing over to her pet seal, she watched as Flotsam's little head lifted up. The seal's nostrils flared as she sniffed the air while staring toward the entrance of the chamber near where Tag stood now. "The Witch has returned!"

"Hide, Tag!" ordered Loken. "Be quick about it!"

Tag glanced about. Spinning around, he dashed over to the cot, dropping on his hands and knees. Tag groaned to see how little clearance there was under the bed. Even if he managed to avoid discovery, were Sin to lie down she'd be resting right on his body, and it would be impossible to escape without waking her.

Pushing up off the ground, Tag raced to the mouth of the sea cave. Staring at the incoming tide, he knew with all probability that he'd be caught up in the currents or a powerful riptide. If he wasn't discovered by Sin, it was likely he'd drown in the freezing sea. Tag cursed beneath his breath. His heart raced as his frustration and panic grew. At this point he couldn't tell if the rhythmic thumping he heard was Sin's approaching footsteps or his thundering heart.

With nowhere to hide, Tag dashed over to the tunnel. Peering down the length of this passage, he spied upon the glow of Sin's obsidian crystal against the dark sky as night prepared to surrender to the coming of dawn. Her back was turned to him as she grumbled to herself. As she stood at the entrance of the tunnel, she removed her hooded cloak. Vigorously shaking off the snow from this apparel before she entered, Sin removed the worst of the accumulation so it wouldn't melt and soak into the fabric, taking longer to dry.

Knowing Sin still possessed Dragonite's staff armed with the powerful obsidian crystal, Tag stood little chance of surviving an attack with nothing more than this dagger.

Staring toward the opposite end of this tunnel, his eyes were met with an all-consuming darkness. He had no idea where this passage led to, he only knew he had no choice. Tag can meet the hag head-on, facing possible death with no hope of rescuing Loken and Elee or he can chance the unknown, hoping to find a place to hide until a rescue was possible. As the Witch tossed the cloak back over her bony frame, Tag made his move.

The 'thump' of Sin's staff striking the ground as she walked grew louder as Tag crept away. His hands traced the rocky wall as he advanced, sinking deeper into the shadows. Probing with his feet, he checked for sudden dips or gaping holes in the floor of this passage before setting them down.

Tag's heart thundered, pounding in his ears as he was swallowed up in this claustrophobic darkness. His fingertips felt the wall of the tunnel abruptly vanish under his touch. Blindly fumbling forward, his right hand grazed against a wall. The tunnel he travelled emptied into some kind of chamber. Following the curve of this wall, he winced in pain as his shin struck up against something sharp. Feeling before him, Tag realized he was in the room where Sin stored the driftwood she collected to dry. Using his hands and feet to determine the size of this pile, Tag quickly determined it offered nothing in the way of a decent hiding place.

He groaned in pain as his left foot suddenly struck up against something hard and flat. Tag almost stumbled over this object that resounded like it was half full. With his hands extended before him, he felt about. He had quite literally stumbled into a wooden container of sorts. Feeling the rough planks of wood, it formed a long, narrow crate. Tag estimated it to be about eight or nine hand-span deep and at least four times as long as it was deep. Running his hands over the top of the crate, Tag determined it was as wide as it was deep. Feeling beyond the edge of this wooden container to see if there was hiding space between it and the wall, Tag was met with more disappointment. There was no space underneath or behind this crate to hide in.

"Aaaarrh!"

The hairs on the back of Tag's neck stood on end. His blood ran cold. This bone-rattling scream sounded from the main chamber to echo through the tunnel and into this dark cave. It was followed by the clatter of the wooden bucket hitting the ground, its contents, the netting and a single puffer fish, spilling out.

"Where is he?" shrieked Sin. She threw down the coils of chain that now dangled loosely around the Mermaid.

"He is gone," answered Elee, delighting in Sin's unpleasant surprise.

Like a raving lunatic, Sin raced to and fro. She dropped on all fours to peer under her worktable.

"Where did he go?" snarled Sin. She loped over to her cot, flinging back the wool blanket and tattered, patchwork quilt.

Nothing.

"Bah!"

She dropped to her knees, searching beneath her cot in case Tag had squeezed beneath. Another scream of rage bellowed forth as she hurled the cot across the cave. Nowhere could she find her escaped prisoner.

"Where is he hiding?" Sin shrieked as she jabbed the tip of her finger through the bars of Loken's prison, almost spearing him on her sharp talon in the process. "Tell me!"

"He escaped!" taunted Loken, as he fell against the cage floor. "Too bad you were so slow. You must have just missed him."

"Liar! He is still about!" screamed Sin.

"Believe what you want," said Loken. "Just know the longer you loiter about, the farther he will get away from this place."

"He is still here!" snarled Sin, her mouth frothing in rage. "I know it!"

In her madness, she dropped to her knees. Slamming the end of her staff against the ground, a brilliant bolt of bluish-white light, as explosive as her temper, erupted from the obsidian crystal.

Elee ducked her head while Loken huddled low in his cage as the bolt of energy ricocheted against the stony walls to fill the chamber with unnatural radiance. Blue sparks burst forth, cascading down in a brilliant shower of light wherever this powerful energy collided against solid rock. This bolt deflected off the ceiling of the chamber to plunge straight into the sea rushing in on a foamy wave. The water boiled and steamed as the bolt of light disappeared into the depths, a trail of luminous plankton glowed an eerie green in its wake like the tail of a great comet streaking across the night sky before fading away.

Sin scrambled onto her feet. Screaming like a banshee, she dashed through the tunnel. Snarling and cursing, she crouched down like a wild animal on the hunt. She searched the entrance of the passage to the outside world, inspecting it for her prisoner's footprints. What tracks there were must have been obliterated by the restless winds or when she had stood here earlier, shaking off the snow from her cloak, or perhaps she was being tricked. Enraged, Sin yanked at her hair with one hand as the other curled into a quivering fist as she punched at her face in self-loathing and frustration.

"RAAAHR!" Sin's bone-rattling scream echoed through this subterranean lair. It rumbled into the empty sky to be carried away by the north wind.

"Damn!" Tag cursed beneath his breath. "Where to hide? Where to hide?"

He could practically feel Sin's heart pounding through the gloom as she turned from the mouth of the tunnel. Driven by desperation, he felt around for a place to hide in case she returned with a torch to search this corner of her lair.

In a desperate scramble he bumped against the crate, forcing the ill-fitting lid to shift. Tag recoiled as the powerful stench of what had to be poorly cured meats wafted up, assaulting his nostrils.

Pushing the lid open a little wider, he reached inside. His hand felt about, touching coarse grains of salt packed in this long wooden crate. Picking up a handful, he lifted it to his nose. His head snapped back, accosted by the mixture of salt, some kind of rancid oil as well as a strange assortment of spices and herbs. Tag determined this had to be Sin's store of food. Surely, the last place she'd look for an escaped prisoner is within her larder of food.

"Where is he?" shrieked Sin, as she raced back down the tunnel. "Where did he go?"

Tag lost no time. He quickly and quietly slid the lid off just enough to climb into the wooden container. Wriggling about, he worked his body into the preserving salts, using his hands and legs to push aside large chunks and portions of meat on the bone to make room. Settling in, Tag held his breath. Sliding the lid back into place, he struggled as the edge snagged on the lip of the crate. Wrestling with the lid, his breath hitched in the back of this throat. He bit down on his lower lip to keep from crying out as his knuckle scraped against a bent nail protruding from one of the planks of wood.

As he lay still in this all-consuming darkness, aside from the beating of his heart drumming in his ears, he swore he heard a drop of blood splash onto the layer of salt beneath him. Tag squeezed the wound on the back of his hand against his leg to staunch the flow of blood.

Against the wan light of the dawn sky the world had been transformed.

Percy exhaled a weary breath as he stopped to rest. A fog of condensation swirled before him. This mist vanished, whisked away on a breeze rushing down through the mountain pass they now travelled.

Silas ventured close on the heels of Halen Ironwood while Loftus and Myron followed, trampling the knee-deep layer of snow. It made for easier travelling for Rose, but Percy ordered Harold Murkins to walk behind him with Rainus Silverthorn.

To Percy it made sense for this large man to take the rear with the Elf Lord. Where Rainus can provide protection from a rear assault, Harold's mere presence can prove to be dangerous. Allowing this behemoth to walk before him would certainly clear a wider path, but should Harold slip and fall, Percy believed he would tumble down, taking all those behind him to their doom. He was not about to chance this as they wandered over this mountain range.

Shielding his eyes from the glare of the sun that set the snow glistening in the radiance of this early morning light, Percy motioned for Rose to continue on.

"Do you wish to rest?" whispered Rose.

"Rest? Me? Of course not!" grumbled Percy. His eyes narrowed in resentment. "I just wish to adjust my cloak against the chill." His gloved hands grasped the edge of the cloak's hood, pulling it lower over his furrowed brows. To lend credibility to his lie, he then wrapped the fabric snugly around his body.

"We can stop and wait for you to catch your breath, if you need to rest," offered Rose, her words spoken in a hush. "It is not a problem."

"I do not need to rest!" snapped Percy, his voice rising in agitation as he flashed an angry glance toward the Wizard. "And if I did, the real problem is that *someone* had elected to abandon our horses than to ride them! Oh, no! We just had to leave those animals behind in a safe, warm barn, while we are made to endure the misery of this arduous, cold climb to lands unknown."

Percy turned with a start as the tip of Rainus' bow rapped against his shoulder. The Elf stood there with his index finger pressed against his lips as he issued a stern warning.

"Keep your voice down, lest you wish to bring these mountains crashing down upon us," whispered Rainus.

"It was not as though I was shouting."

"True, but your shrill voice tends to carry in this thin air," said Rainus. "It is enough to wake the dead the way you jabber on."

Percy reacted with an exasperated roll of his eyes as he nodded to the Elf. Speaking in a hushed tone, instead of apologizing, he offered a flippant, "I forgot."

"Heed my words, Prince Percival," cautioned Rainus, "you are far from the safety of your father's castle. Your forgetfulness or an act of stupidity can get you killed out here and endanger our lives in the process."

"Just because I had a lapse in memory, it does not mean I am stupid!" declared Percy. Against this snowy backdrop, his face burned red with growing agitation. The mortal appeared more rubicund in hue than the Elf thought was humanly possible.

Percy felt the eyes of those in his company suddenly turn on him. He was forced to lower his voice to address the Elf Lord, lest he raise the ire of all. "I promise to be more mindful from now on."

Rainus nodded in approval as Percy's tone was reduced to a discreet whisper. He motioned for him to keep up with the others as his comrades resumed the trek.

Percy drew a weary breath as he turned his eyes forward, noting how Rose had managed to trudge through the trampled snow, unabated as she kept pace with the Elf captain, the Wizard and the men travelling before her.

Inwardly, he was perturbed this lowly girl, albeit one of royal blood, was showing him up before those in their shared company. It was unnatural that Rose was able to travel tirelessly and without a word of complaint when, in his mind, there was more than enough to complain about.

"You heard Lord Silverthorn," whispered Harold, motioning for Percy to advance. "Keep movin'. We don't want to be left behind now, do we?"

Percy snorted in resignation. He resumed his ascent, stepping into the shadow of the craggy mountain that loomed over to their right. Its jagged peak pierced through a shroud of heavy clouds hugging its shoulders to stab into the stark blue sky. Plumes of steam venting through fissures from the belly of this otherwise quiet volcano were conspicuous against this infinite, cerulean canvas.

As Percy hastened his pace to catch up to Rose he wrapped his cloak tightly around his body as the temperature took a sudden and ferocious dip in the shadow created by this mountain. He didn't know which was worse; having to shield his eyes against the discomfort from the brilliant glare of the sun shining on this fresh snow or enduring the biting cold each time his cloak flapped open, snagged by the chilling winds rushing over this mountain range.

As they neared the crest of the narrow, V-shaped valley that formed the pass between these two mountains, Halen abruptly raised his right hand. The Elf motioned for his comrades to be silent as the other hand cupped his left ear. Cocking his head, Halen listened.

"What is it?" asked Silas. He studied the troubled expression on the captain's face.

"I swear I heard a wretched wail – a scream of anguish or pain, perhaps," whispered Halen. "It seemed to carry over these very mountains."

"I heard not a thing!" snapped Percy. With a dismissive wave of his hand, he gestured for Halen to continue escorting them, than to squander his precious time at a standstill in this frozen wasteland. "It was probably nothing more than the howl of the wind blowing in from the north!"

Rainus glared at Percy, growling a muted warning to keep his voice down as he rushed by to join Halen at the front of the procession.

"Tell me you did not hear Tag crying out," whispered Rose, lowering the hood of her cloak from her head to better listen.

"Worry not, my lady. Captain Ironwood's keen hearing could have detected nothing more than the cry of a distant animal," said Loftus. He tried to reassure her as he cupped a hand to his ear, listening for what the Elf heard.

"It could be a dangerous, wounded animal," said Percy, trying not to sound hopeful. "We should not tempt fate. Perhaps it would be wise to turn back now?"

"Silence," ordered Silas. He scowled at Percy. "Stop your snivelling so we can listen in peace. It may well be the Witch."

"Oh, we don't need to be stumblin' into one of her traps," said Harold. Pressing a finger to his lips, he motioned Percy to be quiet. Stumbling through the snow that was crushed under his weight, Harold rushed by Percy to join his comrades to better hear what Halen heard while the Prince stood alone, brooding in silence.

Percy wondered, in hindsight, if just stealing the Dreamstone from Rose or somehow bribing her to hand it over would have spared him the gruelling rigours of this trek, not to mention being subjected to the drudgery of the substandard company he was made to keep. With the exception of Rose when she was being attentive to him, or the Elf Lord when he was engaging him in civil conversation, they presented the only tolerable company in the mix. The rest, Captain Loftus included, left much to be desired.

While the others gathered, ears cupped, head cocked into the wind that blustered as it crested the pass, Percy glanced behind to see how far they had come. His eyes skimmed over the landscape, turning forward to determine how much farther he will be made to travel.

As the sun climbed higher, shortening the shadows entrenching this pass, its rays stretched across the snowy terrain to shine upon the east face of the mountain towering over to their left. Percy squinted as the sun's brilliant light glistened against a now frozen waterfall that was encrusted in ice and snow. Rows of slender icicles clung to outcropping rocks that protruded from where once-running waters flowed.

"Incredible!" Percy marvelled under his breath. He admired the raw power and beauty of nature, revelling in the sheer majesty of the largest ice formation he had ever seen.

And then, true to form, Percy celebrated this moment by lobbing a snowball at the largest of the icicles. It was longer than a spear and as wide as his forearm where its circumference was the greatest. As this tightly packed ball missed its mark, disintegrating against the frozen face of the waterfall, Silas and the others turned upon hearing the impact.

"What the…" The Wizard glanced toward the mortal, just in time to see him launch another snowball at his desired target.

"No!" cried Silas, waving frantically at Percy to stop, but it was too late.

They watched in stunned silence as the ball sailed through the air, striking the large, spear-like icicle Percy had missed the first time.

"Oh, no!" gulped Rose.

The snowball shattered, exploding into hundreds of frozen pieces upon smashing against this icicle.

"Be ready to run," warned Silas, waiting for the spear of ice to fall and set a cavalcade of misfortune barrelling their way.

Their collective breaths snagged in the back of their throats. They waited for the icicle to drop upon hearing a loud crack as the clear ice formation suddenly clouded. Hairline fractures erupted throughout the crystalized water.

The silence was deafening. They waited and watched, but Halen and Rainus wasted no time, searching for a route to possible salvation should the unthinkable happen.

Instead, the icicle remained dangling, anchored to the rocky outcrop.

Rose and her comrades barely breathed. Their hearts thundered, sounding in their ears as the distant cry of a raven shattered the still, mountain air.

"Phew!" said Loftus, as he scowled in disapproval at his royal charge. "What were you thinking, my lord?"

"That is the problem, Captain Loftus," said Silas. "The Prince was *not* thinking when he wantonly endangered our lives with that foolish act."

"Foolish act?" grumbled Percy. "All I did was throw a stupid snowball or two!"

"The snowball was not stupid," averred Myron. " Oh, no! You were the stupid one."

Percy's face reddened as he scowled with anger.

"It is better to say Prince Percy is not stupid," insisted Rose, in a bid to pacify him. "Instead, it was his *action* that was stupid."

"You are not helping my case!" Percy snapped at her.

"Settle down, you dolt!" ordered Loftus, motioning for Percy to stop with his tirade.

"Fetch off!" snarled Percy; his feet stomping like an angry child. "You're the one who should settle down! How dare you call me names?"

Craaack!

All glanced at the giant icicle as it broke away from its hold. They watched in horror as it plunged straight down, piercing into a great bank of snow to disappear in this huge mound of white.

For a prolonged moment that was an eerie silence, and then, as though the mountain had come to life, it seemed to moan in pain. The bank of snow the icicle had speared suddenly broke away, sliding down the east face of the mountain in an enormous, white wave thundering toward them.

"RUN!" hollered Myron.

He seized Rose by her wrist as Percy dashed away, abandoning her to follow the Elves as they jumped, disappearing over the edge of the pass as the sliding snow became a great avalanche rumbling their way.

Percy wasted no time. Racing behind the Elves to seek safety in their company he blindly followed them over the edge. Driven by sheer panic, he made a leap.

His eyes bulged in fright to see the dark chasm of a deep crevasse. Screaming in terror, his arms and legs flailed about as his hands snatched at the empty air.

17
Signs of Life

"Stop struggling, you fool!" shouted Rainus, as he snagged Percy by his wrist.

With this sharp command, Percy froze, allowing the Elf Lord to yank him to safety. None too pleased, Rainus landed the mortal. Like a large trout, he tossed him onto the narrow ledge they had found refuge on.

Rainus ducked to one side as Halen reached out, grabbing hold of Myron. The knight held onto Rose as they made the leap from the path of the rushing snow. Helping Halen to pull Myron onto the ledge, he then reached down for Rose.

Hoisted onto solid ground, she caught her breath as Percy rushed up to her, embracing her in a great hug.

"Thank goodness you are safe!" exclaimed Percy. "It is a good thing I ran ahead to make the leap before you, just to make sure it was safe."

There was no time to contest Percy's version of the truth. Halen reached out, grabbing hold of Captain Loftus as he fell. Rainus seized Silas by the scruff of his neck as he flew over the ledge like a giant bat; his dark cloak fluttered out behind him.

Harold followed right behind the Wizard, squealing in terror to see nothing but a gaping abyss below him as his badger headpiece fell from his head. It shrank from his sight, tumbling down with the great clots of snow cascading over the cliff.

With no thought to his own safety, Myron leaned out. He caught Harold by his hand. The knight cried out in surprise as he toppled over, pulled down by Harold's weight. Silas and Halen seized Myron by his shoulders, preventing him from taking a deadly tumble. Just as Harold's hand, slick with sweat, slipped from Myron's grasp, Rainus and Loftus lunged forward, grabbing hold of the mortal by his wrists. Together, they hoisted him to safety as a wall of snow crashed down before them.

"Thank you, my friends!" Harold nodded in gratitude as he gasped for his breath. "You saved my life!"

"It is what we do," stated Percy, sounding nonchalant like this was an everyday occurrence for him.

"You pompous prig!" scolded Rainus. "You did nothing!"

"I was keeping Princess Rose-alyn safe," argued Percy, "making sure she remained out of harm's way, and yours, so the others could be saved."

"So you say," muttered Rainus, as he and Halen stared with raised eyebrows at the mortal.

"I do! If I had not held on to her, she would have likely met her demise attempting to lift that big buffoon to safety," insisted Percy. "If anything, I kept her from getting in the way during the height of this deadly event."

"Unlike you, Princess Rose was *not* in the way," snapped Myron, shaking the snow from his raiment as he confronted Percy.

"And no thanks to you, your foolishness caused this disaster to begin with," admonished Silas. He watched as the final trail of cascading snow emptied into the crevasse to bury Harold's favourite headpiece far below.

"The point being, we should just be grateful we all survived a potential calamity," reminded Percy. "That is the most important thing."

"It's good to be alive," agreed Harold, searching his pack for another animal headpiece to keep his head warm. Pulling out the raccoon pelt by its striped tail, he positioned it on his cold noggin.

"Considering the option, alive is always better," agreed Myron, as he glanced about the ledge they were perched on.

"Indeed!" said Percy. "So now what? How do we escape this dreadful place?"

"We are safe for the moment, Prince Percival," assured Rainus, "and trust me when I say there are places far worse than here to be stuck in. I am sure of it."

'This is awful!' Tag's mind raced. His heart hammered in his chest as he lay as still as a corpse wedged into a too small coffin.

Not even daring to breathe, he listened.

Not far away the Witch raged. Her obsidian crystal crackled with frenetic energy to match her anger. As she charged down the tunnel back to her lair, Sin was screaming mad, spewing forth a litany of profanities in an ancient dialect Tag was unfamiliar with. He remained still, not moving a muscle even as chunks of coarse salt bit into exposed skin and bony knobs of preserved meat dug into his back and legs.

"Where is he? Tell me!" snarled Sin. She picked up the cage in her trembling hands, holding it to her face as the torchlight served to accentuate every wrinkle, scar and mole on this hideous visage. Spittle flew from her frothing mouth as she raged at the Sprite. "Where did he go?"

"I told you, Tag escaped!" snapped Loken, ducking from the worst of the barrage. "He is probably rallying the forces as we speak."

"Liar!" growled Sin.

"Do you see him about?" Loken's tone was mocking. "While you wasted time searching for him here, Tag took off. If his luck holds, he is long gone by now!"

"He is hiding! Where is he hiding?" With festering anger the cloudiness fogging Sin's blind eye swirled as an image of Tag being throttled by her bony hands formed for Loken to see.

"If he were hiding right now, do you honestly believe I'd tell you where? I'd rather die than help you."

Sin roared, hurling the cage across the chamber. With a loud clatter that set Elee's frayed nerves ever more on edge, she watched helplessly as Loken, unable to brace for impact, was slammed against the steel bars as his prison smashed against the wall.

Like an ungainly animal, Sin loped over to the cage, snatching it up from the ground.

"You better not be dead!" snarled the Witch, staring at the tiny body on the floor of the cage. "If the boy escaped, you'll have to serve as bait to lure the others."

In an agitated huff, she slammed the cage down on the table. Sin's cracked lips curled into a sneering smile of satisfaction as Loken moaned softly. Turning on her heels, she dashed over to the torch next to the entrance of the tunnel. Snatching it from the sconce with one hand, the other grabbed the staff.

"He is gone!" Elee shouted behind her. "There is no point in searching. The boy is long gone!"

Ignoring her warning, Sin slunk into the passage. Glancing to her left, the tunnel delivered her to the larder and storage room. Beyond this small chamber was a dark and treacherous maze. Winding tunnels were sure to guarantee a terrible death to anyone foolhardy enough to venture forth into the depths without the aid of a torch. To her right, the brilliant light of the outside world, made even more dazzling by the freshly fallen snow against the rising sun beckoned to her. At a loping gallop, Sin skidded to a stop at the mouth of the tunnel. Her one good eye narrowed, squinting under the brilliance of the outside world as she searched for footprints she had missed before.

Instead, the restless winds had blown the snow about, concealing all signs of movement coming and going from this tunnel.

Sin thrust her beak of a nose into the air, nostrils flaring as she sniffed like a wolf scenting its prey. There was only the briny smell of the sea. Her fist tightened around her staff as her frustration mounted. Exhaling loudly as she focused her mind, she cocked her head, listening for the crunch of footsteps on the crisp, frozen layer of snow. Sin growled upon hearing only the distant crashing of waves that punctuated the relative silence of this desolate landscape.

Scowling, Sin considered the possibilities. Her instincts warned her that the prisoners were lying about Tag's escape, for why would they ever tell her the truth? A niggling feeling in her gut made Sin think that perhaps the boy had never left the cave in the first place. Perhaps he was still skulking about, his escape pre-empted by her return.

With a snort of indignation Sin turned away from the entrance. Slinking down the tunnel with the burning torch in one hand and staff in the other, she crept through the narrow passage. This time, she carried her staff, not allowing the end to strike the ground as she normally did when she used it as a walking stick. Her angry breath involuntarily hissed as she exhaled between clenched teeth. Holding the torch on high, the flames pushed against the darkness, lighting the way before her. Tiptoeing toward the small chamber where she stored the driftwood, as well as her foods and sundries, Sin's heart quickened, thudding against her thin chest as she prepared to surprise her escaped prisoner.

"A-ha!" shouted Sin.

She pounced forward. Her bony frame and billowy cloak blocked the entrance as she brandished both torch and staff to strike down her quarry. Rather than confronting the boy head-on, she scowled as she stared into a cluttered, lifeless room.

Tag froze. He held his breath.

The light from the torch seeped between the planks of wood forming this tomb and its lid to create seams of golden light shining through. Tag steeled his nerves. He pressed his bloodied hand against his thigh, clenching the dagger to prepare for an attack.

He watched Sin through the sliver of a crack. Her good eye rolled about, searching for signs of life. He could hear the muffled crunch of pebbles underfoot as she crept ever closer, first peering at the jumbled stack of firewood, and then toward the wooden crate resting near to it.

Tag swore he could hear the beating of her heart and the rattling hiss of her ragged breath each time she exhaled.

"Where are you?" Speaking in a singsong voice as though she was attempting to draw a young child out from a game of hide-and-seek, she beckoned to him. "Come out! Come out wherever you are!"

A large lump of preserved meat shifted beneath the layer of salt under Tag's body. It caused the brine to bite into the cut on his hand, stinging it. Wincing in pain, he bit his lower lip.

"You cannot hide forever, you know?"

Tag's breath snagged in the back of his throat as Sin inched closer to his hiding place. He watched as her head cocked from side to side as she listened.

"I know you are here. I can smell your fear."

Tag said not a word. Peering through a thin gap between the planks of wood, he saw Sin staring in his direction.

"If you give me what I want, just a wee bit of your blood, I will set you and your friends free," she lied.

Tag remained silent. He lay absolutely still, wondering why she hadn't obliterated him in his hiding place yet, if she were so sure he was in this crate. He dared not move, waiting for Sin to either abandon her search or to throw the lid off to attack him.

"Come out this instant!" she growled, the feigned playfulness in her voice evaporating into the walls of this cave as her ugly face contorted with unadulterated hate.

Tag had no intention of complying. He waited for Sin to make her move. He was going to take her by surprise. At the most opportune moment, he prepared to attack with his weapon.

"Stand before me!" roared Sin. The obsidian crystal crackled with energy. Its eerie glow filled the small chamber with cold, unnatural light. "Do so now!"

With this command, Tag yelped in surprise. He was forcefully catapulted from the crate.

Sin shrieked in surprise. She jumped back as this mortal landed atop the haphazard pile of driftwood, along with the crate's lid. Tag tumbled off the stack, the wooden lid landing on top of him.

"How can this be?" sputtered Sin. In anger and confusion, she stared at the corpse she had so carefully preserved. "It is not your time to rise!"

Tag gasped in horror, catching a glimpse of the *preserved meat* that had bolted upright to fling him from his hiding place. It was this *thing* that was buried beneath the salt he had been laying on. The cadaver slowly turned its head to stare with clouded, sunken eyes at Sin. Clumps and grains of salt rained down from its dark, oil-clotted head of hair. Shrivelled flesh, now drained of colour, clung to its bony skull. Salt and oil cured skin and muscle accentuated the hollows of the cheeks and the eye sockets while severely crack lips had shrunk tightly around the mouth, twisting it into a sinister grimace to display rows of blackened teeth held in place by receding, lifelessly pale gums. As wretched as the Sorcerer was in life, Dragonite's shocking appearance in death, or whatever this strange plane of existence was now, was even more horrible.

"I am not ready for you!" snarled Sin. "Go back to being dead!"

Instead of obeying her command, Dragonite's head cocked in her direction. He stared at her. Behind these milky, lifeless eyes, Sin was hoping there was a hint of familial recognition for his sibling.

"Sleep, I say! Return to your slumber until you are needed!" ordered Sin. She stared in disbelief, pondering how her brother had risen from the dead without her magic. "I am not ready to deal with you just yet."

Whether it was her angry tone or her demands that set this corpse on edge, it responded by chattering its teeth. Like an angry dog baring its fangs in preparation to bite, a guttural moan rumbled forth from deep in its throat.

"Stop that, you fool! You were never one to listen to me before, but you shall listen to me now!" barked Sin.

Rather than settling down to slip back into a dreamless slumber amongst the hunks of salted pork, Dragonite's dead, but very animated body clambered awkwardly from the crate as Tag watched in stunned disbelief. He was both amazed and horrified.

Standing on unsteady legs, this unwieldy corpse shuffled toward Sin. Like a newborn fawn taking its first clumsy steps on gangly legs, it wobbled in her direction.

Draped in tattered, oil-soaked rags, it swayed like death itself was thoroughly inebriated. Staggering like a drunk, this brought a whole new meaning to being absolutely 'pickled'.

Tag watched as coarse grains and chunks of salt fell from its body and raiment. Remaining huddled beneath the meagre protection of the crate's lid, he clutched his dagger, preparing to attack. He didn't know how this magic worked, but somehow the blood that had dripped from his wound must have prematurely resurrected Dragonite.

The Witch had said before how she required the blood of the one who had murdered her brother to bring him back from the dead. Perhaps the drops that spilled from his hand were just enough to restore life to this cadaver. Whatever the case, it was apparent without Sin's magic it was not enough to restore the Sorcerer's mind. This aberration of nature was indifferent when it came to whom to attack first. At this moment, Sin presented the closest and most easily accessible target to sate his hunger or vent his wrath.

"Back off, you mindless cretin!" cursed Sin, levelling the black crystal at her brother's chest.

There was no sign Dragonite even recognized the staff and its black crystal that was once his most valued possession. Gnashing its teeth in response, another guttural moan rumbled from its throat as it staggered with withered arms extended toward her. Stiff, gnarled fingers uncurled as the corpse reached out for her throat.

"Back off!" snarled Sin. Dropping the torch, the flames sputtered, flickering as it hit the ground. Taking up the staff in both hands, she growled, "Get away from me!"

Unsticking its shrivelled tongue from the roof of its parched mouth, Dragonite moaned, *"Aaains..."*

"Say again," grunted Sin. She was stunned this dead body was attempting to communicate with her.

Dragonite reached for her throat again as a single, hollow word croaked out from between those rotting teeth, *"Raaaains..."*

"Rains? What the heck are you babbling about?" snapped Sin. She backed away toward the entrance of the chamber. "Rain? Water? Are you thirsty?"

"Braaains..." moaned the corpse, gnashing its teeth as he stumbled closer.

"Brains? Of course your brain had been addled!" responded Sin. She used the tip of the staff to bat away the outstretched hands.

"He wants your brain!" shouted Tag. Lifting the lid off his body, he scrambled to make his escape.

With a snarl, Dragonite lunged at Sin.

Brandishing the obsidian crystal, she was reluctant to use its magic to claim his life essence and thereby, lose his potential powers by returning him to the afterlife - permanently. Hoisting her weapon toward this corpse, she attempted to drive it back into the salt-filled coffin.

Undeterred by her threats and the useless jabs of the staff, the monster made another lunge, stumbling only to fall against her.

"No!" cried Sin. Through the staff she could feel and hear the jagged crystal puncture into raiment and leathery skin to pierce through flesh and gristle before penetrating its preserved innards. "You cannot die again, not just yet!"

Just when she thought it was a fatal blow, the assault enraged the aberration that was once the Sorcerer. It growled in anger instead of pain. As Sin yanked the crystal free from this husk of a body, the gnarled fingers with overgrown talons wrapped around her neck to throttle her.

Both the living and the living dead crashed to the ground, wrestling about in the narrow tunnel at the mouth of this small chamber.

"Help me!" wheezed Sin, crying out to Tag as he approached with dagger in hand.

"You're doing just fine," responded Tag. Skirting by the Witch and the corpse, the creature gnashed its teeth at Tag's legs as he scooted by.

"You are as useless in death as you were in life!" snarled Sin. Using the staff, she struggled to direct him toward her escaping prisoner. "Kill him! Not me!"

Glancing over his shoulder, Tag watched this macabre scene play out as the two wrestled: one for control, the other for a meal.

Dragonite growled. Thin, cracked lips curled back to expose blackened teeth that snapped viciously at Sin's angry face as she fought to be free of this creature's tenacious hold.

The thought of killing the dead with his dagger entered Tag's mind, but this thought was fleeting, for it meant contending with Sin and her deadly crystal. Instead, he darted back into her lair. Glancing over to the torch sconce, Loken was missing.

Searching about, Tag spied upon the battered cage amongst the clutter on the worktable.

"Loken!" cried Tag. He dashed over to the cage. Using the blade of his dagger, he popped open the door to this tiny prison. "Loken! Wake up."

Instead, the Sprite lay there in a crumpled, lifeless heap on the floor of this prison, not even stirring as Tag picked up the cage to better inspect him in the poor light of the cave.

Elee twisted about, calling over her shoulder. "I think he's dead."

With a heavy heart, Tag placed the cage back on the table. He was too late to save Loken, but now, he was more determined than ever that Elee would have a chance at life. He dashed over to her side, kneeling by the pillar of stone she was chained to. Taking his dagger, he used the tip of the blade, jiggling it into the lock. With a hard twist, the rust gave way; the padlock fell open, all the while, Sin's angry screams and the corpse's snarling growls sounded through the tunnel to echo through this chamber.

Working with speed, Tag unwound the length of chain. Elee leaned away from the barnacle-encrusted pillar, stretching her weary muscles and excitedly slapping her tailfin against the surface of the tidal pool. For a moment, Tag was shocked. Through the tangle of dull, matted hair cascading down to her waist he could see the cuts and abrasions marring her back, some still bleeding against her sickly pale skin.

"Quickly! There is no time to lose," said Tag. Scooping her up in his arms, he carried her to where the cave opened to the foaming, open sea. He tossed her in on the retreating tide, shouting: "Swim! Get away from here!"

The Mermaid vanished, sinking into the shadows of the jade-green water. Tag watched the churning wave as it rushed in, breaking upon the rocks. He gasped in surprise as Elee burst to the surface, leaping into the air like an exuberant dolphin that had been freed from a fisherman's net. Her hair was glossy and her skin was like luminous porcelain once more; the rejuvenating powers of the sea healing the wounds that had marred her body. As she dove back in with a stupendous splash, the little seal barked at her.

Elee's head bobbed up to the surface of the water as she begged to Tag, "Flotsam! Free her, please!"

Tag dashed over to the seal. Using his dagger, he cut through the net. He yanked hard to widen the opening. The little seal rolled into the tidal pool with feeding on her mind, but upon hearing Elee's urgent calls in a lyrical, high-pitched voice in a language Tag had never heard before, Flotsam awkwardly clambered out of the pool. Like a fat caterpillar, the seal scrambled, awkwardly pitching her body over the rocks toward freedom. With a jubilant bark, Flotsam dove into the welcoming sea to reunite with her master.

"Swim!" ordered Tag, waving Elee away. "Be free!"

"Thank you!" Elee shouted, nodding in gratitude.

He watched as Mermaid and seal dove down together, their shadows gliding beneath the churning waters to dissolve in the depths as they swam away through the opening. A great riptide rushed around them, swallowing them up. The powerful current flowed just beyond the partially submerged opening, sweeping them away to be one with the sea.

Though Tag was saddened by Loken's demise, he was elated that Elee was granted liberty, and now, he resolved to be free, too. Dashing to the adjoining passageway, Tag peeked around the corner to see where the Witch was lurking about.

There she was, no longer pinned to the ground, but instead, grappling toe-to-toe against her dead brother. The two had shoved, pushed, pulled and wrestled their way toward the mouth of the tunnel, blocking Tag's escape to the outside world. He could see their bony frames grimly silhouetted by the light of day. The corpse grabbed hold of Sin, slamming her against the wall of this narrow passage. Rather than slow her down, this act of violence threw her into a fit of rage. She swung the staff about, bashing her sibling across his snarling, skeletal face to send this corpse staggering against the opposite wall.

"You mindless moron!" cursed Sin. She levelled the obsidian

crystal. "Back off, I say!"

As deaf to her demands as it was determined to chew her face off, the creature launched itself bodily at her. Tag watched as Sin retaliated, repeatedly ramming the dark crystal into the corpse's chest and midriff. Black blood as thick as tree pitch oozed from these wounds, but the assault did little to stop this unrelenting attack.

Tag knew there was no chance of skirting by this battling duo, not without getting between them. If he retreated into this lair and attempted to swim through the sea cave, the chance of surviving the riptide in such frigid waters was about as risky as running the gauntlet between the deranged dead and the demented necromancer. Neither held any appeal.

Glancing to his left, a flickering light caught Tag's attention. It was the flames of the torch Sin had abandoned in her larder when the corpse first attacked.

Pressing his back to the wall of the tunnel, he crept down the passage, hoping to go unnoticed. His blood ran cold. Sin spotted him, screaming out to Dragonite, "After him! Kill the boy!"

Tag had no intention of waiting to see if this living nightmare was about to give chase. With his heart pounding, he broke into a full sprint as he raced toward the sputtering torch. He skidded, tripping over his feet as he slowed down, but only enough to snatch up the torch from the ground. Holding the light before him, the flames burned steady once more. He charged down the tunnel, leaving the crazed Witch behind to deal with the dead.

Confident Sin was no different than most animals that take to burrowing into the earth, like a badger or a mole, the Witch had to have another escape route from her lair should this tunnel collapse. It was now just a matter of finding this other exit.

"Come back here!" snarled Sin.

She watched as the torchlight shrank into the darkness as her prisoner made good his escape. With the main and final ingredient of her potion to steal away with her brother's powers disappearing down the tunnel, Sin went berserk. She attacked, ramming the sharp tip of the dark crystal repeatedly into this corpse.

The dead still refused to die.

Instead, Dragonite's bony hands wrapped around Sin's throat once more, squeezing the life from her.

Realizing her efforts were doing nothing except incite this creature to ramp up its efforts to kill her, Sin cursed beneath her breath. She plunged the end of the staff into the chest cavity to pierce its cold heart. Undeterred, Dragonite lunged, snapping and snarling at her face.

In desperation, Sin uttered a spell as she rammed the end of the staff into the corpse once more. Her good eye narrowed as she turned her head away. The black crystal swelled with light shining like beams of sunlight bursting through cloud cover, erupting through the wounds she tore into this body.

With a final twist of the wrist, she drove the crystal in deep. As she spoke the last words of an incantation, this glow became blinding. It expanded, radiating from every natural and Witch-made orifice to shine like beams of blue light shooting out from wounds, old and new, as well as the eyes, nostrils, ears and mouth. The corpse began trembling violently, thrashing to be free of this embedded crystal.

As the percussion of a great explosion rippled through the tunnel, Tag stumbled, falling to his knees. Without glancing back to see what had happened, he snatched up the torch. Scrambling to his feet, Tag raced off toward the darkness ahead.

As the corpse exploded, Sin was flung against the tunnel wall. The staff flew from her hands with the percussion. Splattered by coagulating, black blood and bombarded by flying chunks of flesh, bones and mostly unrecognizable globs of smouldering internal organs, Sin tumbled to the ground. Opening her eyes to the sound of gnashing teeth, she gasped in horror. She lay face to face with Dragonite. She recoiled as this decapitated head continued to snarl and snap at her. To Sin's surprise, even without a body, this insatiable corpse was intent on biting her. Its tongue groped about, finding traction on the ground like a clam using its muscular foot to dig and travel through sand. In a strange and grotesque display, it dragged its head closer toward her horrified face.

Sin scrambled just as this skull rolled down a slight incline, tumbling toward her. Clambering onto her unsteady legs, she snatched up the staff. Turning the black crystal toward the disembodied head, Sin snarled, "Die, why don't you!"

Ramming the jagged crystal straight through Dragonite's left temple, she speared the brain. Instantly, those snapping jaws snapped no more. The cadaver was finally dead.

Sin unleashed a sigh of relief. Checking this head for signs of life, she prodded it with the toe of her boot. Satisfied there'd be no more biting, she pulled on the staff to free the crystal from the skull. Instead, like a sword without a fuller running the length of the blade, it was as though the brain matter glommed onto the offending weapon, refusing to let go.

Setting her boot down on this face now frozen in a permanent scowl, Sin wrenched her staff free. With an angry huff, she kicked

Dragonite's head to send it bouncing and careering down the tunnel. It came to a rest just outside the entrance. The blackened blood that followed laid a stark trail against the glistening, white snow.

Rattled by the bone-bruising percussion of the exploded body, Sin absentmindedly flicked off the remains and blobs of blood from her frock and cloak. Finding a relatively clean section of her garb, she used it to wipe her face of the worst of the gore as she gathered her thoughts.

With the useless corpse now blown to unrecognizable bits, was it even worthwhile pursuing her prisoner into the treacherous maze of tunnels riddling this mountain when his blood no longer serves a purpose? Now that Tag had destroyed her best chance for obtaining real power steeped in magic, the dark magic that was thoroughly entrenched in Dragonite even in death, revenge was a good a reason as any to hunt down and spill the blood of this wretched mortal.

To this end, dispensing a slow, torturous death was the best solution to quell her feelings of rage and dispel the bitterness of injustice that coursed through her veins.

Wiping away the gore clinging to the obsidian crystal, she willed it to glow. Holding this infinite light source aloft, Sin picked her way through the scattered body parts littering the tunnel. Once she cleared the worst of the carnage, Sin galloped, loping like a hobbled, two-legged horse down the passage as she pursued her quarry.

"No point in running, boy!" hollered Sin, her words echoing through the gloom behind him. "If I don't kill you, then what awaits you in the deep dark surely will!"

Tag ducked around a bend in the tunnel, stealing a moment to catch his breath while hiding the glow of his torch from her. Slapping a trembling hand over his mouth, Tag tried to stifle his gasping breath as he listened. He could hear Sin's angry words chasing after him. By the size and intensity of her crystal's glow, he had placed good distance between them, but he knew it would only be a matter of time before Sin catches up.

Before him, the tunnel branched off. Stepping before the opening to his right, Tag held forth the torch, but the light only spread so far. There was no telling where this tunnel would lead. Peering down the opening to the left, the flames flickered and danced, but there was no telling where this passage would lead either. Holding the torch low to the ground, judging from the footprints in the sandy patches where the tunnel he travelled abruptly forked, it was obvious the tunnel to the right was well used. To the left, the tunnel saw little, if any, traffic. Leaning into this passageway, he noticed how the flames of his torch grew and twisted, dancing in the wake of an invisible draft. If his intuition served him well, this fresh air had to be originating from the outside world.

Taking a calculated risk, Tag took several deliberate steps in the tunnel to his right, making sure his boots created clear impressions on the sandy patches. Taking great care, he stepped backwards, making sure his feet set directly over the footprints he just made as he backed toward the fork of the main tunnel.

Turning to the passageway on his left, Tag made a great leap, landing on a large, flat stone. Holding his torch before him, he took another leap onto a rock to avoid leaving footprints in the loose substrate. With Sin's loud, hissing breath echoing through the main tunnel and the thumping of her staff striking the ground as she pursued him, Tag made his move.

With trepidation flooding his heart, he prayed his efforts of deception were enough to send the Witch heading down the wrong tunnel as he rushed off, hoping to be far enough away that the glow of his torch would not betray him.

18
Death by Dragon

"This is madness! Surely you jest, Wizard?"

Percy was dumbfounded as he squinted, staring into the blackness looming before them. The burning torch Halen Ironwood handed to him did nothing to reveal what dangers were lurking deep inside this great mountain.

"I have been known to pull a worthy prank or two in my lifetime, but I have never been one to speak in jest, especially when our lives are put at risk," stated Silas. He willed the crystal mounted atop his staff to glow with steady, white light. "This is the way we are now forced to travel."

"Yes, no thanks to you, my lord," reminded Captain Loftus. He levelled a look of disappointment at his royal charge.

"I am overwhelmed by your sense of loyalty, Loftus. I said it before, I will say it again: It was not my fault that snow came crashing down."

"Yes, it was," countered Rainus. "Had you not thrown that blasted ball of snow we could have avoided the mishap altogether."

"But I – "

"Oh, man up!" snapped Myron, dismissing Percy with a wave of his hand. "You bloody well know it was entirely your fault."

Percy's face reddened. Being accosted by these damning words hurled from all directions set him in a foul mood. Glancing over to Rose, he sought her support, hoping she would call off these hounds she called her friends.

"Tell them, Rose-alyn!" urged Percy. "Tell them I was the victim of boredom, the unrelenting tedium brought on by *their* unwillingness to advance through the mountain pass, when we should have moved on. But no! They had to waste my precious time listening for unfounded danger when the real peril was the treacherous walls of snow surrounding us, waiting to detach had someone even dared to sneeze."

"Sneezing would have been accidental," reasoned Myron. "That cannot be helped, but no one made you hurl that snow. I'd say it was quite deliberate on your part."

Percy snapped at Myron, "I threw it by accident! Is that not so, my dear Rose-alyn?"

"I mean no disrespect to you," answered Rose, "but I do believe you acted of your own free will. Though you did not anticipate the disastrous results, I'd say your actions were quite deliberate."

"Yeah, it's not like any of us told you to test your throwin' arm," reminded Harold.

"Fetch off! I was not speaking to you, you oaf!" Percy snapped at Harold before casting a scowl of condemnation at Rose. It was one that was sure to put her in her place, making this girl more mindful of her choice of words where he was concerned. "I can understand Loftus' disloyalty, for his continued exposure to these rabble-rousers has impaired his judgement, causing him to become small-minded, petty and forgetful when it comes to knowing his place in the order of things. As for you, my dear, I expected better from you, being my future bride and all."

Rose's mouth fell open in surprise as he confronted her with these bitter words of deflated expectations.

"*We* expected far better from *you*, Prince Percival," corrected Halen, with a judicious shake of his head.

"Do not get your tights in a bunch!" snapped Percy, thrusting an accusing digit in the Elf's chest. "I will not stand for such insolence."

In response, Halen thrust out his broad chest, bumping against the agitated mortal to send him stumbling back against Harold. He issued a stern warning, "You are a fool to challenge me, my lord. Do not test my patience unless you wish to suffer my wrath."

"Is that a threat, Captain Ironwood?"

"It is a promise, Prince Percival. Heed my warning and you will be fine; raise my ire and you will be dealt with accordingly, for we are in the midst of a deadly quest. We have no desire to be burdened by your foolish antics and infantile behaviour."

Percy looked aghast as he turned to Rainus. "Lord Silverthorn, your man just threatened *and* insulted me! This Elf of yours is but a lowly captain. He should know his place before royalty."

Rainus glanced over to where Halen stood next to Loftus. It was clear the mortal captain was in total agreement with his Elven counterpart, rolling his eyes in exasperation to hear Percy rant, lashing out at Halen.

"It is apparent to me that both captains are of like mind where you are concerned," answered Rainus.

"There you go then!" said Percy, pointing an accusing finger at Halen, and then Loftus. "Give them a piece of your mind, for I demand respect from all who are my subordinates!"

"One cannot simply demand respect. It must be earned," rebuked Rainus. "But very well, since you insist on me giving them a piece of my mind, then I will."

"I insist! Now, go to it! Give them an earful," grunted Percy. A sneer curled his lips as he waited for the Elf Lord to tell them off.

"Captain Ironwood, Captain Loftus, well said!" praised Rainus, nodding in approval to them. "I fail to believe your words of warning penetrated this young man's thick skull, but failing that, should his future actions be as reckless as before, he will be the one to shape his destiny, not us."

"Indeed!" agreed Silas, watching with mild amusement as Percy's jaw dropped open in dismay. "Now, if you do not wish to be left behind, young man, you best keep up with us."

With a prod from the tip of his staff he steered Percy toward the mouth of the tunnel.

"You first, Wizard," urged Percy, dodging the second prod to allow Silas to lead the way. "You seem quite keen on venturing into the unknown, so get to it."

"Are you admitting to cowardice?" questioned Silas. "Is that why you hesitate?"

"Me? A coward? Of course not! You claim to know these mountains better than us. It only makes sense you should lead the way."

"Dragons," muttered Loftus, with a dismal shake of his head. "Prince Percival is morbidly afraid of dragons. That's what it is."

"Not so!" declared Percy. "Besides, unless this Wizard and these Elves are liars, they claimed the dragons should be deep in hibernation with the first frost. If you look around us, this is no liberal glazing of frost. We are standing knee-deep in snow! The dragons will be embraced in a deep slumber. I know they will be."

"You keep telling yourself that," said Rainus.

"Are you saying you had lied when you told me the dragons would be hibernating?" questioned Percy.

"No," answered the Elf. "With this weather the dragons are indeed asleep, but it is my understanding that just like a bear, these creatures too can be roused from hibernation with enough prompting."

"Great! Wonderful!" snapped Percy. His voice was laced with both sarcasm and dread. "So, you do intend to make dragon fodder of us all."

"Be warned, Prince Percival, should one of these dragons come awake, it is said these creatures are like wolves," cautioned Halen. "They are excited by the hunt. Though a dragon is not endowed with keen eyesight, like an eagle, it will be drawn to movement."

"Meaning?" Percy's eyes narrowed in suspicion as he listened.

"Meaning, if you run, the dragon will give chase, like a hound after a fox," explained Myron. "The more frenetic your movements, the more excited the dragon will be to hunt you down."

"Of course we must run should we encounter a dragon wishing to make a meal of us," argued Percy, as he glanced over to the large and lumbering Harold, sizing him up. "And if we are made to run for our lives, I need only be faster than the person behind me!"

"You run, you die," warned Silas, with a shrug of his shoulders. "It is as simple as that."

"Oh, so we are to die where we stand? Allow a dragon to make a meal of us than to attempt escaping fire and fangs?"

"As Captain Ironwood said, dragons have poor eyesight, but they can detect movement quite easily," said Myron. "Based on our shared experiences, what you should really be careful of is a dragon's keen sense of smell, for it is more keen than that of a starving bear scavenging for scraps of food after a long winter."

Percy's eyes narrowed in doubt. "Hold on here! If we do not run away, that means a dragon is likely to sniff us out, if it doesn't see us first. That only means that I am in even greater peril than all of you."

"How so?" queried Rainus.

"Take no offence, Elf Lord, but I am confident I smell the least offensive of all here, ergo, I promise to be a far more delectable morsel for the discerning dragon."

"Offence taken," grunted Rainus. His eyes rolled in aggravation.

"There is nothing to fear," assured Rose. "As long as we do not smell like dragon food to begin with, we should be fine."

"And just what are we supposed to smell like?" asked Percy.

"Like this," said Rainus. From somewhere in the deep, dark folds of his cloak, he pulled out a small, crystal decanter with a pump atomizer attached to the opening. "This lovely fragrance was created from the oil pressed from the spring blooms of the lavender plant."

"We're to smell like a flower? The lowly lavender at that? I hardly think that will help," said Percy, his tone dismissive.

"I have never known a dragon to eat flowers," responded Silas, "a human or an Elf perhaps, but never a flower."

Rainus held it up to show the liquid of a pale lavender hue in this half-full decanter. Squeezing the bladder of the atomizer, a fragrant, liberal mist wafted over Rose to mask her mortal scent. Rainus then sprayed Loftus, Myron, Harold, and Silas, but when it came to Percy's turn only the faintest of fragrance and a gasping wheeze of air gushed forth. The crystal decanter was now empty.

"Oh, my!" lamented Percy, glancing over to Rainus and Halen. "There is not enough for the rest of us. What are we to do now?"

"Captain Ironwood and I have nothing to worry about, as we always smell of the delightful fragrance akin to that extracted from the attar of rose petals," stated Rainus. "You, on the other hand, have true reason for concern."

"Brilliant!" snapped Percy. "You deliberately waited to douse me with fragrance last, just so this would happen."

"The others willingly accepted my offer. You, on the other hand, were the most vocal in your objections," reminded Rainus, popping the empty decanter into one of the many pockets lining the inside of his cloak. "You were the first to pooh-pooh this fragrance."

"Lovely! Now what will I do?" grumbled Percy, wishing now that he had jumped before the others to be the recipient of a generous spritzing of lavender perfume.

"Pooh, indeed!" laughed Myron. "I have a suggestion."

"One that will work?" Percy stared suspiciously at the knight. "If so, I am game! Whatever it is, I will do it."

"Ewww!" groaned Rose, grimacing in disgust. "You may not be so *game*, and more *gamey*, if you agree to his suggestion."

"What do you speak of?" Percy frowned in confusion. "Lord Silverthorn, can you make any sense of their words?"

"Allow me," offered Halen. He stood near the dark entrance, sniffing as he homed in on the subtle odour lacing the air. Using his boot to scrape away at the snow, he quickly uncovered the boulder-sized midden created by a dragon to establish its territory. Halen continued scraping into the frozen dragon excrement until he reached the layer of moist, pliable dung. His nose wrinkled in disgust as he confirmed it was indeed fresh due to the cold.

Percy retched in his mouth as the acrid smell assaulted his delicate senses. "Surely you jest! That foulness will *not* be touching me!"

"It is either this, become dragon fodder, or get left behind," Halen stated bluntly, inwardly pleased this impudent mortal was about to receive his comeuppance.

Percy considered his options. He was most definitely not getting left behind in this frigid weather, thereby being forced to fend for himself, nor was he willing to become dragon fodder. That left only one possibility, which he begrudgingly accepted.

"Very well," Percy growled, displeased to say the least at what he was forced to endure. "If I must, then so be it."

Plugging his nose with one hand, Percy gingerly dipped the pinkie finger of his other hand into the dung. This miniscule amount of excrement was dabbed behind his ears as though he were applying an exotic perfume.

"That will not do," insisted Myron.

"No?" said Percy.

"Let me help you," offered Harold.

Before he could protest, the large man held his breath as he scooped up a handful of the faeces, applying it liberally to his forehead and cheeks. Percy tried pushing Harold away, but to no avail against this hulking man.

"Interesting," muttered Myron.

"How so?" asked Loftus, grinning as he took certain delight in Percy's misery.

"Prince Percival finally has a shitty exterior to match what is on the inside," Myron snickered.

Loftus bit his tongue, attempting to stifle his laughter. He swallowed in a deep, cleansing breath, composing himself as Harold finished with his handiwork.

"There you go," said Harold, using snow to wash his hands clean. "If you can't be smellin' of flowers, then at least you'll be stinkin' of something a dragon won't be wantin' to eat in the first place, that's for sure."

"Lovely… absolutely lovely," muttered Percy. His eyes watered as he stared at the others. Collectively, they took a deliberate step away from him as the wind suddenly shifted in their direction. This gag-inducing stench hung heavy in the air like a wretched, invisible cloak of dragon repellent to effectively mask his human scent.

"I'm thinkin' it's more disgustin' than anything," said Harold, burying his nose in the crook of his elbow.

"Of course it is!" snapped Percy. He glowered at the big man. "This is absolutely revolting!"

"That is the idea," said Silas, "to make you even more repulsive than you already are."

"Har, har!" Percy grunted in mock laughter. "Aren't you the humorous one, Master Wizard?"

"There was no humour intended in my words," assured Silas. "But enough talk, for now is the time for action."

Halen and Myron followed behind the Wizard, while Harold and Loftus took up the rear, positioning Percy and Rose in the middle of their procession.

With hushed steps, Silas guided them through the maze of tunnels, opting for the narrow lava tubes than the larger passageways most likely frequented by dragons when they are active.

The suffocating darkness that waited to swallow them up yielded to the Wizard's crystal that was set aglow. The flames of the torches carried by Percy and Harold as they followed behind Silas helped to augment its light.

"How much further?" whispered Percy. He switched the torch to his left hand to give his weary right arm a rest.

"We travel for however long it takes to get to where we need to be," answered Silas.

"What kind of answer is that?" whined Percy.

"It is the only one you are entitled to," muttered Silas. "Now keep your voice down."

"I see a faint light up yonder," whispered Halen, pointing ahead into the darkness.

"What is it?" asked Myron, squinting to see what the Elf's keen eyes detected.

"That could be the Witch's secret lair," said Silas, dimming the light emitted by his crystal so it would not betray their presence.

"Perhaps," responded Halen, removing his bow from over his shoulder. "Wait here. I shall advance alone, see what dangers lurk ahead, if any."

"I'll accompany you," offered Loftus.

"No, my friend," whispered Halen. "You shall need the light of a torch to show you the way. Should you advance, it will betray our presence. With my eyes, the light up ahead is enough for me to safely make my way. Better for you to stay here; help keep the others safe."

Before Loftus could protest, Halen was off. With light, quick steps, he melted away, becoming one with the darkness. It was only when he stood at the end of the tunnel, backlit by the eerie red glow he had first detected, were his comrades able to ascertain his exact location. They watched in silence as Halen abruptly vanished from their sight.

"So much for potential danger," whispered Percy, his tone dismissive. "I hardly think Captain Ironwood would brazenly proceed as he did, if there was potential danger lurking about."

"It is a deadly thing to make such assumptions, my lord," said Loftus. "Just be grateful Captain Ironwood had not volunteered your services to scout ahead."

"Your words and tone speak of me as a coward," grumbled Percy. "Had I not been burdened with the honourable task of keeping my future bride safe, I would have boldly ventured forth for the sake of all."

"Keep your voice down," urged Rainus, cupping a hand to his ear as he listened for Halen. "It carries in this tunnel."

"There he is," announced Silas, using the end of his staff to point where the dark silhouette of the Elf appeared against the red glow of light. "Captain Ironwood returns."

"What news have you?" asked Rainus, as Halen became visible in the glow of Silas' crystal.

"Yes, what is that show of eerie light?" asked Rose.

"The news is, there is a large chamber at the end of this tunnel, but it is not the Witch's lair. And that red glow is the light of molten lava."

"That explains why it has become warmer as we ventured deeper into this mountain," said Myron.

"Well, I suppose we shall have to turn back now," said Percy, struggling to contain his joy. "If the way is blocked by molten lava, there is no point in going on."

"The way is *impeded*, not blocked," corrected Halen. "But the lava is the least of our concern."

"How so?" asked Silas.

"There is a barrier we must overcome, and if we succeed, we can continue on our way through a narrow tunnel at the other end of the chamber," said Halen.

"What is this barrier?" asked Loftus. "Is it a vast river of flowing lava?"

Halen drew a deep breath as he gathered his thoughts, determining the best way to deliver the news. "It is worse than that."

"The only thing worse than being consumed by fiery lava would be death by dragon," insisted Percy.

"A dragon?" gulped Rose, her eyes darkened with dread. "Is that what blocks the way?"

"No, my lady," answered Halen. "Not *a* dragon, I am speaking of *four* creatures to be exact, all in a state of torpor in their hibernaculum."

"Say again!" gasped Percy, his eyes melted into large, dark pools of terror.

"Hush," insisted Rainus, motioning Percy for silence. "Better yet, do us a favour by saying nothing at all from here on in."

"Fortunately, those creatures are immersed in a deep slumber. I ventured to within a few paces and none stirred. All remained fast asleep."

"That is a bit a good news," said Myron.

"Yes, as long as they remain oblivious to our presence," added Silas, with a thoughtful nod.

"We get to see dragons? Real, live dragons?" asked Harold. With this prospect, his eyes filled with more wonder than dread.

"Yes, and you shall live to tell about it, if we pass them by unscathed," said Rainus.

"And just how do we accomplish that?" grunted Percy. "It sounds like an impossible feat."

"Most things are not impossible, " answered Halen, as he stared at the sceptical mortal. "If we proceed with caution and no one does anything foolish, we will be fine."

Percy scowled in response, knowing this jibe was intended for him.

"Once we pass them by to enter the tunnel on the other side, should those creatures wake, we will be safe. The way is much too narrow for them to give chase," informed Halen. "Just follow me. Step lightly. Do not speak. Move only when I do."

"That is it?" queried Percy. He eyed the Elf as though Halen could not possibly be serious, and if he were, he had to be absolutely mad.

"Yes. It sounds easy enough, but steel your nerves for we are about to test your mettle, Prince Percival," cautioned Halen. "This task will not be for the faint of heart or those who scare at the mere sight of a great dragon."

"Who said I am scared?" snorted Percy.

"The knocking of your knees betray you," stated Halen.

Percy's hands grabbed his knees to still them as he snapped, "I am shivering with cold. I am not trembling with fear."

"Harold? Princess Rose?" said Rainus. "Are you ready to proceed?"

"Absolutely!" Harold answered with a confident nod.

"Ready, yes. Looking forward to advancing, no. But go, we must," replied Rose, as she drew a calming breath.

"Remember, do not speak," reminded Silas. "Breathe, if you must, but no talking. Advance only when Captain Ironwood deems it safe to do so."

"And should one of those dragons wake before we reach the other side, then what?" asked Percy. He motioned both Harold and Rose before him as he cut in front of Rainus and Loftus to make sure he would be protected, front and back, should a dragon attack.

"Whatever happens, do not run," warned Silas.

"And watch where you tread," cautioned Halen. "There are bones scattered throughout. You do not want to trip. Just keep your eyes on me. Do as I do."

As the brave souls crept toward the mouth of the chamber, several small, bubbling pools of lava cast a red glow to fill this space with eerie light. And though these churning cauldrons were red-hot, due to the size of this cave and the wide passage high above used by the resident reptiles to enter and exit this hibernaculum, it prevented any substantial heat from building up in this cave. It was still warmer than the wintery world outside, but cool enough to lull the dragons into their seasonal slumber until the warmer days of spring returned to the north.

The procession came to a halt as Halen raised an open hand, motioning all to stop. Clenching this hand into a fist, it was a sign for all not to speak. He then pointed ahead to what appeared to be a massive boulder in the centre of the chamber, motioning that they were to go around it.

Percy's brows knitted into a confused frown as he stared at the object of the Elf's interest. As this *boulder* moved ever so slightly, his breath hitched in the back of his throat. Percy's heart dropped into the pit of his stomach, for there lay a great knot of leathery wings, scaly limbs, entwined serpentine necks, and tangled tails. The four dragons were huddled tightly together to conserve body heat, barely breathing as they slept. Above the sputter of churning lava, a dull, rhythmic *'thud'* resonated through the cave floor, amplified by the acoustics of this chamber.

Percy came to realize it was the slow but steady heartbeats of the four dragons, sounding as one, as they lingered in this strange twilight. The creatures' breathing and heart rate were slowed considerably. This reduced metabolism allowed all hibernating animals to enter and endure a prolonged state of torpor, than to starve to death through a merciless winter.

Pressing an index finger to his lips for continued silence, Halen then motioned for his comrades to follow him around this imposing obstacle.

Any hopes of skirting these monsters by moving along the cave wall to give the dragons a wide berth was not possible, not with the piles of bones pushed up and lining the sides of this chamber. They had no choice but to sneak by the dragons, passing directly before their snouts.

Though Halen and Rainus were the very embodiment of stealth, the mortals in their company were not as light on their feet, especially as they tiptoed through the graveyard of bones. Inching closer to the tangled knot of dragons, Halen timed their steps. He advanced, but only when the intermittent noise emitted by the oozing lava as it churned and roiled helped to mask the sounds of their footfalls.

This painstakingly slow exercise in stealth tested their mettle more mentally than physically. Percy was sweating profusely, but it was neither from physical exertion nor the heat exuded by the pools of lava. A constant, cold draft seeping in from the opening above put a damper on the temperature. His perspiration, mingling with the drying dragon dung he was forced to wear, made the reek all the more potent. As the sweat beaded on his forehead, Percy used the edge of his cloak to wipe it away before the rivulet of dung-tainted perspiration could trickle into his eyes. In doing so, he unwittingly removed the dollop of faeces Harold had smeared across his forehead in a bid to mask his scent.

In single file they followed behind Halen. The Elf stopped for a moment, pointing down for all to see. Before them, sprawling directly across the path they travelled was a dragon's tail. Demonstrating how to manoeuvre over this obstacle without disturbing the creature this tail was attached to, Halen raised his right leg high, stepping over this scaly obstacle that rattled ever-so-slightly in time as the mass of giant reptiles slowly inhaled in synchrony.

Silas, Myron and Harold quickly and silently followed Halen. As Rose approached to step over this living barrier, she hesitated. The tail twitched slightly. It was like a cat in the midst of a dream, waiting for the opportune moment to pounce on its prey, but struggling to suppress that telltale, nervous flick of the tail that would give it away. Harold pressed a finger to his lips, motioning for Rose to remain silent. Reaching over, he easily hoisted her up and over the obstacle. Safely on the other side, Rose motioned for Percy to follow her.

For a lingering moment, Percy stood wide-eyed. He stared with unmistakable dread at this dragon appendage that terminated with a half-dozen sharp, bony spikes, each as long as his forearm. It was like a deadly, reptilian mace, powerful enough to smash through any steel armour forged by man or Elf. Percy was filled with an equal measure of awe and terror. Never in his entire life did he believe he'd ever see a dragon, let alone bear witness to four of these monstrous creatures at once, and this close, too!

Waving her hand before his face to break this anxiety fuelled trance, with a flex of her index finger Rose motioned him to continue on. Percy nodded in understanding. Drawing a deep breath to steel his nerves, he prayed for this tail to remain perfectly still as he made his move. Summoning his courage, Percy pretended he was merely stepping over a very large hound as it slept. He raised his right leg on high. Just as he stepped over, gingerly placing this foot down while trying desperately not to let any part of his body or raiment touch the dragon, its tail twitched. It was nothing more than a tremor of muscle as the creature slowly exhaled, but it was enough to send Percy's heart and mind racing in utter fear.

Rose motioned to Percy to remain still, to wait until the dragon's tail came to rest, before swinging his left leg over.

Percy froze. He appeared to straddle this tail when in reality he was hovering a mere finger's-width above this living relic of fangs, muscles and bones, all clad in an impervious armour of scales. He did so more out of fear than the need to obey this girl.

Suddenly, as though the dragon attached to this tail was having a nasty dream, the very tip lashed out. It struck against the wall of the chamber to send the bones scattering and knocking the puny mortal off balance. To Percy's horror, he landed upon this tail. Stupefied with fear, he sat there like he was sitting on a horse.

Fearing the dragons were about to wake, all froze, with the exception of Halen. The Elf frantically gestured at Percy not to panic and above all else, not to move a muscle, even as he straddled the creature's tail.

Percy sat motionless, perched on the very cusp of terror that would cause most to either swoon in utter fear or take flight in complete panic.

Rose reached out, giving Percy's right hand a reassuring squeeze to calm him. Pressing an index finger to her lips, she motioned for his silence. As this dragon settled back to sleep with the others, lulled by the ambient sounds of the gurgling lava, its tail relaxed. It fell limp under Percy's weight.

Rose motioned him to move now.

Steadying him as he cautiously sat up from this scaly perch, Percy shifted his weight and balance onto his right leg. With great care, he eased his left leg up and over the tail. Just as he leaned over, glancing down to secure his footing on solid ground than on a piece of reptile, the beads of sweat glistening on his forehead gathered on his furrowed brows to become one, rolling down to collect as a large, singular drop on the tip of his nose. Before he even thought of wiping it away, the drop of perspiration fell. It came a hair's-breadth away from hitting the dragon's snout, landing with a splash onto a rock before it.

Percy held his breath, waiting for this dragon to wake.

Oblivious, the creature slept.

Percy turned to join those before him.

Suddenly, the dragon stirred. Percy froze where he stood as a loud snort from two large nostrils blasted him with jets of spent, rancid air. The force pelted his boots with loose dirt and pulverized bone fragments.

In a drowsy stupor, it half-opened its eyes that were protected by the opaque, nictitating membrane drawn obliquely over each orb. This third eyelid protected the dragon's eyes when it flew or when it dined on a quarry that was still alive and thrashing, capable of inflicting a blinding injury. Had these membranes been completely retracted, this beast would have been staring directly at Percy. But what this dragon could not see, it most certainly did smell.

The faint, tantalizing aroma of man-meat mingling with the intoxicating scent of fear wafted up from that single drop of sweat that landed before the dragon's quivering nostrils. It was the unmistakable, distinct scent commonly exuded by all its prey prior to being killed. This smell wafted up to stimulate its olfactory senses, instinctively whetting its appetite. It was a hunger that had not been sated in over three months since it last dined, cannibalizing the carcass of a dead dragon.

The creature slowly exhaled once more, its eyelids closing as though it had only dreamed of an elusive quarry.

Loftus motioned for the Prince to advance.

Percy nodded. Taking a step, a fragment of bone cracked, splintering under his weight. The dragon's eyes snapped open. The third eyelids retracted to reveal ebony pupils floating on fiery, amber irises that glowed like burning embers.

Percy's scream snagged in the back of his throat as the large, dark pupils suddenly constricted into narrow slits as the dragon focused on the object standing directly before it.

All in Percy's company froze, praying that he would not run in fright.

Fighting against this rising tide of panic, Percy felt the blood pounding through his terrified heart, surging through his body with each beat. It was so loud he wondered how this dragon could not hear his heart thundering through his chest.

The dragon sniffed at this motionless statue that reeked with the stink of all-too-familiar dung. Percy endured as this creature, like a gargantuan dog, sniffed at him. Another profusion of cold sweat erupted from not just his forehead, but his entire body. He was now drenched in perspiration as he fought the overwhelming urge to flee.

Halen remained still; hoping the pong of dragon dung was still more potent than the stink of Percy's body odour.

The sleepy dragon conducted an olfactory inspection, sniffing the figure standing before its snout. As far as it could see and smell, even this close up, this object was nothing more than a strangely shaped piece of dung, perhaps deposited by one of its den mates. Bringing its flaring nostrils right up to Percy's body, the dragon took a deep whiff.

Taking up the rear, Rainus' hand glided slowly across his body to rest on the hilt of his sword. He waited and watched, hoping Percy would not lose his nerve before the dragon decided to return to sleep.

To the relief of all, the creature slipped back into its slumber and Percy had not bolted in fear.

Rainus motioned for Percy to proceed so he and Loftus can step over this tail that continued to impede the way.

Percy nodded, quick to follow the others as Halen escorted them toward the narrow passage up ahead. Just as he turned on his heels, with a clatter, the very tip of his sword's scabbard clipped the dragon's snout.

Startled awake, with a bone-rattling bellow the creature came to life, rousing its den mates.

As Percy's comrades fought the urge to run, the Prince did not hesitate. Caving in to his instincts, he shot out of there like an arrow. Percy darted into the passage.

Watching the upright piece of dragon dung, now reeking of unmistakable fear, dash away this frenetic movement excited the reptile. It scrambled to its feet, knocking against the other drowsy dragons as the four struggled to untangle their long necks and tails.

"RUN!" hollered Silas. Following Percy, the Wizard passed him. The Prince had stopped to catch his breath, secure in the safety of a tunnel that was much too narrow for even the smallest of these dragons to invade.

As the others rushed by him, before Percy could berate them for their show of cowardice as they ran away, Rainus shoved this mortal, knocking him into a shallow depression in the ground.

"FIRE!" cried Rainus.

Leaping over Percy, the Elf thrust Loftus and Rose against the wall of the passage where it bulged slightly behind a boulder while Halen and Myron dove into a tiny chamber to the right of the tunnel. The Elf and knight yanked Harold and Silas from harm's way as a deafening roar thundered behind them. This angry bellow heralded a great torrent of heat and light as the dragon thrust its snout into the opening of the tunnel. A spark from the gnashing of its teeth ignited the highly volatile gases fermenting in its gut. The creature unleashed this gush of fire as its siblings snapped and snarled, jostling for their turn at a chance to feed.

As the thunderous surge of dragon fire raged, Percy froze in terror. He remained face down in the rocky depression. His cowardice saved his life as the flames billowed, swirling above him. He felt the sweltering heat blazing mere inches above his body. His saving grace was this Elven cloak that shielded him from the cold also spared him from the worst of the fire. The sweat-drench apparel he wore beneath this cloak also did wonders to prevent his flesh from getting seared.

Hearing the dragons fighting amongst themselves as they clawed and dug to enlarge the mouth of the tunnel, Rainus and Loftus abandoned Rose. They raced toward Percy, grabbing him by his shoulders to haul him up onto his feet.

Percy shook off their hands. Fearing another fiery volley, he pushed them off as he dashed deeper into the tunnel. His panic so great, he took no notice Rose and the others as he raced away from the hungry beasts.

"Come back, you fool!" shouted Loftus, watching as Percy became one with the darkness he sought refuge in. The captain was embarrassed, but not surprised by the Prince's action while his comrades, in stunned silence, observed this royal displaying the worst of his true character.

Percy's panicked breaths echoed through the tunnel. It was followed by a hysterical scream as a loud crackling noise sounded from the blackness. This cry was immediately followed by a desperate plea: "Help! Help me!"

"What now?" groaned Myron. He stared into the darkness that had quite literally swallowed up the wayward prince.

"If we are lucky, we have been freed of his foolishness! Alas, I still hear his snivelling cries," answered Silas, willing his crystal to glow brightly. With grim resolve, the Wizard urged his friends away from the hibernaculum, guiding them onward to follow the sounds of Percy's howling.

"Quickly!" urged Rose. "He needs us!"

"My first duty is to keep *you* safe," reminded Myron, his hand resting on Rose's shoulder to prevent her from carelessly rushing ahead as her prospective groom did. "If Prince Percival chose to abandon us in his fear or his desire to be safe, then we shall not foolishly rush off to meet our doom, just because he elected to do so."

"He just panicked," she explained in Percy's defence.

"True," admitted Loftus. "And yet, the rest of us, you included my lady, did not. Sadly, Prince Percival is as feckless as he is a self-serving coward."

"I think you mean to say he's reckless," corrected Harold, adjusting his animal headpiece over his forehead before moving on.

"He is both," Loftus sighed in resignation. Cupping a hand to his ear, he listened as Percy's cry for help resonated through the passage. "Feckless, reckless and more than willing to sacrifice our lives, if it means to escape with his."

"It is a miracle he has yet to get us killed," noted Rainus.

"By his very actions, I'd say that is exactly what he is attempting to do," averred Halen. He assumed his place behind the Wizard as Rainus took to the rear once more as they hurriedly filed down the tunnel, following the sounds of Percy's desperate cries.

Silas yelped in surprised as he stumbled. The ground suddenly yielded to the tip of his staff. It shattered through a thin crust of ash and pumice.

"Steady on, my friend," cautioned Halen, as he righted the Wizard. "It is apparent the floor of this tunnel is not as stable as we had hoped."

"Damn it! Where are you, Loftus, you useless cur?" These anxious, disembodied words floated through the darkness to accost the captain. "Am I to die because of your incompetence?"

"Hold your damned horses!" hollered Loftus. "We will get to you as soon as we safely can."

"Hurry!" shrieked Percy. "For I am the one who is not safe!"

"And whose fault is that?" grumbled Myron. Treading gingerly, he avoided where Silas' staff revealed weak spots on the floor of the tunnel as they advanced.

In the glow of his crystal, where the tunnel abruptly narrowed so all were forced to walk in single file, Silas came across a gaping hole. And in this void, there was Percy. Wild-eyed and dangling into this dark abyss, he clung desperately to the crumbling ledge.

The Wizard lowered the crystal to better shed some light on this royal's predicament.

"You fool!" snapped Percy. "Instead of blinding me with your damned crystal, get me out of here!"

"I have no desire to join you. You require better footing before I pull you to safety," said Silas. "Do you trust me?"

"What kind of stupid question is that? Of course not!"

"And yet you want me to rescue you?"

"I *demand* it!"

"Too bad you have no trust," sighed the Wizard. Instead of extending the end of his staff for Percy to grab hold of, Silas used it to strike his whitened knuckles.

Percy yelped in pain, his fingers instinctively releasing their hold. He fell as Rose screamed, alarmed by the Wizard's action.

Silas burst out laughing, holding his crystal aloft to shine a light on Percy as he landed in the bottom of the hole. The unexpected jolt of hitting the ground that was no more than two or three hand spans beneath his feet was just as shocking to Percy as had he plunged to his death over a great cliff.

Squinting under the glare of the crystal's light, he angrily stared up at the Wizard.

"How dare you?" gasped Percy. With his face burning with rage and humiliation, he scrambled onto his feet.

"You make it so very easy," chortled Silas, stumbling against the wall as Rose shoved him aside. She leaned over the hole to gaze down upon her poor prince.

"Thank goodness you are safe!" exclaimed Rose.

"I'd be safer had that blasted Wizard just stayed away from me!" growled Percy. He brushed off the dust and humiliation from his already soiled cloak. Peering up, he was even more humiliated upon discovering how minimal the drop was. Had he known solid ground was literally underfoot, he would have found a way to climb out of this hole on his own, all in the name of preserving his pride.

"Stand aside, Princess," ordered Halen. As Rose pressed against the wall next to Silas, the Elf knelt down, offering his hand to the mortal. He easily lifted Percy from the hole and into the arms of his grateful princess.

With the grace of a deer, Halen easily cleared the gap. Accepting Silas' staff, he probed the immediate area. Once he deemed it safe for the others to cross, Halen extended his hand, helping the Wizard leap over the hole to land on the other side. Returning the staff to Silas, the Elf helped the others, one-by-one, to the other side.

"Are we ready to proceed?" asked Silas, watching as Rainus gracefully bounded over to join the procession.

"We are now," answered the Elf.

"Perhaps we should take added precautions," suggested Loftus.

"How so?" queried Myron.

"I suggest tying a rope around Prince Percival. Keep him on a short leash to prevent him from bolting, running smack-dab into trouble each time he panics." Loftus spoke in all seriousness.

"Say again!" gasped Percy. He was appalled this captain would even suggest such a thing. "I will not be treated like a lowly mutt in need of correction!"

"Then you must really learn to curb this tendency of yours to flee at the first sign of danger," argued Loftus.

"Had I more confidence in your abilities to keep me safe, perhaps this tendency would be curbed," retorted Percy.

"A tether to keep this royal in check is quite appealing, indeed," said Rainus. "However, I fear if you are on the other end of it, Prince Percival will surely drag you to your death should another frightening situation arise."

"Har, har!" Percy snorted in mock laughter. "I know you speak in jest, Lord Silverthorn, but they are wasted words. We must be on our way with this urgent quest."

"Prince Percival speaks the truth," averred Rose. "If we are to save Tag, we must keep moving."

"I was thinking of resuming this quest to capture the Witch, but yes, if we can rescue Tag in the process, why not?" said Percy, agreeing if only to steer attention away from Loftus' humiliating suggestion.

"Yes, let us not waste precious time with needless chatter," said Silas, as he turned to face the deep dark before them. "Follow me."

"She better not be following me," Tag prayed under his breath. He leaned against the stony wall, his chest heaving as he rested. Glancing to his left, and then his right, there was only suffocating darkness before and behind him. There was no telltale glow of Sin's crystal to betray her presence, no angry shriek of her shrill voice chasing behind him.

So far, his luck held.

Pushing off against the wall, Tag resumed his trek. Not only was he not being pursued, this torch miraculously continued to burn, providing him with adequate light to show the way as he ventured on. With not even a glint of light penetrating from the outside world into this all-consuming darkness, Tag had lost all sense of time and distance as he forged on, searching for an exit.

"Please don't go out on me," prayed Tag. He squinted, staring at the flames that guttered, dancing as a draft whispered through this passage. "I'll be as good as dead, if you go out."

Since he first embarked on the initial quest with Princess Rose, there had been more than one occasion when the torches they carried burned out, leaving them in utter blackness. Being alone, the possibility of this happening played havoc with Tag's mind.

It was bad enough losing a light source when he was in the company of a friend or two, but it was even worse now that he was alone. In fact, the prospects were downright deadly. Without this burning torch he knew it would be blacker than black. He'd have to feel his way forward, praying he did not step off a cliff or land in a hole to break his legs or simply die in the fall. The very real fear of this happening gripped his heart, but the possibility of becoming impossibly lost in such utter darkness in this maze of tunnels was more frightening. Slowly going insane while listening to the panicked beating of his heart and the terror in his voice as he spoke to himself as he wandered lost would be far worse than being dealt a swift death.

"That would be so much worse, indeed," muttered Tag, as he steeled his resolve. "I need to see my friends again. I must stop Rose from marrying that despicable cad of a prince."

Realizing he was talking to himself and the long-held belief that this was the first sign of insanity, Tag ceased speaking altogether. Instead, he journeyed on as he prayed inwardly for the torch to remain burning for as long as he required light.

With renewed determination, Tag picked up his pace. The draft that first lured him down this path was growing stronger. The air seemed fresher. Somewhere up ahead was the source of this draft and possible salvation. His greatest hope now was that he wasn't travelling in circles.

"You have no idea where you are leading us. Is that not so, Wizard?" Percy grumbled as Silas guided them on. "I will wager Loftus' measly life that you have us hopelessly lost, wandering in circles."

"Had we been going in circles, trust me when I say I would have deposited you in the hole we had rescued you from, but only after making it much deeper!" Silas' voice was strained with annoyance at being subjected to this mortal's incessant whining. "It is bad enough we must endure your wretched pong and equally foul demeanour. If it was not for Princess Rose, I'd be tempted to leave you there to rot, while we continue on our merry way, free of your constant nattering."

"I do not natter!" snapped Percy. "And it is not my fault that I reek."

"I'm to blame for makin' you stink, but you got to admit, you sure do complain a lot, my lord," stated Harold. "If you've been listenin' to the Wizard, Master Agincor does have a point. We'd have come across that hole we found you in, if we were goin' in circles."

"So you say, but nattering and complaining is the undertaking of the weak-minded and physically challenged," argued Percy, as he turned his nose up at Harold.

He bumped into Princess Rose as this small procession came to an abrupt halt. Percy glanced about, feeling all eyes turn on him.

"What?" he snapped in annoyance.

"Only the weak-minded would be so blind to the obvious," stated Rainus, with a dismal shake of his head.

"Are you saying I am the weak-minded one?" gasped Percy, appalled by the insinuation.

"Quoting our dear friend, Tag Yairet, as he is not here to speak his mind: It takes one to know one," snorted Myron.

"How dare you?"

"I'm thinkin' it was more of a statement than a dare, my lord," corrected Harold, pleased that he had caught the gist of this conversation.

Percy's face reddened as Loftus began to laugh.

"Fetch off, you mutinous cur!" He glared over his shoulder at the captain. "Stop laughing at me!"

"I will stop when you cease saying such asinine things that make me laugh," offered Loftus.

"Bloody hell!" cursed Percy. "I am surrounded by ham-fisted, larcenous fools!"

"I beg your pardon!" snapped Rose, her delicate brows furrowing upon hearing his insult.

"Of course, I was not speaking of you, my dear," explained Percy. "I was speaking of these ruffians and scallywags you have the misfortune of calling your friends."

"Ruffians and scallywags?" repeated Harold. "Methinks I'm likin' the sounds of that! There's somethin' very rough and tumble about it all."

"Of course you would like being called that," muttered Percy, as he sneered in disdain. "You are a moron, after all!"

"Oh, I'm not likin' the sounds of *that*," said Harold, frowning in disapproval.

Loftus smacked the back of Percy's head as he ordered him on. "Let us not be subjected to anymore of your *nattering*, my lord. Do not tempt fate. Move on before the others lose total patience with you."

"Do not accost me," Percy grumbled as he followed behind Rose.

"Do not give me reason to," grunted Loftus. He impatiently waved this royal on.

Without another word Percy trudged along, brooding in both his foul stink and petulant mood, as the Wizard guided them on.

"Do you see that?" asked Halen. He pointed beyond Silas toward the end of the tunnel they had been travelling.

The passage opened into a massive chamber. Its walls and ceiling looked bloody, illuminated by the river of fiery lava flowing through the back half of this cavernous room.

"I shall scout ahead," said Halen, removing his bow from over his shoulder. "The rest of you remain here. Keep Princess Rose safe."

"Oh, no! Not this time," insisted Loftus. "I am going with you, my friend. I can see well enough to make my way without a torch this time."

"Fair enough." Halen nodded to the mortal. "Then come."

"Yes! Do make yourself useful for once, Loftus." Percy waved the captain on. "And try not to get yourself killed in the process, unless it is to sacrifice your life for my safety."

Loftus ignored this biting comment, moving ahead to follow the Elf.

"It may well be the Witch's lair this time," whispered Myron, his hand instinctively reached across his body to rest on the hilt of his sword.

"We can only hope," said Silas.

"I was hoping to find Tag by now," whispered Rose, unleashing a disappointed sigh as she watched Halen and Loftus venture on without them.

"As was I, my lady. Just be prepared for anything," urged Rainus. He readied his bow as Rose removed the sling from her belt, her fingers digging into the suede bag containing her never-ending supply of ammunition.

Heeding the Elf's warning, Harold reached into his pack. Removing Tag's sword from its scabbard, he clutched the weapon he held in safekeeping for their missing friend.

Seeing all in his company, even Rose, were prepared to do battle against the Witch, Percy felt compelled to do the same, or at least appear as though he was. He reluctantly brandished his ceremonial sword.

"Put that toy away," ordered Silas. "Unless you plan to strut about in a parade, you are more likely to hurt yourself with that *plaything* than you are to inflict pain on another."

Percy sheepishly sheathed the blade back into the equally ornate scabbard as he whined, "Fine! Then do any of you have a weapon to spare? One worthy of a great prince?"

"This should do nicely," said Harold. He placed a weighty rock into Percy's hand.

"What is the meaning of this?" snapped Percy. He stared at this igneous chunk.

"It's your weapon." Harold's words were matter-of-fact.

"Yes," added Myron. "You can beat your foe with it, and should you be overcome by the urge to flee, you can hurl it at your enemy before you do so!"

"Har, har! Ever the jokester," sneered Percy. He hefted the rock, deliberating on whom should be the first recipient of a sound bashing.

"It is better than nothing," said Rose, in a bid to soothe Percy's bellicose mood made worse by this most primitive of weapons. "Even for me, one of my puny steel balls can be plenty deadly when used just so."

"Yes, and though they are tiny, she still has more balls than you ever will," said Rainus, speaking in all seriousness.

"I know what you are insinuating, Elf Lord," grunted Percy. His hand wrapped tightly around the rock, as though squeezing it would somehow calm his growing rage. "And I will have you know, I am more man than she will ever be!"

"I certainly hope so!" A knowing smile creased Rainus' perfect face as he watched the mortal's visage turn ugly, curdling with the venom of anger.

"I will not – " Percy's sentence was cut short as the tip of Rainus' index finger abruptly tapped him on his forehead.

"Look! I know how to make him stop talking," announced Rainus.

"Amazin'!" marvelled Harold, watching with fascination. "Do it again!"

"I said – " Again, Percy's sentence was pre-empted as Rainus tapped him deliberately on the forehead.

"See! He can be made to stop prattling on," said Rainus. "Like one of those music boxes that can be stopped when you close the lid."

"You dare mock me?" snapped Percy, hefting his weapon in threat should the Elf attempt it once more. "You touch me again, and this rock will fly!"

"Oh, hush up!" ordered Silas. "Prepare to advance. I see the captains are on the move."

Percy focused beyond the Wizard to stare through the dim-lit passage. Through slitted eyes he made out Loftus and Halen's dark silhouettes.

"What say you?" queried Silas, as the two became visible in the glow of his crystal. By the patina of sweat glistening on Loftus' forehead, the Wizard anticipated it was heat, rather than fear causing this show of perspiration.

"We have an obstacle to overcome," answered Halen.

"It is great, but it is not insurmountable," added Loftus.

"Lovely! We have yet another den of dragons to contend with," assumed Percy.

"No dragons this time," responded Loftus, "just a chasm of deadly, molten lava to cross, if we wish to journey on."

"Brilliant!" sniffed Percy. With a snort of derision, he tossed aside his primitive weapon. "So, a likely chance of death."

"They said flowing lava, not hungry dragons," reminded Rose, breathing a little easier upon hearing this news.

"Hungry dragons! Molten lava! What is the difference?" muttered Percy. "Both promise a fiery death."

"You really must stop this," chided Rose.

"Stop what?" snapped Percy. "Being the voice of reason in the company of fools?"

"The voice of reason?" scoffed Loftus, his tone incredulous. "Are you mad?"

"No, I am not! *I* am the voice of *reason*. *You* are the voice of *treason*, so fetch off you mutinous cur!" snapped Percy, pointing an accusing finger at Loftus. "And I was speaking to the Princess, not to you."

"And I was speaking to you," stated Rose, jabbing her index finger into Percy's chest. "All this negativity must stop. We, my friends and I, have faced far greater dangers and more frightening odds than this.

If we proceed with caution this river of lava will be no different than the other obstacles we had overcome."

"You sound so very confident, my dear Rose-Alyn, but what do you know? You are but a girl." Percy's dismissive words were laced with cynicism.

Rose fell silent, mulling over this insult that was delivered with a palpable air of arrogance.

"Yes, a girl who obviously knows better than you, my lord," stated Myron. "She speaks the truth. Together, we have overcome obstacles that seemed insurmountable."

"Oh, huzzah!" muttered Percy. "This is not one of those *rah-rah-rally-your-forces-and-we-shall-overcome* situations. In fact, this is hardly the adventure I agreed to."

"You were warned from the start of the dangers, but you chose to come anyway," reminded Loftus.

"The point is, the nature of this quest has changed drastically," protested Percy. "I generously and gallantly offered my invaluable services to help see a common enemy brought to justice. It is now apparent to me this is nothing more than a rescue mission, one to save the life of a shape-shifting miscreant and a rabble-rouser of a knight-in-the-making, both of whom can be easily replaced. And need I remind you all, I am a *prince*, the heir apparent to the throne of Axalon. My life is invaluable *and* irreplaceable."

"But not theirs?" questioned Harold. He was dumbfounded by Percy's comment.

"You are a simpleton of a man. Of course you would ask such a stupid question! I am speaking within the grand scheme of things, you big buffoon. Wealth, title and privilege are paramount. I possess all three. Need I say more?"

"As you are a prince, taking orders from none, we will not command you to journey on with us," said Myron. "You need not go further."

"I am no fool! You mean to abandon me. I will be left to die in this subterranean maze far to the north where none in their right mind will foolishly venture."

"And yet, here you are," muttered Silas.

"The point being, if I refuse to go on, you will conveniently forget about me, undoubtedly fabricating some cockamamie tale to my father of how I met an untimely demise."

"We promise to return for you," offered Rainus. Inwardly, he was hoping this mortal would stay behind so they were free to move forward, unfettered of his incessant whining.

"Very well then!" said Percy, nodding to the Elf. "Princess Rose and I shall wait for you to return for us, once your task is done."

Rose frowned as she addressed him. "Are you serious? I intend to proceed. I will venture on to the end with my friends."

Percy seized her by the wrist, pulling her aside to speak in confidence. "You *must* stay with me. You are my insurance they will return, if not for me, then surely for you."

"I will *not* stay," whispered Rose, wrenching her arm free of his grasp.

"You will defy me to face potential death? And to what end?"

"I will defy death in hopes of saving my friends."

"But if you do not stay by my side, I have no guarantee they will return for me."

"Is that all I am to you? A guarantee of safety?"

"At this moment, yes, for I do not trust *them*, not even Loftus at this point, to come back for me."

"So you must not trust in me, for I am one of *them,* is that so?"

"Do not misconstrue my words," whispered Percy, as he motioned Rose to lower her voice. "I trust you, but under duress, I fear you will abandon all moral scruples. You will be persuaded to leave me behind."

Rose drew a deep breath, struggling to maintain her calm as his words raked at her conscience.

"Truth be told," lied Percy, as he did his best to look pitiable in her eyes, "I do not wish to be left alone. I fear that you shall only meet with harm should you proceed without me. And if you do, then what will become of me? Who will persuade them to return for me, if not you, my love? Either way, I shall surely perish without you by my side."

"Time is wasting," called Silas. "We must be on our way. What will it be, my lady? Will you stay with your prince or will you come with your friends?"

"Yes, what will it be, my dear?" Percy took her hands into his, pressing them to his heart as he whispered, "Will you do the honourable thing? Do what you are duty bound to do?"

"Absolutely. I will do the most honourable thing my conscience will allow." Rose pulled free of his grasp to return to her place in the procession. "I go with them, so we may save our friends."

For a moment, he was dumbfounded, but as the group wasted no time, Percy was forced to scramble. He pushed by Rainus and Loftus, quickly reclaiming his position behind Rose. He muttered to them that he could not stand to be apart from his precious princess, hence the sudden change of heart.

"Follow me while the way is clear," urged Halen. "And I do believe

I have a safe way for us to cross that fiery chasm."

He guided the party toward the mouth of the chamber. It glowed an eerie red as quivering waves of heat rippled and swelled from this cavern. Stepping inside, it was expansive. Rose determined it had to be as large as her father's grand palace and the great courtyard combined. Staring up to the craggy ceiling, it was almost as high as the tallest spire of her royal residence.

"Oh, my!" gasped Harold. "Who'd believe such places exist in this world."

He marvelled at the sheer size of this chamber. What it lacked in architectural detailing that was so evident in the great chamber carved out by the Dwarves in the Mines of Euphoria; the immenseness alone of this cavern was awe-inspiring unto itself.

Jagged, conical stalagmites studded the floor of this chamber. These calcareous protrusions, many so large they towered above them, jutted from the earth like giant teeth. Some were so huge they formed massive pillars where the stalagmite fused to become one with the stalactite that hung down directly overhead.

Harold was certain these great columns were used to support the sheer weight of the mountain, preventing it from crashing down upon this void they stood in now.

"This place is hardly suitable for a secret lair, unless one is the size of a Troll," noted Rainus.

He took up the rear as they followed Halen, weaving through the rock-hard calcareous deposits that were most prevalent along the edges of the chamber while several of the largest floor-to-ceiling columns were situated in the centre of the cave, closer to the edge of the chasm where the lava flowed.

"More importantly, at least this is not a hibernaculum for dragons," stated Percy, glancing about to see there were no telltale scattering of bones.

"Indeed, we shall proceed unhampered once we cross to the other side," said Rose. She breathed easy to see there were no signs of Witch or dragon to be had as they ventured forth.

"So you say, but in my opinion this chasm will definitely hamper our progress," declared Percy.

"All we need to do is cross to the other side," said Halen. He was matter-of-fact as he rummaged through the folds of his great cloak.

"You, you delusional Elf, have a way of making *everything* sound so very easy," grunted Percy. "How do you propose we cross?"

Halen produced a coil of rope attached to a grappling hook.

Percy frowned in bewilderment, perplexed by how and where the

Elf was able to seamlessly store such bulky equipment beneath his cloak. "Where did that come from?"

Halen's shoulders rolled in a shrug, for it was obvious to him. "Like my bow, I never leave home without it."

"And we are to swing over to the other side?" asked Percy.

"That is the plan," said Halen. He scrutinized the ceiling of the cave for a suitable surface the tines of the grappling hook can bite into.

Percy inched over closer to where the earth was riven and the heat from the lava swelled. "You cannot be serious! Swing over to the other side? It cannot be done. In fact, even with your keen eyes, I highly doubt you or Lord Silverthorn possess the necessary aim to properly set that hook."

"Ye of little faith, my lord," grunted Halen. "If I cannot do so, then I have utmost faith in Princess Rose."

Percy's brows furrowed with doubt as he gazed over to his prospective bride.

"Captain Ironwood is speaking the truth," averred Myron. "Princess Rose has a deadly accurate aim, one that would put you to shame."

Rose smiled as Myron gave her a confident nod.

"But first, I shall give it a go," said Halen, as he proceeded to secure the hook to one of his arrows.

"Not if I kill you first!"

Their blood ran cold.

Glancing across the chasm, there was Sin. Her bony chest was heaving as she staggered from the tunnel into the chamber. She was panting as she hoisted her staff, levelling the crystal at the intruders.

Halen dropped the grappling hook, taking aim at her heart. He let his arrow fly across the expanse, but a swell of light like an invisible shield emanating from the black crystal shattered the projectile on impact. The broken shards tumbled into the lava below.

"Give me the boy!" snarled Sin. "He is mine! He is mine to kill!"

"Boy? What boy?" shouted Rose.

"You know whom I speak of!"

"Do you mean Tag?"

"I know you have him!" growled Sin.

"Are you so blind that you cannot see he is not amongst us?" shouted Myron.

"And if we did have that fool, I'd have no hesitation in handing him over to you!" called Percy. He winced as Loftus, in retribution, smacked the back of his head.

"You lost him!" determined Silas, turning his crystal on the Witch. He laughed as he scoffed, "The clever lad escaped from you!"

"Shut it, Agincor!" snarled Sin. She levelled the crystal at him. Her good eye rolled about, scrutinizing the Wizard and his party. As best as she could determine, her prisoner was indeed not amongst them.

"Hey... if you don't have him, then where the heck is Tag?" Harold wondered aloud.

Sin snarled in rage. It suddenly dawned on her that the boy had cunningly deceived her, sending her on a wild goose chase. She now knew which route he had actually taken. She also knew that if she did not work with haste, her chance of exacting her revenge would disappear, if he dares to attempt negotiating his way through perilous terrain to facilitate his escape.

Tag was not about to get away from her.

Sin was determined to vent her wrath, and then when she was done, she'd be free to turn her attention back to these foolish beings that dared to intrude into her domain.

"There is no point in running, Witch," called Rainus. "If you do, we shall hunt you down like the vermin you are."

"Impossible, if you are dead!" snorted Sin.

Rainus and his comrades ducked low to the ground as an explosive flash of light crackled, flying high overhead. This blast of energy erupting from the obsidian crystal missed them completely to obliterate the entrance of the tunnel that had delivered them to this place.

"You have no place to run," cackled Sin, pretending this accidental strike was deliberate. "Now, you die!"

"You wish! I have the Dreamstone. You and the Wizard are equally matched with your crystals, however, with that bad eye, you are a terrible aim," mocked Rose.

"Plus we are eight. You are but one," stated Silas. "You do not even have your pathetic sock puppet to set on us!"

"So you say, Agincor," growled Sin. "But there is no need for a sock puppet when I have *this*."

Rose and her comrades clamped their hands over their ears. The earth shuddered as a bone-rattling bellow resonated through their bodies to steal away their breath and still their hearts. This powerful din shattered several stalactites, sending them crashing down around them.

"Attack!" shouted Sin. "Burn them! Eat them! Kill them! It need not be in that order! Do away with them, my pet!"

The ground beneath their feet trembled as huge talons appeared from over the edge of the chasm. Clawing and raking to find its grip, earth and rocks crumbled from the ledge, tumbling into the churning lava below.

Their hearts jumped to the back of their throats as the head of a gargantuan dragon rose from the depths.

"That is no sock puppet!" gasped Percy. With mouth agape, in wide-eyed terror he stared.

The beast scrambled, rising up over the cliff wall. Like a terrible mirage emerging from a scorching desert, undulating waves of heat radiated from the scales protecting its body as the creature clambered above the red-hot lava.

"It's the mother of all dragons!" cried Percy.

"More like the mother of the dragons we had encountered," determined Silas. At a glance, it was easy to see this behemoth was of the same species, but much larger. Stretching open its leathery wings, the span so great, it cast everything in shadow. The tip of its mace-like tail smashed down upon the edge of the cliff, sending more earth and rocks spilling into the lava below.

"Do we remain still?" gulped Percy.

A sweltering gust of wind sent dirt and dust billowing around them as the dragon folded its wings against its scaly body. Backlit by the fiery glow of lava, the creature appeared even more menacing and intimidating in size. Summoning every ounce of courage in his quaking body, Percy struggled to remain motionless, fighting that overwhelming urge to flee.

"*RUN!*" ordered Halen, as the dragon's head recoiled, its chest expanding with a great breath. "*Scatter! Hide!*"

Halen yanked at the Prince, now frozen in fright. Shoving Percy behind a boulder, the Elf dove behind a large stalagmite. All in his company dispersed, dashing in every direction to find shelter as the dragon vomited a searing geyser of flames.

Hearing Sin's maniacal cackle, Silas dared to peek from his hiding place. The Witch was darting down the tunnel from whence she came to resume the hunt for her escaped prisoner.

Silas threw caution to the wind. He levelled his crystal, unleashing a blistering bolt of energy.

Sin vanished, ducking around a bend in the tunnel as the flash of light exploded against the wall where she had stood a moment before. In a shower of sparks and shattered rocks, she faded into the darkness, leaving behind the hungry dragon to hunt.

"Come back and fight!" shouted Silas.

Instead of drawing Sin's attention, the dragon snarled. Its head swung toward the Wizard's voice. Black pupils floating on amber orbs abruptly narrowed into thin slits as it stared, searching for signs of movement that signified food.

Silas threw his back against the pillar, hoping to avoid the dragon's gaze.

Dropping onto all fours, the beast ambled toward the Wizard. With head tilted and ears upright, it searched the shadows.

Silas remained still. Barely breathing, he mustered his courage. With staff in hand, he waited, anticipating where the creature will show its face so he can dodge its fangs and fiery breath.

Just as Silas guessed wrong, jumping directly in front of the dragon as it neared to pounce, Rainus let an arrow fly. The whine of the projectile slicing through the air caused the beast to cock its head. It was enough to distract the dragon, allowing the arrow to pierce its left ear.

With an angry snarl, the creature shook its head, its ears flapping to and fro. This accosted ear struck against a stalactite directly overhead, shattering the offending arrow as Silas fled, taking shelter behind another stalagmite. A second arrow meant to blind the dragon missed its mark as the creature suddenly turned on the Elf, charging toward Rainus. As it closed in for the kill, Myron whistled, jumping out from his hiding place to draw the creature away as Rainus darted behind a boulder.

Myron waved frantically as he hollered at the dragon, "Here! Over here!"

As one meal vanished and another appeared, the dragon skidded to a stop, spinning about to hunt down this mortal. Its spiky tail swung about like an ungainly counterweight, smashing the column closest to the chasm to send shattered chunks of the once fused stalagmite and stalactite tumbling into the river of lava, as the ceiling above groaned ominously from the shifting weight of the mountain.

Just as the dragon charged at Myron, Rose let a steel ball fly. Her aim was spot-on, striking the dragon's left eyeball. The beast roared with the sting of the assault, its pursuit abruptly halted as it shook off this pain.

Blinking hard, the dragon spun about in a bid to kill this new assailant.

Rose screamed, diving to the ground as the armoured tail whipped over her body to destroy her hiding place.

Rainus raced to her side. Throwing himself over her body to shield her, they huddled beneath his Elven cloak. Blending into the earth, they went unnoticed by the creature.

Frustrated, the dragon roared. It was like a hound trying to chase down a rabbit that keeps disappearing into its warren, only to reappear at another opening.

With his hand over Rose's mouth to keep her from screaming in fright, as soon as the dragon stepped over them, the ground quaking under its footfall to ripple through to their bones, Rainus rolled onto his feet. He pulled her up with him. Together, they ran to hide while Loftus distracted the great reptile from Myron, striking its head with a clot of dirt before ducking back into his hiding place.

With a rage fuelled by hunger, and now compounded by its mounting frustration, the dragon unleashed a bone-rattling roar as it rammed its head against the cluster of stalagmites where Harold had taken refuge.

An attempt to flee unnoticed was impossible for a man his size as Harold hastily lumbered over to the boulder where Percy was hiding. Instead of inviting him to take shelter by his side, Percy pushed Harold away, ordering him to find his own hiding place. A shoving match ensued that immediately caught the dragon's attention. With a swing of its great head, using its snout, it sent the boulder flying to expose both mortals.

Harold and Percy shrieked in fright, scrambling to flee. In a blind panic, both ran to the column Myron was hiding behind. With only enough room for one, all three were forced to run as the dragon gave chase.

Witnessing Rose's assault on the creature, Halen understood the eyes were the most vulnerable part. Taking up his bow, he nocked an arrow. As the three mortals dashed by his hiding place, Halen took aim. As the dragon thundered by, he let his arrow fly, praying the creature wouldn't blink as he did so.

Slicing through the air, the projectile met its mark, piercing deep into the dragon's right eye to impair its already poor vision. The entire chamber quaked as the monster bellowed in agony. As though propelled by instinct, the reptile veered to its right, straight for the source that inflicted this blinding pain.

With its head tilted oddly to see out of its left eye, it charged after the Elf. Halen led the dragon away from the others. Nimbly vaulting over boulders and darting between stony columns, he shouted so the creature would follow the sounds of his voice. By the smashing of everything in its path, Halen needn't glance back to know the dragon was closing in on him.

He skidded to a stop.

A solid wall of rocks loomed before him. Between this wall and the path now strewn with boulders and remnants of shattered stalagmites, there was no escape. With nowhere to run and the dragon charging straight for him, Halen armed his bow. Nocking two arrows, he made a valiant stand.

Just as the beast closed in, its mouth agape to unleash an incendiary blast of heat and flames, Halen allowed the string of his bow to slip off his fingertips. His arrows flew true. They hit their mark, piercing the roof of the dragon's mouth to skewer its puny brain.

In a blink, the fire in its eyes died. Powerful limbs crumpled under its weight, but even in death, the dragon's forward momentum did not slow. With a final, defiant heartbeat, the beast came crashing down on Halen. The Elf disappeared, buried beneath the crushing weight of the behemoth.

As the dust settled around the dragon's corpse, the chamber was consumed by an unnatural silence. Only the laboured breathing and thundering hearts of those made to witness Halen's selfless act punctuated this eerie quiet.

After the shock of it seeped into their bones, all, with the exception of Percy, rushed toward the lifeless mass of wings and scales in desperate hopes of finding the captain alive.

19
Eleven Heartbeats

"No…" groaned Silas. He picked up the captain's bow from amongst the scattered arrows that had spilled from a now cracked and empty quiver.

"That means nothing!" cried Rose, shaking her head in denial.

"It means the Elf likely suffered the same fate as these broken arrows," stated Percy. His tone was callous as he tossed one of the splintered shafts over his shoulder.

Rose's balled fist struck Percy's left shoulder. Tears welled as she snapped, "I refuse to believe he is dead! Unless you show me indisputable proof, I suggest you help us search for him before I really lose patience with you!"

Percy scowled upon being physically accosted, and then being the recipient of this public verbal lambasting by his bride-to-be. "How dare -"

"Over here!" Loftus called out, waving the others over to where he stood by the dragon's neck.

Once again, all, with the exception of Percy, dashed over to Loftus, only to halt in their tracks. A gasp rippled through their small company as they stared upon Halen Ironwood's lifeless hand protruding from underneath the dragon's body.

"There's your proof," Percy muttered.

Numbed by grief, none heard Percy's cold-hearted statement.

Rose covered her mouth to stifle a cry of anguish as Harold, Myron, and Loftus bowed their heads in respect to the fallen captain.

Rainus stood stock-still, his face devoid of emotion as his eyes remained focused on the hand of his dear friend. As a million thoughts and memories races through his mind, his knuckles whitened. His clenched fists trembled as he fought to remain composed.

As all stood in silent respect, Rainus' ears pricked up. A stifled moan, just loud enough to be heard by all, sounded from beneath the dragon.

"Look!" gasped Silas.

Halen's fingers twitched ever so slightly.

"Good gracious!" cried Rose. "The captain is alive!"

She fell to her knees, grasping Halen's hand into hers. With a reassuring squeeze, she let him know he was not abandoned.

"Quickly! We must work with haste before the beast stiffens with death, becoming impossible to move," ordered Silas. He wedged his staff between the dragon's neck and a large rock, using it as a fulcrum. "Help me lift this behemoth."

"Are you mad? Lift this gargantuan carcass? It is an impossible feat!" insisted Percy. He stood alone as the others rushed in to help.

"You say that a lot!" snapped Myron. He hastily pushed by Percy to lend a hand. "Nothing is impossible, if we work together!"

Harold, Rainus and Loftus gripped the dragon by its scales. They hoisted up its neck while Rose and Silas used the staff like a pry bar, easing this dead weight up. It was enough to allow Myron adequate room to work. The knight crawled beneath on his belly, pushing aside debris to clear a path before him.

Hoping for the best, he anticipated the worst. How can anyone, mortal or Elf, survive this crushing weight. Perhaps it was only the lingering nerves of a dying body they witnessed in Halen's hand. And if he did survive, Myron imagined Halen was crushed beyond healing as he stubbornly clung to life.

"Can you see him?" called Rainus.

"Yes! Yes, I can!" answered Myron, seizing Halen by the shoulders. "I have him now."

With Myron pulling and Halen pushing, digging the heels of his boots against the ground to help extricate himself from beneath the dragon, all cheered as man and Elf appeared before them.

Halen stood up, none the worse for wear. Inwardly, he was rattled by the experience, but outwardly, he looked completely unscathed. Myron shook the dust and dirt from his cloak, looking as though he had been the one to be buried alive.

"It is a strange thing how you managed to do that," commented Percy, as he scrutinized the pair.

"I was just fortunate the dragon had collapsed onto those stalagmites," explained Halen, pointing to the shattered formations supporting the creature's dead weight. "They sheltered me from the worst of it when that beast came crashing down."

"No, no!" Percy shook his head. He was in awe of how a single strand of hair did not fall out of place. There was not even a smudge of dirt on Halen's perfect face or a coating of dust on his apparel. "I was speaking of how you Elves always seem to come out looking so… *pristine,* even in the midst of such catastrophes."

"I doubt you will understand, but it is an *Elf* thing," responded Rainus, while embracing Halen in a brotherly hug.

"It'd be a very *lucky* Elf thing," added Harold. His beefy hand offered Halen a consoling pat on his shoulder. "You're luckier than a green-eyed, ginger cat born on a midsummer's eve on the night of a blue moon!"

"I am?" Halen stared quizzically at the mortal.

"Absolutely!" insisted Harold. He nodded fervently as he spoke with conviction. "At least in my world, it most certainly is."

"Well, you are the only one in your wretched, little world," Percy muttered beneath his breath as he turned away from the joyous comrades.

Unaware of Percy's condescending comment, the large man explained, "You've definitely got more lives than the average cat, that's for sure! And a green-eyed, ginger cat born under a blue moon is as rare as they come, in my reckonin'!"

"Whether it was luck or happenstance, I am just grateful you are alive," said Rose, breathing a sign of relief as she hugged the Elf.

"We are all glad you had survived the ordeal," stated Silas, giving Halen an approving nod. "Now, my friend, is that grappling hook still handy?"

"It is," answered Halen.

"Hold on here!" demanded Percy. He spun on his heels to confront the Wizard. "Are you saying we are still going to cross that fiery chasm of doom? Even after all I've been forced to endure?"

"It is the fastest way to catch up to the Witch." Silas' voice tightened with frustration that he was made to explain the obvious to this mortal.

"Yes," agreed Myron. "And we must move with speed, for it is clear she is hunting Tag."

"We must find him before Sin does," added Rose.

"That Witch may well be crazy," muttered Percy, as he released a disgruntled huff, "but to continue pursuing her across this divide is madness!"

"We shall cross this obstacle, one-by-one, and so, too, will you," insisted Rose. Seeing the unmistakable glint of fear shining in Percy's eyes, she offered him a reassuring smile. "We have been through worse. Just do not look down."

ॐ ॐ ॐ

Leaning into the wind, Tag peered over the ledge to stare straight down. A chilling gust buffeted him, stealing his breath and snuffing out the dying flames of his torch.

The craggy, snow dusted outcrop he now stood on jutted over the Sea of Shadows. This great land shelf was balanced precariously above the dark waters capped by foaming, white waves. Over an eon the sheer cliff that once supported this ledge had eroded away from constant exposure to the harsh elements and the unrelenting surf pounding against it during the extreme high tides of winter. How this outcrop withstood the forces of nature without collapsing into the sea below was a mystery to him. Perhaps all that was required was the weight of one errant pebble falling from high above, landing at precisely the right place at the right time to tip the scales of balance.

Sensing his precarious position, Tag quickly and cautiously retreated. He crept back toward the mouth of the tunnel that delivered him to this wind-swept precipice.

Glancing to the north, Tag spied the dark, massing storm clouds looming on the horizon. The brooding sky carried the threat of rain turning to snow, if the temperature continued to drop. It was all he needed to compound his misery. All he could do now was hope for precipitation, in whatever form, to hold off for the time being, but he was not counting on prayers or luck at this point.

His prayer for the torch to remain lit until he found a way to the outside world was answered, but in a cruel twist of fate this exit was nothing more than a dead end.

Tag tossed the spent torch aside.

Inching his way to the immediate left of this ledge, he peered over to see what other cruel trick fate was about to deal him.

It felt like a punch to his gut. Tag's heart sank to the pit of his stomach, for almost two-hundred-feet below was the opening to another tunnel fronted by a smaller ledge. Sure enough, in an ironic twist, there was the escape route he sought! A narrow trail with numerous switchbacks meandered down an additional one-hundred-fifty-feet or so below to where the sea lapped at the rocky shore.

He had no doubt he succeeded in tricking the Witch into taking the tunnel leading to that very ledge and trail that represented possible freedom. However, Tag determined that if Sin had already made it there, it would have been easy to see he had not taken that route at all. She would have spied him somewhere along that treacherous, twisting trail, making good his escape or, at the very least, find footprints pressed into the windswept traces of snow.

Tag knew it'd only be a matter of time before Sin doubled back, finding him here, trapped on this desolate outcrop. Assessing his options, there was no point in turning back. If he did, it only guaranteed an encounter with the demented hag somewhere in the blackness, now that he had no torch. And without light, the chances of enduring a crippling injury were just too great.

He had only one way to go, and that was down.

If he were able to make it to the ledge below, he had serious doubts the Witch will attempt climbing after him, unless she had grand delusions of her physical strength and prowess. If his luck held, Sin will be forced to backtrack in a bid to intercept him below, before he can take to that trail to escape.

Picking up a fist-sized rock, Tag held it over the edge of the cliff. Letting it fall, he counted until the rock hit the water, disappearing into the turbulent sea. It took eleven heartbeats, but he told himself that it had to be less, for his heart was racing. By his estimate, it was greater than a three-hundred-foot drop and more like five beats had his heart been calm. Whatever the case, to slip and fall from this height meant certain death.

And just as death promised to be absolute should he fall, Tag also knew the only way to reach that trail below was to climb.

Scrutinizing the cliff wall, the top half was a sheer, vertical face offering little in the way of secure gripping surfaces to facilitate a safe descent. Whether he fell from this lofty height to somehow land on the ledge below, or missed it, plummeting straight down onto the shore to dash his body upon the surf-pummelled boulders below, he'd likely shatter every bone in his body. However, if he managed to make it a good way down and over, and then happened to slip, if it wasn't from too great a height, there was a slim chance he'd land relatively unscathed onto the ledge below, but of late, luck had not looked kindly upon him.

From this elevation, even for an experienced climber, it would be tempting fate in the most audacious manner. It'd take an incredible leap of faith to tackle the vertical face just to reach that slight slope farther below with all the nooks and crannies that offered a safer climb to reach that ledge. Assessing his chances, Tag figured fate, luck and hope would only conspire against him. The only thing he had left was faith in his own abilities, but even this was hanging by a frayed thread.

Tiptoeing to the right side of the tunnel's entrance, he peered over the ledge to inspect the cliff below. To his surprise, the cliff wall on this side had a very slight slope. Though a fall from here will still mean certain death, as best as he can tell, this rock face offered a better chance.

Even though it promised to be a longer, diagonal climb to reach the ledge and connecting trail, Tag spotted potential handholds in the way of narrow ledges, jutting rocks, and cracks. And where toe and handholds became dangerously spaced, there were even some dwarfed vegetation for him to cling to. Sheltered further beneath this land shelf he stood on, growing beyond the reach of the shadow cast by this ledge, he spied upon these stunted pines. Gnarled and gangly, their tenacious roots were deeply anchored into fissures marring the rock face where scant accumulation of earth provided some nutrients and moisture to gather. He was confident these tiny trees would offer some promise of a secure grip.

Gazing up to the leaden sky, Tag searched for the familiar face of the sun. It was veiled behind gathering clouds. If he were to attempt this climb, he knew he'd have to move swiftly, before darkness settled or the rains came down, making it too slick to hold on to anything.

Flexing his fingers to get blood pumping through them in preparation for the climb of his life, Tag drew in a deep breath, steeling his nerves. "I have no choice." He spoke as though he needed convincing to take that first step. "My friends are counting on me. *I* am counting on *me*."

He peered over the ledge once more, staring down at the dark, churning sea waiting to swallow him up should he fall.

"This is crazy." Tag gulped as his eyes squeezed shut, shutting out the dizzying sight below.

His hands grew hot and clammy as he pushed all negative thoughts from his mind. "My friends are in danger. I must do this."

For a lingering moment, Tag thought on his vow to keep Princess Rose safe. Whether it be a dangerous dragon, a demented Witch, or a snake of a prince attempting to falsely woo her, Tag had made a promise to protect her. And like his father, Tag never made promises lightly. The thought of Percy snuggling up to Rose as he whispered to her sweet, deadly nothings made his blood boil.

Wiping his sweaty hands on his trousers, Tag summoned his courage. Lowering himself over the ledge, he began the perilous descent.

Each move was painstakingly meticulous as he climbed, angling toward the ledge below. Before releasing his grip, Tag secured his hand and toehold as he inched his way along.

So focused on this task, he barely noticed the brisk wind stealing away his breath and tugging on his cloak that flapped wildly with each gust whipping around him.

Must not look down. These four small words churned over in his mind, attempting to convince himself to venture on. *This is easy, like climbing down from a big, old tree.*

Tag pretended this was no different than tackling any of the massive oaks back home, growing large in the County of Wren. As he eased his body down, his eyes caught a glimpse of the three-inch-long, silvery scar marring his forearm. This was a scar he proudly showed off to Rose during their initial quest when boredom made a game of comparing scars and deciding on whom in their company wielded the largest, most unsightly reminder of life's tribulations.

It suddenly flashed through his mind how he became the recipient of this scar in the first place. Tag squeezed his eyes shut as the memory, made all too real by the heart-stopping sensation of falling, replayed in his mind.

Tag bit his lower lip as the tearing of flesh against a sharp, broken branch overwhelmed him. His breath snagged in the back of his throat. His hands ached as he instinctively tightened his grip, holding on for dear life. He can feel the blood pounding through his veins to throb through this scar like it was a living thing, feeding and growing on his fear.

Tag slowly exhaled, thrusting this troubling memory to the back of his mind. Opening his eyes, he spoke in a clear, firm voice: "Do not slip. Do not let go. Do not look down. Do not slip. Do not let go. Do not look down."

These three sentences became his mantra as he resumed this deadly descent. Although they meant nothing to the gulls wheeling high against the sullen sky or to the wind snatching these words from his parched, cracked lips, they kept Tag moving. He advanced, almost rhythmically as he repeated them, speaking with utmost conviction he was going to complete this task and live to tell about it.

For how long Tag toiled, he was unsure. So focused on this mission, he had lost all sense of time. Just as he inched his way to almost directly beneath the centre of this outcrop, his blood chilled.

A wretched wail of anger raked at his nerves. It echoed, sounding through the air before fading into the empty sky. Sin was near.

The Witch dropped to her knees. Raging hysterically, she tore at her hair. Her prisoner was nowhere to be seen. She shrieked once more, her clenched fists pummelling the ground in an absolute frenzy.

Tag froze. He did not even hazard a breath should it alert her of his presence.

Hugging the cliff, he watched as crumbs of earth and chunks of stone from the underside of the ledge crumbled away as Sin vented her wrath. All he needed was to be here in this very place as the hag's demented actions caused the entire ledge to collapse into the sea below, taking them both with it.

Just as suddenly as she had started, the Witch ceased with the hysterics. In defeat, Sin rolled onto her bony back, staring up at the gloom. She watched as several white gulls floated upon the updraft of wind rising against the cliff. One bird tilted its wings, banking just enough to avoid this stony wall before dipping down. It disappeared beneath the ledge only to squawk in surprise to see a human where no mortal man should be. Lifted by the winds to reappear on the other side of this outcrop, fearful of the beings both on and under this ledge, the gull spread its wings wide. It glided toward the safety of the open sea, issuing a raucous cry as it flew away. This loud, grating call seemed to mock the Witch as the bird winged overhead.

"Take that!" snarled Sin.

Aiming her crystal, she fired a dazzling bolt of energy. Sizzling and crackling, it shattered the leaden sky to thunder by the gull, missing the bird's tail feathers as it suddenly veered away.

"Come closer!" She shook an angry fist at the creature. "I dare you to make another pass. I'll roast those feathers clean off, and then I'll devour your sorry carcass!"

Sensing she had no idea how close he really was, Tag resumed his climb. He prayed for her to retreat into the tunnel before he appeared on the other side of the ledge.

For a moment, Tag listened. Other than the steady beating of his heart and the restless wind tugging at his cloak, he heard nothing. The Witch had ended her tirade. There were no more bolts of dark magic being dispensed, nor could he hear the frenzied pounding of her fists. There was not even an undignified snivelling whimper.

There was only silence.

Sin had conceded, surrendering to her defeat.

Securing his grip and setting his toes into a long, horizontal crack, Tag reached for another handhold as he resumed this trek. He yelped in surprise as a chunk of the cliff exploded, disintegrating in a billowing puff of smoke and dust directly below him.

"I knew it!" growled Sin. "I sensed you were about!"

Tag glanced over his left shoulder.

There was her wretched face, scowling at him. She looked even more ghastly and deranged as she leaned over, the blood rushing to her head to wash her face in the most unnatural shade of red. She dangled upside down, straining with her staff for a better aim while the wind blew those greying hairs across her face to obscure her already impaired vision.

"Back off!" shouted Tag.

He scuttled along, climbing higher to hug the bottom of the outcrop in hopes of moving out of sight.

"You wish!" She scooted along, leaning over dangerously as she pointed the black crystal at him. She was forced to act before he was completely out of reach. "Soon, you will be like your friends: dead!"

"Liar! You couldn't kill us before. You cannot kill us now! My friends are *not* dead!"

"Who said *I* did the deed?"

"You lie!" hollered Tag.

"Think again!"

"Your pathetic sock-puppet of a dragon barely left a scratch the last time! You'd be a fool to try that again."

"Yes, that is why I called upon a *real* dragon this time," growled Sin. She leaned as far as she could without pitching her body over.

"I don't believe you!"

"It matters not to me! And it will matter even less to you, once you are dead!"

Tag scrambled, clambering along the crumbling ledge as Sin tried her best to angle the tip of the staff so the crystal would at least destroy his feet, crippling him so it'd be impossible to continue. As she hastily unleashed another blast of power, the unrelenting winds blew the tangle of wiry hairs across her face once more to impede her vision.

This second attempt was worse than the first. Like an errant bolt of lightning, it hit with explosive force. Impacting the cliff well below her target, it struck closer to the mouth of the tunnel and ledge that was Tag's intended destination. The only barrage to accost him was the litany of profanity she spewed. He ventured on, unharmed while Sin ranted, struggling to lean over without falling to her death as she angled her staff for a better aim.

"Bloody hell!" gasped Percy. Stopping in his tracks, his back straightened. His teeth clattered together as a hollow rumble reverberated through the tunnel. "What the heck was that?"

"A volcano?" Harold answered with a question. "Maybe this mountain is goin' to blow!"

"Hush!" demanded Silas, raising his hand to motion for silence. "This whole mountain would be quaking, if it was an erupting volcano."

"So you say, Wizard," argued Percy. "If not, then what was that horrific sound?"

"Just know it was *not* an eruption." Silas spoke with utmost certainty.

"And how would you know?" countered Percy, as Rainus urged him to continue moving on.

Silas spun on his heels, confronting the young man. The steady glow of his crystal accentuated every line and angry furrow etching his agitated face as he snapped, "I know because we are still alive!"

"Perhaps it was a clap of thunder," offered Rose. "To me, it sounded like a bolt of lightning striking the mountainside."

"At this moment, that is more likely," said Myron, as he motioned for Silas to continue on.

Halen's eyes narrowed as he stared beyond the pale sphere of light cast by the Wizard's crystal. "Look, up yonder!"

"What now?" Percy's voice grated with annoyance. "Another dragon? Perhaps a river of molten lava again?"

"Light," answered Halen. "I believe it is light from the world outside."

"Huzzah!" cheered Harold.

"Dampen your enthusiasm, my friend," cautioned Rainus. Cocking his head, he strained to hear the source of the thunderous boom that had rumbled through the tunnel to rattle them to their bones. "Though I have no doubt it was not the work of a volcano, I fear it was neither a lightning strike."

"The Witch?" asked Myron.

"That is the logical assumption," answered Rainus.

"It makes the most sense," said Loftus, nodding in agreement.

"Good gracious!" cried Rose. Her heart raced. "She could be after Tag! Perhaps she has finally caught up to him!"

"Pity! By the sounds of it, I believe we are too late to rescue that poor bugger," said Percy, as he dodged the stinging flick of Loftus' finger meant for the back of his head.

"I hardly think so," countered Halen. "I am confident I detected three explosive sounds. That can only mean Tag is making it terribly difficult for her to strike him down."

"And we know firsthand how bad her aim can be," reminded Rainus, thinking on Sin's blind eye.

"I think you are right," said Myron. "Hurry, Wizard! Lead the way!"

Silas' crystal dimmed as they raced toward the mouth of the tunnel where the light of day beckoned them. With weapons drawn, they cautiously stepped out onto the ledge. They were greeted by a sullen sky dotted by gulls crying mournfully as they wheeled high overhead. There was no Witch to be seen.

"Where are they?" asked Rose.

She crept to the edge where a winding trail meandered down to the rocky beach. There was no sign of Tag with Sin in pursuit.

"Look!" Rainus pointed up to the large outcrop protruding from the sheer face of the cliff.

They heard the cursing before they saw the Witch. When she suddenly came into view, Sin was scrambling about like an animal on all fours as she loped over to the opposite edge of the outcrop. So intent on killing her escaped prisoner, she took no notice of Rose and her comrades on the ledge below. Instead, Sin peered over, hoping her target was making his way closer to her.

"What the heck is she doing up there?" gasped Rose. She stared at the hag cursing like a demented soul.

"There's your answer," responded Silas, pointing beneath the ledge. In its shadow, there was Tag. He clung desperately to the rock face.

"What is the lad doing there?" asked Loftus, as he stared in disbelief.

"I would say he is trying to escape from the Witch," answered Rainus.

"He is trying to get to where we are now," determined Halen, as he glanced to the ragged trail leading down to the beach.

"Well, that poor sod is going to get himself killed," decided Percy. "If he had any balls, he would stand his ground; fight that bloody Witch and be done with her!"

"Fight with what?" asked Harold, his hand patting Tag's sword he carried for safekeeping.

Just as Sin dropped to her belly to dangle over the ledge, she wailed like a wounded animal. A steel ball propelled and guided by Rose's unerring aim struck her high on her bony, right shoulder to send her reeling back with the blow.

"Well done, Princess!" praised Halen. He lowered his bow as Sin momentarily vanished from view.

"Yes, now that crazy woman will vent her wrath upon us all," rebuked Percy, wagging a finger of disapproval at Rose.

"Unlike you, I will not stand by and do nothing!" snapped Rose. She placed another steel ball in the cradle of her sling.

"There are times when the best action is to do nothing at all!" argued Percy. His accusing finger travelled from Rose to the distant ledge. "We are here. She is there. It is obvious her business is with that rogue of a scoundrel! You shall only raise her ire."

"That *scoundrel* is my friend! And I do not mean to *anger* that Witch," growled Rose.

"Then what?" queried Percy. His voice tightened with cynicism. "What do you plan to do?"

"I mean to kill her this time."

Her words were cold and calculating. Rose's wrist swivelled, sending the sling into motion once more, rotating ever faster as she waited for an opportunity to strike again.

Spying on his friends below, Tag hollered, "Get back! Seek cover!"

"Hold on, Tag!" called Myron. "We will stop her."

Silas took up his staff, aiming it at Sin only to have Rainus push the crystal away.

"Take no offence, my friend, but you are sorely out of practice," said the Elf. "You are more likely to bring that cliff down upon Tag as you are to destroy the Witch in the process."

"But we cannot let her escape," argued Silas.

"Put your trust in my finest marksman," urged Rainus, watching as Halen raised his bow, arrow nocked and ready to unleash.

Before Halen let his arrow fly, Sin crawled to the edge of the outcrop. Without making herself a visible target, she blindly aimed the black crystal toward the voices below.

Instead of striking down her foes, with a thunderous clap, the bolt of energy struck the cliff directly over the mouth of the tunnel.

All dropped to their knees.

The ledge they stood on quaked as rocks and boulders tumbled down to seal this opening. Like the percussion of a giant axe biting into dried firewood, it easily split the face of the cliff. The crack the toes of Tag's boots were wedged into widened while simultaneously demolishing the narrow ledge he clung to.

His scream was drowned out by Rose's own cry of fright. She watched him plummet, the wind buffeting him as his cloak flapped wildly like a flag in a windstorm.

Tag's scream snagged in his throat as he gagged. The silver clasp of his cloak jammed just under his chin as his fall came to an abrupt halt.

A rapid succession of four arrows launched by Rainus and Halen had managed to pierce the fabric billowing above Tag, pinning it to the cliff.

"Grab onto your cloak!" shouted Myron. "Hang on!"

Tag reached up, seizing the fabric just as the clasp snapped, breaking under his weight. It 'pinged' as it ricocheted against the rock face before dropping to vanish on the wave lashed shore.

"Hold on, Tag!" called Rose. "We will get you down."

"Not if he falls to his death first," muttered Percy. He winced as Loftus' balled fist thumped his head. The captain shoved him aside so the others could work.

As though dark forces answered Percy's prayer, Rose and her friends watched in horror as Tag dangled helplessly, dropping ever closer to his doom as the cloak began to tear where the arrows had pierce it.

"NO!" cried Tag.

As though the talons of a mighty dragon slashed through his cloak, the fabric ripped, leaving four linear tears. Tag's eyes squeezed shut.

His scream was snatched away by the wind as he fell, plunging straight down.

"Quickly, Princess, use the Dreamstone!" shouted Myron.

Rose fumbled about, reaching for the magic crystal. Clutching the Dreamstone to her chest as she squeezed her eyes shut, her mind raced as she tried to form an image of Tag standing safely amongst them.

Her concentration was broken as Percy shouted to Tag, "Head first! Land on your head! You won't feel a thing!"

Rose's eyes snapped open as Harold erupted with an exuberant whoop.

Tag's hands snagged onto one of the stunted pine trees. His fall ended abruptly, punctuated by a heavy thud against the face of the cliff as the spindly trunk bowed, bending under his weight. He swayed precariously, grateful for this turn of good fortune as Sin raged at his luck.

She dashed over to the other side of the outcrop where she would be out of sight and out of range of the Elves' deadly aim.

"Damn!" cursed Halen, lowering his bow as Sin disappeared from view.

"She's mad! Utterly mad!" declared Loftus, watching as the Witch leaned recklessly over the ledge to take aim once more. "She's intent on killing Tag, even if she dies trying!"

From their limited vantage point, all they could see was the tip of Sin's staff waving about as she angled it beneath the ledge. She aimed it at Tag as he searched about for a safe handhold to continue his downward trek.

"Now, my lady!" demanded Silas. "If there was ever a time to use the Dreamstone, it is now!"

Rose squeezed her eyes shut, blocking out everything around her. Her concentration was shattered again, startled as Sin unleashed another terrific blast of energy at Tag.

This time, it was desperation to hone the Witch's aim as she compensated for her poor depth perception to target her quarry.

"Focus!" ordered Silas. Seizing Rose by the shoulders, he turned her about so she could not see and be further distracted.

Sin lay on her belly. Her lanky body teetered on the edge as she took aim once more. Lowering her crystal, she pointed it at Tag only to shriek in surprise as Halen let his arrow fly. The projectile pierced the staff, biting into the wood just below the crystal to send it tumbling from her grasp.

In a mad scramble, she stretched out, hoping to snag the staff before it dropped out of reach. Instead, Sin toppled over, but her hands latched onto the lip of the outcrop. She watched helplessly as her weapon plunged straight down with the force of a thrown spear.

Enraged, her heart raced as her eyes followed the black crystal. Witnessing its destruction, the staff shattered on one of the many boulders studding the shore. Unbeknownst to her, the chunk of obsidian, still mounted atop the broken staff, flew into the air. The shard of oak it remained fastened to stabbed into a sandy patch to jut from the beach just out of reach of the incoming tide.

Just as Rose conjured up an image in her mind's eye of Tag safely by her side, her concentration was broken yet again. Tag yelped in surprise. The tenacious little tree he clung to remained rooted, but he was left with a handful of shed pine needles as he slipped down to the end of the bending trunk.

Rose screamed in fright as she watched Tag fall.

"Now, Princess!" shouted Myron. "Do it now!"

"I can fix this! Give it to me!" snapped Percy. He reached out to snatch the Dreamstone from Rose's hand, only to have her clenched fist forcefully collide against his face.

He reeled from the blow, staggering back as Rose raced to make her wish come true.

"I can't look!" cried Harold. He turned, averting his eyes from impending tragedy.

"Well, I'll be damned!" exclaimed Silas, smacking Harold's shoulder in glee. "And none too soon!"

Tag tumbled through the air only to land on the outstretched wings of a mighty dragon. He gasped in surprise as he rolled down, coming to rest between its scaly shoulders.

"Hold on tight," ordered the dragon.

With massive wings pumping hard, the leather membrane of each appendage was stretched taut. Like a ship's billowing sails caught in a storm, this creature struggled to gain altitude with this additional weight.

"Loken?" gasped Tag. His arms wrapped around the Sprite's serpentine neck.

"Fancy meeting you here, my friend," greeted Loken.

"I thought you were dead!"

"Sin only wishes. I woke to find the door to my prison open and Elee gone. I made good my escape."

"Thank goodness for that!"

"Indeed!" said Loken, as he banked to one side to avoid colliding with the cliff.

Tag gasped, holding on a little tighter as Loken tilted. Powerful hind legs pushed off against the rock face with this sudden aerial manoeuver.

"I have never been happier to see you," said Tag.

"And my timing was impeccable!"

"As always!" praised Tag. He held on as Loken circled around, before dipping down. He glided toward their friends waiting on the ledge.

"There is not enough room for me to land," warned Loken. "Get ready."

"For what?" asked Tag, squinting as they flew into the wind.

"For this," answered Loken. Just as he neared the ledge, the tip of his right wing skimming over the hard surface, the Sprite veered sharply. Climbing into the sky, he dumped his passenger in the process.

Tag somersaulted onto the ledge. With the grace of an Elf, he managed to roll up onto his feet to stand before the Princess.

Before he could say a single word, Rose threw her arms around Tag, embracing him in a great hug while Percy stared, dumbfounded as he watched this joyful reunion.

"Get your grubby paws off her!" demanded Percy.

Tag responded to his order by hugging Rose even tighter.

"Loken!" shouted Silas, as he pointed to the high ledge where Sin struggled to pull herself to safety. "Save the Witch! Spare her life."

"Are you insane?" called Loken, as he hovered overhead. "She would sooner see us dead."

"But we are not like her," reminded Silas. "It is our compassion that sets us apart from the likes of her."

"She is evil! She tried to kill us not once, but many times over," argued Loken.

"She was not always evil," countered Silas, waving the Sprite off. "Just do it! Do it for me! Let fate determine her end."

All shielded their eyes. The powerful downdraft from Loken's wings, flapping to thrust him through the air and against the wind, created mini cyclones of dust and powdery snow. He circled about, gliding toward the ledge where the Witch dangled, cursing while she clawed at the earth as her gangly legs kicked at the air. In her crazed state, Sin believed if she could only pull herself to safety, there was a still chance she could race down to the beach to reclaim the obsidian crystal, if it was not damaged in the fall and the currents had not yet swept it out to sea.

Instead, the slashing winds and the unrelenting pull of gravity conspired, sapping Sin of her dwindling strength. Though she had no intention of giving up, she was waging a losing battle. Her weary hands throbbed with pain. The earth crumbled beneath her fingers as she clawed at the ledge. She finally lost her grip.

Sin fell back, screaming more in rage than fear, and then she groaned in pain as powerful talons wrapped around her body, catching her in mid-air.

"Well done, Loken!" praised Silas. He watched as a powerful gust of wind steered the Sprite and his reluctant passenger winging over the Sea of Shadows.

Their eyes followed the pair gliding above the turbulent waters and just as Loken dipped low, circling back toward land, Halen and Rainus spotted a rare sight.

"Look! A mermaid!" announced Rainus. He pointed to a tiny figure breaking through the surface of the sea.

"And a seal!" added Halen, spying the small, round head bobbing near to Elee.

"A Mermaid? Where?" asked Harold. Squinting, he stared out over the seascape.

Suddenly, a flotilla of Mermaids appeared, drifting in the surf alongside Elee and her pet. The air resounded with strange, high-pitched, undulating sounds as these beings called.

"If that is their infamous siren song, it is hideous!" declared Percy. He clamped his hands over his ears. "The sailors that had been lured to a watery death must have been drunk to find this so alluring."

"That is no song!" snapped Silas. "It is a summons!"

They watched in stunned amazement. The sea bulged. It grew black, the water churning and foaming. A great shadow erupted from the deep as a hideous creature broke the surface. Loken glanced down upon hearing this commotion just as several monstrous tentacles studded with suction disks armed with rasp-like teeth lashed out. One wrapped around Sin's left ankle while the other two batted at Loken's dragon form. The Witch was yanked from his talons as he was sent tumbling through the air.

"What is that thing?" gasped Loftus. His eyes widened at the sight of the leviathan that stared with an unblinking eye that was bigger than a wagon wheel as the water roiled, splashing around its slimy, boneless form.

"Oh, my! They unleashed the cracked hen!" declared Harold. There was an expression of horror mingled with awe etched across his face as he watched the creature.

"A *kraken*!" corrected Silas. "A monster from the deep!"

He watched as a sinewy tentacle wound around Sin's body, squeezing to stifle her screams of fear and rage.

Loken's powerful wings thrust his body skyward, narrowly avoiding the wild thrashing of deadly tentacles as the Witch was yanked down. These many appendages parted as a huge, beak-like mouth protruded, opening wide. Sin screamed, tumbling into this gaping maw. Snapping shut upon her, the creature sank into the frothing waters.

"Oh, my!" said Rose, her eyes wide in disbelief. "I did not see that coming!"

"Neither did she," said Tag. Watching as the monster became a dark shadow, disappearing to become one with the sea.

All gasped in surprise as the surface swelled, churning once more. The creature surged forth. With a wretched bellow it spat out the Witch before retreating into the deep. Sin landed with splash, frantically swimming to shore.

"She must have tasted especially vile," said Rainus, watching as Sin slapped about, bobbing on the waves.

"Loken!" hollered Silas, as he pointed to Sin. "Fish her out, will you?"

Before Loken could circle around to scoop up the Witch, Elee and her sisters dove into action. Seizing Sin by her hair and her ragged frock, they dragged her beneath the surface of the water with Flotsam barking and snapping at her feet.

"Well, fate did indeed determine her end," said Myron, with a dismal shake of his head as the Witch disappeared with the vengeful Mermaids.

"It was divine justice," averred Tag. "After all she put us through and what she did to Loken and the Mermaid, I can see why Elee and her kin wanted revenge."

"As terrible as this will sound, methinks she had it comin' to her," said Harold.

"I agree." Tag nodded to his friend.

"Good riddance!" declared Rose. "She was a horrible person. She had every intention of killing you, and if she did not, I was so scared you were going to fall to your death trying to escape."

She reached over, taking Tag's hands into hers.

Percy's visage contorted into a hideous mask of fury. He wrenched their hands apart as he pushed his way between them. "And had you entrusted me with the Dreamstone rather than standing there like an blithering dolt of a girl, I could have proved myself a hero!"

"You would not even know what to do with this," argued Rose, holding the magic crystal before his angry face.

"I would have figured it out, in short order," he snorted.

"I'm sorry, but I wouldn't trust you with the Dreamstone, especially where my life is concerned," countered Tag.

"Fetch off!" snapped Percy. "You are just jealous of what we have."

"What do we have?" asked Rose.

"Well, I know what we could have had, but it is obvious you do not trust in me, otherwise you would have handed over that bauble," sulked Percy. "If there is no trust, our love will not survive."

"Hey, it works both ways, you ignorant sod," reminded Tag. "If you trust in her so much, then prove it."

"I need not prove a thing to you!"

"True, but prove it to her," urged Tag. "If you trust her, allow Princess Rose to make one wish come true."

"What is this wish?" asked Percy.

"If your intentions are honest and your love is as true as you claim, then allow her to wish for you to speak the truth, and only the truth."

"She need not waste an invaluable wish on such a petty thing! She already knows I have only the best intentions where she is concerned," insisted Percy. "She knows I can be trusted."

"Can you?" Rose's eyes glowed a deeper shade of violet as she searched his soul for the truth.

"Of course!"

"Then you will not protest should I wish for you to speak openly and honestly."

"About what?"

"About everything, including why you even came all this way when all you did was gripe and complain the whole time," answered Rose.

Myron and the others watched with keen interest, waiting to see if Percy was willing to consent to this.

"Oh, do tell, my lord!" exclaimed Silas, as he gave Percy a knowing smile. "To speak the truth can be freeing, especially if the truth is enrobed in a deep, dark secret wishing to be revealed."

"Ooh! Secrets can be bad!" Harold shook his head in disapproval. "Better to spill the beans, if you get my drift?"

"Secrets? I have no secrets to speak of," insisted Percy.

"Well then, you will have no issue with me wishing for you to speak the truth, for now, I have many questions bubbling to the surface where you are concerned," said Rose. Her hand wrapped around the Dreamstone as she closed her eyes. "I am in need of answers, not assumptions or girlish hopes."

"I answer to no one, not even to you!" growled Percy. "I see what is happening here! I will not be subjected to the indignities of an inquisition."

"You do not trust me?" asked Rose. "Or do you not trust what will spew forth from your mouth?"

"If you trusted me, you would have had no qualms about handing over that Dreamstone instead of punching me with it!"

"In truth, I had considered it," admitted Rose.

Percy looked momentarily stunned. "And?"

"And I decided against it, but as you said to me at the start of this quest, *'it is the thought that counts'*, my dear Percy."

"You insolent, ungrateful girl! How dare you speak to me with such impudence? I am Prince Percival Augustus Chadwick, heir apparent to the throne of Axalon!"

"You may be all that, but your words and deeds of late speak louder than your grand title."

"Grand, indeed! You do not deserve a man like me."

"Very true!" snapped Rose. "I deserve so much better."

With his ego soundly shattered and pride thoroughly crushed, Percy stormed off. He fully expected her to run after him.

Adding insult to injury, instead of pursuing him, Rose waved farewell as she shouted, "Try not to get lost on your way home!"

Knowing they would eventually catch up to him when he next stopped to whine and complain, Rose watched. Percy stomped away, grumbling as he made his way down the path.

"Goodness!" declared Harold. "Maybe I can speak some sense to the young man; patch things up between you two."

"NO!" Rose's companions cried out in a singular voice.

For a moment, her disappointment threatened to overwhelm her as she watched Percy hasten away like a spoiled brat caught in a lie.

"Take this to heart, my dear girl: Never lose sight of all you have in the pursuit of all you want," cautioned Silas, as he glanced over to her comrades.

"No need to pursue him. I can bring him back for you," offered Harold.

"That is kind of you, Harold, but it will not be necessary," said Rose. "Some things are just not meant to be. I believe this is one of them."

"It is a pity Percy's true character was nothing short of disappointing," said Tag. "Just know that you do deserve better, Princess. I just feel bad this was not the happy ending you had hoped for."

Rose nodded, and then she smiled at her dear friend. "Terribly disappointing, indeed, but I take great comfort in knowing that your true qualities never wavered."

Tag felt his face burn, blushing under her kind words spoken with utmost sincerity.

"My dear Tag, you were nothing short of brilliant!"

"I was?"

"Absolutely!" said Rose, as she kissed him on his cheek in gratitude. "As for a happy ending? If I learned anything throughout our shared adventures, it is that true friendship cannot be undervalued and I cannot depend on others for my happiness. I must strive to be happy; to be the master of my own destiny."

"That is quite the revelation," praised Silas, pleasantly surprised by her candid words. "Most people come to this knowledge too late in life."

"I believe this is a lesson one is never too old to learn," said Rose. Pressing the Dreamstone into the Wizard's hand, she curled his fingers around the magic crystal as her companions looked on, nodding in approval.

"So, Princess, are you happy, even though you did not get the man of your dreams?" asked Tag.

"My life is better off without that fool, for Percy was more of a nightmare than a dream," admitted Rose, embracing him in a warm hug. "But who needs Percy when I have friends like you I can always count on?"

"So true, my dear Princess, and it is better to live the life you dream of than to waste your time dreaming your life away," said Silas, nodding in approval.

"For once, you are *not* speaking in riddles." Rose smiled at the Wizard. "Now, let us go home and live the lives we are meant to live."

"An excellent idea, my lady!" praised Silas. "But first, let us head down to that beach."

"To find our way home from there?" asked Myron, as he glanced over to the meandering trail leading to the beach far below.

"Oh, no! Princess Rose can wish us back to where we left our horses, and then homeward from there. Instead, I mean to collect Prince Percival before he finds himself in trouble and I also intend to claim Dragonite's crystal, if we can," answered Silas.

"I suppose we do not need the tides to sweep it out to sea, only to deliver it into the wrong hands," agreed Myron.

"Precisely," said Silas.

"Good thinking, my friend," said Rainus, as Loken, having assumed his Spritely form, alighted upon his shoulder. "We cannot have that happen again."

With Halen leading the way down, his keen eyes searched for the black crystal, just in case it was not yet carried out by the receding tide. Their jubilant voices and laughter as they delighted in their shared company drifted across the sea, rising up to the sullen sky where gulls floated on the restless winds. One hungry bird spotting an easy meal dove down, alighting upon the water where a bed of kelp swayed to and fro with the ever-changing currents. This scavenger greedily plucked up the morsel only to squawk in fright. Surrendering it to the sea, the gull took to the air once more.

Though none can see from the twisting trail, the lost, bewitched eyeball had bobbed back to the surface. For a lingering moment, it floated amongst the seaweed and driftwood, staring at Rose and her comrades. It then rolled about, watching as the Mermaids broke the surface of the water.

Driven by unnatural forces, the eyeball began to swim after them. Its unblinking stare remained fixed on the Witch as Sin was dragged into the murky depths, forever lost in the Sea of Shadows.